Killing the Man

Kenneth B. Humphrey

DEDICATION

This book is for Jennifer, the tumbler that just fits.

MORE BY THE AUTHOR

Young reader series

Raimy Rylan

      Book 1: The World Serpent

      Book 2: Chase of the Samurai

      Book 3: Rylan: Origins (2016)

Adult novels

The Killing Arc

      Killing the Man

      The Killing Face

      Black, White & Killing in Between: The True

      Story of the North Haven Murders

Preface

This book came about in the early months of 1999, when Y2K dominated the headlines and there seemed to be this undercurrent of apprehension among the general populace. Here we were, on the cusp of a new century, wondering what the future would bring. No one knew, but everyone had an opinion. The media enabled this frenzy, of course, whipping up fears of failing technology that would have planes dropping from the skies and microwaves attacking us.

I wanted to personalize this sense of wariness and hope in the adventures of one man, wrapped up in the oldest tale of all: boy gets girl.

Coming back to it in 2014 was eye opening. Texting, iPhones and iPads, LED TVs, social media, the Internet of Things: unknown then, common now. So much had changed in the interim, as if 2000 truly did signify a turn into something wholly new.

I used a font called Century, appropriately enough.

CHAPTER ONE

April 1999

So, get this. In the course of trying to make sense of life, I found my road on the other side of a man who played no favorites. He killed whomever he needed to: black, white and everything in between.

And of course this whole mess also involved a girl, but she wasn't my wife.

Kevin's voice blares to life in my earpiece, knocking me out of my reverie. There's something going on back in the electronics department. I punch a key on the monitor console and the screen instantly changes to reveal five kids walking down the aisle.

My pulse quickens a little and bells dingle-dangle in the back of my skull.

This is what I do. I catch crooks.

In the lingo, people like me are called thief dancers. I don't know where the term originated, but it stuck. Corporations label us with terms like Asset Control or Loss Prevention.

The theft business, like many other human-centric fields, has tipping points where instinct rules the day. It's what separates the good from the great; I like to think my instincts were pretty well honed.

And they are telling me we had some live wires, walking this way.

Kineisha looks over. "You want another angle, Rick?"

That's me, by the by. Rick Johann Killing, Loss Prevention Manager for the Hyper-Mart chain in North Haven, Illinois. Sprawling on thirty acres, a massive complex combining grocery and retail products, it has been touted as the wave of the future, a huge store where everyone can get everything.

Chicago lay seventy miles southeast, just far enough to give the area its own sense of identity but close enough to offer all the big city amenities.

Perhaps due to these factors, the town of North Haven had expanded rapidly over the last few years. People with money migrated out of the overheated Chicago housing market, bringing along their toys, their opinions and their problems. This same story played out across the country as the economy climbed upwards on the back of the Internet dot-com boom, making people wealthy and wealthy people ridiculous.

"Yeah, camera seven," I reply.

She pulls up another angle, viewing the kids from the side. They all look to be in their later teens, early twenties, walking closely in a group. My team and I aren't much older, with me being the elder statesman at a rickety twenty-four years.

I zoom in, looking for the alpha male. In any kind of grouping, animal or human, there exists one that drives on the others. Find that guy and you've just made things a lot easier.

Three males, two females in this pack.

They near the electronics counter and slow down, still clustered too closely together to be natural.

Unless you're looking specifically for it, you wouldn't notice. Most other customers might assume they're just looking around for an employee.

And they were, but for completely different reasons.

Behavioral tendencies, body language, even choice of clothing; these are the stock in our trade, since no thief ever walks into a store holding a sign that declares: "I'm a thief!"

Though I will suggest it to the parents of the next third grader that decides to pocket baseball cards and waste my time.

Eyes are the first clue. We watch the way they dart their vision around, the snap of a head when someone walks by. Nerves are the great betrayer and eyes are the hazard signals for nerves.

Next we watch how they interact with others. In a group, it's easy. They cluster. For single lifters, we often see them avoid anyone else. It's like they are afraid someone can smell the steal on them.

We even watch the paths they take through the store. Certain areas give off a sense of isolation – the thief's refuge – better than others.

I settle on the kid in the middle. He appears casual, yet I can see him whispering under his breath to the others. He's lean and looks fast, which makes my pulse hammer just a little more. I love fast.

Kineisha is chattering back and forth over the radio with Kevin and my other employee Kari, coordinating positions. I tune them out and stare at my new nemesis on the screen before me.

This is how I like to hunt.

The kid wore his ball cap backwards, bill well-curved from years of use. A faded flannel hung loose over a t-shirt and already I can envision how this will play out. He'll stuff something down the back of his pants, pulling the flannel over to hide it.

"Ten on the Sony, Rick," Kevin spouts off in my earpiece. He's betting on the new Sony digital camera that just came out last month. The group mills around that section of the counter, so it's a good bet.

"I'll take that and raise you ten for the Canon." Packaging for Canon digital cameras had shrunk last year.

"Bad bet," chirps Kari. It's the first thing she's said to me all morning. She's quiet by nature.

Alpha male nudges one of his pals. The kid does a slow three-sixty while stepping behind the counter.

Kevin hums a little cartoon song over the radios, in concert with the kid's movement. I can't remember the song, but he also can't carry a tune.

The kid grabs one camera, followed quickly by another. Nice, a two-fer.

All five targets turn as one, hive movement, and walk away from the department. The forced nonchalance and nervous energy is comical. I expect to see one start whistling, as if to show any witnesses that they were just some people out on a casual stroll.

The top of Kevin's head is visible in the background as he stalks along a parallel path.

"Two Sonys. Double payout, right?" He goads me.

I ignore him and turn to Kineisha. "Shall we?"

A smile crosses her face. We bail out of the office to hit the floor. Technology is nice and all that – and if you're my wife, technology *is* all that – but it has limitations. I like the personal approach.

There exists an element of great challenge in thief dancing: Stay as close as possible without being made. For someone like Kineisha, that job comes a little easier. She has a nondescript look, similar to a dozen other girls I might pass at the mall and never remember. With my size, it's tougher, and that's what fires me up. I want to eavesdrop, to smell their cologne or perfume, to invade their personal space.

Everyone gets their kicks in different ways.

Even though we come in all shapes and sizes, there seems to be some common thread, some personality facet, and it's not pure honesty. I'm too cynical for that. Nor do I believe it's the zealous pursuit of justice.

I suspect many of us just savor the chase.

Kineisha and I wind through the clothing areas, communicating with the others to coordinate our placement. Nothing like spoiling a perfectly good 'lift by walking down the wrong aisle at the wrong moment.

That wrecks everyone's day when I prefer just to wreck theirs.

Without a word, Kineisha peels away from me, taking a different intercept angle. We now have the kids surrounded from all points of the compass. Two of the five targets split away from the others. Neither had ever possessed the merchandise, so I dismiss them from consideration.

It could be possible to make a case for them as accessories, but it really isn't worth it. The paperwork is already enough of a hassle and accessories to a crime often degenerate into court hearings.

I dislike having to dress up just to testify.

Kineisha follows them on the chance they have their own agenda or are playing lookout for the rest. If they try to circle around and spot any of us, she'd give a shout.

That leaves the alpha male, his lackey boy and the other girl.

I radio Kevin and Kari to stay on lackey and the girl. A click of the radio transmitter acknowledges my words and also lets everyone know that Kevin stood so close he didn't want them to hear his voice. It's not the most glamorous job in the world, but catching crooks can sure be fun at the right times. I smile in anticipation.

Alpha is all mine.

The three kids move towards an aisle I've nicknamed Lifter Alley. Plastic storage tubs are stacked high on top of the shelving, creating shadows and giving a false sense of security. In reality, I have a perfect sight line.

Standing behind a double-high rack of dress shirts, I parted a couple to look through them. From a casual glance, it probably looks like I'm searching for my size. Anyone watching me for a few seconds more would begin to notice how long I stood, how still I stood and how my eyes never waver. I'm like a statue, because movement attracts attention.

The physical requirements for crook-catching are not what most people assume. Size doesn't really matter because events rarely devolve into a scrum. If they do, you're already in trouble.

Being fast doesn't make or break the job either, although it certainly comes in handy when arresting a runner. Proper planning and anticipation – in other words: backup – neutralizes any speed advantage from a lifter.

For my money, the best asset to have is quick vision. Not just good vision, because glasses can remedy that. Quick vision: the ability to identify, categorize and track items with just a glance. I have a test I administer to applicants that serves to assess this skill. It consists of flash images that create the same fractional glimpses we often get. Not everyone is blatantly obvious like alpha and his crew. Many walk past us palming something small. There are often only little snatches of indictment that propel us into action.

In the alley, my target has finally screwed up enough courage to tuck the camera in the back of his jeans. The other two stand with their backs to him, shielding the view, but his body motion betrays the story.

He yanks the flannel shirt over his butt to hide the bulge.

Finished with his task, alpha switches positions with lackey boy. That's when things start getting funny. And I mean funny ha-ha, not funny strange.

Lackey darts his head around so sharply he looks like a bird. I can nearly see the nervous sweat running down his neck. He gives it a couple of aborted tries and the sound of his nerve crumbling is almost audible. He finally sets the camera down on a shelf. Don't worry, pal, it happens to every guy.

Exasperated, the girl makes a move of bravado that will change her entire day.

She stuffs the item in her purse. It's too big for her zipper to close so she settles for clutching the top with both hands. She gives him a hard stare. Ouch, she's a ball breaker. All three exit the aisle.

Kevin and Kari come to life in my earpiece, predicting how the stop will go down. I've already got my own opinion.

"You two take the girl and chicken boy. I've got alpha."

"Who?"

"The guy wearing the flannel."

I hear Kevin mutter something about me and my weird nicknames. He's covering the mouthpiece, thinking that it's enough. Nice try.

Lackey boy and the girl split off from alpha, heading towards the far set of doors. I let them go without another thought.

Alpha circles around at a leisurely pace, eyes slowly scanning everyone and everything. This isn't his first time. Mine either.

No cherries getting popped today, pal.

He sees me once, but I make sure to avoid eye contact. It's weird, but just as we can often spot a potential lifter based off body clues, so too can they make us. Undoubtedly many of them are moving in a state of hyperawareness and spook easily, but still, it's happened enough that I realize we can quickly ruin a good arrest with one ill-timed stare.

And if they do spook, dump the merchandise, and we stop them anyway, well that's where things can get real ugly, real quick. It's called a bad stop and you only get a few mulligans with them.

Alpha approaches the front of the store. Past him I can see the other two at the far end of the registers. They're stalling. Lackey boy looks like he could faint at any moment.

The electronic doors slide open and the girl marches through them without hesitation. Her spine is rigid, projecting confidence but I'm not impressed. It's all false bravado. Lackey boy follows at a slower pace, glancing backward.

Kari walks casually past him, cell phone pressed to her ear in mock conversation. She blends in so well, she might as well be invisible. He never even glances at her.

After a few more seconds, he proceeds out the door and disappears. I can hear Kevin's voice going through our stop script. He must have went ahead and left Kari inside to follow them. Nice teamwork.

My guy loiters near the door, watching his friends leave the store, presumably waiting to see if any commotion ensues. None does, nor would he see it if there did. We have a separate side entrance to our offices.

Seemingly satisfied that things are cool, alpha turns and takes his first steps towards freedom and capture.

Time to dance, my friend.

Chapter Two

Brand

His body language betrays him in spades: defiant and scared, nervous, volatile. Everything in my experience stated that the kid would not come in willingly. The smart play would be to call for backup.

But everything else in my ego will not allow that. He rankles me, makes me want to best him face to face, to quash his aura of arrogance. He's one of those haughty rich kids with life on a platter, who had everything so easy, and I am just the guy to bring him back down a few notches.

I have a tendency to take some things personal, even if they are imaginary. I don't know this kid from Adam.

Kevin reports that the other two are inside. He asks if I need help. I don't respond, squawking my radio instead. That will keep him quiet.

I wander around the checkout registers, blank look of confusion on my face, a husband on an errand but lost. It's a look my wife agrees I wear easily. It might actually be my default expression.

He nears the door, closing the distance to escape, and there's no turning back now. He's crossed the line and is committed.

Contrary to popular opinion, I don't have to let him leave the store before making an arrest. The intent to steal was sealed when he stuffed the item down his pants and concealed it from view. But by letting him leave, I cement my case nice and tight. There's no way he can argue that he meant to pay and simply forgot once he passed all points of purchase.

Plus, it's more fun this way.

The doors whoosh open at our approach. I'm trailing him by fifteen feet, increasing my stride to reach him once he's on the sidewalk.

Then he snaps a quick glance over his shoulder and our eyes meet.

Just like that, the respective roles in this game are exposed, roles that only I knew before, and everything is laid bare. He knows who I am, what I am and why I'm here.

Without a second thought he explodes from the store, vaulting clean over the sidewalk. His gait is long and straight, his form clean. I bet he had a lot of success running track in school.

That's fine, though. So did I. In fact, more.

My college sprint times qualified me for the 1996 Olympic trials in the 200 and 400 meter races. Back then, only a handful of people in the world were faster. I don't train quite at the same level of intensity any more, but for this job I don't need to. Those people are not likely to steal from me.

I catch up with him near the outer edge of the lot and kick out one of his feet. This sends him sprawling. Because Midwest winters mean lots of snow, sand is a common means to help traction in slippery conditions. One drawback is the accumulation of it by spring, and the length of time it takes crews to come clean it.

Thus far, they had not visited my Hyper-mart.

Alpha slides through the sand in a cloud of dust, instinctively trying to keep his face from scrubbing raw. His hands break his fall and I swear I hear the skin tearing open.

Before he finishes skidding to a halt, I jam a knee into the back of his neck, pushing his face down into the ground. I don't say anything.

"What the fu--?!" He screams, palms pushing against the ground to no avail. My weight is too much.

"Fudge? Fusion? Fulgent? Fusilier?" I pause. "Help me out here. I can't think of any more words starting with 'fu'."

"What do you want?" His teeth grit, but I can't tell whether from pain or frustration.

I yank the camera out of his pants. "Here I thought I was bad, but you're lousy at this game. Guess I'll settle for the door prize."

He says nothing. My sense of humor doesn't always play well to the crowds.

We walk back through the parking lot, drawing more than a few quizzical looks. I keep him in a pain compliance hold, locking his wrist in a bent position. I can't help the stares. People will see what they see, but as long as they don't decide to cross that line, our game stays square.

I bring him through the side door marked 'Fire Exit Only.' It's not supposed to be disarmed, but I have a key and choose to ignore that rule. We need easy access to our domain without having to navigate crowds. Plus, I have a problem with rules I don't understand or agree with.

Our Loss Prevention offices consist of four rooms. One is the camera and equipment room. The other three are given over to processing. Each features a plate window of one-way glass so we can see in without them seeing out. The doors are keyed, to get in or out. Two chairs and a desk occupy the space of each office, but one of those chairs will never move. It's bolted to the floor, in case someone decides to be uncooperative.

The first two rooms are already taken with the other two thieves. They've been separated for better leverage in the interview.

I walk alpha into my office. We're not supposed to have individual offices; I choose to ignore that rule as well. I shove him down into the chair across from my desk and he gapes at me as I cuff him to the welded ring in the chair leg.

"I'm limited to one chase per day. Company policy. You've taken up my quota, hence cuffs."

"Are you serious?" He asks.

I lean in and fix him with my most intense stare, only I cross my eyes. "Do I look serious?"

With that, I leave him alone and walk out into the hall, peeking into the first office. Kari is sitting with the girl – it is professional suicide for a male to be alone with a female in a locked office – and Kevin has lackey boy. I enter Kari's room as she's starting up her report.

Kari is not at all unattractive: smooth skinned, light hair, green eyes, well built.

When we're in a group she avoids me like the plague, but once alone she's much more open. She smiles and actually speaks to me. I don't know much else about her. She doesn't speak of her private life, I don't ask.

The female thief looks at me, but her look is considerably different than Kari's. Her jaw is set and her eyes are red-rimmed as if she's been crying. It happens; I don't let it get to me. I am titanium to women's emotions.

I put on my most disarming smile. "Well, hello there. And how are you today?"

She simply stares back, silent. I glance over Kari's shoulder. The vitals section of her report is blank and no ID is sitting on the desk.

"What's your name?" I try again.

"Ima Bitch. What about it?" Her look is defiant, her accent Southern. I can't place it. Texas, Kentucky, Virginia; they all sound the same to me.

I nod slowly. "So is that Bitch senior or junior?"

"They don't do senior/junior for girls, dumb ass."

Folks, we got ourselves a literal.

The camera is lying on the desk. I pick it up. Retail on this unit is $499, one dollar under felony territory. I suspect it's not a coincidence and that changes my opinion of this case.

Too bad we can't add on tax.

"What's the money for?"

A quick flutter of surprise in her eyes tells me I hit the mark. Maybe she expected me to ask why she took it. Frankly, I don't care.

She shrugs. "Just wanted it for myself."

"Bull. Your friend chickened out so you stepped up. Your other friend has an identical one. You guys stayed right under the felony limit. Looking to refund for cash, I'd guess. Again, what's the money for?"

Another shrug and silence.

"I never got your name."

"That's because I ain't giving it, asshole."

I look over to Kari. She's stifling a smile. "Tell her it's Mr. Asshole to everyone around here."

The lackey boy had been the most nervous. He's my weak link, so I decide to pry at him. I step in with Kevin and moments later I'm speaking with one David Barton of West Virginia. The girl is his sister Casey. Their accents are the only things that match. Maybe they're adopted.

David wouldn't give up anything on the alpha male of their little group, though. Either he's afraid of the guy or afraid of the repercussions of revealing the guy. It's a subtle distinction.

Guess I'll have to do this the hard way.

On the way back to my office I poke my head in with Kari. "Hey Casey, one thing: we'll just need your ID to make things run smoothly from here on out. You can just place it on the desk." I use my most innocuous expression, all pleasantry and smiles, as if we are close friends.

The look she returns is the exact opposite. She knows who just rolled on her.

I re-enter my office. "What's your name, friend?" Maybe, just maybe, I've sized him up wrong and he wants to spill his guts.

He looks at me, then turns his stare to the wall and clenches his jaw tight. I half expect him to shout out name, rank and serial number.

"Listen, you want out of here the hard way or easy? Easy costs, but it's the quickest." I let the hint settle into the room. Sure enough, he picks it up.

"You really think I'm going to fall for that?"

"You're in a heap of trouble. I'm just laying out some options. A guy's got to eat, you know."

He mulls it over then meets my gaze. "Suppose I ask: How much?"

I give a nonchalant gesture. "I answer: What you got?"

"Hundred."

"Then that's what you got."

The kid stares at me, undoubtedly weighing the merits and risk of continuing down this path. I say nothing, letting him work it out on his own.

He nods; a short sharp motion. "I need my wallet."

I kneel down, pinning his wrist to the chair leg. I transfer the cuff to his leg.

"What the hell?" He blurts out.

"Hey, you ran on me."

"But you caught me easy and you're like twice my size."

"Don't forget, twice as smart."

I sit up on the desk and motion for him to pull out his wallet. My legs start to swing in anticipation.

As he removes his wallet, my legs swing harder. Somehow my foot connects with his hand, knocking the wallet free. It flies across the room, contents scattering.

"Oh, crap. I'm sorry," I say.

He reaches for it but the cuff keeps him in the chair and he can't stretch far enough.

"Here, let me get that for you." I truly am ever the helpful guy.

He swears as my game dawns on him. I place the credit cards back, examining each one. He has seven in total. If my wife had seven cards, she'd need a bigger purse just to hold all the receipts.

I count out twenty-eight dollars, carefully placing them in plain sight on the desk. "The other seventy-two in your sock?"

"Fuck you." He sounds pissed for some reason.

Keeping out the driver's license I hand the wallet back to him. "I'll leave your ID out since we need it anyway. You don't have to thank me."

Thus concluded the information reveal phase. The restraints placed on thief dancers are at once liberating and limiting. We're not ordained officers and don't enjoy the same search and seizure privileges. A cop would have just gone into Casey's purse to get the ID for himself. A cop would have patted down my guy and removed the contents of every pocket.

I don't stand on such firm footing.

But on the flip side, I'm not encumbered by things like Miranda rights. I can ask them anything with no warning for how the information will be used. Hell, half the time I don't even bother to announce that they're under citizen's arrest.

I start filling out my report, easily the worst part about an arrest. The fun part's over, now we're left with crappy handwriting and narratives. All our reports are still manual, which drives my wife crazy. If I mention it, she'll start prattling away on methods of automation. My eyes glaze over in seconds. I can barely work my cell phone.

"Mr. Todd Layton, of Otway, Ohio," I recite, looking at his ID. My mike is still open. Now Kari and Kevin know all the player names.

"Hey," I lean forward. "If someone asks you for directions, do you ever tell them to go 'otway'?"

He fumes in silence, still pissed at my bribery ruse. I always find that funny. They steal but I'm the bad guy for tricking them? Yeah, right. I should be the one pissed. I almost got ripped off for seventy-two bucks.

We banter back and forth for a while. Well, I banter and he remains defiant. I complete my report and place a call to the police. We tend to prosecute 99% of all crooks, but I'd also once heard that 74.17% of stats are made up on the spot.

So take that for what it's worth.

A check on Kevin reveals he's as bored as me, also waiting on the cops. The adrenaline of a bust doesn't last long. I know he's envious that I got the runner, since he lives for the action as well. I also know Todd would have left him in the dust. Kevin can catch crooks with the best of them, but an athlete he is not.

We once played racquetball and I could barely move from the laughter of watching him try to hit a little bouncing ball.

As I check in on Kari, I notice a mark on Casey's neck. High up the back, just under the hairline. She sported the shaved sides and back/longer hair on top look made popular by many female softball players. That's the only way I could have seen it. I lean in close behind her, thinking it's a tattoo.

No, it's a brand.

That had to hurt, getting stamped on the back of the skull like that.

Casey spins in her chair. "What are you doing? Pervert."

"Smells like someone farted in here. Just doing a sniff check."

I brush aside Kari's quizzical look with a short shake of my head and leave. On a hunch I step back into my office and use a pencil to flip off Todd's ball cap. I ignore his obscenities, palming his head and pushing it forward. Sure enough, same brand, same place.

"What is that?" I ask aloud, not really expecting a response.

And Todd does not disappoint. A simple 'fuck you' is all I get back.

Casey's brother David doesn't have the mark and he claims ignorance when I ask. I can't tell if he's lying or not.

So I leave everyone sitting on their respective haunches and head out to the sales floor.

I feel bothered by the brand. It's new. It's not something I've ever seen. We may not be urban gangster central in North Haven, but we have our share of activity. We also catch a number of people with some kind of affiliation.

Usually it's a tattoo, sometimes crude, sometimes elaborate. Anyone can get one and with modern instruments even soft Gap-generation kids can handle the pain.

But a brand?

That's hard core. Or at least harder core. Especially on the back of your neck.

I find myself staring at the registers, lost in thought, until I realize that a bunch of the cashiers are staring back. I'm making them nervous, making them wonder if there's something wrong.

Entering a hallway to the second floor of the building, I take the steps two at a time.

This area is where all the other managers live, separated from normal human interaction by taupe-colored cube walls.

On a late Saturday morning it's empty. Everyone is on the sales floor.

My mailbox is overflowing, with envelopes internal and external, and other such junk. Some of it might be important. I grunt in confusion. I've always thought that if you ignore a problem long enough it will go away. The mail gods must subscribe to a different theory.

Another hallway lurks past the common cube area and I turn my feet to there. This is the true power center of not only the store, but all the stores in the region. Corporate players with titles like Regional General President and Regional Marketing

Director reside here. A light is burning down at the end from one of the offices and I smile to myself.

Sure enough, Jay is in.

I give a quick knock as I enter. "Jay Dub! What's up, you dog you?"

Jay looks up from his stack of papers and returns my greeting. His last name is something incredibly difficult, like Wickeszechalewsky, which caused me to call him Jay Dub for short back when we first met. His title is Regional Operations Director – Hardline, whatever the hell that means.

Jay's the guy that took a chance and hired me as a freshly-minted college graduate two years ago. We quickly formed a friendship. He isn't much older, but better at tracking his lanes on the career highway.

Actually, most people are better at that than me.

We chat for a bit to catch up. Due to his travel schedule, I don't see him as much anymore. He shows me fresh pictures of his daughter.

I glance at the clock on his desk. Cops should be getting here any minute now. But first: "Do you still do work with troubled youth at the civic center?"

"If I say 'yes', what does that mean?"

I sketch out a crude copy of the brand on Todd and Casey's neck. "Ever seen this mark before? Maybe on the back of someone's neck?"

Jay studies it then shakes his head. "Doesn't look familiar, but –"

"But what?"

He chews his lip and stares at it. "Last year I studied the etymology of gang symbolism, trying to get a better understanding of their origins. I don't think this is a sign attached to the normal gangs we see around here. But that's just my hunch."

"I thought etymology was the study of bugs?"

He laughs. "Such a smartass. Where'd you see this? Why are you asking?"

I shrug with forced nonchalance. "Just thinking about a design for my forehead."

This time his laugh is a little faked. I can tell he doesn't believe me. I leave with the promise that we'd play some racquetball soon.

I snag a donut out of a box leftover from a morning sales meeting. Normally I'm very strict about my food regimen, but hell, everyone needs a cheat day. Plus, I had other concerns about this day that could only be put off for so long and a single donut wasn't one of them.

CHAPTER THREE

Horsepower

By the time I trot back downstairs, the cops have arrived. Officer Allan Borden is in with Kevin, while another one processes Casey.

"What's up Allan?"

He looks up from the paperwork. "Rick."

We shake hands in the tradition of two men who know each other well, but not to the point of sharing off-duty time together. Matter of fact, we've been acquainted since grade school, when I used to pick on him. We're friendly, not friends.

Kevin doesn't need my help with this part of the bust, neither does Kari. They're both experienced. I know a fifth wheel when I see it, so I excuse myself.

I open my office door to find Todd standing, still shackled to the chair, staring at the bookshelves lining the wall. He jumps, obviously startled, and a guilty look flashes across his face.

"What are you doing?"

"Nothing. Stretching. Can't believe you shackled me."

Everything is in its place on the shelves. Stacks of magazines, mostly of the *Road & Track* variety, model cars, some mandatory work manuals that have never been opened; a knock at the door interrupts my thoughts.

I let in Allan. He's seen plenty of my reports, enough to be comfortable with the way I prepare them. A few cursory questions for Todd, a quick glance at the paperwork, then he flips open his citation book and starts filling it out.

"He got violent with me," Todd suddenly blurts, holding up his hands to show the scrapes and dried blood.

Allan looks up from his book. "Did you run?"

"Yeah, because he scared me."

"He scares everyone. Dumb move on your part anyway. You can't outrun him."

The compliment, backhanded as it is, catches me by surprise. That's not our relationship. It also emboldens me.

"Hey," I say to Allan, clamping my hand over Todd's head and forcing it forward to expose the brand. "What do you make of this?"

Allan leans in closer to peer at it. "How do you see these things?" He mutters, but makes no other response and goes back to his citation.

"It's new. The girl in the other room had an identical one. Are you hearing anything about new gangs in town?"

Normally gangs arose out of opportunity, boredom and self-protection. Kids, coming together from points of strength and weakness – the strong bullying the weak, causing the weak to get strong – and attracting others searching for that sense of belonging.

Usually they were self-contained, fairly small in scope, with a limit to their lifespan.

The differing accents on Todd and Casey could be nothing more than coincidence. A worst case scenario would have a large regional gang coming into North Haven to recruit and settle in. Don't ask me why though, there's nothing special here.

Allan looks up at me. "What are you doing?"

"Huh?"

"The thinking. I can hear your mind racing already. It's a brand, the new thing for kids. It's something they'll regret in twenty years, a reminder of a dumb decision. Don't make it anything more than that. The world has enough hobby cops."

I bristle at the rebuke, but shut up. I don't even know how to articulate what I'm thinking, much less explain it. I needed to mull it over some more.

After the police leave, I sit back in my office and let my mind wander. Shadows and whispers of conspiracy bang around in my skull no matter how much I try to ignore them.

Eventually I realize that sitting around won't help me and putting things off will only make matters worse.

So I tell everyone I'm leaving and walk out to my car at the far end of the lot. She's a Mustang Cobra, my pride and joy. And probably the only woman in my life that gets me.

I sit there in neutral, listening to the deep exhaust note while pondering things significant and otherwise about life. Honking and a squeal of tires knocks me loose from my reverie.

Over at the next entrance a Mercedes signals and turns into the lot, piloted by a distinguished-looking black gentleman in a bow tie. I decide he looks like a professor. It's a really nice car, one of the S series.

Hugged tight to his bumper is a beat-up wagon. The old man pulls over a few slots, making way. In response the wagon surges forward and skids to a stop in front the Benz, blocking any further progress. Something has really pissed off that driver.

My hackles rise and I engage the Cobra into gear, pointing it towards a potential situation. Anything attached to the Hyper-Mart is my territory, so I feel perfectly within my rights to stick my nose where it perhaps wouldn't normally belong.

The wagon driver leaps out of his car, rushing around to the Mercedes and raining down a torrent of obscenities. I catch the gist of it between spurts of profanity: the Mercedes wasn't moving fast enough.

You know your trigger is light when something like a slow car can cause you to explode.

The old man looks up at him through the closed window, unwilling to roll it down and respond. Can't say I blame him; it's getting to be a weird world out there.

I slow my car ten feet behind the maniac. He ignores me; or is completely unaware, too consumed by his rage. The old man meets my stare and I can see the concern in his eyes. He isn't afraid yet, but teeters on the edge.

"Hey!" I shout when the wagon driver stops to draw a breath. He has a stocky build. Any former muscle earned in younger years now gone to chub on a nightly habit of beer and burger. It wouldn't surprise me if he was still drunk.

I tend to get judgmental that way.

He spins. "Whaddya want?"

"Is this really necessary?" I ask in a neutral voice. He's maybe a shade over six feet, tall enough that I have to crane my neck slightly to look up at him from my seated position.

"Go fuck yourself."

I clamp down on my emotions and let just a little edge seep into my voice. "Say that again."

He looks over his shoulder at me, perhaps rethinking his tone. "This ain't none of your business."

"Or maybe I need to make it my business. Why don't you try someone who can handle it? Or do you just do easy prey?"

I want to deflect the focus from the old man to me, move the fight to someone more willing – and able – to carry it.

My ploy works. The maniac swings back to me, teeth clenched, eyes squinting. "The hell you say to me? You see what's going on here? This piece of shit is driving some fucking fancy car, thinking he's got life made when he's probably just living off welfare, buying this shit on our dime. That's the way it works with these people. Fucking..."

He then drops the N-bomb.

I hate racial slang, especially that word. My best friend in life, a guy that stood by me through thick and thin, is black. We'd had our fights, like all friends do, and will probably have more. But in the end we bleed for each other. Anyone coming between us has to go through me first.

"Yeah. My fault. I didn't make myself clear. I meant to say: You are a lowlife. You pull in here like this, bringing your hate. In truth, if your pops had just pulled out, then we'd all be better off."

The man reddens and starts forward. Behind him the Mercedes driver watches a racial confrontation between two white guys.

Before he can reach me, maybe throw a punch through the open window, I shove open my door and rear up. Like my car, I too possess a fair share of horsepower. He hesitates as I unfold to my full height. People who meet me often ask if I play football, but usually just those who don't follow the sport or know my story.

This guy must have been a fan to some degree. He stares as I step forward and a spark of recognition flares on his face.

"Hey, aren't you – "

I cut him off. "No, I'm not. Walk away before you find out who I am."

His attitude falters, as is often the case with a bully; especially when looking up at someone who outweighs him by thirty pounds. He doesn't like the odds.

With one last attempt at bigoted dignity, he spits on the lot near my feet and stalks back to his car. He pauses just long enough to point accusingly at the old man before roaring off in a cloud of exhaust. The sound of a ratty muffler shreds the ambience of a nice Saturday afternoon in April.

The Mercedes window starts to roll down, perhaps the old man wishing to offer thanks, but I just wave him onto his day.

My mood has soured.

Like many other young people, I too had arrived at a turning point in my life; that place where all roads diverge and each choice made would prove significant in some manner.

When I look back, this was the day it all began.

CHAPTER FOUR

Maya

The ten mile drive home usually takes me twenty minutes, mostly because there's no direct route. I follow side roads, some lined with white fences as a nod to the past when this was horse and cow territory.

I live in the village of Marewood, an exclusive community with street names like Devlin's Way, Deep Crossing Lane and Meadow Prance. Lawyers nod to doctors over neatly trimmed hedges, in turn those doctors wave to corporate executives across the street. It is – shall we say – a high tax base concentration. Little of it comes from me, understand. My forty large wouldn't even cover the property bill and utilities.

Our family income is heavily weighted towards my wife. She's one of the tech people fueling the Internet engine. As a computer consultant, she averages somewhere in the neighborhood of two hundred dollars an hour.

I thought it was an exorbitant amount, but 1999 had brought this unbridled, almost irrational, sense of exuberance about all things technology. People with those skills are making money hand over fist.

And then there's Rick Killing with his hopped-up Cobra and low rent retail job, fouling the waters.

I'm on autopilot, letting my mind continue on its wandering ways, when the radio breaks the news.

A man had been found murdered on the outskirts of town, in a bare field. Suspected cause of death was the wooden stake driven through his eye socket. Drawn around him, in the freshly turned dirt, was a circle of red with a white cross inside. Inside the cross, a red blood drop. It's a symbol adopted by the Ku Klux Klan many years ago. The man was white.

I pop in one of my favorite college CDs in an effort not to listen to any more. The band is Afghan Whigs and I rumble down neatly trimmed avenues of North Haven with songs like "*Crime Scene, Part One*", "*Bulletproof*", and "*Honky's Ladder*" pouring out. The choice of music is not lost on me.

Thinking of the news irritates me. Murder sucks. My driving grows aggressive, the tires chirp when I shift gears. Told you she understands me.

The victim was one Donald Sutton, esquire, a big-time lawyer from a nearby town.

Left behind were a wife and two small children, which made me ache. My wife and I haven't been blessed with the pitter patter of children, but we are both still young and many years stretch ahead. Of course, Sutton probably thought the same thing.

The implications in his death were stark. Someone, somewhere, wanted to send a very public message. And that message said, 'Our turn.'

It felt weird to think of the Klan, to think they played a role in the daily life of my town. Did they even still exist? In my mind they were one of those stains on history, a chapter in our nation's adolescence that many would rather forget. The year 2000 is right around the corner; the Klan is a relic from a far gone time. Those two things are mutually exclusive.

Aren't they?

The KKK was one of those topics that got thrown in the blender with other artifacts, like the telegraph machine or Pony Express. We'd come up with newer, better mechanisms to replace them, relegating their legacy to school lessons and museum tours.

If the Klan truly lives around here, who will be next?

Unfortunately, Sutton wasn't the first. I figure he isn't the last either. Two others preceded him in the last month. Three deaths didn't generate much news in places like Metropolis or Gotham. But North Haven is none of those places and hopefully never will be.

Still, the manner of death deserved more attention. These were not drive by shootings, muggings or DUI-caused accidents. All three men fit a profile; all three men were used for a particular purpose.

Victim One had been hung from a tree, iron collar and shackles placed around him just like the slaves of old.

Victim Two had been draped on a cross, burned alive, covered by a white satin robe and matching hood. The material was traced to a Klan Grand Wizard who disappeared over a year ago.

Then Victim Three: Sutton with his new eye implant.

All three were white, middle-aged men of power and influence.

I'm white as white gets, with lineage that traces back to Denmark. When I get home I'm throwing away my fluffy white cotton robe, just in case.

Two large stone pillars emerge from the horizon, a wrought iron header arching overhead. The name Windermere Fields is spelled out in the iron, ornate and ridiculous to me. What the hell is a windermere anyway? The developer should have stayed literal and named it Corn Field Estates or Former Pasture of Crap from Animals.

Except this place is as far from crap as I've ever been. The median house runs about 4000 square feet, with all the attendant amenities such as brick paver driveways, built-in irrigation, basement wine cellars, and Shaker-style roofs.

I wind down the street, passing houses filled with people I barely know, but know about. A couple of executives from a local pharma company lived side by side, but they hate each other. Something about competing divisions or such. There were some lawyers, computer geeks like my wife working off fat contracts, a CEO for a small downtown start-up. We even had a writer whose stuff I never understand and who I can't tolerate for more than three seconds. Writers are a weird flock.

In all, Windermere Fields contains fifty families in various states of bliss, decay or devotion to the almighty dollar, perched at the precipice of a new century. And we all rarely speak to each other.

A median splits the road down the center, a manicured island boasting ornamental trees, flowerbeds and a park bench that has never been sat on. The ridiculous association fee paid for upkeep on it and I can see my money at work: A crew of Hispanic laborers are yanking weeds and planting the colors with which we'd usher out the old century and advance into the next.

My vagrant thoughts on race and the passage of time are replaced with other considerations as I pull up to my house.

We live at 620 Hunter Run. Past our house the road split into a series of cul-de-sacs, each with a weirder name than the last. In the nine months we've lived here I've wandered around a few times walking my dog.

The wide driveways sport the latest Audi, Mercedes or Lexus and seem to exude a certain desperation, as if keeping up with the Jones just raised a new bid and no one was sure whether to match or fold.

What made it worse is that I no longer own a dog and people look funny at me as I drag an empty leash.

Of all the houses, ours probably stood out the most. Not because it was the largest or nicest, but because it has a unique architecture. Built in 1996, it's a Mediterranean-style villa with stucco and a red slate roof. It would look great on a hillside in Italy. A perfect place to get away from the pressures of life, the realtor said. Everything a growing family needs, the realtor said.

I bet she didn't have a clue as to what our family really needed.

The garage juts out from the front of the house, doors perpendicular, which creates a kind of courtyard. I trigger one of the three garage doors and crank my steering wheel left to enter. I leave it open in case I need to rush out later.

My wife's Jeep inhabits the first stall; my two motorcycles sit in the middle. One is a Honda SuperHawk, a crotch rocket in slang terms. The other is an older Honda SuperMagna that I keep for sentimental purposes since it was my first bike. Super this, super that. What a super day.

Four steps lead up to the veranda fronting the house and I take them one at a time, unlike my usual single bound.

Three sets of doors line the wall, leading into the dining room, main foyer and den. I twist the knob on the middle door and enter.

My shoes scuff on the tile as I pass through. The aforementioned dining room on my left holds a long cherry wood table and matching chairs that we've never used. I have no idea where the furniture even came from.

On the right sat my wife's home office. She's not in there, which I find surprising because it's her favorite room in the whole wide world. She can spend more hours staring at a computer screen than anyone I've ever known. My grandparents – God bless their souls – would have declared that so much staring could only drive her blind and crazy.

I can attest that she's not blind.

I toss my keys on the center island in the kitchen. All the appliances are stainless steel, which kind of confuses me since they aren't as shiny as our silverware. I once hinted that maybe my wife had been ripped off in the purchase, resulting in a wonderful knockdown fight. We were driving at the time and she actually pulled over a couple miles away and ordered me to get out and walk home. I didn't.

I ran home, because I'm fast, but she still beat me. That pissed me off.

Tucked off the side of the kitchen is a hallway leading back to our bedroom. The realtor called it the master suite, a great lie. I can't get my wife to call me master anywhere, especially there. She's not in that room either.

Likewise, the master bath is empty. It has one of those all-glass showers for twenty of your closest friends. The whirlpool tub can hold another dozen. The last time we used it was during a fight, not to be confused with the stainless steel altercation. My wife retreated to the bathroom and filled it, floating in the water with her snorkeling gear to block out my words. It was monumentally irritating until I poured a cup of water down the snorkel tube.

Then it became quickly hilarious, at least to me.

I retrace my steps and don't bother to check the loft or second floor bedrooms. She won't be up there, I'm not sure she knows they exist. She'll be downstairs.

Our basement holds a workout room, rec room, bar area and all the other usual suspects. French doors lead out to a paver block patio, which in turn is covered by a wooden deck from the kitchen area above.

Pausing at the bottom landing, I look across the open space to find her, my blushing bride. Maya Mananoa Killing. Petite, intelligent beyond my understanding, dark-haired and dusky-skinned; gorgeous enough to make a man's eyes bleed.

Hawaiian-Filipino heritage gifted her with skin that stays tan all year round, black silky hair that would probably never turn gray and a slim frame that didn't need much help to stay that way. Her genes also provided a youthful look. We are eight years apart but she looks younger.

Oh, Maya, you have so many things working in your favor.

She stretches out on a yoga mat, clad only in white Lycra pants and matching sports tank, and the outfit showed her off in a most brilliant way. Her hair, tied back into a long braid that hangs nearly to her waist, rolls off to one side of her back as she leans forward, touching forehead to kneecap, fingers to toes. I wince. If God wanted me to touch my feet, he would have put them a lot closer to my hands.

Her back is to me, thankfully. I sip a deep breath and hold it a second. Exhale. "Hey, babe. I'm home."

The singular lack of response tells me everything I need to know in that instant. Check that. There is a response: Her back stiffens ever so slightly. It's subtle, but I know what to look for.

Here we go.

I step off the landing and walk slowly over to her. "I thought you were going into the city to work today."

Maya slowly draws herself back up to a sitting position, holding it for a few seconds before standing. Maybe she needed to calm herself. She grabs a towel from a nearby weight rack and dabs at her brow.

She has a face to match her body: exotic, mysterious, hinting of secret promises that you might be lucky enough to learn. A tiny spattering of freckles across her nose is visible when there's no makeup. In all, her normal expression is of serenity and poise, as if she knows something that no one else does.

"You're a dick," she says.

Well, that everyone knows.

"Why would you go into work?" She continues. "You know what today is."

"International Hamster Appreciation day?"

"Bastard," she mutters, eyeing up one of the ten pound dumbbells.

I needed to be careful here. Last winter she had heaved a five pounder at me and missed. But she hit one of the French doors square in the middle. I spent the next hour shoveling snow off the carpet, cleaning up glass and taping plastic over the hole until a guy could come out. She even made me pay for the repair.

I know very well what today is, despite my smart quip. It's her birthday. Hamster Day isn't for another week yet.

Today she turns thirty-two. I vaguely remember her talking about spending the day together but for some reason I still chose to go into work. Some shrink, somewhere, probably could charge us thousands of dollars to diagnose our – my – issues. I don't think it's all that complicated.

However, no one likes to be attacked, to be confronted with his own dick-headed nature, including me. I take it one step further and escalate.

"Of course I remember the day. But you know what? You spend every Saturday either in the city or parked in front of that stupid computer. Why should I think today is any different?"

To back up my words, I employ my most intimidating glare, the one I use on crooks to get them to confess. I tower over my wife by more than a foot, so my height works into it. I narrow my eyes.

"Stop staring at my chest, asshole."

Man, what a tough cookie. It *is* a nice chest, though. I avert my look and try a different tack. "Why didn't you remind me this morning?"

"I was still asleep."

"Stop trolling the web 'til all hours and you could wake up at a decent time and remind me." There might have been a touch of sarcasm in my tone.

"I shouldn't have to remind you. You're supposed to know things like that already."

"Well, if I wouldn't have to take care of everything else around here, I'd have more time to remember the little things." Oh, crap. It just slipped out.

"Little things? *Little things?*"

And just like that we descend into our weekly fight. It usually takes place on Sundays, but hey, we're flexible adults. I honestly don't know what prompts these verbal sparring sessions, but I have a few theories.

I used to think it was due to us always having Sundays open. Since I often worked Saturdays, she did too, leaving Sunday to become the day of our discontent by default. Maybe we just can't spend that much time together. That's theory number one, flimsy as it is.

Theory number two, sad to say, is my suspicion that every time we look at each other we think: *I shouldn't be here*. Maybe that's more me than her, I don't know, but sometimes I can see hints of it in her eyes.

Our relationship only had six months under its belt before we took the plunge. A short courtship, as my parents would say. She was enrolled in a Master's program at the University of Illinois, I was big man on campus due my athletic achievements. I guess she wanted to be the girlfriend of a sports hero.

In my senior season, she got her chance.

I broke off from a long-time girlfriend and within weeks Maya came calling. We danced around each other for a while, although I danced considerably less: My knee had taken a serious shot in the fall and just like that my pro sports future turned cloudy.

So instead of finding riches at the end of my personal rainbow, she found a gimp and it culminated in a wedding after graduation. Maybe she thought I'd pick it all back up one day. I wasn't sure what my motives were at the time, aside from the physical attraction, but I have a sneaking hunch that they were not as admirable as they should have been.

When I think of my wife, a sense of something broken accompanies the thought. Like I had one chance to make my life right and I fumbled the ball before crossing the goal line. I often wonder what it would be like to be free of this marriage, but I don't want to be tainted by the entire experience. A part of me – that stubborn part – is determined to stick it out through all the trials, because that's what you do. But I can't always hear that voice clearly.

I don't want to be a divorced man, don't want that label, because that's not the way things were supposed to be. Also, it would confirm the magnitude of the mistake I made one fateful night in college and I'm not sure I can bear that realization.

Our fights usually follow a similar pattern: She bitches about my insensitivity, pig-headedness and inconsideration. I claim innocence and turn everything around by counter-bitching on her lack of affection, work obsession and nagging. I know it's an immature reaction, just as I know it's probably a common theme in other relationships. But everything changes when it's your fight.

So we spar back and forth in our preset modes, rehashing old hurts, opening wounds too thinly healed. A glance at the clock across the room reveals the time. It's almost four. Enough nonsense. We need to move on from this.

"Look, babe," I say. "I'm sorry I forgot. Okay? It wasn't intentional. What do you want me to do to make it up?"

A step towards her demonstrates the depth of my sincerity. Shrinks probably call it 'bridging the gap' or some other such silly metaphor.

It signals her turn to let loose a tear or two. Strangely enough – or sadistically for those of that persuasion – I like the way my wife cries. No puffy eyes, no snotty sobs. Just silent runnels of emotion tracking down her cheeks.

It probably says something about my inner state, and Lord knows I have plenty of flaws, but I can only be who I am. In a definition of the word pathetic, we seem to require such hateful fights in order to bare our souls and touch each other in the way man and wife are meant to.

But enough drivel.

The end of a fight also signals the beginning of something else, that great equalizer which temporarily salves all wounds: make-up sex. Only with the foreplay of damaging emotion are we able to unfetter the bonds that trap us tightly all other times. Only then can we press flesh to flesh in an attempt to heal the ever-widening rifts in our marriage.

And that's my third and final theory on our relationship. We know if we fight, we can then be intimate and one day a week is better than none at all.

So I take her hard and rough right there, on the yoga mat used to promote good health and feelings of harmony. Only there's none of that between us; we find our spiritual center by other means. By naughty words and forceful actions and sweaty grunts.

Unfortunately, relationships predicated on such flawed foundations can never last.

CHAPTER FIVE

Surf 'n Turf

By five o'clock the growling in my stomach cannot be denied and it makes me antsy. Maya could probably lounge around the house naked for the rest of the night – and that holds its own promise – but the restlessness in me is too much. The afternoon sun glistens off her tan thighs, until I give one of them a slap and tell her to get moving.

Our post-coital glow has once again knit together the wounds for another week.

We share a quick shower and I end up wandering the house as she begins the detailed process of making herself presentable to John Q. Public. My feet take me out to the front veranda and I lean up against one of the columns that flank the stairs. Our house faces east and the lowering sun creates long shadows across the front yard. I've replaced my working attire of jeans and a t-shirt with something a little more formal for dinner: I added a belt and my t-shirt now sports a classier logo.

As I stand there, the sound of a car turning into our street rolls over me. The garage blocks my view of the subdivision entrance so I play my mental game of guess the car based solely on engine sound. It's a big V8, but unfamiliar. Not domestic, not German. Definitely not a truck.

A Jaguar sedan appears seconds later, purring contentedly along.

The driver looks my way, almost as if he expects I will be there, and gives a small wave. I nod back and watch as he continues down another half dozen houses and pulls into a driveway on the opposite side. It's a monstrous Victorian tucked into a corner lot, with a wrap-around front porch and garage nestled in back. Maya and I had glanced at that place during our search but a glance was all. Even her salary couldn't swing the nut. Jaguar man moved in a month ago.

From the few times I've seen him, he reeks of corporate power: CEO, business consultant, lawyer, something like that. If I'm a movie director looking to cast the role of President, he would be it.

I haven't yet introduced myself, but it's on my list of things to do. Right after painting the garage floor mauve. I'm not big on meeting new people.

It occurs to me, watching my new neighbor park his car, that he fits the general profile of the murder victims, at least from what little has been reported. They all shared common traits: successful, middle-aged, white men of power, living a supposedly clean life.

None of them hid a history littered with vices like gambling, drugs or prostitutes. Even the connections to white supremacy affiliation were not confirmed. Maybe the men had been targeted solely for what they symbolized: white upper crust society, the echelon to which many youngsters aspired in their mad dash to the new century.

I wonder if my neighbor is worried for his safety.

Occasionally I ponder whether I could exist in that corporate world, making decisions that affect the lives of many, carrying the fates of people I would never meet. At times it seems pretty cool.

But I'm also realistic enough to acknowledge my true talents. They are in a very different field, far away from corporate boardrooms or streets called Hunter Run. To get back to that place where my skills matter means a long hard journey, one I fear I lack the strength to make.

And for that I hate myself.

Maya can't stand the Cobra – too noisy and cramped, never mind the fact that I wedge myself into it daily – so her Grand Cherokee becomes the family ride by default. I don't mind, it's a pretty cushy ride, fully optioned.

When we go places, I usually drive, if only to prevent her from dumping me on the side of the road again.

As we roll through the manicured lanes, I try to engage her about the North Haven murders, talking things out in an unconnected ramble, my way of brain storming. Maybe by doing so, my psyche would latch onto some small detail overlooked by everyone else and I'd become the hero for figuring it all out.

Mind you, there is no evidence that I possess detective ability or experience, but I refuse to let minor details get in my way.

Maya, bless her self-absorbed soul, hasn't been paying attention to the news. She didn't even know a third murder had been reported, which leads me to suspect that she truly did spend the day glued to her computer and ignoring everything else. I almost jump on that suspicion, but that would only lead to another fight and then I might never get to eat.

So I recap the pertinent information about Sutton and proclaim my belief that it is minority types lashing back at whites for things that happened in history.

A slightly pained look crosses her flawless features, meaning that she has to entertain thoughts about something other than bits and bytes. "I didn't realize the Klan was such a problem around here."

And just like that, her finely tuned intellect cuts to the quick of my theory. I've lived in North Haven for my entire life, apart from the college years, and there is no track record of racially charged activities.

We don't have minority gangs, we don't have white supremacists.

We don't really have much of anything except story book suburbia life, especially if you read the town's promo material.

Since I've never heard of race-related incidents in my town, I assumed there really aren't any. I'm not fully naïve, I'm sure there are occasional fights where someone spews hateful words, but that's not the same as an organized effort. Maybe some new movement has surfaced and some minorities are trying to cut it off before it grows too powerful. Maybe Sutton is their latest shot across the bow.

In any event, Maya's simple statement causes some doubt. I need to think on this more.

I pull the Jeep into the lot of a local steakhouse, a place called Kyle's. It's your typical neighborhood haunt, run by Kyle and his wife Ann, full of dark wood, dim lighting and fantastic red meat. Despite my careful intake of the "right" foods, if I could eat there every day I'd die a happy man. Fat, but happy.

It's a usual Saturday night, filled to the brim with a line of people waiting outside the door. Warm weather brings people out in droves, especially after the Midwestern winter.

I tow Maya through the crowd, skipping the wait list, and head straight to the bar. Because of my size, I generally have little trouble parting a crowd. Maya had once confessed to enjoying the reactions of people when I did that. She likes when someone recognizes me, probably because it's her own tenuous link to fame as well, a gentle tug on the life she desires.

Myself, I ignore the looks.

We grab the last two barstools. As soon as Ann sees us, she trots out our drinks. We're frequent enough that she knows our preferences without even asking. Captain Morgan for me, some fru-fru drink for Maya. I lift my glass in silent toast to my friend the Captain as both girls start talking girl stuff. For some reason, even though they are complete opposites in every way, Maya really likes Ann.

I swivel my stool and let my gaze roam the restaurant.

One of my occupational hazards is the inability to *not* watch everyone around me. Call it compulsion, but I study faces and body language when in public. It's not that unusual to see someone I've busted. The look on their face when we cross stares is often priceless. Shame, embarrassment, sometimes hostility.

Maybe I'm good at my job because I remember people, or maybe I remember people because of my job. Or maybe, just maybe, I enjoy that bit of voyeurism that comes from knowing a dirty little secret.

Many people have committed one of the so-called "common" crimes: speeding, bouncing checks, even DUI. These confessions will come up at a party, usually with a shake of the head and promise to avoid next time. But ask someone if they've ever stole and it's a different matter; it treads a different ethical line. You can trust someone who got caught speeding, but if someone admits to being a thief, suddenly they get looked at sideways.

No one is as defensive about a code of honor as they are when caught breaking it. Integrity exists only when no one is watching. Unfortunately for some, I *always* watch.

My eyes scan the room, trying to figure out who will one day succumb to the temptation of something for nothing.

A group of kids occupies a corner booth across the room; a typical gaggle out loose on a Saturday night. Although, I use the term "kids" loosely. Several of them look close to my age, they just don't have the grown up lifestyle that I so dearly enjoy.

Cigarettes, glasses, plates and laughter litter the table as they perform that ageless dance. Girls were checking out other girls in the room for competition. Boys were also checking out other girls. A few glances are sent Maya's way; she remains completely oblivious to the attention. It doesn't bother me. I'm not the jealous type.

The kids are all faceless to me, features similar to a hundred others I see on a daily basis. The races are mixed. Two blacks, an eastern Indian and the others white. If these kids can set aside racial and cultural differences to hang out and have fun, why is it so hard for anyone else?

Why does someone have to unearth the ugliness in our nation's past and remind us of what we once were?

And if there truly is a new surge of racial supremacy growing in North Haven, what would it do to these kids?

That's probably what bothers me the most. The image of my childhood town was being threatened, corrupted, forever changing the color tint of my memories, staining also the sentiment that accompanies a past so cozy. I never want to lose that softness inside that comes when I roll the streets I've known my entire life.

The trouble starts just after our food arrives. We'd moved to a table; in front of me sits a massive steak. My third or fourth drink also sits in front of me, the Captain joining in my wife's birthday dinner.

I raise my glass in a silent toast and drain it. The magic of bars is that I know another will somehow appear.

Maya has ordered one of those dinners of steak and shrimp. It has a really cool nickname, but my mind is growing fuzzy and the name escapes me. I snatch the drink off my waitress's tray before she can even set it down and take a gulp. Maybe this will jog my memory.

A group of Asian-looking people walks in through the door; couples mostly, with a few youngsters in tow. They're speaking whatever their native language is. Even though I'm married to a Filipino bilingual woman, I don't pretend to know the differences in appearance. It probably makes me racist to say they all look alike.

However, Maya is inherently – no militantly – proud of her heritage. And she has strong opinions on other ethnic groups, so she's the true racist in our household. And, as luck would have it, this particular group is on her shit list.

I hear the sharp sip of breath, followed by a hissed comment to me: "Look at them, Rick. They're Japanese. I hate it when they do that. They're in our country, they should speak our language."

For some odd reason, Maya cannot stand anything Japanese. She once stated that it had to do with World War Two. Apparently Japanese soldiers came to her mother's village in the Philippines and did some of the terrible things that get done in wars. Nothing, fortunately, to Maya's mother, a young woman then. And definitely nothing to Maya, who was not even a consideration yet.

No one she knew had been harmed all those decades ago, yet that bred an intense hatred I've never understood. She insists that you can't trust them, that they're underhanded and sneaky. Not even a great dinner of surf and turf can erase that hatred –

Surf 'n Turf! That's the cool name! I smile at my innate brilliance and signal for another Captain, since my current one must have tipped over. It's empty and that is the only way it could have happened so fast.

"What are you smiling at?" She asks suspiciously, as if by my expression alone I've aligned myself with her mortal enemies.

"Nothing, babe."

"You think this is funny?" A dangerous glint sparks in her eyes, but I don't fully recognize it. Something is making my vision blurry and inaccurate.

As stated, Maya can be a tad irrational despite her intimidating intellect, and that tendency is only exacerbated when something triggers her dander. The glint warns that her cream is rising and God help anyone in the line of her fire.

Just after we met, she was car shopping and selected a nice Acura. But when she found out that Acura was a Japanese company, she accused the salesman of tricking her and walked out. Never mind that Acuras are probably made in Ohio, Canada or someplace other than Japan.

The new RCA widescreen in our family room is a direct result her insistence that I get rid of the Mitsubishi. I really liked that TV, and now it sits unused in our basement storage room.

As the Japanese group files to a table behind us, Maya tears off a chunk of food and flicks it over her shoulder, hitting one of the women.

Oh, man, here it comes.

The woman looks back at us, but Maya's already averted her eyes. That leaves me to meet the confused gaze, which I could only do for a moment because my eyes keep crossing. I simply and slowly point to my wife with her head down in a land of surf 'n turf.

Maya mutters under her breath in her mother's tongue. I don't understand the language, but I recognize swear words when I hear them. Maybe round two of our weekly boxing match will take place at my favorite restaurant.

The woman stares a second longer before turning away. I can hear her whispering to her friends and a few glances float our way.

"Why did you point me out?" Maya says lowly. Her fingers are shredding the food. Actually, not shreds. Ammunition.

"You didn't have to do that."

"They're Japanese. You can't trust them. They're sneaky and underhanded."

"You don't even know them."

"I don't have to. Don't want to."

Experience has taught me the harsh lesson of prudence over valor. I know better than to prolong the discussion; it will only end in a bad way. I shake my head and notice another drink before me. Told you there's magic.

Maya flicks another piece. The lady spits out a garbled word and throws it back. Is everyone in this place insane?

I get up and bring my drink to the bar. I'm no longer hungry, but at least I've got the Captain. He'll keep me company.

That was my last coherent thought of the night.

7:34am

I groan and roll over, falling off the couch. Mornings always appear twice as fast when you really, really want them to take their time. I squint and peer at my watch, but it tells the same story.

A peek in our bedroom reveals Maya fast asleep so I close the bathroom door quietly. My face throbs on both sides and there is all kinds of racket in my head as I brush the flannel off my teeth.

A note is stuck to the mirror: *You were a jerk last night. By the way, surf n turf is steak and LOBSTER! Asshole.*

Vague memories come flooding back, of the drive home, chanting about how cool it was to have a food nickname that rhymed.

I'm not much of a drinker, never have been, mostly because I'm really bad at it. Also, taking care of my body is a lifelong habit and doesn't leave a lot of room for harmful ways.

Last night's bender was unlike me.

I can only attribute it to the restlessness that lives inside me; the feeling that comes from deep within and causes me to think all sorts of thoughts that I really shouldn't be thinking. Maybe I'm truly standing at my own crossroad and will need to soon decide a path.

The message indicator on the phone blinks incessantly as I top the stairs to an office area above the garage. I have my own line up here, which only a few people know. I'm fairly sure I know what the content of those messages will be.

It's spring, the time of year when the annual NFL draft rears its head. Football prospects around the nation are running, jumping and lifting for pro scouts, praying and begging for a chance to get drafted. The machine that is professional football is in full swing, putting into motion plans that will result in one championship team to end the season. I once believed my future consisted of being a key cog in that machine, but with every passing year the gulf widens until I'm no longer confident I can make the leap.

With one deep breath I plop down into my desk chair and press Play. There are numerous messages. Apparently someone misses me.

The first three are from my agent, feeling me out for my state of mind once again. That's not exactly what he says, but I can hear the underlying theme. His name is James DiCiprano and he's been my agent since college graduation. I wouldn't call him a friend exactly, but we're friendly.

Beyond that, he's hung in there with me despite everything; he has displayed a certain faith in me that many others don't and for that I appreciate him.

Perhaps the promise of a big payday keeps him around, but I doubted it. Kids come out every year and he could easily dump me for one of them.

But keep me on he does. His messages name several teams that are interested. I don't understand how they know to call him about me, but I assume there exists a huge list somewhere showing who represents who. I have to be at the bottom of that list.

All I need to do is return his call, give him an enthusiastic thumbs up, and start jumping through the hoops arranged by interested teams. One single call will start the engine and change my entire life within weeks.

One call.

I delete all his messages.

The restlessness inside isn't sourced from football, at least not all of it. No, it's something deeper, and I need to resolve certain things before I look into those other corners. There are enough shadows that I can only shed light on a few at a time.

My mother had snuck a message into the string, delivering her weekly updates since my father would never lower himself to such levels. Delete.

A few more were work-related, all several days old. Kineisha, calling to tell me about a liquor thief from the other night; Kari, just saying 'Hi'; my manager, asking why I never return any of her calls.

Delete, delete, delete.

And just like that I sever a few more ties in my life, cutting myself off in a cycle of entrapment. Bit by bit I back myself into a corner from which the only escape will be a long hard fight. Don't ask why I do such things.

Maybe I have a chip on my shoulder the size of Texas, seeking to prove my worth in a way meaningful only to me.

Maybe I'm trying to force a boiling point in my life, creating situations that will burn me if I don't move.

Or, just maybe, at my crossroad, I stood waiting, waiting for that thing to come along; a thing that would define me as a husband, as a person, as a man.

CHAPTER SIX

Dee

Two hours later I pull into the lot of the North Haven Athletic Center, parking out at the edge. An early run on the trails behind our neighborhood had worked some of the fuzziness out of my head, although the first fifteen minutes were painful.

I yank my bag out of the trunk. Jay is sitting in his parked Lexus near the entrance. They're cars for men who like manicures, in my opinion.

He had obviously received my last minute voicemail about racquetball. The guy has no idea what kind of harvest I'm about to reap on his ass.

We shake hands when he gets out. His gym bag sports a bunch of worn-out racquet gloves dangling from the strap. It's an honor badge by experienced players, to show off your prowess, kind of like notches in the belt of an old gunfighter.

My own bag has no such declaration. I prefer to beat the unwary with stealth.

Jay glances back out at my car on the perimeter. "Were you driving without a seat belt?"

"Not only that. I'm carrying a dead prostitute and 20 kilos of cocaine in the trunk."

"Seriously, you should be more careful." Since the birth of his daughter, Jay had gotten ultra conservative to risk. Apparently kids can do that to you.

"I only live a few minutes from here, chief safety."

"Still. I read somewhere that over ninety-three percent of accidents happen within five miles of your home."

"Really? Shit, did I ever buy in the wrong neighborhood then."

I sign Jay past the front desk and we descend the stairs to the locker room. I keep a standing reservation every month on center court, the one with a back wall of glass and raised seats for an audience.

We bang the ball around for a bit, warming up and taking subtle notes of each other. Jay knows his way around a court. He snaps the racquet, extracting a ton of torque from a short action. He's not as tall or fast, but his lightning quick steps serve him well in a tight space.

So I smack him in the back of the leg with the ball. It's like moving a batter off the plate by throwing heat too close to him. He'll think about that later.

Ten minutes later Damonti Davis enters the gym. My friend from way back, the black man who forces me daily to rethink my stance on black men.

The desk clerk does a double-take and greets him. Dee – as I'd called him since age seven – nods back and approaches our court.

In my head, an announcer's voice rings loud: *Batting second, from nearby North Haven, Illinois, third basemen Damonti Davis.*

Nearly one year ago, the life of my friend Dee had been irretrievably altered. The Chicago Cubs lost a starter at third and decided to call up one of their future prospects. After being drafted right out of high school and toiling in the farm leagues for five years, Dee finally got his chance in The Show.

He never looked back.

He exploded onto the Major League Baseball stage, ripping off highlight reel catches, batting up a storm, and in the process solidifying his place at one corner of the diamond. The Cubs rewarded him with a three year deal worth $4.8 million.

And just like that he entered a life both of us had always wanted, even as punk kids running the sidewalks and emulating our favorite sports stars.

Spring training folded just the other day and it's the first time we've seen each other in a month or more. We bump fists. I introduce him to Jay.

Jay looks a little startled. "Rick said Dee Davis. I didn't make the connection to *the* Damonti Davis. Nice to meet you." Even though Jay's not a baseball groupie, he follows sports enough to recognize the face.

It's a hard one to forget. Black as night, with one gold tooth peeking out and eyes lighter than they should be, Dee represented his race much in the same way I did mine. We are salt and pepper, but never has it come between us.

If anything, it makes us more loyal to the other, determined to stay tight in a world seemingly intent on separating whites from darks and washing each at a different temperature.

After a little small talk, we decide on best five of seven, cut-throat style games where one guy is against two in a rotation.

I toss the little blue ball to Dee. "Game on, bitch."

Two and a half hours later we finally call an end. The series had run to ten games, with Jay squeaking out four wins. He's a better player than I thought, experience making up for lack of athleticism. Dee and I each won three.

I shouldn't have run my mouth at every turn.

As we exit, a small throng of people are gathered outside the court. They cluster around Dee, requesting autographs. A few glance my way, probably wondering why I look familiar. My own story is not that far gone.

Since Dee is still new to the celebrity game, and since he generally is a nice guy at heart, he indulges everyone. Jay and I retreat to the juice bar up on the second level. From there we can look down at the crowd. I sit back with my bottle of grapefruit juice and watch. If I said it didn't gnaw and make me a little jealous, I'd be lying. At the same time, I feel happy for him.

Problem is, I don't know if I'm happier than jealous.

Dee, like many, isn't all that comfortable in front of a crowd of people staring at him, expecting something. Factor into that his natural shyness, which he covers with a surly exterior, and he can come off as a typical thug.

Seen from a distance, without the benefit of a lifetime friendship, I understand the perception.

That, however, causes Dee to carry a chip about the plight of the Black Man. In the last year, he's made a lot of new friends, not all of them true, and I could sense their influence. His inner rage at racial injustice has gained a sharper edge, slicing just that much deeper.

After a while, everyone leaves and he joins us, motioning silently to the juice girl for a bottle of water.

"Aren't you the popular guy," Jay comments.

Dee nods and pulls on his hat, adjusting it crooked on his head. What a dumb look. "Now, sure. But not always. That'd be my man Rick there." He smiles, a megawatt grin that splits his face. There's a hint of malice in it.

Jay glances over at me, then back. Under the duress of a game, they had dropped the veneer of corporate executive and sports star thug, becoming two guys playing a game. It's common ground, providing a form of relationship.

"Meaning?"

"How long you known Killer?" Dee asks.

"Just a couple years."

"Been around here your whole life?"

Jay shakes his head. "Up and down the west coast most of it."

A nod, processing the reply. "Well, Rick be what you call a hometown sports hero 'round here. When we was growing up, nobody could get 'nough of that boy."

I interject. "Yeah? I've had enough already. You can stop now."

"You pouting 'cuz you didn't win all the games for once?"

"And ruin the fine example you set as a sore loser? Perish the thought."

Dee flicks a bead of sweat at me and turns back to Jay. So much for accommodating me. Thanks, friend.

I get up and wander over to the bar. The girl smiles and sets down another bottle of juice before me. If there's a message in her eyes, I'm not seeing it. I'm a bit distracted.

Maya will likely be home when I get there, still pissed. As evidenced last night, she holds a grudge longer than anyone else on the planet. Her actions towards those ladies would be dismissed as proper self-defense of her culture, while my liquid indulgence would be categorized as a husband wrecking his wife's birthday.

Jay's voice cuts into my thoughts. "Hey, you never told me that, Rick."

Like I tell him my every dark secret.

I return a blank look. I don't know the subject, although knowing Dee like I do, I can guess.

He waits a second, expecting me to respond. When I don't: "The ninety-six Olympics. You could have gone?"

I just grunted in dismissal. Not my favorite topic.

"Well, what gives?"

"Nothing gives, Jay. I hurt my knee and couldn't compete. Those spots are precious, so I gave mine up for someone who was healthy. It's ancient history."

Dee snorts. It sounds evil. "Hurt, my ass. More like balked. Chickened out. Choked."

He switches to a really good slave impression which, surprisingly, I find less humorous than he does. "Po' boy, don' wahn talk 'bout all dem *fay-yeh-lures.*"

Turning back to Jay, he reverts to plain old thug. "You shoulda seen this boy. Track, football, basketball, baseball, didn't matter none to him. Skills upon skills. What you can only imagine, he did. We done tore up the town back in high school, me at running back, him doing quarterback. He gets a full ride to U of I and switches to wide receiver. Sets school records in football and track. Swear to God, man, he is the fastest white boy I ever seen. Fast enough that folks come visiting, talking medals, talking about representing America."

Dee takes a breath, but just a short one so I won't interrupt. I'm trying to tune him out; I know I can't shut him up.

"Then, a month before finals, not the Olympics themselves, just the final time trials, he done twists his knee playing basketball. There was still time afterwards. All he had to do was run his normal split and he's in Atlanta for the 200 and 400. Instead my boy pulls out. I bet teenage boys take more time pulling out than he did. Lord."

"Did he break it or something?"

"Shit, no, man. Barely sprained it. He was playing against me and I saw it all."

Now the smile from the juice girl has something more to it and I hate that. I don't need false pity. It makes me crabby.

"You want to fill in the rest, Killer?"

No, I don't, jackoff. But I say nothing, trying to ignore him. My best friend who, at the moment, seems to be talking his way out of that category. I can hear the taunting smile in his tone. What a bastard.

"So a few months later, November. My man is working on the college record for single game receiving yards. I can't even remember how many he had at half..."

One hundred and sixty eight. The record was two hundred fifteen, set in 1981.

Not that I was paying attention or anything.

"Third quarter and he goes over the middle on a quick slant. His specialty, turning that short gain long with all that speed o' his. It's an eight yard catch, first down. He's kicking in the afterburners and then, bam! You could hear it across the field. Worst sound ever. The knee bent all sorts of wrong and his season is done. Just like that. Junior year, scouts talking first round pick, multi-million dollar contracts coming in and now he blows it for real."

Jay makes a sound in the back of his throat.

"But that's not where it goes bad, hear?"

"He seemed to be moving fine in our game." Jay is fully engaged in the tale of my demise.

"Yeah. Blown knees ain't good. But his wasn't as bad as it looked. Partial ACL. Guys have them repaired every year and come back. All he had to do was rehab, stay in school another year and then go pro. He'd probably drop a round or two in the draft, but he'd be playing in the game. *Playing in the game, man.* And even if he couldn't ball out like before, he still could have worked back to the 2000 Olympics. All the boy had to do was buck up and try a little hard. So what's he do?"

By now Jay is completely silent, enraptured. I just keep my back to them.

"He takes a flyer. First train to Loserville. Drops out of school, sports and life, even though the surgery worked. He dumps his fine honey girl, comes back here and starts chasing baseball card thieves for a living. Dude coulda been tearing up the league, but he dove straight for the smallest pond so he could be the biggest fish."

Jay sits back, odd look on his face. In the years I've known him, we've never broached this topic. Mostly because I don't like to talk about it with anyone, especially my wife, who was there for the aftermath and rarely missed an opportunity to remind me of what could have been.

So. There you have it.

We all have dirty secrets, things which cause us shame and which we carry in silence. In my day job,

I traffic in the dirty secrets of complete strangers while holding one of my own. In a way I'm a hypocrite. I expose the secrets of others, yet there is no one to hold me honest to my own.

Well no one except my bestest friend Dee.

I guess I could have become something else as a result of my decisions. I could have become a thief, a drug user or a guy desperate to hang onto whatever fame he had. Instead I did something far more abhorrent to me.

I quit.

I bailed out on the thing that meant the most to me; my future. And it was a future that held a lot more than football. Many reasons could be found for my actions but I think it is clear cut: Either I am afraid of failure, or I am afraid of success.

The end result: a life of daily irritants, like a wife who thinks I'm an asshole and a friend who loves to tell the tale of mighty Rick's downfall. It doesn't mean I've given up on making the big score in my life. I think circumstances will create the crucible I need at the right time.

And then I'll be tested once again.

People wonder why I stay friends with Dee when he likes to humiliate me in such a manner. Like any other relationship it's a complicated thing. He's a young, rich athlete, with a golden glove and a big bat in America's favorite pastime. He attends parties with supermodels and people from magazine covers. He drives a big Mercedes with tinted windows, gold wheels and a booming stereo. He embodies the right and wrong of sports at the end of our century.

But if anyone thinks that gives them a full picture of the man I call friend, they are wide of the mark. Way wide.

One of the things that bothered Dee the most about my fall was the way I crumbled after looking at the long climb back up. No one struggled harder to keep me going; he picked me up so often I lost count. I think he took it personally that I failed. In a way it was also his failure. He was one of the few back then who truly knew my potential. Coaches could shape, scouts could predict and reporters could go blah, blah, blah. Only Dee could look at me, see where I came from and understand where I could be someday. He wanted me to succeed and it bothered him to see it all go to waste. It still bothers him. That is the type of friend everyone needs at least once in their life.

Then there is the flip side, his mean streak.

Dee has always resented me to some degree. Call it competitive grudge, call it plain old jealousy. I'm taller, faster, stronger. My body carried me to greater heights. We both wanted that high school quarterback position, I won it. I was the one who started appearing on national scouting mags. Even though he's become The Man by virtue of his Cubs deal, there was time when my name *always* came first.

Though he's not slow or untalented by any means, no Olympic scout ever asked him to try out, no college knocked on his door with a scholarship in hand. He was just not extraordinary.

So now that I'm living on an injury waiver, the competition is over and I've won by default. No one will respect a guy beating down a handicapped competitor. We may never know who is better in his respective sport, and that's something I can understand. It's robbed him of the chance to best me on a larger stage.

The title is mine.

If the roles were reversed, I might have acted the same way. Hell, considering how I act much of the time, I may have been worse.

So that's why we stay friends. Someday, we'll be even once again.

Jay stares at me with that same fogged expression many get upon hearing my story; like they can't understand how someone could walk away from all that. Little did they know how long the walk actually was.

But enough melodrama and history. Time to switch subjects to something much lighter.

"Hey," I say, drawing their attention. "Did you know that in Wisconsin, state law mandates that the maximum penalty for a violent crime will be increased for hate crimes? How cool is that?"

Dee and Jay look at me like I'm a lunatic.

"What the hell...?" Dee states.

I interrupt him. "It means, pal, when you finally explode and beat down a white guy up at Lake Arrowhead, they can extend the years of sentencing."

"No, dawg. That ain't it. They'd do it just 'cuz I'm black. No other reason."

Jay looks sidelong at Dee, probably trying to judge his seriousness. Unfortunately, whenever Dee begins spewing racial tripe, he is always serious.

They are conversations that don't often turn out well between us.

"You don't really believe that, do you?"

Dee gives a look like Jay's mentally unable to understand. "How can you know, bro? You white, almost as white as Killer there. Cops don't care about you, they just want to ride up on a brother."

"That sounds a little persecutory."

"What? *What?*" This sends Dee off on a tear. He will indulge a debate with anyone, any time, regardless of who they are. I remember one time when he visited me in college. We were stone cold drunk outside a bar and it started snowing. All of a sudden he's in the middle of the street screaming about how racism exists everywhere and if any more proof was needed, just look at how the white snow covered the black pavement.

Oddly, his argument made sense at the time; that is, until the cops showed. I don't remember how much the disorderly conduct fine was.

I cut him off before he can climb any further over Jay. "You want to know the truth? Check out the site for the Southern Poverty Law Center. They track all sorts of hate crimes and racist groups. They even have a legal assistance division that could get you raw stats."

Dee stops and looks at me. "What do you know from the SPLC?"

"Enough. Did you know there is over a thousand different hate or race groups in this country, all with some type of agenda? You got your Neo-Nazi groups like the Aryan Nations and the National Alliance. You got skinheads in the White Aryan Resistance. You got groups against the Jews, like Posse Comitatus. It's all around us."

"Now you're reading this stuff?" His eyes are skeptical.

"Of course, there is the Klan and all its offshoots; the World Church of the Creator and real odd ones like Stormfront and the White Order of Thule. Supposedly the FBI is expecting some of these whackos to use the whole Y2K thing as a cover to blow shit up."

Jay nods. "I did a paper for my Masters. Some have intricate pagan rituals affiliated with ancient warrior rites. Hitler used that same approach to connect with his followers, even though he was pretty dismissive of the old ways. People still practicing true paganism really have nothing in common with racist ideologies, but groups like The Order of Thule have sublimated it to the point it seems like a natural part of white supremacy extremists."

Dee looks a little put off that we actually know something about this. He's used to being the standard bearer. Take that, friend.

This conversation naturally leads us into the North Haven murders, the reason I started reading up on white hate groups in the first place. I don't know a whole lot, matter of fact I pretty much blew through my wad of knowledge already.

We each have our own opinions. Dee sums it up the most succinctly: "They just killing the Man. That's what it is."

"What?" Jay says.

"You know, the Man. The establishment. They just getting back what's theirs, what's been taken from them over the decades."

In the end we all agreed that it was a phrase that effectively covered the scope and swatch of violence happening in quiet North Haven.

Killing the Man.

We adjourn with handshakes and hearty laughter all around. Well, at least handshakes. I promise Jay I'll redeem myself next time.

I really hate losing.

As per custom, Dee and I make our way to my house in separate cars for an afternoon of hoops and grilling. It's a sport we both played in high school but neither of us ever considered it a career option. I'm white and he has the vertical of a Beluga whale.

So we drive, two men bound by shared history, unaware of what the future holds, charging minute by minute ever closer to a new millennium.

I keep glancing in the rear view mirror at his Mercedes with max tint windows and gold colored accents. Dee is barely visible behind the wheel, submerged in the dark interior. One hand can be seen on the wheel, sporting a large ring, but nothing more. Such imagery might be threatening to a single white girl from the Heartland out on her own for the first time. Especially with the heavy thump of rap music rattling his windows and most of the zip code.

Dee rails against anything resembling a racial stereotype, yet he does nothing to dispel it. That seems a bit hypocritical in my book.

I leave the Cobra at the entrance of my driveway so we have plenty of room in front of the garage. Dee does likewise and emerges from his car, phone pressed to his ear. His smooth operator persona is in high gear and I roll my eyes. Playing the field has never been my strong suit. In high school I only dated three girls and one of them became my college girl.

She was one of the things left behind when I traded my future for a present wrapped up in Maya ribbons. Boy, what a great choice *that* was.

As I kneel to tie a shoelace, a door slams farther up the block. Since I'm an observant cuss who makes his living watching people, I glance over by reflex.

My Jaguar-driving neighbor has decided to make an appearance, the first time I've seen him outside. He strolls down the driveway at a leisurely pace. Just another high-powered executive taking a break from ruling the world to enjoy a warm Sunday.

Behind him paces the largest dog I've ever seen, like the lovechild of a Great Dane and a Clydesdale. It maintains a set distance behind its master, stopping when he does.

He catches sight of me and gives a firm wave, staring in my direction. After a moment, he strides in my direction.

Dee swears softly under his breath and snaps his phone shut. The chirp of a low battery sounds. "Killer, where your phone? I got to finish that call."

I motion distractedly to the house. He knows very well where I keep my phone. In fact he could just swap batteries since we have the same model.

My neighbor approaches and I watch silently. He winds between the two parked cars and sticks a hand out in greeting. He's close to my height.

"Hello, I am Geoffrey Stephenson Moller. Nice to meet you." His light gray eyes, matching the gray at his temples, pin me and his words are carefully cultivated. I decide in an instant that life could be worse than looking like him when I hit fifty.

I set down my water bottle and return his grip. "Nice to meet you, Geoff. I'm Rick Killing."

"Please, I prefer Geoffrey."

"Great, I prefer Rick." Our handshake drops, leaving two men to square off like prize fighters.

"And this is Tyr." He motions to the mutant animal behind him.

"Yeah, I recognize him."

"Indeed?"

"I put twenty on him to place during last year's Kentucky Derby."

Moller looks at me for a long moment. Either he doesn't understand my humor, or he doesn't like it. I get that a lot.

He gives a cool smile. "I wanted to come introduce myself. I have not yet met anyone on the block. When I saw you, I thought there truly is no better time than the present. You would agree?"

Despite the stiff formality of his manner, I find myself admiring the way he speaks, so educated and in control. He's wearing a short sleeve polo and khaki pants, the casual yet elegant choice of executives everywhere.

Before I can reply, he casts an eye over my shoulder. "You have a lovely house. I once owned a Mediterranean and did not relish leaving it. Truly a peaceful place."

"Thanks, yours isn't too shabby either."

I motion for us to sit on the bench that flanks the driveway. Tyr pads around behind and settles into an alert pose. The canine eyes apprise me, probably for supper. "If he takes a dump, let me know. I got a backhoe in the shed."

The smile comes more easily, indicating an ability to adjust quickly. He reaches back and pets the neck. "Tyr has been with me for many years now. It is if as we are brothers under the skin."

I shift gears. "So, Geoff, what do you do?"

"Geoffrey, please." He crosses his legs in proper CEO-style, sinking into a pose that looks natural. "I own a consulting firm."

"Really? Like computer consulting? My wife does that stuff, maybe you can hit her up for a good gig."

He shakes his head in a measured manner. "No, there are many consulting disciplines. My arena is in management consulting. Diversity clinics, development initiatives, resource planning and other such behavioral skill matrices."

I had him until the word 'my.' No wonder he gets the big house. "Lofty stuff. Way over my head completely."

His return smile is warm, the kind a father gives to a son who just can't seem to grasp the intricacies of a split-finger fastball. His eyes crinkle at the corners, revealing a fine web of wrinkles. He's getting tan from somewhere, either a salon or some other country. Other than that, he comes off like an okay guy. Maybe I'll stop busting his balls.

Maybe.

"And you, Rick? What is your specialty?"

"I'm in management with the Hyper-Mart retail chain." I generally don't offer specifics on my job to new acquaintances, just in case, you know.

Moller lifts an eyebrow. "Indeed? My firm is currently in negotiations with your corporate offices about conducting racial diversity and customer relation seminars. I am sure you are aware that many minorities feel they are viewed as inferior to whites. There are daily instances when a white man or woman will look with distrust upon a person of color, perhaps to the extent of making disparaging remarks. That is the genesis of all racial barriers, Rick: In the heart of one person at a time. We are proposing a series of classes to expose people to the differences – and similarities – of color, for it is only those ties that will bind us tightly as a nation."

I suspect I've just heard the closing statement of his marketing pitch to the officers of my company. Boy, would Dee love this guy.

"Interesting." Not really. "What's the name of your company? Maybe I can drop a dime for you."

"Asatru Convergence, Inc. But I would rather you not mention our connection. I want to avoid the appearance of impropriety; if we are awarded the bid, it should be because we offer the best program. Not because I happen to live near someone who knows in which ears to whisper."

I nod and we move onto other topics. He does nothing to dispel my initial notion of him.

CHAPTER SEVEN

Hobby Cop

The front door slams as Dee emerges and strides across the drive towards us. Moller practically leaps to his feet. I follow more leisurely and motion between the two men.

"Damonti Davis, Geoffrey Moller."

Dee nods silently, back to his truculent persona and sticks out his hand to shake.

Moller grasps it in both hands. "A pleasure, Mr. Davis."

"He lives down in that gray Victorian," I add, pointing.

Dee shrugs. He doesn't care. He doesn't even know what a Victorian is. The moment becomes awkward as no one speaks. Moller is the one who patches things over.

He swivels and walks to Dee's car. "You have fine taste in autos, Mr. Davis. As a German, I take pride in all things from my country. Mercedes is an excellent example."

I frown. "I've seen you in a Jag."

"Only here. I have an E-series at my other home. Jingoistic pride in German engineering does not preclude me from appreciating, or even owning, other good automobiles."

"Yeah, dawg," Dee interjects, eloquent as always. "Benz rules. Twenty inch BBS wheels, Pirelli 40-series, AMG suspension, Brembo brakes. Full hookup inside with DVD player. *This* is a ride."

Moller seems a little put off by Dee's name dropping. A distasteful look flashes across his face, subtle. If I hadn't been looking right at him, I'd never have seen it. Don't blame him, I dislike name droppers too. He looks over at my Cobra, then to me, perhaps expecting a similar litany of mechanical bragging rights.

I shrug. "Ford. It means Fix Or Repair Daily."

That brings a laugh from both men and suddenly we are having ourselves a grand old time.

"I must confess," Moller says. "I find it refreshing and quite heartening that you two, men of different races, can maintain a friendship."

Dude, you make it sound like no one else has ever ventured outside their color to make friends. But I don't say it aloud.

"It is a harder and harder thing to do in today's society. Rick, if I may, what is your heritage?"

"All Scandinavian. Grandparents on both sides came from northern Europe. Denmark and Norway, to be precise."

"No surprise there. You carry your Norse blood well. I doubt anyone would mistake you for a son of the Far East." Moller gives a laugh but Dee and I simply stare. Maybe we didn't get the joke. Or maybe it just wasn't funny.

"Anyway," Moller continues, moving past our lack of response. "I commend you two for staying together. It seems the world tries very hard to separate people."

"Especially when the white folk getting killed," Dee spouts.

"Yes, unfortunate. What do you make of it?"

I interject, before Dee can reply. "History, coming back around. Some blacks have a hard-on about racism, especially the Klan, and want to send a message about it."

"You know the victims were associated with the Klan?" Moller's eyebrow rises. "I had not heard such."

"Well, there are rumors," I stammer slightly. Did I really know, or had I meshed some of my ideas together with reality? "Plus, it just makes sense. Look at the way they were killed. It has to be retribution for the things the Klan once did."

Both men look at me intently. Dee's lips compress, meaning he is irritated. Probably because I assumed blacks are behind it all. I can't read Moller's gaze, but it's no less intent.

"There are many presumptions in your words, Rick. That can be a dangerous slope."

"It's a dangerous time. Especially for white men who fit a specific profile. Like white, successful and of certain age. Like, um, you, Geoff. I hope you didn't dance with the Klan recently."

His face flushes under the tan, the first time I've seen him not in complete control. He gives a short laugh. "No worries there, Rick. Plus, from what I can tell, North Haven teems with men like me. If anything, I have the advantage of great numbers amongst which to hide."

I shrug. "Your life."

Dee is uncharacteristically silent. He seems either awed or intimidated by Moller. It's not often he gets like this.

Motion at the periphery catches my attention. From Moller's house a young man steps out and looks around until he spies us. He begins to walk with a gait that has an unnatural smoothness to it. Lilting, swiveling from the hips, like a male gymnast.

He's barely out of the driveway when another young man rushes down the driveway and leaps on his back. "Horsey!"

They both go down in a tumble.

"Lance! Get off me," the gymnast pulls away and continues towards us. His hair is shaved tight to his skull, leaving a layer of fuzz blonder even than mine. I estimate late teens, early twenties. He's in khakis and colored shirt; I swear they are pressed.

Lance laughs and trots to catch up, chucking his shoulder into him when he does.

I think Moller sighs.

"Gentlemen, these are my sons Nathan and Lance."

Lance bounds up the driveway to shake our hands. His blond hair is longer, almost shaggy. Where Nathan has his father's lean build, Lance is more rounded, giving the impression of hunching. Both are pale skinned, and any family semblance is in the nose and eye shape.

Nathan stays at the end of the driveway, indicating in his body language that he has no intention of coming closer. His eyes pierce through and through, way too serious for someone his age. He appears old before his time.

His stare flicks back to Dee. "I know who you are. Watch your inside shoulder when you get behind the pitch count. It started dropping after that road series with the Reds late last year."

The comment catches Dee off guard. He mutters an 'okay.' It's not often he accepts criticism without firing back, especially to a common fan.

Nathan's narrow eyes return to me. I can see Geoffrey's color in them, but that's where the similarity ends. He seems like he's looking right through me. It's unnerving and I don't like it, but before I can take the offensive with some quip, Geoffrey clears his throat.

"Please excuse Nathan. He tends to think he knows more than he really does. It's one of his failings."

Wow, and here I thought my father was an asshole. Well, he is, but for different reasons.

If Nathan cared about his own father speaking to others as if he were a child, it doesn't show. Matter of fact, nothing resembling emotion shows on his face. The guy is cold-blooded.

"Your flight is booked. Six-thirty eight in the morning." With that, and with nothing else, Nathan spins and begins walking back home.

Lance points to my car. "Sweet ride, man." He gives a peace sign and runs to catch up with his brother. This time he doesn't tackle him. He does, however, slap him on the back of the head as he sprints past.

Nathan does not even react.

Moller watches them for a second before turning back with a wan smile. "I have tried to work with him, but he is so serious. Focused far too sharply. It is rather disappointing."

"Well," I say. "Us sons are around only to wreck our dad's life." I don't hold back the sarcasm.

Moller doesn't respond to that. He clears his throat and looks down at his dog. "Well Tyr, shall we? I have much to do for tomorrow."

He rests a hand on Dee's fender and addresses us. "It has been a pleasure speaking with both of you. Perhaps we can gather again when time is not so pressing?"

"Sure. Why not?"

At the end of the driveway, Moller stops and swivels back, as if something has just occurred to him. "You two are obviously car aficionados. I need a reference line in my opening statement tomorrow, something pop culture oriented. What is your dream car?"

Without hesitation, we reply in unison: "1967 Corvette Stingray with the L88 engine." If either of us could sing, we'd sound like Simon and Garfunkel. Dee would be the funny looking one.

Raw surprise leaps across Moller's face. "My, that is not the answer I expected to hear. What a coincidence. I happen to own one. Marina Blue with Standard black trim. Four speed."

I think, at that moment, the cracking sound echoing across the yard comes from two sets of jaws hitting the pavement. Drool quickly pools up around our feet.

What are the odds? I have a model of one. I stammer: "But there were only a few made. Twenty that I know of."

"Yes, I am in a select group, apparently. It is currently down in a shop in Houston for detailing."

Dee looks ready to pass out. Funny how men can salivate over the silliest of things. He's a millionaire and couldn't get his hands on one if he tried.

We are far from perfect creatures, but nonetheless amusing at times.

Moller dangles his carrot just a little more. "How about this: I will return in two weeks. The car is scheduled to be ready and delivered to a Chicago holding house by then. Let us meet at my house, perhaps grill out, and you can take it for a few hours."

If he follows up the offer with a request that we jump off a bridge, I will knock Dee out trying to get there first. I think I strain my neck nodding so hard.

With a parting smile, Moller takes his leave – and his pet rhino – and walks back to his fortress.

Dee and I just stare at each other and smile.

Two days later, on a dreary Tuesday, the inevitable lash back happens. I hear it on the police scanner in my office.

A man named Jerome Carter had been found hanging naked from a tree. Crude swastikas were carved into his skin. His wallet, still containing twenty-eight dollars and several credit cards, lay nearby on a stack of his neatly folded clothes.

Carter was forty-six years old, twice divorced, four children by those two wives, and black. He also had worked at the same place for eighteen years, with spotless attendance, and had turned down numerous promotions. He lived in a renovated house in Chicago, along with owning rental property.

No one knew why he was in North Haven. He had no connections to the area.

By all accounts Carter appeared to be a model citizen, well-liked by those who knew him. His co-workers spoke highly of his work ethic. Both ex-wives wept openly together and said good things. A young white couple renting one of his units banded with the ex-wives to raise money. Five thousand dollars to anyone with information leading to an arrest of his killer.

Of course, all that news would surface over the following days after his discovery.

This morning, I heard only a few grim details spoken in cop shorthand over the airwaves. North Haven has hovered around the periphery of national news the last few weeks. Carter's murder will change that and propel us to front page status, for all the wrong reasons.

I spend most of the morning scrounging the internet for more information, slowly giving myself over to the obsession growing inside me. I didn't know what it was at the time, didn't understand what drove me on. Only in hindsight did it become obvious.

I surf to the major sites, both local and national. The *Chicago Sun-Times* has a story up within hours, although lacking many details. By lunchtime *USA Today,* *CNN* and *MSN* have joined the wave.

The massive media machine is gathering momentum and turning its attention to my town.

Carter's murder will not be the last. I'm convinced of it. It's actually an escalation in a war that many don't realize has already started. Today it's Jerome Carter. What will Thursday bring? Friday?

Where is this leading and where will it end?

If I can get my hands on the details, I'll understand the picture. This is the seed of my obsession.

Information is my biggest obstacle. Unfortunately, I'm not a detective. Hell, I'm not even a cop. However, I am resourceful and annoyingly persistent, and I have access to people with the goods. I just have to tap into my network.

Aside from the beat cops that come out to take shoplifters off my hands, I also interact with detectives, usually in the case of forgery, credit card scams and the like. Whenever a bunch of crooks hit town with stolen cards, my store is on the short list of targets. We have our state of the art surveillance system and more than once I've been able to provide footage to detectives, giving them their first look at the suspects. It's always made me feel like a key component of the case.

I've also managed to build some relationships that way.

North Haven has a relatively small police force, and only one full time detective assigned to fraud. His name is George Warren and we've solved a few cases together over the last year. I fish up his number and dial it. He can be my bridge to the guy working the murders.

I absently push one of my model cars across the desk as the phone rings. It had been moved and I wondered which one of my employees did it; they know not to touch my stuff.

"Warren," comes the curt greeting on the other end.

"Hey Warren, it's Rick Killing."

A slight pause. "Killing," he repeats slowly. Guy must have a short memory; it's only been a few months since we crossed paths.

"Yeah, from over at the Hyper-Mart. Loss prevention department."

"Oh, yeah, sure. The Hyper-Mart."

"Hey, I'm wondering if you can put me in touch with whoever is working the latest murder, the Carter guy from this morning. Is it your case? I might be able to help."

Another pause occurs, in which I can imagine him rifling through his address book for the number.

"Wait a minute. You the big blond guy? The ex-jock from...where was it? Northwestern?"

A sinking feeling comes to me. "Actually, it was U of I."

"That's right. Now I remember. No way, no way in hell. You're a pain in the ass. Last summer when all those counterfeit twenties hit town, you made us look like idiots. Why the hell would you dress up as Andrew Jackson and stand downtown asking people if they've seen you lately? Do you know how many calls we received on that?"

"I was trying to help, think outside the box a little."

"Well, you didn't. Ninety-nine percent of the public can't even tell you that Jackson is on the twenty in the first place. Plus, it was a shitty costume. People thought you were Mark Twain."

"I just wanted to help..."

"No, what you did was make our jobs a lot harder. For every call we receive, we have to burn time checking into it, even the stupid ones. Cases are made or broken over little details, so we can't just ignore a call. That ended up with us having to explain the difference between Twain and Jackson over and over. People are stupid. You know what you got, pal? Hobby cop syndrome. It's bad enough I got the FBI standing around here waiting for me to fetch their coffee, now I got guys like you..."

I slowly place the phone back in the cradle.

So, Warren won't be any help.

I sit there a second, thinking, undeterred. Lifting the phone again, I punch the main number to the cop shop. The lady that answers is much more polite and I ask to be put in touch with the lead detective in the murders. I have a lead.

After a moment on hold, she comes back. "Sir, he's on the other line right now. Can I take your name or put you into his voicemail?"

"He wouldn't by chance be talking to another detective, would he?"

"Yes, I believe so."

I mumble a thank you and hang up. Apparently my reputation precedes me.

Feeling stupid, I start calling my employees instead; poking at them for anything they might have heard. Local kids are often a good source of information and we touch enough of them in our job that gossip has a way of making it from the mean streets to our ears.

Although with names like Willow Lane and Whisper Court, I don't know exactly how mean our streets are.

Unfortunately I reach only Kevin and Kari, and neither seems to care much about it. Kari's voice jumps a notch when I call, so I keep it real short.

I leave the office and spend the remainder of the day wandering around the store, eavesdropping. It may seem like a silly way to take the pulse of a community, but I stand by it. You can't get a more random sampling of citizens. White, black, rich, not-so-rich, young, old...you name it.

Sometimes I'd linger close to a group, donning my 'stupid husband on an errand' persona. Other times I'd stay behind a one-way mirror and listen to whoever came close enough. I even sat in the men's dressing room for thirty minutes, waiting for enlightened men to enter, try on jeans and discuss the plight of this town with their friends.

But all I get is a kid's tale of woe at a party gone wrong. Based on what he told his buddy about the damage to his parents' house, he'll be in debt forever.

In the end, I come away more concerned than before. Blacks are angry that one of their own has been murdered, though not a single one seemed surprised by it. I find the outrage rather curious. In the truly mean streets of Chicago, young black men die every day, yet those events barely rank a page three mention. Perhaps because it's accepted as a fact of life in the big city and not major news any more.

In North Haven, it's the only news.

Black people are outraged. White shoppers carry a growing sense of concern. They've already been targeted in the previous three murders, now what will this latest bring? Many feel certain that another white guy will be next, in a more gruesome manner, soon. There's apprehension in their eyes and they watch everyone around them even as they talk. They are worried about the next target; any white person is fair game.

I glance over my shoulder, just in case.

Any Hispanics I came across didn't have the same concern. Then again, they mostly spoke Spanish and I couldn't understand a word. But they pushed their carts in a very concerned manner.

Maya hasn't come home from work when I pull into the garage. It's only six; on days when she works in the city, she often doesn't return until eight or later.

I rummage through the fridge for dinner. We're both pretty nutrition-conscious and rare is the junk food found in this house. I really could go for a Twinkie, though.

In the end, I settle for chicken breast, cottage cheese and fruit, chased by water. Yum.

As I sit there by myself, perched on a stool I still think is too high for the counter, I realize just how quiet this place is. I could hear the tick of the grandfather clock in the front hall. Even with Maya here, it stays quiet, she doesn't make a lot of noise. She doesn't work to loud music, speak loudly or need the TV on for background chatter.

Yet, without her, a key component is absent. This leads me to wonder what it would be like without this component on a daily basis. My future seems so muddy, so hard to understand or see, that I truly have no idea what it would be like.

As a youngster, making all the silly plans that kids make, I always thought I'd be a parent by now. Looking back with the benefit of hindsight, I realize how ridiculous the thought is. I'm not in any shape to be a father.

I still want kids, but when I see Maya's face in that picture, it scrambles everything. I can't envision her that way. There's no way we could even afford it in our current condition. She makes a lot of money, but it's never about how much comes in, only how much goes out. Between the nut for our ridiculously large house that she had to have, and her penchant for spending, we're slowly losing ground.

Her credit card debt grows every month, but whenever I set a plan to pay it down, she blows it off saying there will be more money to come and we can do it then. Secretly I thank the stars that we maintain separate accounts. I work to pay for my car and miscellaneous house expenses, she pays for everything else.

I push the empty plate away, once again disgusted with the state of my life. Plate glass windows, expensive furniture and endless tile floors surround me. The pitter-patter of children's feet would not echo gladly in here.

There's been only one other time I've lived with a girl. My college girlfriend. We had a moderate two-bedroom rental. My athletic scholarships took care of us well enough that we didn't have to crimp for every penny. As college kids we lived like kings.

Even though that little apartment provided less than a quarter of the space of my current house, the memory seems warmer, more inviting. It could be the gloss of nostalgia, sanding off the edges of a younger time. Or it could be the company I kept.

Her name was Kimberly Katherine Tadisch, and when I left her behind she faded from my life but not from my heart.

CHAPTER EIGHT

Activist

Over the next couple of weeks, North Haven stays quiet. It doesn't matter though. The news monster has found us.

Crews with famous logos plastered to the side of vans start trolling our streets. Many of the vans come with roof-mounted dishes. People are accosted on the sidewalk, diverted from their walk by smart-dressed men or women seeking an opinion by shoving a mic in their face. Local dignitaries, such as they were, are interviewed to speak for the town. We lead off the evening news cycle.

In an odd way, the town benefits. Restaurants start booking up early, hotels fill up. Suddenly little North Haven grows up, like a boy who has just gotten attention for his dance moves at a wedding reception. He wants more, so he tries new moves and inserts himself into the circle. At some point, the adults stop thinking it's cute and his time is then marked.

The weekend in which Moller promised to return and bring back his Vette coincides with the NFL Draft. For the last several years the weekend has held special significance for me. In 1997, it should have been my coming out party, the start of something special. Instead I found myself watching it from my parents' couch, wrenching in my gut.

I've spoken to my agent James several times leading up to this weekend. There are teams with interest, and that makes me feel better. I know all I have to do is give the go-ahead to him, allow him to submit my name to the league. Maybe a team takes a flyer on me in the late rounds, hoping against hope that I still possess my skills and that my knee is whole once again. If they are wrong, they've only a burned a low round pick and those guys don't often make the team anyway.

If they guess right and I'm still the guy from the University of Illinois, well, lightning in a bottle is a great thing to have.

More than once, when talking with James, we come to a point in the conversation where he falls silent, and I know what he wants. He wants the signal.

I just can't give it. Not yet. The shape of my life is skewed and until I straighten it out, I'm not square.

So I spend the third weekend of April 1999 with one eye on the television. Students get their name called and with that call, graduate to the pros.

One of those names could have been Rick Killing.

By the time Sunday afternoon rolls around, I've had enough wallowing in self-pity. I turn off the TV for the first time.

Restless, I join Maya in the laundry room while she folds shirts and mutters under her breath. Probably about me. We've been getting along well, meaning no fights, and it's really frying my nerves. With her, the calm truly precedes the storm and I know it's only a matter of time before Mount Maya blows.

"Hi," I say, picking up a bra. How the hell do you fold one of these things? I tuck the straps into the cups and then bend it in half.

"Seriously, Rick." She pries it from my hands and tosses it into the clean basket.

Our domestic bliss lasts a few more minutes, until she shoos me away because I folded a shirt wrong. But she does it in a subdued manner, kissing me on the cheek for my effort. Her niceness is making me ready to freak out.

I exit the house in time to see Dee's pimp-mobile pull into the driveway. We give each other a shoulder bump. He's wearing some offensively-colored warm up suit but I can't begin to guess the color. I suspect it was once a shade of purple. His hair is fluffed out into an Afro and so much gold hangs from his neck that I'm seriously concerned for his spinal integrity.

"You hear Gretzky is playing his last game today?" I ask when I get bored of mocking his outfit.

"So? That a white person sport. The brothers don't watch that."

"Way to shatter the stereotype."

"Truth, man, truth. Like it or not."

"Only because there's no ice in the ghetto and you got some freaked up genetics that prevents it." Never mind that Dee grew up in the same "ghetto" streets that I did.

"Now why you got to go and play the race card off the draw? Don't you know better?"

"Is it true or not? Why are there almost no black hockey players?"

"'Cuz it comes from Canada or some other shit cold place. Ain't no blacks dumb enough to live there. We stay where it's warm."

Yeah, like the upper Midwest winters are so mild.

I pick up a basketball from inside the garage and toss it to him. "Bull. There's some weird ankle design problem. Admit it. You people can't skate for shit."

Dee fades away and drains a fifteen footer. "Crazy talk, dawg. It's a culture thing. Ain't no different for basketball. Why so few good white boys playing?"

I grin and we chant together. "Because white men can't jump!"

Taking his rebound, I launch myself towards the basket, dunking it with both hands. "Or at least some can't."

"Showoff."

Before we can further indulge our shared immaturity, the staccato sound of a big-block engine cracks the air. We both snap to attention as Moller idles past us in his 1967 Stingray. He smiles and nods with his head for us to follow him down. Lance is behind him in the Jag and he gives the horn a long honk. The neighbors have to love us.

Dee and I, with forced nonchalance, stroll down the street without saying much. We don't have to; we know what the other is thinking. Most women don't understand car obsessions, and we can't explain it.

The smell of raw exhaust fills the air, from a brutal, politically offensive engine that doesn't give one shit about emissions, global warming or saving the whales. It probably runs on the sap of endangered trees.

Moller the elder leaves the Vette at the end of his driveway as Lance pulls around him into the garage.

"Gentlemen," he says as we approach. "Good to see both of you again. As promised." His hands give a small flourish to the car, making him look like a game show girl.

We notice the error right away and it's confirmed when we pop the hood. "This isn't an L88," I declare.

Moller stares at me then darts his eyes to the engine. "You can tell just by looking?"

"Hells, yeah," Dee chimes in.

"It's the 427 V8, minus the L88 option. Who'd you get this from?"

"A..ah, private seller on the east coast."

"Well, you got ripped off. Hope you kept your receipt."

Moller doesn't seem too put off by the revelation, once he gets past his initial shock. Must be nice to have so much money that an error worth tens of thousands doesn't matter.

As for Dee and I, it doesn't matter either.

We spend the next couple of hours farting around town, taking turns and generally burning the tires right off the thing. Stupid grins are plastered to our faces.

By the time we return, Nathan has made his appearance from the nether world and set up shop next to a grill on the back patio, plate of steaks ready to be thrown on. It surprises me to see him in this setting. There must not be any children to torture right now.

Lance is behind an outdoor bar, Geoffrey perched on a stool before him, drinking some kind of liquor on the rocks. That doesn't surprise me, he seems like the type.

What does surprise me is Maya sitting next to him, waving a beer bottle around as she talks. She leans her head back to laugh at something. Her legs are crossed elegantly, showing off the tawny skin beneath cropped khakis. A white tank top displays her upper assets to their fullest.

"Hey, what brings a girl like you to a joint like this?" It's my way of asking how exactly she ended up here. To the best of my knowledge she has never met the Mollers, elder or younger.

"Geoff came over and invited me, since you didn't." She pours the last dregs of her bottle into her mouth.

How come she gets to call him Geoff?

I shrug and toss the keys to him. "It'll do. Too bad you were scammed. I can take it off your hands for twenty bucks. Least I can do."

"Make it thirty, with a full tank of gas," Dee pitches in.

Moller smiles, a thin tolerant expression. "Generous opening bids. You are too kind. However, I have a man on the east coast I need to speak to. Your insight is appreciated."

Lance holds out two bottles of Budweiser's finest. "Boys, our finest ale, on the house." He says it with an old English accent. What a weird kid. How can he and Nathan be brothers?

Dee and I clink bottles, a silent toast to friendship and things that – on that night – we didn't know. With his wild hair and gold jewelry, he seems utterly out of place in the company of four white men and one crazy Filipino. But he might just end up as the most normal of all.

In any event, we end up sitting around on yet another fine April Sunday, two groups of people nosing their way through a maze of getting to know each other. The food disappears quickly, as does the booze. But the mark of a good party is how seamlessly new liquor replaces the old. In our case the magic elves made sure we never went dry.

We compare histories and stories. We trade on the coin of personality, seeking that elusive common ground, an element which will survive a captured moment on Moller's patio and propel us forward to other settings.

I can be pretty funny in my normal state of being. Tuck a few in me – not too many though – and I can be downright hilarious, no matter what Maya says. I use that talent to good effect, telling tales, playing puns and scoring...scores. The Mollers laugh, even Nathan. It doesn't look like it pains him too much, and my original opinion takes on modifiers. The guy has the personality of an eel, but if he knows when to laugh and what to laugh at, that's worth something I guess.

As for Moller the elder, he remains one cool dude. Everything about him – body language, speech patterns, the attentive listening – spoke to a man spilling over with charisma and assurance. I could picture him sitting in a jazz club with a woman on each arm as easily as I could in front of hundreds conducting a seminar.

I decide that when I grow up, I want to be just like him. There is powerfulness in his aura, unflappable, aware and highly perceptive.

Maya likewise seems to appreciate the man. When he speaks she falls silent, something she rarely does with me. She might even have been listening. If nothing else, that in itself earns Moller enormous respect; no one can enthrall my wife.

Even Dee looks more at ease; a purple clown at ease. He drops the gangsta persona, washing it away on the beer flowing through his system. He reverts to the guy I knew and grew up with, before adult pressures, batting averages and millions came between us.

It's nice to have him back.

As the afternoon wanes and the sun slides toward the horizon, we perform our own slide into oblivion. Whenever the conversation slows, Geoffrey sparks it back up with some seemingly random topic. The breadth of the man's knowledge is incredible.

Lance remains the same, a charming – if somewhat goofy – post-teen trying to play with the adults.

It's Nathan who changes the most. I don't know if it's the liquor, or something forced, but he grows intense to a fault. He laughs harder than anyone else, he nods his head in agreement or shakes it vehemently in denial. His teeth bare with each gesture, making him look feral.

After the sun sets, Maya gives a shiver at one point and Moller invites us inside for the ten-cent tour. I can only suck my teeth at what the place holds.

By way of being nosy, I remark, "So Moller, you keeping the missus locked in the basement or something?"

Nathan barks out: "She's not here."

"Oh, thanks Einstein. Thought I was standing on her for a second."

Geoffrey steps in. "My wife Katrina is still at our other home with my daughter. Allison is finishing up her last year of high school and we did not want to pull her out. We will all be rejoined at some point."

That's got to be tough, living apart from your wife and daughter, I think. Then again, he has the warm and woolly Nathan to make up for their absence.

We finish our tour with little other fanfare and retreat to the game room in the basement. As with the rest of the house, it's appointed in jaw-dropping fashion. Billiards, air hockey, darts and assorted other games lining the walls. A massive projection TV sits in one corner, opposite a massive oak bar.

It's a great space, but I'm not sure who it's really for. I couldn't picture Nathan loosening up his bun enough to come down and play. Lance, maybe. It certainly fit his personality, but seeing how terrible he was at everything told me he didn't spend much time here either. And Geoffrey seems fairly unaware of the purpose of everything except the TV.

The bar is fully stocked with all kinds of liquor, many I didn't even recognize. So we helped ourselves. Myself, I abandon the beer and start with the harder stuff, all the while chanting silently: *Mix your liquor, gonna get sicker.*

The corner TV is on a local news channel when follow-up information on the Jerome Carter murder airs. Nothing more than a fluff piece, playing to the horror of the story and exploiting the emotions of suffering family members.

Suddenly it seems important for me to talk about it. I call for everyone's attention but from the confusing looks, my words must have been garbled. So I repeat them, loudly.

Maya swings to me. "What are you squawking about now?"

"Nothing. Not you. Them." I motion in the general direction of our hosts.

Geoffrey catches my gestures and turns. "I'm sorry. Were you speaking to me?" He doesn't even look phased by the drinks we've all consumed, but that can't be true. If I'm drunk, then he has to be too. That's the way drinking works.

"C'mere," I slur.

He breaks off conversation with Dee and makes his way over. There's hints of unsteadiness, which makes me feel better. His two sons follow like good puppies.

After a moment Dee notices he's speaking to thin air and ambles over as well. Maya reacts the opposite and collapses on a couch in the far corner.

"Say again." Nathan demands. It's his form of a request, minus the question mark.

"That," I motion to the TV, which had since gone to commercial. "It's crap."

Lance looks at it and his forehead creases in confusion. "Pepsi is crap?"

"Is not," Nathan counters, ever the contrarian. He belches loudly and tries to say the alphabet. He gets to E.

I squint for a second, resetting my vision. "No, no. Pepsi is fine. The murders. Those are crap."

Geoffrey is clearly delighted with my pronouncement. "Really? And why is that?"

"Because, that's why. Because people are dying. It's wrong."

"The Man must pay his bill!" Dee yells to no one in particular.

Geoffrey gives my friend a piercing look, equal parts inquisitive and questioning. Or maybe he's having as much trouble seeing straight as I am. He turns back to me. "Which is worse? The three white men, or the latest of the black man?"

"All bad."

"And I agree. But if there is a kind of rank to assign, which was more rationalized?" It sounds like 'rushanized.'

"Well, if those guys were Klan-types, racists and that sort of thing, then they deserved it more. Carter sounded like a normal guy just living his life."

"Interesting. The media paints a picture and sells it to all takers. You are not to blame for accepting their product, it has been designed for easy consumption. Ashk...ahem...*ask*, yourself this: Has there been any actual proof of racist activity from any of those men? If all three were Klan members, do you not think evidence would have been found? Instead the fourth estate has presented conclusions based on the manner of their death, not their life."

"You talk like you knew them."

Geoffrey leans back on his stool, crossing his legs. Though I can see how bloodshot his eyes are, he still assumes a power pose easily. "Actually, I did. Donald Sutton. Not well, but my business had crossed paths with his several times over the last year."

"He wear a hood to meetings?" Dee asks, then laughs.

"Absolutely not. He was as normal as you and I. Kissed his wife and children goodbye in the morning; ate dinner with them at night." He pulls his corporate cape a little closer and goes into Moller mode.

"The media is washing the story to the lowest common denominator, herding everything together into the Klan tent. While they are the most well-known supremacist effort, one that traces their lineage to the childhood of our country, they are not the only one. Nor are they the most dangerous."

Geoffrey swirls his glass slowly, staring at it for a second. He's been drinking Maker's Mark. "We near the end of the 20th century and many other factions have emerged over the last decade or so. Liberals call them the Far Right, falling into the same fallacy of grouping everyone together. Hammerskins, 14 Words, Totenkopf; these groups carry far sharper swords than the Klan. Extremist is not an incorrect term for them."

"Well, I don't lump them all together. I know --"

He cuts me off with a wave of his hand. "Let me finish, please. Not all hate movements chant cries of death and dance around bonfires in costume. Some internalize it into religion, draping it in words that seem innocuous. Like the news media, they create an idea that is easy to digest. No one gets hurt from words; this could be the underlying rationale."

Now Geoffrey is warming up, clearing up his speech, focusing his mind. The rest of us are cross-eyed students nodding at a lecture but too afraid to admit we lost track of the teaching point. "Have you ever heard of the Celtic Cross?" He asks me.

"Never."

"Hate the Celtics," Dee says. "Go Bulls."

"They believe in the superiority of the Aryan race as represented in the blood lines of all Nordic cultures. You yourself could be a poster boy for their physical ideals. Tall, white and strong. Pure. It is that image they sell as a product, but there's a stain on the underside, hidden from casual glance. They speak to the religious piety found in ancient pre-Christian warrior cultures. It's transformed into a religious movement, not a racial one. However, in their eyes, true Christianity has been adulterated by Jewish influence."

"Yeah, but...Jews are not a race." I'm suddenly uncertain, his knowledge is causing all sorts of turmoil in my brain.

"Correct. The Cross does not make a distinction. They also decry violence and suppression, preferring secession over domination. It makes their mission seem passive and keeps them from a harsh spotlight, but at the core, they still share a segregation agenda with declared groups like the Klan. Ask yourself which is more dangerous: The threat you can see, or the one lurking in the background?"

At that moment I realize Geoffrey has far more insight into the North Haven problem than I originally thought. He's also far more educated and smarter than anyone I've met. I'm so overmatched it's not even funny.

Geoffrey sees the blank look on my face. He's lost a student and he knows it, I can tell. He turns to Dee.

"Damonti, as a man of color, what is your true reaction to this? Not what the general outrage is, but what you feel deep in yourself?"

Nathan crowds closer. Over in the corner, Maya and Lance are babbling to each other, clinging to the threads of a conversation neither understands.

Dee readjusts his stance and drawls out by way of answer: "Sheeee-it."

Unfortunately no one really gets his response, not even smart Geoffrey. So he starts over.

"The Man got it coming. Too long the brothers been on the short end. You ask me, those guys got what they ordered the first day they stepped into some whitey meeting. Hammerskin, Church of this or that, Aryan Nation this or that...it all the same: the Man hating on other colors just trying to make things equal. Carter is the tragedy. He lived in a victim's place: the color of his skin. Nowhere for him to escape or make himself not a target. If he lived the same exact life but in white skin? He's still alive right now. Know what I'm saying?"

As garbled as his delivery is, Dee makes some sense. Carter was just me in different skin. And that's a really frightening thought.

Geoffrey leans forward, intense and attentive. He sets down his glass. "Do you think there will be more?"

"Hell yeah. You watch. This will become tit-for-tat."

I snicker and take another gulp. He said 'tit.'

"And what will it take to stop?"

"Stop what? The killings? The racism?"

"Both. Either."

Dee shakes his head. "They got to catch the guy first of all. Can't be but one or two killers. It's too big to stay a secret if a whole bunch know. Word would leak. Maybe they a part of some hate group working on their own. Maybe they a whole new group trying to make a mark."

Geoffrey nods and leans back. "Possible. I too predict more action lurks on the horizon, and not just more deaths."

"Meaning?" I say as Dee moves behind the bar for a refill. Lance scrambles up to help him. I hope he doesn't have a game tomorrow; that could be brutal.

"I think we will start to see the unintended consequences of the messages inherent in these murders. Smaller, localized crimes spawned. Fistfights, two groups of kids who normally would pass each other without comment suddenly notice the racial difference and it escalates. Muggings or robbery pinned to an opposite color, whether true or not. Minority business targeted for vandalism, or eyeing up customers for intent apart from purchase. Ideas breed mistrust, breeds emotion, gives birth to hate. If enough of these confrontations occur, it becomes a new norm. Eventually it broadens, spills outward from race to class. Now it's more than your color, it's your standing in society, it's the perception of your lot in life. A monster is created that encompasses everyone. In a large crowd, all driven by resentments of their own creation, potential outcomes range the gamut."

Geoffrey drains his glass in one swig. "I would not relish being attacked simply because I'm a white man driving an expensive car."

I've never projected it out that far. In his scenario, Dee is a target for being a rich black man.

I'm one for being a poor white man. Our association with each other will not provide any kind of protection.

This pisses me off to think about. My current state may be helping that, though. I challenge back: "So what do you think needs to be done, smart guy?"

The liquor makes me belligerent, the reality makes me afraid.

He pauses, staring down into his empty glass. Nathan snorts in derision, to who knows what, and joins his brother and Maya.

"I firmly believe that one person needs to emerge from all this uncertainty and unite the community. Force is not a resolution; education and acceptance is."

Dee responds as he rejoins us. "Say what?"

Geoffrey stares at him. "And I believe that person could be you."

"*Say what?*" Dee screeches, perhaps a little too loudly, a little too panicked. I merely give him a 'you go, girl' fist pump.

"Hear me out, Damonti. This is not such a wild idea. You have already demonstrated an activist mindset. You are a sports hero playing for a cherished institution. Even if you no longer live in the area --"

"Who told you that?"

"You are a public figure now. That information is readily available. When you speak, you do so from a platform that encourages people to connect and listen. In another place like Los Angeles or Seattle, you would just be an athlete trying to make a difference. But here you are a son of the town, one of their own. And this town stands on the brink of a situation that has the very real potential to worsen before it heals. North Haven is crying for someone to carry the burden and ignite our healing."

"That is, unless," Geoffrey says, setting the hook. "Your words are posturing and you do not really live those ideals. In that case, you would be a poor choice."

"You kidding, right?" The shock is plain on Dee's face, but there's something else there. A spark deep within, waiting to grow into flame.

"I would never kid on a subject as serious as this. Would you?"

Dee reverts to his ignorant gangster, a protective reflex to uncomfortable pressures. "I don't know nothing about that stuff, man." He pronounces it 'nuffin'.

"Fortunately, I do. It is what I do, and fairly well if I may brag. We coach people as one of our business products. I can coach you."

"You so good, then you do it." There's petulance in Dee's tone. We all have different fears and we all react to them in different ways.

"I do not have the credence that you do. I am not from here. I have no celebrity status. More pointedly, if I may be so, I am not a minority. I am of 'The Man', to use your phrasing. I would be shouted down where you will be heard. It must be you, Damonti Davis."

"Dude, I ain't no Malcolm X."

"Neither was he, until he *became* Malcolm X. Before that he was Malcolm Little, convicted felon. His climb to the light was much farther than yours."

"Aw, man..." Dee trails off and we all watch an internal war. His natural reluctance fought with his desire to make a difference, something that extends past the baseball mound. He's always admired transcendent athletes like Jim Brown or Muhammad Ali, men who used their fame to say the things that needed saying. North Haven, small and removed from the big city glare, but currently undergoing its own growing pains, provided him an ideal jumping off point. He could practice his craft here, polish up his skills and plan how to expand to a larger audience.

It's like the situation has been tailor-made for my friend, and I don't see how he can say no.

He flicks his gaze up to me and holds it for a long second. I stare back, then nod. We both know what the answer must be.

"How does this all work?" He says to Geoffrey.

The Moller collective smiles and there is a palpable release of air in the room.

"I will arrange for one of the local network affiliates to interview you. Your status will open those doors easily. We will have to work fast, so it may happen as soon as tomorrow night. We'll start small before approaching the syndicated shows, like *20/20* or *Dateline*. Truly, Damonti, only you determine your ceiling."

Dee's eyes grow wide as the implications sink in. Geoffrey stalls him with an upraised hand.

"I will find you a speech coach and assemble a question list. This is the way we control the interview and ease you into it. I've found that helps reduce the initial anxiety."

Geoffrey smiles, a full wide expression revealing grace and appreciation. "This is a good thing you are doing, Damonti. North Haven will be a better place for your role."

He turns to the rest of us. "A toast."

We all raise our drinks.

"May the eye of your wisdom grant me courage. May the strength of your arm grant me strength. And may we effect change as a result."

I don't think anyone really knew what he meant by all that. But we answered his toast anyway, because we were all drunk and had no idea what the promise of a brighter tomorrow meant to each other.

If only we could have known.

Chapter Nine

Kimber

Monday brings several surprises, a hangover the least of them. That's twice in one month; I'm practically an alcoholic.

First I catch a kid stealing. That, in and of itself, is nothing unusual. The unusual parts surround it.

I pick up his scent as he carries the most expensive drill we sell from the back of the store, around the far end of registers, to the returns desk where he attempts to return it without a receipt. It's called refund fraud, a difficult thing to catch, hard to prosecute. These cases are ones where we need to observe the crook enter the store empty-handed, select the item and attempt to make a refund.

It takes a set of nuts to commit refund fraud. You're staring an employee in the eyes telling them you just want a return, without knowing whether they saw you enter without it, whether they saw you swing around the end with it, and while they take their own sweet time.

Someone engaged in this kind of theft has graduated from the impulse lift to a premeditated action. Money is the object for these crooks, not gratification of something for nothing, not the thrill of stealing. That leads us down different roads for motivation and can reveal rather interesting stories at times.

A customer service girl named Sarah assists him. Obviously he has no receipt and something in his mannerism must have triggered her internal alarms. She picks up the phone to call me and we cross stares as she listens to it ring. I'm already behind the crook.

I wink at her.

She presses the hang-up button. To complete the charade and avoid spooking the kid, she pretends to order a box of blank refund slips from the warehouse.

Her role is played perfectly. She informs him that without a receipt, she can only refund the lowest sale price. Store policy and all that, you know. Since it's all free money, he doesn't object. They rarely do, and the ones that do can barely walk for the size of brass balls between their legs.

He dutifully fills out the paper form and smiles as she counts out the cash, laying it on the counter so the overhead cameras can record the amount.

The second he touches it, I move right behind him. And I mean *right behind*. I never let anyone leave the store after a refund, no need to. The deed is done at that point.

The guy senses my presence behind him; he sort of turns and makes to sidestep me. I slam a hand against the counter, blocking his path.

"Hi there," I say in my most neutral voice.

He looks up at me, confused and not a little apprehensive. I will readily admit to a perverse pleasure in the reactions of suspects when I stop them. He looks like he wants to run, but as he looks up, I can see him mentally wilt. I lean in closer; intimidation of size can be a great benefit.

I escort him back to the offices and begin his arrest paperwork. In the process I learn his name is Andrew Barton. He looks nothing like Casey or David, and a nagging voice in my head won't let it be coincidence. Finally I give in and check the back of his skull. The kid is meek, he doesn't protest.

There it is. The same brand.

Red and inflamed, as if recent. "What is this?"

"A tattoo." His tone is not convincing.

I flick it with my finger, causing him to wince. "Awfully tender for a tattoo."

"Leave it alone." He pulls away.

I give it another flick, fully intrigued. "Where'd you get it?"

"Some place downtown. Why?" He doesn't meet my eyes, fixated instead on his fingers as they knot and twist.

"What does it mean, Andrew?"

"Nothing. I just saw it on some other guys and liked it. That's all."

"I don't believe you."

Our conversation is interrupted by a cop knocking on my door. I don't know this one well, so I keep my thoughts to myself. There's some thinking that needs to be done here.

Andrew remains meek and cooperates fully.

The surprise hits me later that night at home. I flipped on the TV while fixing some dinner and there's Dee's face, filling the screen.

Seeing my friend on TV doesn't faze me. He's done plenty of interviews over the last year, especially for the local outfits.

What gets me is his appearance.

Gone: the hair. No more Afro, no more braids; a clean-shaven scalp gleams under the studio lights.

Gone: the gangster apparel, the old baggy jerseys, the dripping gold. Instead he wears a soft, cream collared shirt, open at the top button. The contrast to his skin is stark. Each ear sports a single diamond stud, but even these are subdued for him.

Mostly, the change is in his speech. No ghetto slang. He forms fully articulated sentences, modulating his tones, occasionally flashing a smile that shows off his gold cap. I hear Moller in his words and the difference in my friend is night and day.

I stand there, butter knife in hand, listening to my childhood friend address the population of North Haven and surrounding areas. He pleads for tolerance, citing examples from previous decades when violence begat more violence,

It's a fact, I'm certain, that Dee has no idea what 'begat' even means.

He mentions Montgomery, Alabama, and Kent State. He quotes Martin Luther King. He denounces the activities of the Klan, past, present and future, while also condemning the apparent retribution doled out to Sutton and the two other victims.

The door leading in from the garage opens and Maya enters the house. She must have left work early.

"Look at this," I say, pointing with my knife and dropping a glob of peanut butter on the floor.

She comes up beside and silently watches.

Dee sits in a backlit studio, across from a local reporter. His posture is comfortably erect, straightened from his default slouch and he looks the reporter in the eye. He is the image of a composed young black man appealing to the community with words of idealism.

But this young black man I know; I can see the falseness of his body language, the forced casualness, the nervous tremors that clatter up and down his spine.

Whatever Moller may be, and that includes a guy who raised two weirdo sons, I have to give him credit for the makeover in one day. I've been trying to get Dee to form full words for years.

"What's he talking about?" Maya asks.

"The Carter case. He's telling people not to seek revenge, not to escalate the hostilities, because that's not the answer."

"Why?"

Jesus, Maya.

"Because if some blacks decide that they need to send a message for Carter, they'll probably go hunting a white guy to even the score."

"But that wouldn't make it even. There have been three white men. Plus, they started it."

I can only laugh. The whole threat of a racial conflict escapes her; she sees only the number disparity. By her count, two more blacks need to be victims. Talk about elementary school logic.

I nod my head towards the screen and suggest she share her viewpoint with our newly appointed town activist.

She just sniffs dismissively and heads to the bedroom to change.

The capper of the day occurred later in the evening, proving that truly the best things are saved for last. But only if you could count this as the best thing.

Maya and I are downstairs working out. She's running on the treadmill. In her hand is the latest gadget she purchased. I didn't fully understand her explanation at the time, only that she could save songs to it and no longer needed CDs.

It seems like a great idea, except that now she sings off-key to music only she can hear.

I lay on the bench, working my chest. The TV behind me plays one of my favorite movies: *Better Off Dead*. I recite the lines from memory.

Footsteps sound upstairs as someone enters. It doesn't alarm me. Our neighborhood is pretty safe, plus I can instantly tell they belong to Dee.

Apparently the remaking of his image didn't extend to teaching him not to shuffle his feet.

Another set follows his and these I don't know. I grunt out one last rep and sit up to towel off my forehead.

The two people cross through the kitchen, tracking us by the screeching wail of my wife. Dee descends first, still clad in professional wingtips. He must have come straight from the news studio.

Behind Dee is James, our shared sports agent. A hint of dread washes over me, foreboding that a day so long in the coming has finally arrived. He's come to sever our working relationship, setting me adrift from my NFL dreams. I should have just given him the okay for the draft.

He reads my face and sees something there. "Surprised, Rick? It's not often I catch you speechless."

Actually, I feel defensive and more than a little mad; he's here to personally dump me. It's not his fault, but still I'm irritated. "Just say what you have to say." It comes out more forceful than I meant it.

James smiles at Maya as he crossed her line of sight. His eyes dart along her body, quick and furtive. He looks willing to forgive her awful singing for a glimpse of what her attire conceals.

Buddy, there's a price for everything and wait until you see her bill.

Maya glances at him with an unreadable look. They've met before and she has to know something different is going down.

Dee plops down on a couch in the center of the room. He looks at me and his face is a smirk. The bastard is enjoying this; he probably thinks I deserve it too.

Pulling a stool up to me and sitting, James looks hard at me. Most of our communication is over the phone, so I don't know his tells.

He begins without preamble. "You've been drafted. The Minnesota Vikings."

In times of utter shock, I like to think I come off all cool and collected, maybe with a snappy retort. In reality, probably sounded like: "Wha...how? What? WHAT?"

James gives a short laugh and holds up a hand. "Don't hurt yourself thanking me. You're welcome."

I take a deep breath, hold it in for a ten count, calm the internal churn. "Explain how that can be."

He scratches his neck, a habit I noticed at our first meeting. His complexion is swarthy, with whiskers that overachieve by hitting the five o'clock shadow mark well before noon. Because of this, he always looks like he needs a shave. The collars of his shirt have to irritate his skin.

"Let's start by saying that the organization only drafted your rights, in the seventh round. If you don't sign a contract with them prior to next year's draft, you become eligible again and some other team can make a try."

"But I never declared myself eligible in the first place."

A delicate cough into his hand. "Yeah, about that. Damonti and I made it happen. I do have some papers that I need you to sign and backdate to make it legit. If you don't, I'm in big trouble, so at least do that for me.

I stare at him. I stare at Dee. My stomach does barrel rolls. In equal parts I feel barely bridled excitement and overwhelming pressure. My dream of being a professional athlete has just been thrust upon me – in a most underhanded manner, mind you – and I only have to run with it.

Yet, along with that excitement came the old horsemen chasing me. Doubt, insecurity, a sense that I was not yet square with my life. These cast great shadows over me.

Taking my silence for refusal, Dee gets up. "Killer, think about it. The Vikings, man. Back in the pads, flying downfield for the sixty-yard bomb. You could be in game shape by August. People will know your name by October. Know what I'm saying?"

Yes, I do. But you don't know, and I can't explain.

In high school the whole town would turn out for games. Thousands of fans. That pressure I could handle. Then came college and suddenly thousands became tens of thousands, became televised games. As graduation loomed, draft potential became my world. I couldn't turn around without someone asking me where I was going. Bar, grocery store, hair cut salon, gas station. No place remained proof against the inquisition, and it started to squeeze me.

My father didn't help. He picked at me constantly for a decision that met his approval, critiquing each game and translating any mistakes into life altering events.

Both Dee and James hold on for an answer, but I have none. My life has been flipped in the last ten minutes; I need time to digest everything.

They spend another half hour slogging through details, tossing around possible scenarios. I don't say much.

In the end, they leave me with a sheaf of papers waiting on my signature, the initial step in my transformation. I simply hand the stack to Maya, who gains a sparkle in her eye once she understands what they represent.

I can sense the change in her; it's nearly a visible aura reflecting her anticipation of a life she's always desired. Or felt she deserved. That's just one more pound of pressure.

In one way a path has just opened up before me, terrifyingly clear. Yet, it's also quite complicated. I need to boil it all down into the things that matter most, the immediate priorities of my life.

One: To be or not to be. Enter a realm of sweat, fame and pigskin glory, or remain a faceless worker bee dancing with thieves. It's all there, encapsulated in a bundle of paper. A few John Hancocks and it all becomes a truth. It will take more strength than I have to lift that pen.

Two: Stop the madness infecting North Haven. Maybe I won't be the hero who ferrets out the killers and brings them to justice. This is real life, after all, not some book or movie. But I want to play a role, some kind of contribution to speed the resolution. This is my hometown, the place of my childhood, and it bothers me to see it stagger under the burden of Big City problems. If I'm to leave for gridiron fame, I want to have North Haven at peace; it will always be my anchor.

Three...

I look over to my wife, perched on the couch flipping through the pages with fervor. She goes back and forth, comparing points, looking for Lord knows what buried in the legal jargon.

My wife.

I repeat it in my head, attempting to recapture the sentiment that accompanied the 'for better or worse' phrase of our marriage vows. A sinking feeling steals upon me as I look at her and try to see farther down the road of my life.

Only hard decisions await.

I need to think. Maya keeps pestering me with questions about the contract, as if I've signed so many in the past. I can't sort things out with her yammering at me every few minutes, so I exit outside.

The street rests comfortably, lights burning in windows down the block. Moller's house sits dark, the only light a post lamp in the front yard.

A ride will clear my head, I decide. I roll the Super Hawk out of the garage. The V-twin engine fires to life and within minutes I'm heading west, chasing the sun past the sleeping horizon.

It starts out as a wandering journey, a metaphor for the aimlessness of my thoughts, yet somehow all my roads lead to one place. Despite my denials, they always had and one day I'll have to address it.

Rolling into a sleepy village thirty minutes west, I cut the engine and let the bike coast to a stop under a street light. It's an older neighborhood, probably erected in the Sixties. Mature trees line the block in gauntlet formation. Many of the houses are Rambler-style with garages tucked underneath. The street runs straight and true, like those who live here. A few lamps provide illumination, splotches of light amidst the night.

There's a sense of peaceful comfort here. It's like lying in your bed at night and listening to the familiar sounds of a house that holds all your memories, that knows you deep inside.

I stand next to my bike for a long time, summoning the courage to take that fateful step, to trod the sidewalk to something familiar.

As it turns out, my courage comes to me instead.

Footsteps sound on the concrete behind me. A chain clinks and I realize she's been out walking the dog. She always did at this time of night.

I turn. "Hi, Kimber."

The dog lunges forward to the end of its chain, a silky chocolate Lab. I knelt down to pet it. "Hey there, Sebastian. How's my buddy been?" He licks my hand eagerly.

Kimberly Katherine Tadisch levels a steady gaze at me, studying. "Rick, you can't keep doing this."

I cock my head and grin. "It's been a couple of months. You can't go that long without me."

"Irrelevant. I assume you're still married and I'm still with Jeff. That makes all this a moot point."

"And how is Jeffy? Besides being a complete twit, that is?"

Kimber – only I get to call her that – deigns to answer my question. She merely stares, so I stare back. As mentioned, we shared a life together for a time, until our paths diverged. She went on to counsel troubled teens with her sociology degree and I, well that tale has been told in nauseating detail already.

While not breathtakingly beautiful in the same vein as Maya, Kimber is no slouch either. Her blond hair is usually wound into a ponytail that bounces and sways with her walk. The body honed by becoming a nationally ranked doubles-tennis player has lost none of its vigor or shape. That's how we originally met.

Jocks tend to run in the same circles.

Life emanates from her every movement, character brightens her face. Her green eyes flank a nose strong and stubborn; her jaw cuts a fine line, more so than mine even. We could pass for siblings; friends used to call us Barbie and Barbie's brother.

We were far from it, however. Lovers. Best friends. Perfectly carved for each other. She is soft where I'm hard, she lends the strength I lack. Cliché or not, we are soul mates.

Well, once we were. Until fear clouded my vision. Until I no longer saw what was in front of me and foolishly looked for other shores and the mirages in the distance. Hindsight teaches harsh lessons, not the least of which is the fine line between running towards something and running away. Two years ago I was one of the fastest men alive and when I decided to run, no one could catch me.

"How are Jack and Jill? Still up on the hill?" Kimber's mom is actually named Joann, but it has always been an inside joke between us.

"If you expect me to say they're asking how you are, think again. Parents can be prickly when it comes to guys who break their daughter's heart. Even a couple years on."

I open my mouth, but she cuts me short. "You didn't ride all the way out here to ask about my parents, my brother, my sisters or to pet Sebastian. Last time it was to wish me a happy birthday. What's this time?"

Annoyance snaps in her tone. She's one smart-ass quip from punching me, I can tell. So I stop playing around. She's spent the last two years being angry with me and doesn't need any more fuel for that fire. I'm tired of being the lug that dumped her.

"I've been drafted."

Instant change. Astonishment flares to life in her face, unabashed and real. "To the NFL? Rick, that's incredible. What team?"

One of her greatest strengths, something that humbles me every time, is Kimber's ability to revel in the success of another. She truly is unselfish that way. Even Sebastian jumps and yelps, which is good. He used to be mine, so it's the least he can do.

"The Vikings."

"Oh, Minneapolis is wonderful. I wished dad hadn't sold our condo there. The music scene, the lakes; I miss that place."

"Yeah. Your dad didn't mention it to you, huh? Kind of surprising. He's always followed the NFL so I figure he would have seen it over the weekend."

She shrugs and gives the leash a short yank as Sebastian tries to wander off. "I saw his number on caller ID earlier, but haven't called him back yet. Guess I know now what he has to say."

In her happiness for me, Kimber's abrupt tone has given way to the girl I remember. It creates a bittersweet tang deep inside of me. I glance over my shoulder, to a small Cape Cod partway down the block.

"Is he there now?" I ask, referring to the current man in her life, a guy I once met and instantly disliked. I think he felt the same way; at least I got that impression from his 'go fuck yourself' comment to me.

"Yes."

"You let him move in yet?"

"No."

Planning on it?"

She sighs and in that sound evaporates the moment we shared. "The answer is the same, Rick, the same as every other time you've asked. I don't know. The last guy I lived with really spoiled me. And then he tore me up."

For those keeping score, that's me.

I move a step closer, trying to break that imaginary plane erected when former lovers have to re-define their roles into something else. But Kimber steps back in lockstep, either anticipating the move or possessing the reflexes of a super ninja.

"Don't," is all she says.

What I want her to say is something altogether different, but I don't know how to get her to say it. Nor is it really my choice. Two years ago I set her aside like used goods and now have to play the cards such a move left me.

Of course, the difference between knowing the situation and accepting it are two separate things.

"Are we always going to be like this?" I ask.

"As I recall, that didn't matter at one point. Or don't you remember emptying out our place of all your things? I came back on Monday to find you gone. No note, no word. Next thing I know, you're making time with Maya."

"And I've apologized endlessly for it."

"I didn't – I don't – want an apology. I wanted an explanation, instead of having to piece it together myself. I'm okay now, Rick, really I am. I know why you did that and I can even understand it somewhat, though I'd never do such a thing to someone I cared about."

"Well, if you understood my motives so well, why didn't you let me in on the secret? Help me square up?"

"No, no. That's your cross to bear. I will not enable your weaknesses nor will I shoulder the burden of reassembly. That's all on you."

We both stare, at impasse, with different purposes. She shakes her head gives the leash another tug. Sebastian gives my hand one last lick as she backs away.

"Go to Minnesota, Rick. Win your battles and you could be the best, you're the most incredible athlete I've ever seen. I promise to watch every game."

The words are meant to bolster me, to lend me some of that marvelous strength she holds in abundance. But that's not the kind of promise I want. In her words I hear a finality that burns.

Nothing comes out of my mouth in reply as she turns away. These are not the arguments I do well in. I'm built for hit and run comments.

Kimber passes from the circle of light cast by a lamp overhead, into the shadows. In seconds I can no longer see her.

It's a metaphor for our relationship and crucial to my understanding.

I'm just not very good at accepting things I don't agree with.

CHAPTER TEN

Odinism

Within twenty-four hours the media machine stirs to life and begins the task of tracking down the Vikings' surprise draft pick.

Me.

Normally sports reporters are pretty efficient with the information they dispense during broadcasts, but the facts are focused on just a few names and everyone else is treated as second class.

And then there are shocking selections, like mine. By the time my name was called, public interest had waned. Only the diehards stick around for the late picks. Even the major networks like ESPN struggle for storylines in the last couple of rounds to keep fans tuned in.

Additionally, as far as the sports world was concerned, I'd become persona non grata. I'd dropped off the radar, becoming just another face in the crowd that caused people to look twice and try to remember where they've seen me before. Like that maniac from several weeks back.

Rick Killing has been living in the "Where are they now?" file, a footnote or trivia question.

All I know is that when my name got announced, I was knee-deep in the brew and heated debates with my new neighbors. Although all our tongues were pretty garbled by then, so who knows how it really sounded.

James fulfilled his agent duties leading up to draft weekend, fielding the annual calls about me, providing non-committal responses, drumming up interest in case of a selection.

I don't feel bad for letting him take the brunt of scrutiny from the press. It's his job. Plus, he got me into it in the first place, let him sort it out. Regardless, I sign the papers and become a Minnesota Viking.

No calls come to our house from the media, which is not surprising. Everything is in Maya's name and her number is unlisted. That won't deter reporters completely, but it does slow them down a bit.

Eventually I will open the door one morning to find cameras and microphones staring back at me.

But it's not this morning.

I skip the news and head straight into work. I don't bother checking my machine in the loft either. James has that number; he'll let it leak to a select few as part of the publicity game.

As I rumble into the parking lot of the Hyper-Mart, I replay last night's encounter with Kimber. I know it's wrong to go to her, on many levels. It betrays my wife, who thankfully had not waited up for my return. It casts a wrench into Kimber's life with her pudding-headed boyfriend (although that I'm fine with.)

A part of me doesn't care. The heart and mind don't always speak the same language.

The camera room is dark. No one was scheduled last night and suddenly I'm glad of that fact. I need some alone time.

In my office I skim through all the major sports sites. Many have done commentary features, playing to the human element since no one knows how I am anymore.

Can Rick Killing overcome the devastating injury two years ago and become dominant once more?

Two years ago the nation buzzed with clips of Rick Killing killing it on the field? What will he be next season?

Those were the positive agenda storylines.

And there were negative stories too. I try to ignore them all.

How can Rick Killing expect to compete after being away so long?

The game is changed now. Rick Killing will be lucky to earn a roster spot and should probably just go play in the Canadian league.

Jay is the first person I see. He knocks on my door and simply stands there. "Wow."

"Surprise."

"Are you going to quit?"

"Rookie contracts are in the two-fifty, two-sixty range. You think I should add my pittance on top of that?"

He grins. "That was kind of a stupid question, I guess. What if things fall through? Re injury and such. What's your contingency plan?"

"Move in with you."

And so it went. The remainder of the morning passed in a whirlwind of calls. My cell phone vibrated every minute it seemed; I never knew so many people had my number. A few co-workers stopped me as I walked through the sales floor, questions ranging the gamut from when I would quit (why did everyone care so much?), to what I'd think it would be like (ask me in a year), to whether I could autograph something for their kid (sure.)

I took care to guard my words because I knew the dangers of misquotes, even among those with no ill-intent. If I'm in a news controversy, I want it to be because I meant to be, not because someone took my words out of context.

Amusingly enough, several people who don't know me well commented on my size and how it made sense, as if the only criteria for the NFL was size. That's like saying all tall people can play pro basketball.

My boss even called from her remote kingdom, wanting to know if I was the same guy her husband had read about. She picked and pried about plans for my Hyper-Mart career, undoubtedly worrying about having to backfill my spot. Then again, maybe she was glad for the chance to be rid of me.

I danced around the issue and remained non-committal, just to annoy her, because I'm a bit of an asshole.

By early afternoon, I know I've got to escape. Kevin and Kineisha make their appearance. They're unusually subdued around me and it feels uncomfortable. I don't like that; I'm the same guy I was last week, nothing has really changed. I don't know how to say that to them in man-words, though, so I say nothing.

Dee's on a three game road swing, so he's not an option for hanging out. Maya, even if I wanted to spend one-on-one time with her, is working down at a client site. Kimber...well, even I know when to leave well enough alone.

It's disheartening to realize how few true friends I have.

My eyes fall on the arrest report for Andrew Barton, sitting on top of a stack of papers. It was only yesterday, but it seems a lifetime ago. Here's something that can give me a focus and keep my patterns unpredictable to any news hounds hunting me.

I jot down all the different addresses for the Barton clan, noting the similarity.

Next, I log into the company network and search for shoplifters by the same last name. My three cases come up first, indicating they are the most recent. Todd's name appears again, notated by Casey's name as an accessory who was not cited at the time. It happened a month ago at a store farther south in the western suburbs. So they had tried the same thing, but Casey had rode shotgun instead of playing Bonnie to his Clyde.

I hit print on this report.

As I exit through the side door at the front of the store, I spy a news van sitting up against the front sidewalk, in the fire lane. A FOX affiliate logo adorns the side.

I slink through the lot, using other cars to hide my escape and call the police to report the illegal parking job. Again, just because I'm an asshole.

As I snap closed my phone, I note the number of waiting messages. One of those will be my father. He never calls the house.

The store where Todd was caught is roughly sixty miles away. I place a call to my Loss Prevention counterpart there, a lady named Michelle. We've spoken a few times in the past, but never face to face. She picks up the phone on the third ring.

"Michelle, Rick Killing from the North Haven store."

"Oh, hi. How weird that you called. Hey, how's the football career going?" She gives a laugh and I can't tell if she's being funny or really doesn't know. Before I can answer she plunges on.

"I heard it mentioned on TV this morning and thought 'Hey, I know someone with that name. What a coincidence.' Wouldn't that be the life? Making millions of dollars to play a game. Talk about easy street."

So she's a little oblivious. I rush forward onto another topic. "Yeah, great life. Listen, I need your help with a stop you made last month. Guy named Todd Layton. Do you have any video on it?"

The sound of a keyboard tapping can be heard, then: "Yep. I remember. One of my part-timers caught him and he tried to run. Why? You get him too? That's quite the distance to drive."

"I think so, but want to make sure. You going to be around in another hour or so? I can swing by."

"Oh, no need to do that. I can just send you a copy, should only take a couple of days."

"That's okay. I'm in that area for something else anyway and there's a bit of a time crunch."

A few moments of silence. "Alright, sure Rick. Is there something going on?"

"Nothing special. Just my curiosity getting the better of me. I'll see you in a bit." I hang up and pull into a sandwich shop.

After ordering a tuna and lettuce sub on wheat – no mayo please, you know what that stuff does to you? – I perch on the hood of my car in the back corner of the lot, chewing and staring off into space. The cell phone sits next to me, flipped open, staring up with expectation. The message icon blinks steadily, a countdown to the many things I don't always want to remember but can only ignore for so long.

Clearing my throat, I pop in a piece of gum to mask tuna breath and start working my way through the messages. The first three are from James. Four and five are from a local sports reporter, probably the same guy stalking me at work in the van. He'd profiled me on several occasions during my high school years. Once my career seemingly crumbled, though, he no longer had interest. There was always the 'next big thing' to chase.

I didn't mind.

Message six is from my father. I skip over it to seven and eight. Just a couple college buddies who I still talked to. Neither of them had made the NFL, though they kept the dream alive by working out for teams every year. Maybe one day we'd be on the same field, but I doubted it.

Hopping back into my car, I roll down I-294 towards the far west suburbs of Chicago. I scroll the message list to number six and play it on speaker mode.

"Rick, it's your father. I just got a call from that reporter at FOX 6. He says you were drafted this weekend. Is that true? I hope for your sake it is. This is your chance. Call your mother and me when you get a chance."

Click.

No congratulations, no goodbye. God bless, pops. The message header indicated he had called early this morning.

I delete it.

Michelle's store squatted in a suburb called Wheaton. The trip takes about an hour, not counting my sandwich stop. Thankfully traffic is light at 2pm on a weekday and I make good time.

Most Hyper-Marts were built along the same scale, modified little by little as the years trotted past. I pull up in front of the Wheaton location and see it's a mirror image of my store, if a tad bit smaller. I whoosh through the electronic doors and cut across the store front. I give a quick two-tap on the Loss Prevention door and twist the knob.

It's locked.

How come she can get her employees to listen?

The door opens to reveal a plump woman of roughly forty, clad in a denim shirt hung loose over jeans. Her cheeks are heavily colored, to accent the reddish tint of her poofy hair. She looks more like a bake sale mother than a thief dancer.

"Whoa, nelly!" She exclaims, looking up at me. "Who let in the Hulk?"

Her expression goes blank for a second, followed by: "Holy crap. It *is* you. Oh my God..."

With a sense of chagrin, I realize my t-shirt is one of those generic 'Property of' athletic logos. I guess mine would be coming from the Vikings from now on.

"Jesse over at the Schaumburg store said you were huge, but I never made the connection. Oh God, Rick. I feel so dumb."

I wave her off. "No worries. Thanks for helping me out here."

"What are you still doing here?"

"You haven't let me in."

"No, I mean, in this job? Shouldn't you be somewhere else?"

"There are a few things I need to clean up first." I'm talking as if my NFL career is a certain thing. Maybe I've come to accept that it is and there's no turning back now. "Can we go inside?"

"Oh, yeah, sure. Sorry about that. I'm just shocked. Come on in."

Her set up is identical to mine, with three offices sporting one-way glass along the hall. It didn't look like she's taken one for herself. She pushes open the camera room door and we enter. Her desk occupies one corner of the room.

That would suck; I'd go blind trying to read things in this low light.

"You got anyone else on today?" I casually ask, eyeing up her arrest board. The numbers are quite a bit lower than mine.

"Nope. I'm a small-staffed, lower traffic store." She fishes out a slip of paper from her jeans and peers at it, punching in numbers to her digital recorder. I had read the report before leaving, but those were just the bones of the arrest. I needed the flesh and blood, which comes from behavior and watching the guy in action.

A screen scrambles and flares to life. The recording swings around wildly, zooming into the hardware department. Whoever had been running the rig had probably received a call to check someone out and we are watching the results of his efforts to locate the person.

After a couple more gyrations, a young man leaps to center screen. His back is to the camera, his head whips side to side, presumably spooked by passerby. No wonder he got caught.

When the coast clears, he grabs a box of something and walks down the aisle towards the camera.

It's not the Todd I busted.

He walks to the front of the store. My mind says 'refund fraud.' As he nears the end of the registers, preparing to make the turn towards the service desk, something spooks him. He looks over his shoulder then sprints out the door, still carrying the box. A heartbeat later another figure follows him.

"That's Danny," says Michelle. "He got made somehow, but finally caught the guy out at the edge of the lot. Both guys got pretty scraped up."

"You know you're not supposed to pursue that far," I remind her, knowing smile creasing my face. Like any thief dancer worth his – or her – salt could just pull off. "Company policy."

"Oh, you're a fine one to talk," she retorts with a laugh. "Jesse says you'll chase them all the way across town. Didn't you get into trouble last year for knocking on someone's door and asking for the stuff back?"

Apparently Jesse talks. I'll have to watch what I say around her, at least for the near future.

I shrug. "Maybe." The house was on my way home anyway.

Michelle punches another key to rewind and freeze the frame of Todd's close-up. "So, is this the same guy?"

I shake my head. "Not even close. You think this was a refund?"

"I'm not sure. Danny didn't think so, but now that you mention it, I can see it."

"Pull up any refunds under his last name. Add in Barton too."

Michelle sits down at her desk and starts tapping away. I notice how well-worn the fabric of her chair is. It seems like she spends quite a bit of time in here.

Her screen fills with entries, dozens of them, all bearing the names of Barton or Layton, and close derivations, like Burton, Landon and Bayton.

"Holy..." But she doesn't finish. I can read her thoughts: She's embarrassed that no one noticed.

I lean closer and scan the list. Casey and Todd appear several times. David, once. The merchandise choice is what betrays them. All had returned similar items, often more than once. Todd had even returned the same drill Andrew tried to boost from me yesterday. Most interestingly, all the addresses listed were a variation on the same theme.

Deeper and deeper. What am I looking at here?

In all, we identify nearly twenty transactions in the last ninety days, worth thousands. I'm willing to bet there are many more we don't find, under names we don't know yet.

"You know you can set your system to filter by occurrences of a name, so it will kick out a report, right?"

"Yeah, I know," she laments, sounding suddenly tired. "But there's so many Bakers and Smiths and Jones to wade through..."

"That's the point of it."

She mumbles the same reply everyone gives when they are caught in the inertia of their own laziness. It's not my mission to change her, so I thank her and take my leave.

I wander the sales floor for a while, mulling things over in my head.

Todd Layton was not the same Todd Layton I busted. I supposed there could be two, but I didn't buy the coincidence. Casey Barton, using an address similar to the first Todd's, had also used an address similar to the second Todd's, in a town sixty miles away. Andrew had given an address new to me, until I get a load of some used here.

There's no question these kids are piling up refund fraud with fake information. The traffic is heavy at this store. Because it's easier? Most of the addresses were closer to my store.

And why did they need such quick money?

The common reason is drugs, but it didn't fit this time. I've arrested plenty of people stealing to fund their next fix and these kids did not fit the profile.

Maybe they're financing something. But what? The money they'd secured from Michelle's store wouldn't do much more than bankroll a spring break trip. I can't picture fast Todd partying up a storm at Daytona Beach. It has to be something else.

The brands flash back in my mind. It's a group thing. I abruptly turn my feet back to Michelle's office.

She's still there and I sketch out a crude rendition of the brand. "Ever seen this on any of the kids you caught?"

"Odinism," is all she says.

"Who?"

"Not who. What." She points to chair and I sit, intrigued.

"My family is mostly Swedish, with a little Irish thrown in for parties." She gestures to her pomp of red hair as if that proves it. "My sister dated a guy who was really into his Norwegian heritage. He studied a religion called Odinism. It's about following the old ways, believing in a lot of what those old warriors did. Like everything else, it's been 'modernized,' into things like nature worship, vegetarianism and all that tree-hugging stuff. I thought he was a crack-pot, personally. He'd pray to the king of the Norse gods Odin, hence the name, and make symbolic sacrifices to the other gods. God of the hearth, god of crops, god of war; things like that. It goes without saying that I'm glad they broke up."

I sit back. "Safe to say then that it's a white person's faith?"

"Guess so, since it traces way back to a mostly white area of the world. But nothing can stay 'white' any more. Now you have to include the blacks and Asians and Hispanics or risk being called a racist."

I hear the underlying tone of her words, but ignore it. My mind is busy jumping from dot to dot. "Is it a white power religion?"

"I don't know. I'm sure skin head and neo-Nazi types have used it, but that doesn't make sense to me. At its core, Odinism preaches non-violence, communing with nature and such. It's not a very good fit with people trying to stir things up."

Stir things up.

Is that what the murders in my town boil down to now? Just some people stirring things up?

Her view of white supremacy is a little narrow, but I get where she's coming from. Any faith founded on peace wouldn't mix well with groups striving for non-tolerance and subjugation of other races. Then again, religion is one of the most easily corrupted concepts. Look at all the killing in the Middle East, done in the name of their Holy War, or Allah, or whatever. Look at the Crusades.

Odinism being peaceful wouldn't prevent white power types from adopting it. They'd just mold it to their cause.

I take my leave of Michelle, for good this time. By the time I hit the interstate, rush hour is building.

My return trip will take longer and there's a stop I need to make on the way.

My progress slows to a crawl as I enter the confluence of three major arteries, affectionately known by the locals as the Hillside Strangler.

My mind races far ahead, putting together the pieces.

Chapter Eleven

Colonial Estates

I get there just after seven. Even small fringe towns have a lot of acreage to cover when you don't know where you're going. The sun is low, leaving the roads to wallow in shadow. And of course, I'm a man, meaning I don't stop to ask for directions.

Zion Hills is nestled alongside Lake Michigan, just under the Wisconsin border, a little spit of population hidden off the main highways. I've never been there, even though I grew up less than an hour away.

I motor through the silent streets, passing an occasional car, wishing my Cobra was just a little quieter for once. It feels like I've intruded on a town locked into 1950. Small houses front Main Street, deep porches guarding the entrance, garages tucked off alleys to the rear. Lights burn in many of the windows, muted by curtains. As I cruise around, I notice that many of the 20th century icons are absent: Starbucks, Applebees, Target, Walmart. The time-frozen aspect of Zion Hills has rebuffed all efforts towards progress.

Or it was just too small for notice.

The stores are of the Mom and Pop variety, often with half-functioning signs proclaiming their purpose. I pass Tucker Foods, Alice's Restaurant and Smiley's Bait and Tackle. Smiley hadn't bothered to spring the coin for a fancy design, his was just a white placard lit by a spotlight staked in the ground. It hangs suspiciously from what looks like a Century 21 signpost and I can only shake my head.

These people wouldn't know the 21st century even when it smacked them across their collective backsides.

I finally find my destination on the north end of town, an apartment complex hidden off the main drag by a thick cluster of woods, fronted by a fading sign saying Colonial Estates. I pull over and kill the engine.

This is the location of several of the addresses. I don't know if any of them really live here, but I sure would like to find out.

Sitting for a second, I try to think what I will really get out of this wild-hair impulse, but nothing comes to mind. That has to be the sign of a great idea, right? Maybe I can just nose around a bit. If something strange pops up, hopefully I'll look at it and think: Yeah, that's what I was looking for.

I get out and close the door with a quiet click. In the trunk are some workout clothes destined for the washer. I need something dark to cover my light t-shirt. An old sweatshirt with faded lettering on the chest will work. I flip it inside out to hide the letters and pull it on.

Phew. If someone gets too close, maybe the smell will warn them off.

The entrance lane to Colonial Estates curves through the pines for a half-mile. I jog slowly down it, noting how none of the buildings are visible from the road. Even though there's no outward indication, everything in me screams conspiracy. These were all clues to support my theory.

Problem being, I didn't even truly know what my theory was. Just some half-baked ideas of nefarious activity.

Nefarious.

Great, I'm starting to sound like Snidely Whiplash.

The apartment buildings look old. A dozen of them are arranged in nested crescents that surround a central courtyard. It seems the builder wanted to honor old Colonial architecture, but ran out of patience, money or both. Small traces of the design element can be seen in decorations over doorways and in the dried fountain that holds point amongst the courtyard.

A massive American flag soars high above the fountain, lit by a spotlight staked into the ground.

I wonder if they got theirs at the same place Smiley did.

A sidewalk leads from the drive to the courtyard, and then branches off to each building. The drive circles the outside of the ring, leading into a parking lot. The whole layout is nice and neat, one way in, one way out. Trees ring the complex, thick in the darkness, ominous.

My imagination is starting to run wild.

There's no noise to hear, despite the number of windows that are lit. I sidle off the driveway and stand under a tree, descending into what I call 'quiet mode.' It's a stillness of the body that I use often when watching crooks. It's more than holding still; it means pulling your aura inward, like disappearing, as goofy as that sounds.

I keep my eyes slightly downcast, letting my secondary sight detect any movement. I don't have to wait long.

Across the courtyard, someone moves. He reaches up and scratches his jaw. My vision picks up the motion instantly and my eyes dart in his direction. He's in the blackened lee of one building, motionless just like me, but facing away.

I know why I'm standing still. Why is he?

My first reaction is a guard. But you only post guards when you have something to protect. Or when you have something to hide.

Turning my eyes away, I wait. If I'd continued staring, he might have sensed me staring. Don't laugh, it's real, but I have no idea how it happens.

Worse, if I had continued peering at him, my vision would have started playing tricks on me, creating shadows and movement where none existed.

After a few minutes, three figures detach themselves from the shadow of a building, walking towards my guy. They converge upon him. A moment later, three leave. I can't be sure, but it looks like they just rotated watch.

I need a closer look, but my nerves are starting to fray. This is way over my head. The smart thing would be to report my findings to the police; allow men trained for this sort of thing to do their stuff. Then again, what would I say? That I saw some people acting in a suspicious manner, when it could just be a neighborhood watch group.

With my track record of going off half-cooked, that would play *real* well. I could just imagine the detectives laughing over the latest episodes of Rick Killing while munching donuts.

That will never do, not at all. I'm no one's laughing stock.

Not anymore.

That leaves only one option, so off I go.

Backing slowly into the trees, I skirt the edge of the forest, moving slowly, paranoid that other guards might be lurking in the trees. At least my dark clothes help me blend in, even if they smell awful. Score one for thinking ahead.

I maneuver myself in line behind the one guard I can see, staying to the trees. Now I can see what he sees. It looks like some kind of assembly is in process in the clubhouse building. The doors are closed, but through the picture windows I can see the proceedings perfectly. Kids of both genders – most appear younger than me – sit in rows of folding chairs, listening to a lecture from a man standing behind a podium. There has to be a hundred people in the room.

Two flags hang behind the speaker. One is the American flag. The other bears the symbol for Odinism, painted in blacks and reds.

Yes, validation. Of what I'm not yet sure, but it means I'm on the right track.

I can't see the face of the lecturer. A smaller version of the flag is hung near the window and it blocks my view of his upper body. I'll need to change my angle if I want to get a look at him.

I slip forward, hoping that my pulse isn't as loud on the outside as it sounds inside. Edging along the building, I find a vantage spot behind some bushes in need of trimming.

He's an older guy, drill sergeant type. Gray hair shaved close to the scalp and permanent scowl give him a no-nonsense attitude. He's got a stern look as he speaks, eyes piercing the all-white crowd before him. It's easy to picture a uniform on him, a chest full of medals and complete intolerance for anything not like him.

Even though I can't hear his words, I understand perfectly his message.

He epitomizes all that is white hate. He didn't need the massive tattoos, the thrash metal music, the Nazi symbols. A promise of violence is within him and no fashion choice can hide it.

I wonder if the blood of Jerome Carter stains his hands as they grip the lectern.

I'll admit it: I felt weirded out.

And confused. Todd, Casey, Andrew; none of those kids carried hate vibes. They were as normal as you'd expect, apart from being thieves. Do they really march to the beat of this guy's drum? Is this some kind of cult? Are they disenfranchised youth looking to be part of something different and will eventually grow out of it?

Or are they much more dangerous than that?

I leap to the assumption that the three dead men were attached to this group. Somehow their association made it to someone's radar, someone who didn't like the idea enough to take drastic action.

It doesn't get much more drastic than death.

Thing is, what's so special about North Haven that a group – any group – of supremacists would settle in? And not just the white folk, but also the people willing to kill to send a message.

A stake through the eye pretty much says: "Go away."

How could all these militant racists be running free and not go noticed? I wonder if Allan Borden and his buddies know about Colonial Estates. If they don't and I'm just uncovering it...my mind spins. Rick Killing, detective, savior of North Haven.

Cool.

I need to find the opposing group. If I do, then maybe I can tie the activities back to them, show a cause for the conflict. My head swims with possibilities and scenarios, most of them me proving to everyone I'm not such a putz after all.

There's not much left for me here. The speaker is still speaking, the kids are still listening. I'm not willing to wait around for cookies and punch.

Re-tracing my footsteps, I back away from my hiding spot, peeking in the windows of any lit apartments. None offer up anything other than a place inhabited by kids. Posters, Playstations and pizza boxes. Hell, that was my first dorm room in college.

As I slink around the corner of the building, my head lost in plans and thoughts, I get careless.

I stumble directly into the guard.

He'd moved his position while I watched the assembly. We are both in the process of walking and turning, so we smack into each other face to face. Just like when Scooby Doo and Shaggy run into the monster.

I'm not sure who is more surprised. Probably him.

There isn't much to say, no handy quip.

So I shove him as hard as I can, up against the brick wall. His head slams against the stone and a yelp of pain escapes him. He drops to his knees, grabbing at the back of his head. The other hand makes a feeble attempt to latch onto my pant leg, but I kick it away and react as any sane man would in this situation.

I run.

A shout chases me as I sprint across the courtyard, abandoning stealth for speed, dissolving into a dark blur. I hear answering calls from another direction and guessed they were from the other three patrols.

It doesn't matter. None of them could catch me if we raced for fun; running scared like this gives me an extra gear.

My stride lengthens as I tear down the entrance drive. Weakening shouts come from behind as they fall back. A shape suddenly emerges from the trees lining the entrance, nearly causing me to yell in alarm. He's quite a bit smaller so I don't bother slowing up and barreled into him at full speed.

He goes sprawling back into the woods, tumbling head over heels. A ragged gasp comes from him.

I have to reach my car with enough of a lead that they can't see my plate. Thankfully I don't have those automatic lights, so my plate numbers won't be lit up when I start it.

Never has an engine sounded so good as when mine fired up. With one foot mashing the Go pedal to the floor, I dump the clutch and tear away in a cloud of tire smoke. That should also help hide my plate numbers.

As I row through the gears, one kid skids to a halt in the road behind me, but I'm far enough away now and still accelerating. He quickly shrinks in the rearview mirror. I wait until he's out of sight before turning on my lights.

With a racing pulse and shaking hands, I wind my way home.

Chapter Twelve

Dinner

For couple of days I mull over what I now know,
trying to decide what to do with this information.
I've learned a lot; I haven't learned what it all
means.

Fact: There is a new brand in play around North
Haven.

Fact: The brand is associated with a pagan religion.

Fact: Kids with this brand are committing acts of theft.

Fact: These kids are traveling, willing to drive an hour or more to steal.

Fact: There is a gathering of people around this brand and someone thinks the gathering needs guards posted.

While the facts all meshed together in my mind and pointed to something peculiar, maybe even deadly, they might not necessarily mean the same thing to another person. I've added in too many of my own suppositions.

Assumption: The brand, and spirit of what it means, has been corrupted by a group of white people.

Assumption: This group believes in racial separation.

Assumption: This group is intertwined with the murders somehow, which if true, makes them more dangerous than anyone realizes.

Assumption: The kids are stealing to generate money that they need for some reason. It's more than spending cash or the thrill of easy funds.

I can't go to anyone in an official capacity with this information. Given my history, I need iron-clad proof before revealing anything. I don't need to look like an idiot.

Again.

Unfortunately, no plan springs immediately to mind, no matter how much I squeeze my eyes shut and think hard. Maybe I should let things percolate for a bit.

It just needs to happen sooner rather than later.

Meanwhile, North Haven continues to descend into civic suspicion and rumor. Flyers start appearing on telephone poles around town, decrying the violence. At least the pics of the lost dogs get covered; those always make me a little sad.

Several small rallies came together spontaneously, black and white folk standing on a shared platform, shouting for the world to hear. I don't know exactly what benefit rallies bring, but it's nice to see people trying.

Too bad I could walk a couple of blocks and still feel the tension between groups of people eyeing each other across an intersection. Maybe they hadn't heard the rally speech. A megaphone could help that.

Right on Jordan Way, someone fronted the cash to erect a billboard that simply said "Stop The Madness." The background of the sign is blood red, letters black. The symbolism is subtle.

Dee calls me late in the week. "Dawg, you catch me on Angela Harris?"

"You should close the bedroom door. My eyes will never be the same."

"What?"

"Never mind. Who's Angela Harris?"

"Lady with a local show on CBS Chicago. Plays at 1pm."

"That's primetime soap opera. Are housewives and stoned college kids your target market now?"

He ignores my bait. "An' next week I got a shot at Oprah. She been watching. She understands."

"She should. She's black and this is about as cut and dry as it gets."

I could picture Dee in his new persona, sitting on Oprah's couch, conversing about critical social topics...wait, no I couldn't. This is the same guy that wore his clothes backward after those two young rap Kriss Kross kids did *Jump, Jump* when we were teenagers.

"If you do Oprah, I'm calling in. I swear, Dee."

That tamps him down a bit. "You wouldn't do that. Would you?"

I don't answer, letting him swing in the wind. "Anyway, what else is going on?"

"Everything, man. Hundred miles an hour. This thing with Moller has exploded, more than I ever thought it would. I even bought some advertising. Guess the theme."

"'Stop The Madness'."

He pauses. "How'd you know?"

"I saw the billboard. Let me guess, you contributed the idea. It's a line from that one movie you used to quote all the time back in high school. You couldn't think of anything more original?"

"That was a kicking flick. Loved that thing." The intent of my comment is lost on him.

"Well, try not to let your Martin Luther impersonation get in the way of everything else."

"What you say, killer?"

"Don't ghetto talk me. I watched the Mets game last night. Your error in the eighth…that's a play you make in your sleep, Dee."

"Yeah, shit happens. What you want me to do? Besides, I hear you the one with real problems. Like this Sunday."

"You talked to Maya?"

"Yeah, tried you at home first. Wanted to do some racquetball this weekend." He laughs. "But she got you tied up all the way."

I make a dismissive sound. "It's just dinner."

"Yeah, whatever. Have fun." Click.

Problem is, dinner is with my parents.

For most people, going home means reliving the moments that went into creating the person they became. That's true for me too, only not all moments are equal. We all take different paths to reach our destination and sometimes that trail can leave marks.

"So, why are we doing this again?" I ask for the umpteenth time as I steer the Jeep out of our neighborhood and point it north. Maybe I could just drive until we hit the North Pole.

"Because," Maya replies with great exaggeration. "We haven't visited in months and they want to talk about your wonderful news. Since you refuse to call them back, this is the only way."

"My dad just wants to make sure I don't fuck it up. That's all."

She slaps me on the arm. "Rick! He wants to help. And anyway, you need someone to prod you along."

That pisses me off, even if it is true. No one likes to admit they don't do such a good job of managing the direction of their own life. Matter of fact, I have plenty of direction. Unfortunately it just keeps changing.

But hey, that's not my fault.

I cast a sidelong glance at Maya. She's staring ahead with a contented look on her face. It's a look I've seen a lot more since the draft and I know why. She's giddy over me returning to football, returning to the tableau where she's admitted in the past she liked me best.

Problem is, I'm not sure she's happy for the right reasons.

Over the last couple of years she has watched me slip farther and farther away from the things I excelled at. I think one thing that bothers her is not that I wasted my potential, but that she's wasting hers on me. In her mind, she belongs with someone who deserves her; not the other way around. It's not a wrong viewpoint; it speaks to her self-worth and how she values it.

If I return to the Game, I come one step closer to being that person. It's not about fulfilling my destiny, it's about fulfilling hers.

She is so different from Kimberly I sometimes wonder how I could be attracted to both types.

Maya stretches in her seat, arching her back. Her short shirt lifts to reveal a tan and flat stomach. Oh, there's the attraction. Now I remember.

I hate being shallow.

My parents raised me in the heart of North Haven, living a life based on the principles of company loyalty, proper attendance and job security, in that order. To them, this is the sequence of a career.

In return, both were afforded the opportunity to take early retirement. My father leapt at the chance. It allowed him to sink into his favorite hobby: woodworking. He'd spend mornings carving out rocking chairs, or birdhouses, or porch railings. Where all these things ended up, I had no idea. Afternoons would find him in front of the TV catching his shows, one of which was a soap opera. I found that humorous.

My mother didn't make the break as easily. Her career as a doctor's secretary parlayed into freelance medical research. Her days were spent poring over arcane journals and trade articles. If anything, she is busier now than before, rarely leaving her den before supper.

Since I have no siblings, my parent's obligations to any offspring began and ended with me. That can be good, but more often than not, bad. Good in the sense that they were able to focus on me and my life. Bad, in the sense that they were able to focus on me and my life.

Last year they left North Haven for good, building a new house in Wisconsin, two hours north. In that move, I lost an anchor to my past, the place where I'd grown into a man. The new place is plenty big for them, with all sorts of new amenities absent from the old house. It is not, however, a home. At least not one I recognize.

I pull up the long driveway just after four. The house sat alone on a few acres with no trees. At some time in the recent past, this plot was part of a cornfield. Carving a yard out of such a flat landscape struck me as ugly and distant.

I stop the Jeep in front of the garage. It's open, revealing both of their cars. Dad putters around in the back half where he'd set up his wood shop. He's pretending to inspect a pine board, but I know in reality he is just waiting for us to show.

He sets the board down and waits until we stop before he comes out of the garage. His gait is stilted, an old injury from his younger days. I'd never gotten the clear story on what exactly had happened; it was one of those family folklores that had been repeated so often the origin is no longer known.

I did know that the injury kept him from competing at an athletic level, which was too bad. The guy has amazing coordination and reflex. One of our pastimes used to be shooting hoops, like games of horse with him limping from position to position. Invariably, he would make at least one jaw-dropping shot per game. His favorite is to pick a spot at random, glance at the basket, then close his eyes and make the shot.

Much of my own athleticism comes from him. Among the catalog of good youthful memories were nights spent in the driveway, shooting hoops in companionable silence. But the catalog grows thin at the point where I started making decisions that didn't meet his approval.

I glance around the newly paved drive and notice the absence of a hoop. That says something.

Roland Killing limps towards me, hand stuck out. "Hello, son. You don't return your calls."

I accept his proffered grip and give it a short shake. "Been busy."

He still holds the ramrod posture of a military rearing, courtesy of my grandfather, and his eyes remain steely. I'm only a couple of inches taller, but the gap seems larger every time I see him. He'd always had a lean frame even though he could not exercise like other people, but I can see evidence of a paunch under his sweatshirt.

This strikes me as somehow sad, like noticing a childhood tire swing that's faded, rope frayed, and realizing it will never again hold your weight.

Maya comes forward and hugs him, whispering a greeting. He accepts it only because it's good manners; I know deep down he isn't too crazy about her. Not that he dislikes Maya, but Kimber had been his favorite. In his estimation, we were once the perfect couple.

Once.

Together those two turn and make for the house. I take a moment to spin slowly around, looking back down the driveway. The sun hides behind heavy cloud cover. A hint of cold rides the air and it mirrors my mood. This house isn't my home, I didn't belong here, and I didn't want to be here. I vow to leave as soon as supper is over.

Stepping through the front door, I hear my parents speaking in a low whisper to Maya, back in the kitchen towards the rear of the house. I enter the kitchen and force a light tone to my voice. "So, what's the whispering about? Ancient Chinese secrets?"

"Hi, honey." My mom comes forward, standing on her toes to hug me. Like my father, she's fair-haired and pale, with the movements of someone who knew physical activity. She'd been a standout collegiate swimmer and could still lap me like I'm treading water. I swim like a dog. A dog with weights strapped to his tail.

"Hi back at you. What's for dinner?"

"Your favorite."

"And what exactly would that be?" Even I'm not sure. Moms have selective memories and you have to gut-check them at times.

She swipes at me with a potholder. "You know, prime rib with steamed vegetables and twice-baked potato."

I *did* like that. My arteries hardened just at the mention. "Great, wonderful. Since I missed the first part of the listening game, why don't you tell me what you were all talking about when I walked in?"

My father, in the process of moving towards the dining room, spins back. "Rick, stop being so suspicious. We were talking about you."

"That I gathered. What I want to know is what about me warranted the hush-hush voices."

Maya shrinks away from the discussion. Alone with me, she has no problem going toe to toe, but in the presence of others she tends to avoid confrontation. Unless they're Japanese, of course.

Mom opens her mouth to speak, but dad cuts her off. "If you must know, we were wondering whether you'd made the decision to play for Minnesota or not. Maya said she didn't know. There. Does that make you happy?"

"Not as happy as if you'd just come right out and asked me first. For the record, I have signed the papers, so at least that part is settled. Now are *you* happy?"

Dad shakes his head, disgusted. "You're going to piss this one down your leg too, aren't you?"

"If you say so, pops. Then you can have the satisfaction of being right once again. I know how important that is to you. Don't bother thanking me, it's my pleasure."

Funny how families can so quickly enter the same old rut even when they only see each other occasionally. Isn't absence supposed to make the heart grow fonder? I saw it once on a Hallmark card, so it has to be true.

I could take these exact words and match them up against all the other countless arguments between us. In his eyes I could only screw up, and I was tired of trying to live in accordance to his expectations.

In more sentimental moments I ponder the dynamics of our relationship. I figure we just don't know how to talk to each other without expectation and subtext. If there's a day on the horizon when we'll strip away all the crap and speak openly, I'm not holding my breath for it.

Sometimes I'm not even sure I want it.

Maybe I do belong here. Sure feels like my house growing up.

"Rick, honey. Stop." Mom lays her hand on my arm. She has ways of defusing things, and plenty of practice over the years. "Rol, show Rick the basement."

He pauses, probably debating the merits of just pushing me down the stairs, then grunts. "Come on. You might like this."

I follow my father down. An ornate railing decorates one side of the stairs and I wonder if he carved it. But I'm not going to give him the satisfaction of asking.

The basement leads out to a back patio. It overlooks a deep slope, much like my house. Fading daylight leaks through the French doors, giving the space a nice glow. Dad stops and points to the far corner where a bar sits.

It had been carved from dark wood and featured the requisite brass foot- and hand-rails. The surprise centerpiece is an aquarium. It sat in the face of the bar, in a cutout. Brightly colored fish swam lazily in circles.

"Huh. That's interesting. What made you think of that?"

"Your father's a genius, that's what," he replies, giving evidence to the origin of my smart ass nature.

It's his way of offering an olive branch, a way to say he no longer wanted to fight. It has always been this way; he uses metaphorical words to convey words he lacks the courage to say.

Only I've never really understood the message.

He spends the next few minutes dissecting the manner of construction, as if I needed to know the detail so I could run home and build my own. I let him go on, wandering away in my mind, thinking indistinct thoughts.

Mom calls us for dinner a few minutes later and dad breaks off his litany mid-sentence. He's just as eager to get this meal done as I am. Then we can once again go our separate ways.

We arrange ourselves in a cross pattern at the table: Maya across from me, mom and dad facing each other. Without preamble, thanks or a pre-meal prayer, he begins loading meat onto his plate while the rest of us watch in silence. When he's done, he hands the platter to me. It moves clockwise from there.

Outside of the occasional comments on the food, it's quiet, so after a bit, I decide to change that.

"I discovered a white supremacy group living in North Haven and they could be at the center of all the crap going on back home."

Everyone gives me a blank stare, even Maya, who I had not kept in the loop as to my extracurricular activities of late. She'd only have scoffed at my ideas anyway and tell me to focus on football.

I toss out another nugget since this is a tough crowd. "I think the three white victims belonged to this group and they were retribution murders. Jerome Carter was the answer for their deaths."

My parents stay on top of local news despite the distance. It's an old person thing, I'd decided a while back. So eager to leave for different shores, yet unable to let go. There's probably not much gossip up here in Nowhere, WI.

Lastly: "I'm going to solve the murders."

Dad sets down his fork and stares at his plate. "Dammit Rick," is all he says. It's enough.

"Does this mean you won't play football after all?" Mom asks. "You were so good at it."

Maya, being the smartest person in the house, looks me in the eye. "What are you trying to prove, Rick? And to whom?"

I don't answer. I think we both knew that I wanted to do more than simply solve a set of mysterious murders, that it represented a rung on the ladder I needed to climb. Deep down, she probably fears that my ladder will take me higher than hers, and where would that leave us?

A sigh comes from dad, like he's decided to indulge me in some childish game. "And what makes you think you can find out something the police can't?"

"Because I'm looking in different places. Places where they won't bother."

"Like the criminal masterminds that steal baseball cards and trinket jewelry? Are they graduating from petty theft straight into murder now? Or is there a stop off for kidnapping, drug running and extortion?" He hates my dead-end job.

"Actually, there's a run on refund fraud going on. They are pooling money to fund something big and that's my trail back to the source."

Maya's eyes sharpen, as if suddenly understanding the depth of my conviction. "How do you know this?"

I give an offhanded shrug. "I've spent a few days poking into some things, like addresses." I keep it vague, trying to project a casual vibe. If she takes interest, she'll drive me nuts with questions. She'd probably insist on creating a database for it and spend a month worrying over the correct font to use.

"Why does the address matter?"

"I think they congregate together, like a closed community. There's a complex by the lake and another just north of there that I've been able to find." For those not from the area, the 'lake' always meant Lake Michigan.

Dad raises an eyebrow. "You visited them?"

I nod. "Just one, the other night."

"And did you take this information to the police? What about that friend of yours? Borden?"

"To tell them what, pops? That I found a bunch of kids living in an apartment complex and I think they belong to a hate movement? Think about how flimsy it sounds. I need more yet."

"You're not going to drop this, are you?"

"How often do I quit something important?"

His withering glare is my only response. When I refuse to take the bait, he switches topics.

"I saw Damonti on the Angela Harris show this week. Since when did he decide to get into this stuff?"

"Just recently, on a Sunday night not so different than this one," I say. Maya suppresses a smile, probably remembering how drunk we all were. She hadn't gotten out of bed until noon the next day. It was fun, but look where it's taking us all.

"Does he think he's going to be the next Jesse Jackson?" Dad leans back and crosses his arms, as if he's just driven a stake into the heart of the debate.

"Would you rather he does nothing? You know Dee. He's always been touchy about race subjects. In case news doesn't reach you up here in the Land of the Bumpkins, we've got dead bodies piling up. The latest was a guy who probably got targeted for nothing other than his skin color. Of course Dee is going to take up that banner. I don't blame him."

"But the other three deserved it?"

"No, but if they were actively involved in hate crimes, it's a little easier to understand the motivation."

Dad processes that, staring through me as he does. His eyes have always been unnerving and he knows it. "You think there's a black gang that decided to go after this white group just to make a point?"

"Well, it could be any minority, but I'd guess blacks, yes. All the symbols about the Klan send a message."

"And you've uncovered the racist group you believe these men belonged to."

"I've found *a* racist group. Whether they were part of this group or not, I don't know. But think about it. How many can there be in North Haven? It's a pretty safe assumption."

His tone grows aggressive. He's hearing something he doesn't like. "Then how will you find this black group? Paint yourself and sneak into the ghetto?"

"Better than whittling rocking chairs and watching soaps all day," I fire back. My pulse quickens as I finally take his bait. The bastard knows the right buttons to push. I feel the heat rising.

But we've already hit our quota of arguments per visit. I should save something for next time.

Taking a deep breath to bleed off the pressure inside of me, I wave him off and focus on my food.

After dinner, dad takes Maya downstairs in order to victimize someone else with his woodworking knowledge. I stay and help mom clean up. It's our time-honored ritual, our bonding time.

"Are you really so unsure about playing football?" She asks at one point.

"Yes and no."

She wipes a glass carefully. Despite the presence of a brand new dishwasher behind her, she still prefers to hand wash anything glass. "You'll have to expound a little more than that, honey."

I stop and lean against the counter, staring out the window. Across the backyard there's nothing but young grass leading to retired farmland. Clumps of trees can be seen in the distance.

"I've pretty much made my decision. But there are some other things going on that affect it. Things that need to be squared away."

"You're not still worried about your knee, are you?"

Of anyone, she knew the severity of my injury. Or shall I say, lack thereof. She knew I had copped out on an excuse but never took me to task for it. Moms can be great that way. I shake my head. "Knee's fine."

"Is it this gang thing? This obsession you have with getting involved in things that don't affect you."

I could debate the merits of whether white men being murdered in my hometown affected me, but I understood the gist of her question. "Maybe a little."

"You know, you don't have to solve all the world's problems. No one will think less of you if the murders are solved by men who are paid, and trained I might add, to do these things."

"Yeah, I know. It's just something I want to do, but it won't hold me back from anything else."

She nods slowly, taking her time to place a glass up in the cupboard. "Then it must be Kimberly."

That catches me by surprise and I shoot her a look. "Why would you say that?"

"I ran across her last week."

"What? How? You're a hundred miles away now..." The logic snaps into place. "You called her."

"Actually, she called me. She wanted to know if everything was alright in the family and one thing led to another."

Kimber knows exactly how nothing is ever 'alright' in the Killing family. Although our problems, in the greater scheme of things, weren't terrible. Dad didn't drink, beat mom or cat around with other women. He did nothing to threaten the stability of our family.

He is just a rigid, self-righteous asshole who resented a son that wasted golden opportunities never presented to the father.

"So what did she say?" I can't help it.

Mom smiles her special smile, that one every son has seen before, meant only for him. "Rick, I'm not going to broker this for either of you. You are married to Maya and, while I like her just fine, you know my feelings towards Kimberly."

I did. Kimber was everyone's favorite. It's me that's on the shit list.

"But," mom continues. "You have to understand that your actions will affect more than just you and Maya. Kimberly has a life now too. She hasn't been sitting around waiting on you. Your father and I can't take sides in this. We won't place our values on what you have to do to make yourself happy."

"I know, I know. Thanks."

She laid a hand once again on my arm, this time with a different touch. "She still loves you, though. Moms have a way of knowing this. I could hear it in her voice."

"Yeah?" My pulse grows loud suddenly.

"Yes. But you have a lot of ground to cover. You have to be the man that deserves her, the man she can admire. That goes far beyond being the best wide receiver, which we all know you are. It goes beyond fame and fortune. Everything in life has come so easy for you, Rick; you've never really been tested. And when you finally were, you failed. That causes you to lose respect for yourself, which causes others to do the same."

She presses two fingers to her lips, as if holding back a belch, but her face is too thoughtful for that. Plus my mom has manners.

"It's not too late to get your life back where you think it belongs. You are so young yet. It's not too late to remake yourself, to escape this self-pity malaise you've been wallowing in for the last couple of years. Stop rattling around inside yourself and figure out just who Rick Killing is."

I feel the tightening in my throat. Moms are so true. The loop of denial and pity has become a circle I run endlessly. If I don't do something, I'll find myself there forever, wearing a groove that eventually becomes too deep to climb up.

I bend over and hug her. I was wrong before. Maya isn't the smartest one in the house after all.

CHAPTER THIRTEEN

Breaking Away

We're quiet on the way home and I can't decide if it's comfortable or awkward. Had Maya and I degenerated to the point where I can't read her anymore? Further, can she still read me? Can she see what's gnawing my insides, and if so, would she even make a comment?

I no longer know, and that in itself is a statement of things.

So we remain silent, Maya and I, separated by a gulf of private thoughts and fears, a husband and wife who really don't know each other, only what angers each other.

As we turn into our neighborhood, I flick on the high beams out of habit. They reflect off something farther down the block that catches my attention. Dee's Mercedes sits in Moller's driveway. I'd know those ugly rims anywhere.

I feel a strange twinge. Why is he there late on a Sunday night? Getting more advocacy training?

I've been cut out of the loop. Without me, Moller would never have had access to Dee, but now that he does, I'm out. They've known each other only a few weeks; it's happening fast.

For Dee to make the trip up from his Chicago home meant there was a purpose, yet he didn't call to let me know he'd be a few doors down. That's not the norm. I get the feeling that Moller doesn't want me present for whatever they do together, and it makes me irritable.

Maybe I'm just being petty.

After we park, I tell Maya I need a quick walk to settle the red meat in me. Her only response is a soft grunt and in that reply hides many words I may never hear.

I wander down the block. The night is chilly and I can feel goose bumps on my arm. The smell of damp earth soaks the air and it feels like I'm the only person moving in the stillness.

The hood of the Mercedes is cool to the touch. I walk up the drive, noting the lack of light in the house. Moller's Jag sat outside the rear garage. Of the Vette there is no sign and I wonder where he keeps it. I hadn't seen it since that Sunday.

Taking the steps two at a time, I bound up on the front porch and jab the doorbell.

After a long spurt of waiting in which I'm tempted to ring it again, Nathan yanks open the door. There's no sign of welcome on his face. I bet the Girl Scouts never sell to him. "Yes?"

"Dee here? Whaddya guys doing?"

"Playing Twister."

He says it with such a straight face that I almost take him seriously. Funny quips are my domain. I suddenly get a glimpse of how other people feel. "Can I join?"

Nathan gives an uncaring shrug. "If you must."

He turns without another word and stalks back through the house, leading me downstairs. Not long ago we had ourselves a merry old time, but it may as well have been a lifetime back. Nothing looks the same.

What once was recreation and game space had been given over to another purpose. Gone is the pool table, the wet bar, games and leather couches. They've been replaced by a half-dozen TVs in a rack against one wall, tuned to a variety of news outlets, national and local.

The opposite wall features a bookcase filled to capacity. I flick a glance at the spines; the common theme seems to be American culture in the twentieth century. It gives me a horrific shudder as I flashback to high school government classes.

Geoffrey and Dee sit in the far corner, at a massive oak table. Piles of books and papers litter the surface; several desk lamps provide reading light. Both are in collared shirts and ties, sleeves rolled up to show everyone just how hard they are working.

Geoffrey looks over the rims of reading glasses perched low on his nose. "Hello, Rick."

Dee looks up from the book he's reading, slight surprise in his eyes. "Killer! Wassup?" We shoulder bump and clasp hands in the same manner we've done for years.

"And what are you boys playing at?" I pick up a paper from the table titled *1998 Crime Statistics in the South Atlantic Region*. Numbers and charts sprawl the across the pages.

"Just research," says Dee, sitting back down and motioning to a chair for me. "There's a lot of shit going on, especially with this whole Y2K thing."

"Such as?" I plop myself down, pushing away a book in front of me bearing the title *A Bleeding Nation*. Nathan sits across from me. Of Lance there's no sign and I wonder where he's at. I've never seen the brothers apart.

Geoffrey speaks first. "Have you heard of the Megiddo Project?"

"What's it rated?"

"It's not a movie. Megiddo is the ancient site of many battles. It had multiple incarnations as a fortress city and is even referred to in the New Testament as the place where the final battle for good and evil will happen. In Hebrew, *megiddo* forms the base word for Armageddon."

"That movie I did see. Cried at the end."

"Humor me a moment, Rick. That was merely background information." He pushes the glasses farther up the bridge of his nose with one finger. "Last year, the FBI launched Project Megiddo. The objective was to gather evidence of any terrorist actions designed to coincide with the turn of the millennium. What they discovered was that we have as much to fear from within our own country as from external terrorism."

"Such as..."

"Such as Times Square. A video recently surfaced, confiscated from a little known white power group. It featured footage from several different angles around the Square, concentrated in the spots where people traditionally gather for the ball drop on New Year's Eve. On the tape can be heard military jargon, firing lines and escape routes. These were no backyard bigots randomly lashing out while drunk, there was serious planning and multiple contingency plans. They were lethal."

"So they'd just open fire, slaughtering anyone in the way? That doesn't sound racially motivated, it's more like mass murder. What if white people were hit? Wouldn't that defeat the purpose?"

"Crossfire casualties, I believe, is the term used. Unavoidable, but by associating with minority races they placed themselves in the line of fire and risked their own lives."

"Sounds a little harsh."

"It is indeed. That's the mindset of these people, Rick. No compassion, no attempts at understanding. They will justify their goals no matter what. Consider this: That was just one plot unearthed by Project Megiddo. How many others like it exist?"

Dee nods. "Killer, there's so much going down that the average folk like you don't know. Everywhere we turn. The stuff will stagger you."

Geoffrey creates a sense of impending doom with his words, but it has a plastic feel, like the threat is to someone else and not tied in with the events of North Haven. I know I should be alarmed, or at least worried, but there's just not enough impact on me. "Guess I better go arm up. Luckily Hyper-Mart is having a sale on grenade launchers this week."

He removes his reading glasses and taps a sheaf of papers with one bow. "You must understand something here. The United States is a unique nation, one born of melding a wide variety of race and culture. The population diversity makes it unlike any other place on earth. We daily walk among so many minorities, with their attendant ethnic patterns and habits, that we don't even notice it. Most of us anyway. This can lead to greater appreciation of the differences that separate us, but it can also inhibit acceptance of the commonalities that bind us."

Geoffrey leans back. "In 1990, law enforcement agencies created a joint effort to begin collecting data on events that could be categorized as hate crimes."

"Will there be a test on this?"

"No. Almost ten years later, over 12,000 agencies contribute data from forty-eight states. The sheer volume of this information results in a comprehensive gathering of intelligence on all cultural groups. As an output, we gained the UCR."

"Unexpected Catering Results?"

"Uniform Crime Report. It is published by the FBI going back to 1995."

He's doing a fantastic job of ignoring my smart ass comments, so I give him credit. "And what does this wondrous UCR reveal?"

Geoffrey smiles and hands the ball over to Dee. "You can answer this now, can't you?"

"Killer, you got to look at some of these numbers. They are ridiculous. Did you know that last year alone nearly four thousand of my brothers were assaulted in some way simply because of their skin color. You compare that to four hundred Japs and six hundred Mexicans and you can see the problem."

I can see, sure. But Dee can't see the irony in his use of derogatory terms to describe other minorities. Maybe once you're a member of that class, you have immunity from being called a racist. Maybe discrimination is a uniquely white affliction, something we can call our own and don't have to share with anyone else.

If only. Life would be much simpler when problems could be easily identified.

"So how do you know it's white on black, or white on some other color? Do your reports tell you that?" I challenge him.

"Because the numbers don't lie." He rummages through a stack of papers, pulls one free and skims the paragraphs. That's how I know it is new information to him. His memory is pretty good.

"The Southern Poverty Law Center puts out the *Intelligence Report*. Used to be called *Klanwatch*, but I guess that didn't cover enough. There are over eight hundred groups classified in the patriot movement. These are the true haters: The Freemen, Klan, Christian Identity, along with anti-abortion nuts and conspiracy freaks. Right here in the Midwest is a big hotspot. Action happening under our noses, in Wisconsin, in Michigan. Indiana had huge Klan activity way back when. You put all those numbers together and it's obvious."

I frown. "Not really. No, it's not. It's like saying drunk driving is on the rise because GM or Ford is cranking out more vehicles. Cause and correlation are two different things. What's going on around here boils down to the actions of a select few. Telling me that crime against minorities is on the rise doesn't tell me anything about why three white men were killed here. Isn't that where you should be concentrating? Think local, move global or some such shit?"

Dee nods absently, only hearing part of my reply as he flips pages. Somewhere in there he thinks is one stat that will explain everything and which he can hang his hat on. I know how my friend argues, we've done this dance before.

But, he apparently can't find it. He stops looking and just stares back at me, waiting. I'm not going to be the one to blink first.

I am, however, suddenly tempted to reveal what I know of Colonial Estates and the other apartment complex, of Odinism and the assembly I witnessed. You can't get much more local than that.

But for some reason I back away. My instincts tell me it's just not time yet.

"You know," I finally say. "You have all this evidence of white groups and their missions, but you're forgetting one thing."

"Like what?"

"It takes two to tango. Your outrage has been sharpened by the murder of Jerome Carter, but there were three men before him, three men who supposedly belong to the very movements you are researching. You cite examples of white on black crime, but ignore the reverse. White supremacists aren't offing their own, so by your logic, it must be blacks. They started all this."

He opens his mouth, but I override him.

"What some brothers did to those three men is every bit as bad as the Klan. They acted in a premeditated manner, calling out some kind of link

247

these guys had to white power, just to send a message. Who is the message to? What is the grand scope of this all? There are pawns and kings, Dee. Pawns and kings. Which one are you?"

For emphasis I point to a chess set in the far corner. It's the only game leftover from the purge.

"It don't have to be one or the other," he replies.

"Sure it does. You either know what's going on or you don't. And the 'don't' crowd is pretty large."

"You taking sides now?"

"It's not about sides. It's about seeing the entire game. We don't know the motives behind these deaths, making us fools flailing around in the dark to the person who started it all. Make no mistake, someone, somewhere, is playing North Haven for the fool. You and I are in that class."

Dee suddenly stands up, slapping down the paper. I can tell the pawn comment took a while to sink in and piss him off. He hates even the notion of being used.

Both Mollers remain silent, sitting back and watching a developing confrontation between friends. I think they were afraid to get in the middle.

"A few brothers take it on themselves to strike back for the pains of their ancestors and you think it no different than the Klan?" In his rising anger, he's reverting to ghetto speak, meaning my words hit their mark. When it comes to the plight of Black Man in modern America, he doesn't always think straight.

"Two wrongs don't make a right. Look, all I'm saying is that if some black guys are targeting whites solely because of color, regardless of any group association, isn't that the definition of racist?"

"You don't know, man. You don't know..." He shakes his head, a sure sign that his debate train has run out of steam. It's never been his strong suit, a major flaw for anyone who wants to be an activist. He's always relied on pre-determined quotes and volume to win his arguments.

"Then educate me. Is there something about racism that I don't know? Is it a one-way street marked only by white signs?" We've had this conflict many times in the past, never with resolution.

Geoffrey stands up and takes a step forward. "Rick, please --"

"Sit your ass back down," I haul out my mean glare. It isn't hard, I'm pissed now. My old angers are resurfacing, petty resentments that have nothing to do with the current topic and everything to do with Dee and I.

Geoffrey sits.

I spin back to Dee, sweeping my arms wide to encompass the room, the multiple TVs flickering silently, the bookcases full of cultural America. "What do you think you're trying to do with all this?"

"Trying to make a difference, that's what."

"As in Jesse Jackson, Al Sharpton difference? You can't stand those guys. You think they stick their noses in where they don't belong and make things worse, not better. Is that your plan?" I stand and tower over the man who is my brother in every way except blood. "How are you going avoid endorsing reverse racism?"

Dee stands as well, rising to my challenge. "Step off, Killer." He shoves me to emphasize his command, undoubtedly intending to push me back down into my chair.

I take one step back, absorbing the force. Then I push back. Hard.

Maybe too hard.

Dee goes reeling back, crashing onto – and collapsing – the oak table. I ate my Wheaties this morning.

Geoffrey leaps to his feet with a startled sound. Words hang from his lip, but this is not his arena anymore. We've accelerated past his comfort zone of correct words and tones, to one of aggression and muscle. He has no place here.

Nathan also skitters out of the way, although his exclamation sounds suspiciously like a curse word.

I stand there, somewhat startled, knowing that we've crossed that barrier of civility. It's not the first time we've done it; won't be the last either.

If Dee has similar thoughts, he hides them well. Instead he scrambles to his feet and charges, catching me in the gut with his shoulder, lifting and carrying me back.

We land hard on the floor, breath exploding from my lungs as Dee's two hundred pounds comes down on me. Both of us are big men, the amount of damage we can do is significant.

I shove him to the side and his leg smacks the rack of TVs. One falls off the top row, smashing on the floor.

Panted words are leaking from his lips. He's so angry that he can't even speak clearly. He thinks I'm belittling his cause; I think he's blind to reality.

In a way, we chose that exact moment to evolve into different people. Whether we knew it then or not, that night forever altered the state of our friendship. Maybe we would become tighter for it, or maybe it would be a fatal crack that could only grow wider.

I knee him in the side and double him over. In a flash I'm on top, smacking him in the face. Once, twice; his head bounces off the hard floor and his eyes roll back, dazed. I push up from him, planting both hands on his chest to keep him down. My shirt is ripped from neck to sleeve.

Dee rises to a sitting position, blood streaming from his busted lip. "Go 'head, Killer. Pound the black man. You jus' jealous 'cuz I the pro, not you and all your skills."

"What the hell is wrong with you? Do you really think I'm the bad guy here?"

Both Mollers are shouting, but I shove aside the noise. What they have to say doesn't matter. They're intruders here, not me. They've been around a few months; I've been here my whole life.

Dee gives a sullen look and doesn't answer. I hold out my hand. "Come on. Let's get out of here and talk."

He accepts my grip. As I start to pull, he yanks forward and clocks me with his free hand. I stagger back, light bulbs flashing bright behind my eyes and ringing noises suddenly going off in my ears. One of the bookshelves halts my motion. Several books fall to the floor.

That's going to leave a bruise.

"You ain't never known what it's like, Killer. Never. You come from a different world."

"You dumb ass. We grew up three blocks apart!"

"I ain't talking location. Color is not geographic. Moller's been teaching me and it's opened my eyes. I can't believe I been so blind. I knew stuff before, but now it's all fresh again. People got to change."

I rub my jaw. "And you're going to be that change?"

"Maybe. More than you for sure. At least I'm trying. If you ain't part of the solution, you part of the problem."

I'm not hearing this. I turn to Geoffrey. "Have you been loading this crap into his skull?"

He raises his hands in a warding gesture and takes a half-step back. "Rick, I assure you, Damonti's thoughts are his own. We are just exposing him to the larger picture. It starts somewhere, with context for one to grasp. In this case, North Haven, because tragedies are happening and no one knows who the next victim will be. If we can prevent even one murder by standing up and begging for peace, will it all not have been worth it?"

I can sense the slickness of his words. They sound so good, but there's something there that makes my skin itch. I lack a response. Really, what can you say back to that?

If I was better than Dee at debate, then Geoffrey is better than me in the same skill by the same margin. In this, his arsenal holds more ammunition. I could always just punch him to even the field, I guess.

I look over to Dee, but he doesn't meet my gaze. He stares down at the floor. "You should just go, Killer."

Before I can respond, Nathan steps in front, playing the tough guy by placing a hand on my chest. "You heard him. Leave."

"Go piss yourself."

I shove him. Since he weighs significantly less than Dee, my effort has a significantly more pronounced result.

Nathan careens backward, smashing into the TV rack. He tumbles awkwardly down and I hear the crack as his wrist breaks on the floor. I've been around enough broken bones to recognize the sound. His cry of pain confirms it.

As the elder Moller rushes to his son's side, I turn and stalk up the stairs. Dee watches me go in silence.

I slam the door to our house, loudly enough to startle Maya in the den. She leaps from her chair, annoyance written across her face. "What the hell is the matter with y—Oh!" It changes as she sees me.

"What kind of a walk did you take?"

I give an irritated wave. "You're not funny." And I'm not in the mood.

As I stomp back to our bedroom, my thoughts careen wildly. Never have Dee and I come to blows over race; it's always been the unspoken safe ground. Usually it's just wrestling until someone cries 'Uncle.'

Or until I give him a Wet Willy. Those things gross him out.

This was different. Dee's lifelong grudge against all things racist isn't buried too deeply, so it would not be hard for someone to key in on it. But still, Moller seems to have awoken a whole new beast. The grudge now bears a sharp edge and cuts a wide swath. Somehow he had nursed it from heated words into direct action. What kind of influence did he wield?

I stand for a long time at the window, old shirt removed and hanging from my fingertips.

Something had to be done to ensure Dee doesn't get in over his head, and it would have to be done by me. I might be an asshole, but I'm a loyal asshole. One lousy fight isn't enough to sever the strands of our friendship. I owed it to him to find out how deeply the web extends, to understand the nature of the animal he was attacking.

If it all goes bad, I might be the only one who can save him.

Footsteps sound on the floor behind me as Maya enters our bedroom. She walks up behind me without a word, long fingers tracing lines from back to front. They turn south and my stomach contracts involuntarily from the sensation. For all her quirks, the woman sure knows how to seduce a man.

"Big tough Rick. Fighting and getting dirty."

Apparently the awkward ride home was a figment of my imagination, or no longer mattered to her.

Maya loves it when I'm physical with anything; in some warped way, it's a turn on for her. Games, exercise...hell, struggling with the lawnmower; all these triggered her.

I think she likes feeling helpless, being thrown around and grappled hard. We've never discussed just how far her fantasies go, I'm not sure I want to find out.

Turning in her arms, I look down at my wife. She stands on her toes to kiss me, but I snarl my fingers in her dark hair, yanking her head back and exposing her throat. She moans softly.

"There's something I need you to do for me."

"Anything." Her response is husky and full of promise. Her hands continue their work on me, trying to bring me up to her level. I can almost smell her arousal.

Unfortunately the answer is not what she expected.

"Help me investigate someone on the Internet."

Chapter Fourteen

Felony

Where to start? First things first. My
investigation into the murders – if that's what you
can call a private citizen overstepping his bounds –
needed to idle for a bit.

I'm sure Moller has all the best intentions, I just
need to make sure he's capable of walking the walk,
because I know he can talk the talk. I should be able
to backtrack his trail and see what kind of success

he's had at previous stops. If it turns out he's in over his head too, well then I'd have to figure out my next step.

Once Maya began speaking to me again after being slighted in the bedroom, she showed me ways to look up the information I sought. To her, the Internet is a daily tool that she has known for years, understanding of its ways and comfortable with its nuances. For the average guy like me, it's still this uncontrolled space where clicking the wrong thing can send you spiraling down a rat hole.

My experience is limited to major news and sports sites. I wouldn't know how to look up someone's identity if you paid me.

I found some things about Moller, like the house purchase and utility hook-ups. He had titled the Vette just a week before bringing it home; he was listed in a directory of executives for some kind of social club located in the southeast. A picture of him and Lance, standing next to each other at a formal event, both men in suits, from several years ago.

After that, things quickly ran dry.

I know Maya told me what else to do, but I hadn't listened well and didn't take notes. And I certainly was not about to call her at work and ask for directions again. From that she would extrapolate the idea that I dismissed her knowledge, which meant I didn't really respect her, which would lead to another argument...

No, I needed to figure it out on my own.

Luckily I have a habit of snatching victory from the jaws of defeat, not from skill mind you, usually just through random occurrence.

In this case, Dee came through.

Well, not Dee himself, but his ways.

The Cubs were on a three-day road swing out west. Whenever he travels, Dee leaves his car at home. He's also not much of a stickler for cleaning it.

I sneak out of work during the week and drive down to the city.

Dee lives north of downtown Chicago in an area called Ravenswood. It's a young single person's locale, with fits and starts of gentrification. Clubs, restaurants and close proximity to both drew him in. He purchased a renovated two bedroom condo on Clark street for a cool half million. It had all the latest Scandinavian-inspired design elements that a young black player from the far suburbs needed to maintain his street cred.

I pull up to the underground garage entrance. Hopefully he wasn't mad enough at me to change the access code. I punch it in and the gate swings inward.

Idling the Cobra into the dark interior, I aim the wheel towards the back. Dee's Mercedes sits by itself in the slot nearest the elevator. I shut down the Cobra and get out to sight down the front passenger fender.

In the glare of overhead lights I find what I'm looking for.

The day we met the Mollers, Geoffrey had rested his hand on Dee's car. Thankfully my lazy friend only cleans it a few times a year; he pays for someone to detail it rather than washing it himself.

In the black lacquer sheen – whoever does his work really gets this thing to shine – I can see several prints.

With strapping tape, I transfer two complete prints. It feels underhanded to dig into Moller's past this way, as if he's a criminal, but Maya has her methods, I have mine.

On the way home I call the main line for the North Haven station and get through to Allan Borden.

"Rick, what can I do for you?" His words sound friendly enough, but I detect an undercurrent of reserve. Maybe he heard about my call to Detective Warren and is wondering what I need now.

"I'm hoping you can help me with something, as a favor."

"Depends on what it is." I decide he has heard.

"Just a print trace," I say, lying through my teeth. "We got a guy we're tracking at the store. He's burnt us a couple of times, but I was able to pull some prints off a shelf he touched. I just want to cross reference his name and see if he's been picked up anywhere else."

This is a gray area for us. I've made similar type requests in the past, for information available only to cops. While it's not quite illegal for him to provide it, he tends to get skittish over it. He's a Boy Scout and breaking rules makes him nervous, even if those rules don't exist.

"I guess so. Want me to swing by the store? I'm only a few miles away."

"Uh, no, not right now. I'm on lunch and won't be back for a while. How about later on?"

"Just call me when you're going to be in." He gives me his cell number and we hang up.

Of course, typical in my screwed up life, Fate decides to conspire against me a little more, make things just a tad more complicated.

I'm at home on a Thursday morning, still unsuccessfully pounding away at Maya's keyboard in my search for Geoffrey Moller, when the bell rings. I lurch up from the chair with a barely restrained sigh of relief; my eyes are crossed. Maya is in the city on one of her many Y2K meetings, which ends up being a good thing.

Allan is standing there when I open the door, strange look on his face.

"Hey," I say. "You didn't need to bring the print results. I'd have been happy to come to you."

"I'm not here about that. They are with Warren but I don't know if he's submitted them yet. You'll need to talk to him."

My hope sinks. Based on our last interaction, I figure those prints are at the bottom of a round file now. "So, what's up then?"

He clears his throat and looks me in the eye. "Rick Killing, you're under arrest."

My mouth gapes open. *"What?"*

Allan flips open his notepad and skims it. "You are being charged with assault against Nathan Moller."

"But, but...that was an accident. The other night..." Words dry up on my tongue as the implications of a felony start to roll through my mind. "Why you?"

"Because I know you. As a favor. You know how these things can blow up in the media. Your face has been on the news a lot recently. You think those vultures won't have a field day? I can at least try to keep it quiet. Now I have to read you the Miranda." He removes a card from his breast pocket and glances at it. "You have the right to remain silent. Anything you say can and will be used against you..."

I tune out his words, drowned by the thunder in my own brain. There's no love lost between Nathan and me, no secret there. I would have thought Geoffrey could have moderated his son's reaction.

Actually, maybe that's what happened and this is the best he could do.

I wonder if Dee knows. He has to. Did he do anything to keep it down? I feel a sense of betrayal. If he did nothing, leaving me to hang in the wind...

The effects of the arrest could be severe, aside from the actual conviction. If I'm found guilty, there goes the Hyper-Mart. My boss dislikes me enough already, but I'm too good for her to fire. After this, I'm fair game.

Then there's the other career. The new NFL cares about character as much as talent. No one wants a player who carries a label. Regardless of the severity or outcome, I would always have that sign hanging over me.

That's if the Vikings chose to even keep me on the roster. They could easily cut their losses and my contract.

I worried what Kimber would think. Maya I'm not as concerned about. She'll believe whatever I told her, as long as it did not ruin her image of marital and social – as in a pro athlete's kind of social – existence.

Kimberly has no such bindings on her. She wants nothing from me and as such, would only believe me if the facts supported it. More than anyone else, she knows my habit of creating trouble with the best of intentions. It's a byproduct of my personality and all my protestations to the contrary would not sway her. She's heard the excuses before.

I could imagine her shaking her head and thinking: 'There goes Rick again. When will he ever grow up?'

But, I *am* trying to grow up. Trying to be a man worthy of more than what I have. An arrest is a major setback in that quest.

Allan winds down with his Miranda litany and I force myself back into focus. I could just knock him down and run, but even I know a move that stupid when I see it. I could make his job tougher by being an asshole, but that doesn't do either of us any good. He made the drive out of consideration for me, I owe him.

Deep down, I'm just scared.

I give a single nod. "Let's go."

Walking ahead of him, I run scenarios through my head and stop at the passenger door of his cruiser.

He looks like he wants to put me in back, but the thought passes. He holds open the door as I get in. My neighbor across the street is washing his car, paused with a soapy rag in one hand, watching this all play out. He'll have something to talk about over dinner.

Allan settles into the driver's seat and backs out of the driveway. His radio squawks intermittently with chatter from other officers. He speaks into it, giving a numeric code that probably meant he'd arrested me and was coming in.

I needed to right myself, put some semblance of normalcy back in my head so I could think. "Do I still get my one call?"

Allan nods.

"Just one?"

Another nod.

"Well, can I borrow against a future arrest and get two?"

He gives a short bark of a laugh, but I can tell he doesn't think it's all that funny.

Allan walks me through the booking process. I waive my rights to a lawyer and give a statement of events, being as truthful as possible. Officers mill around, staring, making me nervous. I keep my eyes averted.

At one point Allan leaves me alone as he fetches something. An older cop approaches immediately, probably just waiting his chance. He's cut right from the stereotype catalog: gruff appearance, paunch overhanging his belt, three days of stubble.

I tense myself, ready for anything.

He pulls up before me, staring at me hard. He's even got a toothpick dangling out one side of his mouth. This is going to be bad.

"Hey. You did it."

I'm not about to confirm his statement. I keep my eyes focused straight ahead.

"Never thought it would happen. But you did it. Can I get your autograph?"

I snap my gaze to him. "What?"

"Me and my kid watched you all the way through college. Never thought you'd come back after that knee. But you did, man. You did. He was so excited when your name was called, says he has a new favorite team. Can I get your autograph for him?"

With a shaking hand, I produce something that looks like a chimp penned it. Then again, it didn't look to different from my normal signature.

As if that were some type of signal, suddenly I find myself surrounded by the other cops, fielding questions, giving autographs. One asked if I'd met Randy Moss yet.

When Allan returns, he tells me to either post bond or be remanded to the custody of the court. That meant I needed money. Unfortunately I didn't have enough. He directs me to a small room for my phone call. I dial, thinking how pissed she'll be.

My fingers drum a beat on the table, nerves creating their own rhythm. When she answers, I nearly explode with relief.

"Hi, Kimber."

A sigh. "Rick, why are you calling me?" Annoyance edges her tone. She doesn't like to be called at work. I can hear yelling in the background, kids.

"I'm in trouble."

"Now what? Where are you?"

"The police station in North Haven."

"Oh, Jesus. What did you do this time?"

"It's a long story, one I'll explain when you pick me up."

"Shouldn't you be calling someone else? Like Damonti? Or better yet, your wife?"

I scrub my eyes. "Kimber, please. Just help me out here. Promise I'll explain. Oh, and bring your checkbook."

She cups the receiver and I can hear muffled conversation. The yelling continues unabated as she comes back on the line. "You owe me for this one. A big one."

I brighten. "Like the big ones I used to give you?"

She pauses and there's a lot of meaning in that space. She might actually play along. "Give me a half hour."

The line goes dead before I can respond.

"You're busting my allowance wide open," Kimberly says as we walk out of the station. "I don't budget for bail money."

I simply raise my arms and cast my head back. "But I'm a free man at last. You don't know what it's like inside, minutes turn to hours, days to weeks, and before you know, most of your life has passed."

"You were in there for an hour and half, you dip. And you spent most of it answering questions about the NFL. Seriously though, I can't afford that money. You know how little I make trying to heal the world's damaged kids."

"Don't worry. I'll pay you back, with interest."

"I know about your interest. Keep it far away from me." But she smacks me lightly on the arm to take the sting out of her comment.

"It's noon. Let me take you out to lunch. It's the least I can do."

"Well, that's probably better than the *most* you can do, given your history, but I can't. I've been gone too long already." She fishes keys out of her purse and double taps the remote. Her car chirps in response.

Kimberly ferries me home, keeping me at bay with light banter. I know she's not up for any more soul-searching conversations. We've had enough of those recently, they no longer serve a purpose. I knew the things to say, but not always the things to do, and that's what has always mattered to her.

Now that I know the things to do, she no longer cares.

In short, she doesn't trust me and has every right to that opinion.

So we parry with each other, verbal jousters reveling in a relationship worn so well. We slip into the roles of two people who mesh in the most fantastic of manners. The drive home takes seconds.

"Come on," I cajole her as she pulls into the driveway. "I'll make something to eat. You haven't even seen the house yet."

She doesn't put it into park, looking at the imposing facade of columns, stucco and landscaping. Her eyes turn to mine, searching.

"I'll tell you why I got arrested," I throw in as added incentive.

"And write me a check before I leave."

"Absolutely." I wonder where I'm going to get the money.

Kimber shuts down the car and we enter Casa de Killer.

I spend a few minutes walking her around, trying to avoid Maya's name as often as possible. Kimber's hair smells of fresh shampoo and it makes the gulf between us wider.

We settle on chicken Caesar salad and take it out to the back deck. The sun creates little beads of condensation that roll down our glasses.

"Nice house, by the way. Ostentatious as hell, but nice."

"Osten...hasten...tayshush," I slur, mocking her vocabulary. But seriously, I don't know what it means.

She dips a finger into her glass and flicks water at me. "Smarty boy. So where's your wife today?"

"Down in the city. Why? You checking to see how much time you have to ravage me?" I know I'm pushing the envelope again.

"Time is not the issue. I just don't like to be interrupted."

I cast a sidelong glance at her, gauging mood, but can't tell. It almost sounded like flirting. I decide to leave it alone, in case I'm wrong.

"And where's Jeffy?"

"Working, like normal people should be."

"Yeah, us felons have flexible hours." Good thing today happened to be my day off. Getting perp-walked out of your own store is bad for the career.

"So," Kimberly says. "You were about to tell me why I had to come bail you out of jail."

"Hmm, I was, wasn't I?" Picking up our now empty plates, I bring them into the kitchen and refill our glasses.

Kimber stares reflectively out over the backyard and I stop to take it in. God, she is beautiful.

"Did you see Dee on the news last week?" I set her glass down in front of her.

She checks her watch and nods. "It's a good thing he's trying to do. These murders are terrible and a lot of people are on edge over them. Someone has to be the sane voice trying to bring back peace."

"Well, I'm not sure if he's sane or just misguided. You do know that someone is directing and feeding him answers from the background, right?"

A shrug. "Isn't that always the way it is? Look at politicians; it's almost required for them. That still doesn't tell my why you're a criminal at large."

"Oh, that. Call it a slight mix up between Dee's handlers and me."

"And so you assaulted them? What did you do, punch someone?"

I shake my head and hold up one wrist. "Oops."

Kimber's eyes go wide. "You broke some guy's wrist? Rick! That is bad. This could all backfire on you. You haven't even started your football career yet and it could be gone in an instant. You know how little tolerance the league has for that stuff nowadays."

"I know, but it's all secondary."

"Since when? You were always meant to go professional; you just needed the right time. What could this possibly be secondary to?"

"To Dee. You know I would never bail on him. I don't know if he knows exactly what he's getting himself into with all this public persona advocacy stuff. I need to know he's in good hands. The guy that's tutoring him, he seems good, but I don't know that for sure. I'd hate to see Dee steered wrong and ending up looking like a fool. It could hurt his career too."

Kimber holds up her hand for me to stop. "Let me understand clearly: You are willing to risk a career millions of men would die for, on the off chance that your friend is being led astray in his efforts to do civic good? Do you realize how that sounds?"

So I told her everything. The stakes in this game, the brand, the kids, Odinism. I unloaded it all in a stream of consciousness. I'm sure I came off as borderline lunatic, but if anyone would understand, she would. No one else knew me better.

When I finish, Kimber gets up without a word and walks into the kitchen. I can hear her speaking on the phone, probably to someone from work.

She returns to the deck and I expect her to say goodbye. Instead: "You think there is a white racist group present in North Haven. They've had three of their members killed and you think Jerome Carter is retribution for that. You've caught some kids stealing and the brand is their mark. This brand may be the symbol of the white group, but you cannot find any evidence of an opposing group who would have done the first three murders. On top of all that, you worry that Dee is being controlled by a guy who may or may not be qualified to do it. Because of that, you got into a fight, got arrested, most likely will have to go to court and could possibly lose your dream career. Have I got everything straight?"

"Well, when you say it like that--"

"Have I?"

I hear a lecture on the horizon. Maybe I deserve it. My reasoning isn't always the best but I try to come from a good place with it. I accept the inevitable thrashing of my actions once again with a simple nod. No matter where I turn, someone is telling me I'm wrong.

But it's Kimber who holds the surprise.

"Sometimes I wonder if I even know you anymore, Rick Johann Killing. You could be working out for the Olympics next year. You could be on the roster of a pro football team, on magazine covers and idolized by millions. You could be anything you choose and yet here you are, running around half-cocked on the vague notion that your friend may be in over his head. Do you have any idea how that sounds?"

Kimber's eyes are glistening as she comes to stand in front of my chair. Her hand reaches out runs along my jaw, a gesture that harkened back to our time together. "You make it so hard to believe in you. And even harder not to love you."

She leaves the house without another word.

CHAPTER FIFTEEN

Run Riot

The remainder of the afternoon was spent in damage control. Well, actually, James spent the rest of his day that way; I simply called to let him know his newest Viking had been arrested for felony assault. He probably wanted to swear at me, and profusely, but since he technically worked for me, he bit his tongue.

In the end I agreed to do some spots for ESPN along with meeting league and team officials to explain my side of the story. It wouldn't happen for a few weeks yet so I had time to prepare. Still, it will be a doozy.

Maybe I should have just recorded my disclosure to Kimber as proof that at least one person understood it.

Maya arrives home twenty minutes after my call with James. Her demeanor hints of anger. The clues might have been in the way she walked, the sharpness of her actions, but more likely they were in the way she threw her purse at me.

"And what did *you* do today, Rick?"

I caught the projectile easily. Hey, I'm a professional receiver now, it's expected of me.

Was she talking about Kimber or the arrest? Suspicion is in her nature, but there's no way she could know about lunch, could she? I put nothing past her. I phrased my answer carefully.

"What did you hear?"

"Everything. On the radio, the Score 670."

Okay, that makes me feel relieved. I'm pretty sure my personal life doesn't make news. "Since when did you start listening to sports radio?"

"Since my husband finally became an athlete. They've been talking about you for the last two weeks. Why wouldn't I want to listen?"

Finally became an athlete.

In the most technical sense of the term, I'd always been an athlete. What she means is that I finally became a paid athlete.

I choose not to pick that particular thread and try to give her a full explanation of what happened. By the time I finish she no longer looks like she wants to pelt me with household objects.

"That's it?" Is her initial comment. "Nathan pressed charges because of that? What a wimp."

I agree, if only to avoid re-igniting her wrath. She slips into the bedroom, returning minutes later in shorts cut from old sweatpants and a tank top. As I move into the family room and flip on the TV, she heads into the kitchen. Too late, I realize my error.

"Who was here today?" She asks.

"What?" I force nonchalance into my voice and pretend to be absorbed by the TV. It's a clothing commercial.

"I said: Who. Was. Here. Today. There are two sets of dishes in the sink. Did Dee come over?"

"No." I offer nothing more. This line of dialog is doomed already.

"Then who?"

"Why are you getting all suspicious?"

"Why are you avoiding the answer? That means it was a girl. Tell me who."

I sigh, but not loud enough for her to hear. "You don't want to know."

The commercial ends, replaced by the evening news and what do you know, my face appears next to the reporter. They have a file photo taken from college. I try to focus on what's being said but the sound of Maya's stomping feet hinders my efforts.

"You brought her here?" She asks, eyes narrowing dangerously.

Maya knows the ghost of Kimber hangs over our relationship. She's extremely jealous and has a right to be. She doesn't know how much right she has.

"Maya, she bailed me out. We ate lunch here, it's the least I could do."

"Why didn't you call me? Or Dee? Or someone, anyone else?"

"You were downtown, Dee is on a road trip and may not want to hear from me anyway. I didn't trust anyone else."

Maya makes a sound of disgust and storms back into the kitchen. The slam of dishes follows as she fixes an angry supper she will never eat. I know she's thinking about Kimber and me together; the image would drive her crazy until she just had to ask--

"Did you kiss her?" She yells.

"No. Nothing happened."

"Did you want to?"

"Knock it off, Maya. You're going nuts over nothing."

The clatter of cutlery being thrown into the sink echoes out to me. "No, you're making me nuts. Get over her, Rick. You're a married man. Married to me."

I don't respond.

In any war there are times of conflict and times of peace; action and silence. And make no mistake, North Haven was in a war. Not of political ideals, geographical boundaries or religion, but of color and history and something no one but the architects and generals knew.

After a brief quiet period, after existing at the edge of suspense and apprehension, the town exploded.

It occurs on a Saturday evening.

I sit in my office, paging idly through a file on my "investigation", when Kari bursts in, frantic look on her face.

"Rick!" She heaves. "Something's going on out on Jordan. Couple of blocks from here."

'Something' in Kari's parlance could mean almost anything, but she's not the type to go off half-cocked, unlike her boss. I take one look at her face and follow her out into the parking lot. The sun bounces along the horizon, leaving a strip of red lying across the earth that's just enough to see by.

Screams and loud noises float over the buildings packing the retail strip of Jordan Way. They block my view. I light out on foot, accelerating quickly away from Kari. She gives a couple of gasps for me to slow down but I ignore her and keep hauling ass.

Rounding the corner of a grocery store, I skid to a halt. The store stands at the intersection of two main roads, Jordan and Steeplechase Avenue. Across the intersection, under the harsh glow of a stoplight turned red, I see a mob of people, shouting, yelling, screaming.

A car sits abandoned in the crosswalk, blocking traffic, doors flung open. Other cars are idling at other points of the compass, horns blaring, lights flashing, doors left hanging open as their drivers join the tumult.

I'm not sure how long I stand there. Probably just a few seconds. But it feels like an eternity as I watch the pent-up anger of a town erupt into an uncontrolled scene in an area I know so well. The throng of people moves and surges, an entity with violent life of its own. In no way can I see who or what lies at the center. God help whoever it is, though.

In the distance sirens sound, ricocheting off buildings, making it impossible to determine where they are or how long before they arrive.

Kari catches up to me. Her breath heaves in huge gulps and a gasp escapes as she sees what I do.

"Oh...my God. Rick--"

The yells grow louder as we close the gap and individual voices begin to sort themselves out. I hear the gamut of human emotion: anger, pain, fear, loss.

My gut flutters. No good can come of this, I know; this is not the mark of progress.

If I had time to sit back and plot my actions, the smart move would have been to stay clear, let the authorities handles things. After all, being caught in the middle of a violent mob mere days after posting bail for assault is not a great plan for anyone.

But I can't just sit on the sideline and watch. This is my home.

Kari and I wade into the mix, noting that every face we see is white. I grow fearful then, for who I'd find in the middle. The crowd sways and jostles, a thing alive. Kari takes an errant elbow to the face and squawks in pain and surprise.

I turn to see her lower lip dripping blood. "You okay?" I yell over the commotion.

She nods and waves me forward, wiping at the blood with her other hand. "Just go!" She yells back.

I use my size to clear a path, pushing and shoving bodies away. Several people look up at me and some give a reaction. Most try to shove back, attention focused towards the center.

There have to be over two hundred people crowding the scene.

A short heavy guy in shirtsleeves and a tie resists me by leaning back into my path. I give a second heave and he disappears under the mass of feet.

The inner ring of the crowd consists of a bunch of white kids hunched over four huddled forms. They're black. Blood smears their clothes, the asphalt and yellow lane stripes, all spilled under the guise of racial division. Whatever Dee hoped to accomplish with his activism has little to do with this.

These people are after something else.

The kids continue to rain down blows, shouting and encouraging each other, keeping anyone else away by pushing back. A half dozen people are trying to pull the kids off, but with little success. One woman bleeds profusely from her nose but doesn't seem to care. She cries, polished fingernails ineffectively pulling at the back of a shirt. The kid just ignores her and laughs with his buddies.

I tangle my fist into the hair of one kid and yank back. Hard. He yells and swings wildly with his fists, but I avoid them and throw him down. Instantly he's pulled away by the crown, overwhelmed by greater numbers. I throw another back in the same manner.

From the bottom of the pile one of the victims punches back, trying to gain his feet for better leverage. He's instantly mauled. I watch a haymaker split the skin of his forehead, just above his brow. Blood splashes.

The wail of police sirens swells as cruisers round the corner a few blocks away and race towards us. I pull away two more boys and one of them spins to square off with me. Bloodlust fills his eyes and I'm not even sure he sees straight. He manages to catch me in the ribs with a fist. It hurts, but my adrenaline is flowing strong.

I crack him across the bridge of his nose. Immediately his eyes water, messing up his vision, so I punch him in the gut as hard as I can, just to return the favor. Punk.

I'd be lying if I said it didn't feel good. All the angst haunting me, the unresolved issues in my life, the questions on my future and hurts of my past; all these came together, resulting in a punch that lifts him off the ground with a whoosh and a cry.

He crumples down, tucked into a fetal position. I reach down and twist his face away from me.

There it is. The brand of Odinism.

I'm not surprised. Half of me expected it, the half that suspects there is some larger plan to all this. These kids are being manipulated somehow, heeling to some order or cause that calls to them. Is it really racial division? Or something else?

The kid looks up at me, pain and fear replacing the naked aggression. He's just a year or two younger than me, but it may as well be decades. There is nothing in common there, aside from skin color.

I'm disgusted and cuff him on the side of the head.

Clouds of tear gas roll over the mob, changing fight into flight as people start tripping over each other to get away. The canisters continue to rain down and soon everything is smothered.

I feel my eyes watering, stinging horrifically, and retreat. I can't tell whether I'm headed back to my store or in some other direction. All the landmarks are hidden by tears and smoke.

Megaphone orders blare forth, from cops using their best in-command voices. I don't know that I've ever been so grateful to hear such a thing.

I stand on one street corner, watching from a distance as the cops slowly restore order and try to sort the mess. Good luck with that.

Kari's already back in the store, cleaning up her busted lip. I had told her to just go home.

Hundreds of people are milling around outside the police cordon, engaged in the same activity as me: gawking. More arrive by the minute, dwarfing the size of the original mob. God help everyone if another clash were to suddenly break out.

There seems to be this sense of disbelief, a low buzz that drifts in threads among the crowd. I hear it in snatches of conversation and random comments. Person after person tries to speculate on what had started it. None of them are probably close to the truth, but no one lets that stop them.

Behind me a man loudly proclaims to anyone within earshot that more trouble will follow; that some "uppity blacks will attack back for this and we should all do something before that happens."

I look over my shoulder at him, letting the anger show freely. "Shut your pie hole or I'll do you the favor."

Something in my face must convey the seriousness of my intent. He backs down and stalks away, undoubtedly seeking a more sympathetic audience. I should do something more to keep him from inciting others, but I have no idea what that could be. Would Dee's words have an effect on a guy like this? I have my doubts. Whose words would have an effect? Or is he already a lost cause?

I watch him go, noting the expressions around me. Shock, anger, dismay, sorrow.

Not a single face, though, is black.

Blood marks my shirt. I'm not sure from whom though. It's a weird feeling, like a stain that will never come out, a reminder of the night my town cracked.

Thunder rumbles in the distance, one of those common spring storms, and it seems achingly appropriate. A storms nears North Haven alright, perhaps it already has. People are dead and the front has yet to reach us. Soon the thunderheads will be rent apart by brilliant streaks of lightning, flashing for a moment in the darkness and disappearing.

If the searing light touches off a conflagration, everyone burns.

Out of habit I let my eyes roam the crowd, wandering among the many faces packing the sidewalks. Streetlights spill a garish glow, split at regular intervals by police strobes whirling in silence. This turns everyone into flickering ghosts. Red, blue, red, blue...

As my vision bounces from face to face, I see Nathan Moller. He's staring right back at me. It's one of those moments where my thoughts are far afield and my reaction is delayed a second or two.

I dart back my gaze. He's already gone.

I leap from the curb and sprint across the street in pursuit.

Chapter Sixteen

Rally

No luck. He's disappeared down a rabbit hole. I wander up and down that side of the street. I know I saw him. Or was my adrenaline surging so high that my mind played tricks?

It's probably a good thing I didn't find him. I might have broken his other wrist.

With a conflicted sense of awareness, I trudge away from the scene.

Over the next twenty-four hours, pieces of the puzzle emerge, peeling back the sequence of events. It also has the side benefit of burying news about my arrest to the back pages.

North Haven now had bigger fish to fry.

Apparently a joke had ignited the fire. A carload of white kids shot paint pellets at a bus stop. It wasn't a new prank, although more prevalent of late. In this instance, the majority of waiting riders happened to be minorities. And both sides had been charged up by recent events.

When the victims shouted and hurled curses back at the car, it screeched to a halt, the occupants bailed out and it was on.

On any other night, under more normal circumstances, a few blows would have been traded, some blood spilled and a few people cited for their actions. Usually the escalation is limited.

Not this time, though. Dozens of other white males were nearby and witnessed the exchange. They joined the fracas, outnumbering their counterparts four to one. That was all the fuel needed.

Injuries to both sides were numerous, although one group definitely came out worse. Lacerations, busted teeth, even a couple broken bones. One black kid landed in intensive care and would be there for a month; plastic surgery would help repair the damage to his face, but he'd never look quite the same again.

Thankfully no guns were drawn, a small favor amidst a horrible event. Problem is, next time someone would. No one wants to be a victim.

I keep trying to call Dee, but his phone goes straight to voicemail. His new trip is back-to-back swings through Cincinnati and Los Angeles. It bothers me that he's not taking my calls. We've gone through similar spats in the past, but this time the reasons are more significant.

So I change my tactics.

I wait until I see Moller's Jag roll down our block. When I pound on his door, Geoffrey answers. His eyes widen. "Rick, what are you doing here?"

"Where's your kid?"

"Lance or Nathan? I presume Nathan."

"Of course."

"He's at a conference in the southeast. He left several days ago. Based on recent events, I thought it best he absent himself for a while."

Which would cover the mob night. Maybe I did just imagine I saw him.

Moller glances past me to the street. I don't know what he's looking for.

"You are endangering your case by coming here. Please know that I counseled Nathan against pressing charges, but he is very stubborn that way--"

"I don't care about that. What are you and Dee doing? What are you telling him?"

"How do you mean that? I'm simply tutoring him on the manner in which to best speak to this town, to use his stance to help see people through. There is no coercion on my part. You know as well as I that he has always nurtured an advocacy and a desire to effect societal change. I am merely providing new channels for him. Whatever problems have arisen between you two is beyond me. I can promise that he has not said a negative word about you in my presence."

"I don't believe you. There's something else going on. He's never shut down on me like this. What are you really doing?"

Moller levels a stare at me, and I can see the wheels turning. "What have I done to earn this mistrust? You are a cynical young man, Rick Killing. That is your cross to bear, not mine. Do not presume to place your problems at my doorstep, relabeled in a manner convenient to you."

What the hell does that mean? I swear this guy reads a thesaurus for fun.

"Look, whatever your stake in this is, whatever you get out of 'helping' Dee, I'll find out. If this is a ploy to make you look better so your company gets more business, I'll drop the hammer on you so fast it will make your head spin."

His eyes narrow. "Shall I receive that as a threat?"

"No, as a promise. Play him straight or else."

"For such a physically large man, you certainly are small and petty within. You hide behind a wise cracking routine, but you fool no one. Is your entire existence rife with conspiracy? I do not fear you, Rick, however I do pity you. Seek peace, not conflict."

With that he slams the door. I thought about pounding on it until he answers again, but I didn't know what I'd say. Maybe I could tell him I wasn't petty, he was.

Am not.

Are too.

I didn't speak to Maya until later the next day. Sleeping in separate rooms tends to inhibit conversation. Eventually she'd come down from her anger at my lunch with Kimber, but until then I keep to myself upstairs. I had bedrooms, bathrooms and a TV room.

She finally calls me as she's heading home from work. "I'm listening to ESPN1000."

"Don't. There's nothing to learn from them, they stopped being about sports long ago and are mostly about what they can do to create news."

"Still. They're talking about you, about your upcoming interview. There's a lot of questions. How will you be in the locker room? Has the time off made you a different person? How rusty are your skills? That type of stuff. The arrest is big news to them."

I ignore all that. "They say anything about Saturday?"

Maya stays quiet for a second. "There were a couple of people who called in and said they saw you in the middle of things. One said you were helping, another said you beat him up. No one's really sure, but there are a lot of negative comments."

"So? What do they know?"

"Enough to call into a sports station and spread bad karma about you."

"Well, it happened two blocks from my store--"

"That's another thing. Most rookies aren't in full time jobs, being a ball player is your job."

"And when a contract that pays me something is offered, I can make the transition."

"You should quit now. It doesn't look good. I can support us for a couple months and then you'll get your contract."

I hear the true message behind her words but I don't address it. I'd rather not be more reliant on her. She wants the opposite.

"Anyway, did you think I'm just going to watch what's happening a couple blocks away and not do anything?"

"I know that. You *always* have to get involved, and that's where the trouble is. But at least you could consider what the perception of your actions will be. I don't want you to endanger your future."

You mean 'our' future.

"Hindsight management, that's all you're practicing Maya. Easy to look back and say what I should or shouldn't have done. I hate that. You weren't there." Suddenly I'm no longer in the mood to talk, even if it means bringing back some level of harmony to our life. The bed upstairs is just fine.

She's quiet for a moment, maybe regretting her choice of words. When she does talk, her voice is lighter. "So, when do you tape for ESPN?"

"Not sure. James will tell me."

"Are you excited about it?"

"No."

"Do you know what you're going to say?"

"No."

"Okay," she draws out the second half of the word. "What's the plan tonight? I'll be home in forty-five minutes."

"Don't know. Nothing planned for me."

She sighs. "Do you want me to let you go?"

"Yeah, my pizza is burning."

"Wait, what? You don't eat pizz--"

Click.

We didn't talk that night. By the time she got home, I was long gone on a solo ride. I accidentally may have wandered over to Zion Hills and another small town over the border in Wisconsin, but things were quiet at both places. With motorcycles, even boring roads can be interesting and it's easy to just ride without aim. Hours can pass quickly.

She is in our room when I return, so I retreat upstairs and don't come down until long after she'd left in the morning.

Guilt starts to eat at me as I stare into my cereal bowl. We may not be destined for folklore, but we are in this life together. I can at least be...not petty. Fucking Moller.

Maya's working at one of her clients today, a Motorola location thirty miles away. I decide to drive down there and surprise her with a spontaneous lunch. If my boss only knew how often I left my job, she'd have all the reason to fire me that she needed. That is, if I ever return her calls. She doesn't have my cell. If she wants to talk, she'll have to come to me.

Judging by the number of voicemails waiting on my desk phone, I think that day will be soon.

I pull my car into the visitor's slot near the front door of Motorola. The place is corporate template design: brick and glass, fancy enough to satisfy employees without concerning stockholders. If I can ever figure out where Moller's company lives, this is what I expect to find.

The receptionist looks up at me. We've met before, but neither of us can remember the names.

"Don't tell me," she blurts out. "You're here to see...um..."

"Maya Killing."

She snaps her fingers. "Right, I knew that." The nameplate on her desk reads Christine, and just like that I'm one up on her in the name game. Though it probably counts as cheating.

After a few key punches on her computer, she looks back up. "She's out of the office right now."

I'm a little freaked out that they can track people so easily. "Really."

"Yeah, I saw her leaving with Tom a while back. They're probably at one of those long offsite meetings."

I take a random stab. "Tom North?"

"Who's Tom North? No, Tom Simmons. They work close."

"Thanks," I say and leave.

I could just call her phone, set up a lunch meeting somewhere nearby. That would be the rational thing; it's probably what I should have done in the first place. But something propelled me to show up in person. Now the moment has passed.

I don't bother calling.

On the way home, a local radio station runs a public community announcement. At six-thirty tonight, a rally would be held for victims of the mob attack from Saturday. It is scheduled to begin at the spot of the attack and wind its way through the older parts of town until arriving at City Hall.

There, all marchers would hold a silent vigil in support of the injured. Everything would end with a symbolic signing of a peace treaty by all participants, a pledge to be delivered to the mayor's office.

Best of all, the rally would be led by North Haven's newest advocate, Damonti Davis.

Wow. Since when did Dee learn how to organize a rally? Or even conceive of one? Then it hits me. Since never. This has Moller written all over it. Dee must be flying back special just for this.

On the surface it sounds like a good thing. The cynical side of me wonders otherwise. So what if a bunch of people sign a petition? Do masterminds behind the murders care one whit about some social contract? If there's some background agenda – and I'm convinced there is – then what a cross section of citizens thinks or signs has no bearing. They've brought out the existence of hate in North Haven, made everyone aware that evil trespasses here, but there's got to be more to their mission. After Sutton they went dark. Why? Biding their time or planning for more?

My instincts said something would happen at the rally. Question is: What?

I keep one eye on the clock as I drive, calculating my activity and chunks of time.

A motorcycle will be perfect, so I return home and grab the SuperMagna. This is Harley country, so there are bikes everywhere, all the time, even January. I'll blend in and still have more maneuverability. I yank on a full face helmet with tinted shield to hide my features and roll out of the garage, trailed by the rap of my tailpipes.

It might be my imagination, but I sense expectancy in the streets as I pass, like they pulse with life. For sure there are more people milling around, strolling as if they have nowhere else to go on a fine Thursday evening. I cruise past the intersection near my store and see the beginnings of a gathering along Steeplechase Avenue. A few dozen scattered people – mostly of black persuasion – stood together in clusters, despite the fact that the rally wasn't scheduled to begin for another hour. That gives me just enough time.

The trip out to Colonial Estates eats up half that cushion. I pull over to the side of the road, close enough to see the entrance sign but hidden to anyone leaving the place. If any of the inhabitants have plans to do something at the rally, I want to know.

Hopefully I'm not too late, in which case I'm just a guy sitting on his motorcycle in the middle of nowhere.

I keep one eye fixed on the entrance through a gap in the trees, while I check messages on my phone. Before I can even play the first one, it rings. I answer without looking at the caller ID.

"This is Rick."

"Why the hell haven't you returned our calls?"

"Hi to you too, dad." I'm a little surprised he made the effort to call himself, but it makes sense. He wants to yell at me in person instead of translating through my mom. More satisfaction that way.

"What are you doing?"

He doesn't mean right now. He means in a generic life-altering consequences type of way.

"It was an accident. Don't worry about it."

"The news says 'felony.' That's more than an accident. You know how teams scrutinize every single thing nowadays. Don't give them any free ammunition."

"I said don't worry about it. It's my problem, not yours."

"Your problems *are* mine, especially when they become public. They reflect poorly on your mother and me."

"I'll do my best not to tarnish your pristine image. My agent is handling it."

Dad is silent, mulling this over. "Does your agent have this happen to a lot of his clients?"

"Enough to know it's not the end of the world."

A grunt comes in answer, the closest he will come to saying 'Okay, I overreacted.' Having worked himself up into a lather, he cannot simply throttle back and let it go. Good old dad.

Movement at the entrance to the apartment complex catches my attention. Cars begin exiting in a line.

"Listen pops, much as I love to get lectured, I need to go. Important life-saving plans here. Love to mom."

"But Rick--"

I yank my helmet back on, waiting until the cars are almost out of sight before firing up the bike.

I'm casual about tailing them, fairly certain I already know the destination. I need to get a look at the cars and how many there are more than I need to know where they head. I ride far behind, hoping for the best, expecting the worst.

As we enter North Haven, the cars peel away from the procession one by one and that alarms me. There's premeditation in such a maneuver, reflecting a plan. I don't know which one to follow and so stick with the lead car.

The traffic grows thicker and thankfully I start seeing police presence.

I lose sight of the car for a bit and by the time I catch up, the occupants have disappeared. It's parked in an alley ten blocks away from the starting point of the rally.

None of the faces stand out to me as I slowly idle the bike around. In the hour since I left, crowds have formed, knotted together by a common cause. News vans and smartly dressed reporters are sprinkled throughout the scene.

Orange cones divert and block traffic, so I pull over to the side and sit on my bike. The helmet stays on my head; last thing I need is anyone recognizing me. That could quickly become another negative sighting. Context is everything.

Local cops, sheriff's deputies...even State Troopers are in heavy supply, although they keep to their respective squads and don't mingle. Snobs.

A muted roar draws my attention away from counting badges. People whoop and cheer as a car with tinted windows slows to a stop in the middle of the blocked road. Dee exits and makes his way to an impromptu platform staged on the sidewalk.

He's once again draped in conservative, corporate colors. I think I prefer the guy with chains and goofy hair. Him, I know. This guy...

He speaks for ten minutes, words of finesse and meaning and consequence. I hear his handlers in each one and the uneasiness settles in my stomach. But I can't see any of the Moller clan. Strange. You'd think they would like to watch their protégé in his first live action scene.

Dee finishes his intro and moves with purpose to the head of the crowd. Police hold everyone back to clear his path.

He pauses, rather dramatically I think, before beginning to walk with a measured stride. A hush falls onto the throng of people as they fall in behind him, arranged into three lines by the cops. An official – and completely artificial – mood settles over us all. Those in uniform straighten up just enough to show respect. Those in attendance remain silent, stepping to the beat of their new civic leader, in rhythm with his intent, if not result.

If anyone wanted to spark a racial fire, right now would be the best, or worst depending on your view, time. I almost hunch up in expectancy, like a guy reaching his finger out to test whether an electrical wire is live or not. You don't know what's going to happen, but if it does, it's going to sting.

After ten minutes they've barely covered ten blocks. Christ, at this pace the bad guys will age out.

Tough to instigate a race war from a retirement center.

Dee pulls even with my spot. He knows my bike, he knows my helmet. But if he realizes I'm sitting twenty feet away, he gives no sign. His head is lowered in reverence for the thing he's trying to do. I can respect that, I can respect the desire to make this a better world; I can't respect the forced way he's doing it. Plus, he looks a little ridiculous.

I'm glad for the helmet, it contains my snickers.

There are hundreds of people in his wake now. I'm impressed to see the size and makeup. Not just minorities, but a true mix. Maybe there's hope after all and I'll be the fool by the end of it. I can live with that.

The silence floats ahead of everyone, like a cloud slowly expanding, and it's a good sign. It means acceptance and recognition. It means peace.

It, however, does not mean permanence.

A scream rings out. Back where the car from Colonial Estates had parked.

CHAPTER SEVENTEEN

Insider Trading

The screams come from the rear of the crowd, because predators hunt where vulnerable prey is found.

Plus, most of the police presence was at the front, clearing the route. In nature and law enforcement, the weak are left behind, sacrificed so that the strong may live.

I rip off my helmet and sprint towards the scene.

A young girl is kneeling in the street crying, clutching her head where blood seeps between little fingers. A chunk of brick is lying next to her, job done now. She's black, of course. It couldn't be the two white boys trying to help her, dressed in gangster clothes, or the white guy in a collared shirt and tie, standing over her fierce and protective as he sends his stare across the crowd. Those targets imply a different message.

Someone has good aim.

I skid to a halt near the girl and the man spins around to me, hostility and anger writ large upon his face. I hold my hands up in peace and kneel down next to the rap boys.

She's bleeding heavy, but the cut is not deep. Scalp wounds look worse than they are.

As people yell and descend upon us, things start to crumble. Some cops run back to assist, leading other cops farther out front to look. Those cops falter in their duties, attention diverted. The march stumbles at its head, slowing to an uneven crawl, losing momentum like a slowing train. Soon it stops and begins to reverse course in ragged movement.

We're in that undefined gray area where everyone knows something just went wrong, but not quite sure what it was. The police need a clear action to react against, a crime to pursue; a suspect to charge. They have only one of those things.

People in the crowd need more and they weren't going to get it. Left to public decision, justice is harsh and aggressive. It seeks swiftness when consideration is required. We all fall into the trap.

The mood instantly shifts into overdrive, switching from show and support to hunt and kill. I'm swept along.

Another chunk of concrete sails out from behind the crowd; barely missing us and finding a woman facing the opposite way. It hits her in the upper back with a meaty sound, followed immediately by her cry as she falls forward.

In a flash I'm up and running towards the general direction of the throw. This is how I will make a difference tonight, Dee.

As if my movement flipped a trigger, the street explodes into sound and action. The intent and organization of Dee's moment vanishes in wink. Now there is only primal vengeance, against the perpetrators of the attack, against the perpetrators of those events that brought everyone together in the first place.

Each side has their cause. Jerome Carter. The youths from the mob. Donald Sutton. The boy in the hospital. Martin Luther. Rosa Parks. Bernie Goetz. Those were the distinct ones, the concrete examples of why we stood in the street and marched. They brought friends, less defined emotions that follow us through each and every day.

A long-held grudge from some distantly remembered event.

The feeling of impotence in front of a mindset tough to understand, tougher to change.

Natural prejudice. Simple hatred. Crowd mentality.

Suddenly the street is pure chaos. People yell and surge, shout, throw punches and wrestle one another. Rage is unleashed and it flows over us all in a tidal movement, pent-up pressure finally released and drowning everyone in its path.

I shove bystanders from my path as I reach the sidewalk. Something hard smashes my back, igniting a flare of pain just under my shoulder blade. It drives me to my knees. Something else smacks the back of my head, ringing my ears and bringing the taste of copper to my throat.

I realize I've bitten my tongue. A hand grabs my arm, tries to yank me up, disappears. Fog rolls over my vision as I stumble to my feet. A tunnel forms, black and white faces flashing by on either side, disconnected from the sound of their passing.

Like a man drunk on too much of a bad thing, I'm fixated on the spot where the second concrete missile originated. I'm yelling at no one in particular, just yelling, and it goes unheard beneath all the other noise banging up against my head.

The attackers are long gone. People knock me from my intended direction, spin me around, bounce off and fall down

Something tangles my feet and down I go again. Tiny pebbles and grains of sand grind into my cheek. A hard-soled dress shoe smashes my fingers but it causes the owner to trip and fall himself. Ha. So, there.

All around me legs and feet are scrambling, kicking, running. I tuck into a ball, arms over my head as a kick lands on my elbow. One strike, then gone.

Hands clutch me and try to lift. "Hey, get up man." It's a male voice. "Get. Up."

I do, with his help, staggering awkwardly over to a building. It's a Subway restaurant.

He follows me. "Hey, are you okay?"

"Just...banged my head. Need a minute."

His face slowly rotates into focus and there's a spark of recognition in my brain. It's tiny in the roaring storm. I squeeze my eyes closed, clutching his shoulder as if for support.

Then: He was the guy with Todd and Casey, the one who separated from them with the other girl before the bust went down. Told you I'm good with faces.

There's an opportunity staring me right in the eye, so I take a stab in the dark. "Thanks for the help. You from Colonial Estates?"

His stare locks onto mine, startled and instantly wary. "Maybe. You?"

"No, I have a place, but I hear good things."

A teenage girl is pushed and stumbles into him. He shoves her away without breaking eye contact. ""You know about the place?"

"I know that it's good for some people who want the same things in life."

Before he can respond, the melee washes over us. Bodies, stinking of sweat, fear and anger crush up against us. Cops are yelling, but no one's listening. We both sidestep an older black guy rushing by, blood streaming down his cheek. He looks like he's just trying to escape the madness.

My rescuer kicks at him with snarl, glancing off the thigh, but the man doesn't even notice. He keeps moving.

A wild swing comes out of nowhere. I block it with my forearm and shove back. It's a young kid, Hispanic-looking, no more than fifteen if a day.

The action spins me towards the street and I cross stares with Dee. It's a happenstance thing. He must have come back to the heart of the commotion, trying to restore order to his own rally.

We lock eyes, two men of shared history, two friends trying to break the mold of their lives in order to grow. We know each other so well, but in that moment we are strangers across a fence, separated by the things that shouldn't matter.

A punch catches Dee from his blindside, coming out of nowhere from a guy sporting a loose tank top. He's missing one boot. His arms are skinny, but his hands are large and gnarled at the knuckle.

My instant reaction is to run to help Dee, smash that one-booted bigot in his face until the rest of his teeth fall out. Dee crashes backward but regains his balance. His eyes turn murderous, red and wide. He's going to break the man in half.

I turn my back on him. I can't let this chance slide by and if my rescuer is who I think he is, running to the side of a minority leader will not help my cause.

"We need to get out of here," I say, spinning him towards the alley next to Subway. "Cops are going to start using smoke."

"Yeah, probably. Come on."

"Hey, what's your name?" I shout over the din as we wind around dumpsters.

"Galen Schroeder. Yours?"

"Rick. You follow sports at all, like football?"

If he thought it a weird question, he didn't react. "Nah, can't stand them. You must though. You look like a jock."

"Nope, just like working out."

Galen – pudgy, pale and furtive – turns out to be a willing conversationalist. No, scratch that. He's a motor mouth. He most certainly doesn't fit the stereotype of a neo-Nazi skinhead with their shaved skulls, tattoo hostility and death metal music.

I guess the white power industry has changed just like any other entity that relies on the human experience to exist. Nothing stays the same forever; adapt or die.

Too bad though. It makes the monsters harder to see.

Galen is that kid that other students picked on because he lived inside his head. He was the first knockout in dodgeball because he wasn't paying attention. I bet he was bullied a lot.

I steer him towards a bar and grill a few blocks away. The sound of police sirens and bull horns follow us, growing fainter as we walk.

I'm not going to get a second chance at this, so I jump right in. "You know what I hate? I flip on the tube and there's Jesse Jackson with some black family. He's trashing government for how expensive utilities and taxes are, how social assistance doesn't provide enough for the average family to live on. Yet mom's standing there in a fur coat with gold-capped teeth, fingernails all done up. Maybe if they'd stop pissing money to 'front' an image, they could pay some of those bills and stop sucking money from guys like you and I."

And actually, that's true. Only it isn't confined to one particular color, it's about a certain mentality; that entitled mindset that you deserve something without having to earn it. Those people don't belong to just one race.

Galen nods his head as we enter Vandy's Grill and take a booth in the rear. My back is killing me so I don't lean back. That must have been some rock I got hit with.

"They eat their own, just like other animals. Look at all the ghetto crime and who lives there? Niggers. They create their own troubles, destroying themselves in a cycle of poverty. If we could just section off parts of the country and ship them all there, the world would be a better place."

I resist the urge to put my fist through his face and order us drinks. He likes Ketel One vodka with Diet 7-Up. He calls it a Ketel 17 and uses a straw to drink. I call it a pussy drink, just to establish that he is dealing with an alpha male. I may need this guy's help to find things out, but I don't have to curry his favor. He makes it easy for me to be an asshole.

He goes on. "You know what else I hate? Stupid Arabs. They come over here, clog up our schools with their oil money to learn computer science, take all that knowledge home and undercut our workforce because pennies on the dollar makes them rich in their shit hole desert. How are we supposed to compete with that? We're shipping so many jobs overseas to a bunch of immigrants that can barely speak the language. You ever call a support hotline only to not understand what the bitch on the other end is saying?"

"No. Sounds like you have though."

"Man, I used to have a kick-ass job. Designing web sites at forty bucks an hour. Didn't have to do shit. I could drag it out for billing and give the client back some piece of shit site I threw together in a day. Then they outsource my group, so I end up answering calls for half that wage, five days a week. And get this: they decide to send that job overseas as well, so here I am on the street trying to find a job. Some bitch was so happy because she could finally go back to Pakistan or wherever and transfer with the company so she'd have a job still. Fucking dot-head."

"Yeah, you got shafted." In actuality, what I want to say is: *You were a twenty-something punk with a good job you didn't deserve and now you're pissed because reality kicked you in the balls.*

Maya's told me about the Galens of the world. People who managed to learn just enough programming language that they could sound credible during interviews. And because the dot-com boom needs fuel, companies hire them. Maya dislikes them due to their lack of formal training and sloppy code habits, whatever that meant.

As I thought about it, Galen was like the woman in my story; he'd been given the opportunity to improve his life and still didn't think it was enough.

"Still looking for a job then?" I take a slow draught from my beer.

"Fuck, yeah. But there isn't shit out there, unless you want to become a tech writer or help desk robot. No thanks. Those jobs suck. I need something better."

I feel so little sympathy for him it truly cannot be measured.

My turn to drive. "So, sounds like we are coming from the same place. Tell me more about your group. I've been involved with others before, but they all went soft and lost direction. I want to be part of something that changes the way things are going. You guys into that?"

"Abso-fucking-lutely," Galen sucks the dregs of his drink through the straw. I signal the lone waitress for another. Truth serum really is nothing more that liquor injected directly into the blood stream. People with their drink on will say whatever comes to their mind. "Check this. The Covenant has this membership model--"

"Covenant?"

"Yeah, Covenant Church of the New Millennium. That's the name."

"Sounds more like a religion." Thinking about the brand, I throw out a hook, gambling again. "Do they practice any of the old world stuff? Like Odinism?"

"You know about Odinism?"

"Hell, yeah. Been practicing it for years."

"That's too cool. Then you already know most of what the Covenant preaches."

"What a coincidence, huh?"

"No kidding."

Now for the line.

"So how does this group work? How do I get in?" I motion to the waitress for yet another Ketel 17. Taking my cue, Galen drains his glass and belches. His eyes are a little glassy and I figure he isn't much of a drinker. Not that I am either, but at least I'm not a punk.

"Well, first you have to be sponsored by someone in the group. They need to do the checks, make sure you're legit. Once that happens, then you need to come up with the join fee. Past that, there's the monthly dues and work that's assigned to you."

"Okay. So then you'll sponsor me." I make sure that I say it as a statement, not a question.

Galen hesitates, but like most soft geek-types avoiding confrontation, he bends instead of straightening. "I guess so, sure."

Sinker.

I lean back, feeling a rush of success. This seemed like a breakthrough, something more I can add to the folder. Pain flares up in my shoulder, making me wince so I lean forward again. There's not much of a plan in my head yet, I hadn't figured it would be this easy. Once inside, then I'll think of something.

All the best plans come from winging it.

"Tell me more about the monthly dues?" I wondered what exactly they provide. Living space? Food? Or were they gone forever, like church offerings, something that's used for the 'good' of the institution.

Galen sucks yet another drink dry and this time he motions for himself. Apparently he's comfortable spending my money now that we're pals. He knocks over one of his other glasses and I catch it as it rolls off the table.

"Whoa, dude. Nice reflexes. Dues. Yeah, they are what they are. You can't bring change without ringing up some charges, right? A thousand to enter. If you don't have all of it, you just pay five hundred and work credit the rest. Then it's anywhere from three to five hundred a month after that."

So there's the refund fraud. These kids needed money. "And you pay it?"

"No choice, you have to. Don't pay, don't stay. Don't stay, find your own way home."

"And where's that?"

North Dakota. East Dunseith, North Dakota, population 500. No way I'm ever going back there."

"So you pay."

"I pay. They move us around a lot though, to build relationships with the other chapters."

Other chapters? "How big is this Covenant?"

He shrugs and stirs his straw, staring down in the drink. The liquor is working fast on him, creating mood swings. "Don't know. I've only been around since December. Big though."

I can see I'm not going to have him for much longer. At some point liquor changes from truth serum to something else and it seems we're approaching that point quickly. Leave it up to me to get a lightweight. He better not puke on me. Then I will definitely punch him.

Time to speed things up. "So who's the guy at the top? Who do I talk to about joining?"

"You're talking to him."

"No way." Galen is a total putz. I refuse to believe he has any authority within the Covenant.

"Well, just about joining. We can sponsor people on our own. In fact, bringing you in earns me a discount on my dues for three months."

What is this? Amway?

He continues. "Head of our chapter is some guy named Wagner. I haven't met him yet, just attended a few of his lessons."

It's apparent Galen Schroeder takes his commitment to the white cause as seriously as he did his former "kewl" web design job. I get the impression he stays because he's too weak to go, too afraid to return home and because it gives him a sense of belonging to something.

He fishes a scrap of paper out of his pocket. It's a gas station receipt. He scribbles down a phone number.

"You want to find out more, let me know. Meeting Saturday night. I have to go."

He slides the paper across the table and gets up. His exit from Vandy's Grill is rather unsteady, in fact he smacks his shoulder against the door frame and almost falls down.

I retrace my steps back to the rally. Things have settled down. Hundreds of people continue to mill around; the police presence is still strong, warding off another flare up.

The hate and anger from earlier has dissipated. Now it's just the gawkers and gossips, the bystanders who claim to have seen nothing and the ones who know everything.

Covenant Church of the New Millennium.

The financial set up intrigues me. Someone at the top is pulling some serious bank from these kids. It's little more than a pyramid scheme. So how can a financial scam play into a race war? I don't get that part.

Galen hadn't seemed too concerned that it was a scheme, but the dues wore heavily on him. He mentioned them more than once. Bringing me on as a new member would lessen that burden so he has a vested interest in making it work.

It is also my best path forward. I want to check out these Church goers for myself.

I keep my head down as I move along the sidewalk. Trash is everywhere, storefront windows broken, knots of people clustered together. No one pays much attention to me.

The Honda was tipped over at some point during the action, irritating me. The SuperMagna model had only been made for two years, over a decade ago. Parts are getting hard to find. I can see the mufflers are now scratched and dented, a corner of the seat torn, broken mirror. My helmet has disappeared as well.

A whiff of gas floats over me and it's strong. The bike must have flooded lying on its side like that. I'll need to let it drain a while.

So I sit there, watching the interaction of people, the cops patrolling, the business owners shaking their heads.

"Rick?"

Allan Borden approaches me, decked out in riot gear: black jumpsuit, matching helmet with clear face shield, body armor emblazoned with the word 'POLICE' on the chest, carrying a Kejo riot baton with shock capability.

I didn't even know North Haven had that kind of equipment. Bet it's the first time he's worn it.

"What are you doing here?" He stops a few steps away. Behind him are two other storm troopers; they stand facing away, scanning the crowd.

"Heard there was a street party. Looks like I missed a hell of a good time."

He doesn't respond to my poor attempt at humor. We're both grim over the night's events, if for different reasons. Or maybe the same ones.

"You mixed up in any of this tonight?" His wave takes in the general mess.

"No, just took a ride down to watch."

"Then why are you bleeding? Your shirt is ripped and stuck to the blood." He reaches out as if to tug on my shirt, but I twist away.

"I cut myself shaving."

He points to my bike, the damaged pipes. "That looks recent. What happened?"

"Left it parked and someone tipped it over. I'd like a thorough investigation headed up by you personally. Let's nail the bastard."

"Rick, be serious for just one second. Don't make me ask again."

All sorts of replies fly through my head. I bite back on them. He's really my only ally in the police force. I could be a shit about him arresting me, or I could put it aside and act like an adult. It goes against my default setting, but I can probably fake it.

"Let me ask you something instead. This is me being serious," I say. "Have you ever heard of the Covenant Church of the New Millennium?"

"No. Who are they?"

"They're a white group living out in Zion Hills and other pla..."

He cuts me off. "Oh, them. Now I recognize the name."

My pulse quickens. "So you have run across them."

"Not specifically, just awareness. They are one of those groups that talk about segregation between the races; that hold mini-rallies and generally cause a nuisance. They all have names like that. The Christian Identity, White Knights, Christian Knights of the Order, Coven of the White Rule, White Covenant of Order...You get the idea."

"I do. You think they could have had something to do with this tonight?" A large fragment of glass falls out from a broken window across the road. It shatters with a loud crash. No one looks.

"No, not really. The kids belonging to those groups are mostly losers, hanging out in the woods drinking Jack around a bonfire and bitching about the state of the world, but never doing anything about it. Back when we were in school, those kids were the grunge gangs you used to pick on. Like that one guy you taped to the principle's car when he pushed down little Libby Leffler. What was his name?"

"Allan Borden."

"Ha. Asshole. I can't remember his name...Anyway, most of these supposed white hate

331

groups are attractive to kids like him, who can't hold down a job, so they shave their heads and join. It makes them feel better to hang out with others who have the same loser mindset. None of them can plan a meal, much less something like tonight."

"But what if they were? What if they had some head guru who organized them with a mission and a structure and discipline?"

"We'd have heard about it already. North Haven isn't that big. Contrary to your opinion, the police in this town try to do their jobs and most are pretty good at it. We even have a small gang unit. It's their job to track this kind of activity."

Allan's dismissal bothers me. He's arrogant like I've never seen him before. Did he really think there wasn't a growing problem? "Is that what you'd call tonight? A couple of gangs clashing?"

"Trust me, if there were two groups going at it over color, we'd know." A few people pass us. Allan swings his baton and gives them a curt nod. His patrol partners have wandered off and are now a block away. "But you obviously think otherwise."

"Three white guys murdered in outrageous ways. One black murder in retaliation. A bunch of white kids pummel some blacks within an inch of their lives. Now, the first peace rally in North Haven and it ends in a riot. All in the last six months. Doesn't that seem a little too coincidental to you?"

"Anything's possible Rick. That doesn't mean it's probable though. We have to go where the evidence leads and so far it doesn't lead us anywhere. We can't chase down every conspiracy."

There's no use debating further. Allan isn't changing his mind and neither am I.

Sending up a little prayer, I thumb the ignition on my bike. It fires up. God bless Hondas.

I stop Allan with one last question. "What happened to Damonti tonight? He okay?"

"I don't know. Never saw him after everything started."

"You should put out a call. If he goes down, this town will explode."

I roar off down the litter-strewn road, not bothering to hear the answer.

Chapter Eighteen

Aftermath

I walk into the house and let the door slam. In the den, Maya slaps down the phone and spins around.

"What happened?" She's got a flustered look on her face. I'm not interested enough to probe her about it. The following conversation would likely just end up in an argument, one more log tossed onto the bonfire, and by now the flames are licking at the ceiling of our time together.

"You didn't hear? There was a peace rally near the store, where those kids got beat down last week. It turned into a riot."

Maya grunts. I don't think she really cared one way of the other, which I find irritating. She's capable of great apathy towards anything that doesn't touch her personally. She needs to yank her head out of the Y2K crisis long enough to look around. Malfunctioning clocks may be the least of our worries in another six months.

To emphasize the severity of the night's events, I twisted my torso to show the torn shirt.

She sips a quick breath. "What is that?"

"I think I got hit with something thrown. Maybe a brick or broken bottle." The wound is throbbing more now that I'm paying attention to it.

"You were in the middle of it? Of course you were, what am I thinking?" She lifts my shirt and I raise my arms so she can remove it. The shadows around me move as she tilts the desk lamp for better light.

"Oh…my god. Rick, that's not just a cut. Someone stabbed you!"

"What? How do you...?" I twist my head, as if I'm part giraffe and can actually see back there. I can't.

"Part of the blade broke off and is still there under the skin. I can see the broken edge sticking out. It's lying kind of flat. You need to get to a hospital." She pokes and prods with her fingers, sending sparks of pain along my shoulder and arm.

"Ow. No, stop that. I can't. If it gets out in the news...No. How deep? Can you pull it out?"

She makes a sound under her breath, part disgusted, part fearful, and the sparks flare into full-fledged lightning bolts. "Almost there," she whispers through gritted teeth.

Why is she gritting? I'm the one with a knife stuck in me.

"There!"

I exhale and turn to see. Nearly two inches worth of blade had been left in me. It looks like a cross between a butcher and steak knife. Who attacked me, Mrs. Butterworth?

"Oh, it's really bleeding now." Maya dabs at the wound with my shirt. I can feel the blood trickling down my back into the waist of my jeans.

I look down at her. "Where's your sewing kit?"

Fourteen people were arrested in connection with the riot. I am surprised it wasn't more, but then again, those were fourteen the cops caught in the act. Many more probably got away in the confusion. Estimates placed the size at four hundred participants. Stores in a five block radius had been looted, cars vandalized, small trees uprooted, one very cool motorcycle tipped over.

Fifty-two people were treated for injuries that could be traced back to the action. No one else reported being stabbed with kitchen cutlery and I wondered what I did to deserve such an honor.

Of Dee there was no word other than his role as leader and figurehead of the march itself. I took it to mean he didn't get arrested or seriously hurt. Although I bet his face hurts from that roundhouse punch.

The Cubs are playing a home stand against Atlanta, so he should be around the area. I'm tempted to call him, but I keep seeing the look in his eyes as I turned away from him. Betrayal. Abandonment.

I don't call.

USA Today has coverage on the front page, albeit in the lower half. The top spread is once again reserved for Y2K topics. Now they are saying that cars might stop running if their internal chips don't recognize the four-digit year. Lord, that's all we need.

I lean back in my chair, wincing slightly as my wound stretches. In addition, my hand is swollen from being stomped on. Two of the knuckles are enlarged and it's hard to bend the fingers. The risks to my NFL future appear here and there, in little notches, but I'm not wavering.

I keep telling myself I'm doing the right thing. Everything else will work out as long as I do that.

Hopefully.

The phone rings and it's my mother. "What is going on down there? Are you okay?"

"Yeah, I wasn't in the area." Even as adults we don't like to disappoint our parents and lying is the easiest route forward.

"Well, that's a surprise. Normally you wade into things like that with a smile on your face. How's Damonti? I saw that it was his rally."

I debate telling her the updated version of what I know. Because she's mom and moms always listen. Moms also worry way too much.

"He's okay too. We talked this morning."

After I end the call, I slide the paper with Galen's number around the desktop in figure eight patterns. I don't care what Allan says. He's wrong. The Covenant is organized and large. They were behind disrupting the rally, although it only seemed to be a few kids. But what if the entire organization was this way? Maybe they only have a few members assigned to different actions in order to fly under the radar.

If they're focused on staying out of the public eye, that tells me there is something else planned, much bigger.

And now I'm officially worried.

Someone has to do something. It's not going to be the police, judging on Allan's stance.

I pick up the phone and call Galen.

Right away, he throws me a curve ball. "Yeah, I can bring you to a meeting. I need to see your place first."

"My place...why?"

"See how you live, see where you live. I'm not wasting my time sponsoring someone poorer than me." He gives a fake laugh.

I fumble around mentally. "Yeah, sure no problem. I...oh, shit. Another call coming in, from work. I have to get that. I'll call you back and we can set it up."

I hang up before he can respond.

He's probably suspicious. But he's also desperate. He needs my membership fee to lessen his. I just have to make sure I dangle enough interest to make him think I really want to join. That should dampen any warning signs he's feeling.

I look over the wood railing of the loft to the tile and granite kitchen below. Obviously bringing him here is not a consideration. One look at my Filipino wife and the game is blown. White supremacists don't get the hot wives. I think they marry their sisters.

I'll have to come up with an alternate.

Saturday afternoon, 5pm

Kimber answers the door of her house wearing dress shorts and a faded twill shirt hung loose. She looks like she stepped right from Eddie Bauer's house.

"Why do I let you talk me into these things?" Nice greeting.

"Because you're just that kind of girl?" I respond.

"I must be out of my mind." She steps back and invites me in with a flourish of her hand.

"Probably, but this is something I have to do. You, of all people, should understand. You stay at that underpaid, overworked job of yours because it makes you feel like you're making a difference, right? What I'm doing is just a variation on that theme."

"You spook me when you're trying to be responsible, you know that?"

"Absolutely."

She sits on the couch and motions for me to sit across from her in the chair. "This isn't some ploy to get in my pants, is it?"

"Would it work?"

No answer. Maybe she's considering it.

"I can respect what you want to do, Rick. But why can't you be normal about it? Volunteer at a shelter, donate clothes to Goodwill, write a check to Red Cross. Why do you put it on yourself to expose an organized movement only you know about and the police don't believe exists?"

"Slow night on TV?"

She sighs. "Anyway, you remember the place, right? I don't need to show you around."

"Yeah, I remember."

It's a small cottage. Cozy would be the realtor term. And by cozy, they really mean ridiculously tiny. The living room would fit in my walk-in closet. Well, Maya's closet. My stuff hangs in one corner.

But the house emanates a sense of privacy that I like, something my tile echo chamber lacks.

"We're not going to be interrupted by Jeffy are we?"

Kimber doesn't respond to that, carrying a vase of flowers into the back kitchen and refilling the water. She always had flowers displayed somewhere when we lived together.

Ten minutes later the doorbell rings. I open the door to Galen and nod him inside. Kimber is cool to him with her answers to his questions, but I don't think he cares. His eyes keep drifting to her tennis legs.

I can tell he's been given a script of questions to ask. Things like religious affiliation, background, job and more. If they were designed to ferret out a fake racist, they never would. Terrible questions. On top of it all, Galen asked them in a half-hearted manner, never following up on any cues Kimber gave him when she hesitated.

He wouldn't last five minutes on my team. We are all ruthless interrogators.

Finally his questions wind down. Kimber did not hide her dislike of him and I think that also prompted a quicker ending. Racist or not, I don't think she'd like him in any form.

At the door I give her a peck on the cheek, like any devoted boyfriend would. That's our cover. Thankfully I never wear my wedding ring. "Don't wait up, honey. I may be late."

She stiffens for a second then grabs my face in both hands and plants a kiss full-force on my lips. "Oh, I'll wait up alright, stud. I'll even let you do that special thing you like so much." Her eyes glint in a devilish manner. She spins back inside and slams the door.

The hell...?

Galen's mouth hangs open. "Holy shit, dude."

I push his shoulder towards the sidewalk. "Not another word."

He stumbles and recovers his balance. An old Nissan shitbox is parked in front of the house.

"You can ride with me."

"In a Jap car? No chance. I drive American muscle. You should be embarrassed." Plus, I want to be able to escape if necessary.

I follow him north out of town to yet another cluster of apartments, this one in the town of Antioch, Illinois. How many places did these Covenant kids occupy? It felt like one of those invasion movies where aliens slowly infiltrate our population and no one realizes they are disguised as us. Only this time the aliens *are* us.

The complex is old and worn, but like the two others I found, it sits tucked back from the road, hidden from casual view. Railroad tracks cut through the town and behind the apartments. It must be hell trying to get a good night's sleep with train whistles flying by.

The parking lot is packed with cars, most old, junk or both. I'm attending a gathering where they hate blacks and drive pieces of shit. Great, just my crowd.

Galen parks as close as he can get to the door, wedging his car between two pickups. There isn't enough room to open the passenger door. I hope the driver of the blocked-in pickup gets pissed and pounds on my new friend for a while. I'd stay to watch that.

I leave my car out at the perimeter, out of habit and out of caution. Last thing I want is some punk arriving from Colonial Estates and saying: 'Hey, that looks like the car from the other week. Let's key it just in case.'

When we enter the clubhouse building, people are milling everywhere. Most look a few years younger than me, which I'm learning is the sweet spot for recruiting. Clusters of kids create a winding path to the other side. These must be their cliques and I wondered if there were cool racists, nerd racists, outsider racists and all the other archetypes from *The Breakfast Club*.

Pausing by the door, I let my eyes travel the crowd, settling my nerves and scanning for anyone I might have busted recently. If Todd or Casey is here, that would make for an interesting meeting.

Fortunately, I don't recognize anyone.

Unfortunately, someone recognizes me. "Holy shit," exclaims a squat boy. "Aren't you Rick Killing?"

CHAPTER NINETEEN

Blue Dragon

I look down at him, sifting through the assortment of responses and attitudes. I settle for Unfriendly Prick.

"The fuck are you?"

His face washes red, but whether from intimidation or embarrassment, I can't tell. "Dude, you're coming back to the game. That is so awesome!

I'm for sure picking you in the first round of my league."

Okay, he's not intimidated. It's worse. He's a fantasy football geek. Those guys are annoying. "Whatever. Stop talking to me."

"So what are you doing here? Joining? No way. That's completely awesome. I'm going to tell all my friends."

I lean down to him. "You breathe one word of me being here and I'll hunt you down. You won't make it to your fantasy draft." That's a pretty clear threat, in my eyes anyway.

"Hey, do you think I can get a picture with you?" He turns. "Hey, hey! Anyone got a camera with them?"

What the hell is wrong with this kid?

I slip into the crowd while he's distracted. There are over a hundred bodies crammed into the room; I should be able to place a few of them between him and me. No one is as tall as me, so I settle for hunching to avoid detection.

Snacks and drinks fill a table against the far wall. Chips, salsa, vegetables, a great looking guacamole dip; no sign of any liquor. The offering is all sodas and water. I feel like I'm in a gag show. This is a white supremacist gathering?

I could be at a Tupperware party.

No one displays evil-looking tattoos, no black leather; the soundtrack is crappy 80s bubblegum rock. I don't spot one shaved skull.

These kids wore jeans and khakis and Polo and Reebok. They are not the collection of losers Allan Borden believed them to be. They're a Democrat's wet dream. How in the world could this white bread slice of Middle America produce someone willing to kill a man like Jerome Carter?

"Hey," Galen says as he approaches and hands me a diet Pepsi. "Meet anyone yet?"

"Just some nitwit by the door."

He peers around me. "Short fat guy in the faded red sweatshirt?"

I nod.

"His real name is William, I think, but everyone calls him Seal. He'll talk forever about something completely stupid and he uses his hands so much, he ends up looking like a seal clapping for dinner."

I nearly smile, until I remember where I am.

"Why is he waving to you?"

I ignore the question. "So what's going on tonight? How does this all work?"

"We'll start with the pledge. There will be some housecleaning talk, dues, living arrangements, that kind of thing. The main sermon is about that nigger rally the other night. We can't let that stuff get out of control."

The casual way he used the word catches me off guard. I nearly choke on the Pepsi in my mouth. "What stuff? Like the violence?"

"No, the blacks, the spics, the nips. We start letting them march and pretty soon they'll start thinking bigger, start demanding more, taking larger chunks out of our nation. We don't need any more welfare cases. There might be some plans discussed tonight."

"Plans?"

He nods and stuffs a handful of potato chips into his mouth. No wonder the kid is in terrible shape. "Like the thing over on Steeplechase. That was us." Chip fragments spray as he talks.

"Oh, yeah. Some guys from Colonial told me about that," I lie. "You get in on that?"

"No, but I know how it was drawn up. Some of us kept spraying losers at the bus stop until someone finally reacted. There was a bunch more Convenants hanging out down the block, just out of sight but close enough to join in the fun once it started. Man, we stomped some black ass that night. Wish I'd been there."

Better that you weren't.

Well, I least learned that North Haven had been played for a fool. That was no chance scrum; it had been designed. But for what purpose? Just to create a fight? That didn't make much sense.

A man emerges from the back and steps up on a makeshift podium. His hand slaps the wood three times, slow and loud. The talking drops off after the first slap.

He's well into his forties, the oldest person associated with this group that I've seen. His outfit is torn from the pages of Executive Monthly: pressed white shirt, subdued tie, sharply creased pants. The guy doesn't bark out any orders or perform any distinct salutes. He simply leads us in a prayer.

It's a subverted version of the Pledge of Allegiance. I recognize the rhythm but not the words. None of the voices are in alignment. I catch some pieces about protecting the honor of America, of purging impurity and resisting a liberal government that would allow the core of our country to be diluted by criminals and immigrants.

It ran long and didn't rhyme.

Rows of folding chairs had been arranged in front of the podium and we filled them in an orderly manner.

He introduces himself as Jonathan Wagner, 8th Level Blue Dragon in servitude to the Supreme Grand Dragon himself.

Wow. That's not going to fit on a business card.

Wagner speaks for thirty minutes on recent events, wrapping them up in colorless words that failed to capture the sheer chaos and social disorder. His tones are measured and his sentences complete, discussing the degradation of a race as if it were a declining stock option.

At least neo-Nazis foamed at the mouth so you could see who the lunatics were. Wagner is controlled and unreservedly dispassionate. He looks like he'd wear the same expression whether pulling the trigger on genocide or holding a baby for baptism pictures.

Goosebumps stand up on my arm.

If this guy is an example of the leaders of the Covenant, then everyone has severely underestimated them; myself, Allan, the entire police force. Their agenda hides behind the faces of cannon fodder with names like Galen and Seal, clueless nincompoops searching for a sense of belonging.

I sneak a glance around me, identifying all the exits, just in case this turns real bad, real fast.

The next agenda item is for new attendees. Wagner asks for all new people to stand and be recognized. I really don't want to do this. Galen nudges and raises his hand, pointing me out.

I slowly stand.

A few others stand with me, providing a false impression of security in numbers. Wagner starts with a girl on the far end, asking her to reveal name, address and a reason for being here tonight. As she spoke, a man sitting behind Wagner scribbled down the information.

My nerves stutter as I realize the implications of handing over Kimber's address. I sneak a sideways glance at Galen. Hopefully he didn't commit the address to memory.

When my turn arrives, I straighten and look Wagner in the eye. "Name's Rick Killing."

In the back, Seal gives a whoop. "Killing, going long, long...touchdown!"

Everyone ignores him but I quickly reel off house numbers that are transposed. The guy gives a short shake of his head as he writes and I'm hoping that he didn't hear them well over Seal's shouting.

Wagner levels his gaze at me. "Your face has been in the news lately, Rick. What is a professional athlete doing here?"

"It's because I am a professional now. Gangster jocks are ruining sports like basketball and football. They roll around in their trucks with over-sized rims, wearing old jerseys and spouting off about being 'old school.' Most have no clue what that even means. They're busy wife-beating, crack smoking and gun toting. Baseball is letting Asians and Puerto Ricans fill up the ranks, pushing out the farm boys that grew up in their own field of dreams. Boxing is all blacks and Mexicans; the great white hope is a myth. Hockey is the only major sport that stays true to its roots, but no one cares about it because it's full of Canadians and Europeans. I'm here as an American athlete."

The field of dreams thing might have been a little much.

The space between Wagner and I shrinks as he stares at me. I can't read anything there. Finally: "Most eloquent, Mr. Killing. Is that a spontaneous comment?"

"I used mental notecards. They're bright green."

He seems like there's something else to be said, but stays quiet and moves onto the remaining people. I can tell he's not really listening to their introductions.

Afterwards, he continues his speech, expounding on my theme. The word 'contamination' appears more than once in his diatribe, however he never used the N-word, which I found interesting.

Nor did Wagner allude to any further action against the black community. He railed against color, but never suggested what could be done about it. So from a persuasive argument standpoint he failed miserably. On the other hand his audience was captive and they all shared his mindset, so maybe he didn't feel the need to preach to the choir.

Worst of all, he did not implicate himself or anyone from the Covenant in the murder of Jerome Carter. Bastard. I want a signed confession.

At the end of the service, when everyone is mingling and trying to find a graceful way to exit, Wagner approaches me.

"Why are you here?" He demands, granite eyes fixed on me.

I turn from the barking of Seal – the kid will not leave me alone – and face him. "What?"

"Your attendance tonight. What brings you here?"

"I already said in my intro."

"It does not add up. None of the other members are from here, so they wouldn't know, but I've lived nearby for years. I have a nephew just a couple years younger than you. Danny Wagner. Ring a bell?"

It does, but I don't want him to know, so I shake my head.

"He played against your team the year you won the state championship. I saw a number of your games that season and you know what I remember? Seeing you and Damonti Davis. The star quarterback and his sidekick. Local papers ran a number of stories on both of you and the theme was your connection to each other. Now you expect me to believe all that has been cast aside? How can you be a soldier in the army of purity when you've been tainted for years?"

I want to put my tainted foot right through his mug. "High school was a long time ago. Are you the same person you were at seventeen?"

"I'm quite a bit farther removed than you."

"Doesn't matter. People change. My sports career was aborted back when some jealous black guy took out my knee. I've burned the last two years rehabbing in order to get one shot at the NFL. Two long years. You won't read that in your papers, but I have a story to tell. Now that I'm finally back to where I was, I'm just taking care of mine. No one is going to take that away from me again."

Wagner takes a step back from my intensity, looking me up and down. I can tell he doesn't buy my words, but he apparently believes in keeping your friends close and your enemies closer. He jabs out his hand to shake, but there's no trace of warmth in his expression. "Welcome to the Covenant Church of the New Millennium, Rick Killing. It will prove interesting to have you around."

Damn straight it will, pal.

CHAPTER TWENTY

Person of interest

I've ridden Galen as far as I can. He got me in
the door, his role as ground level recruiter was done.
Now it's up to me.

I get Wagner's number from Galen and set up a
meet for Wednesday night after work. Let's see if I
can work him over for some new information.

Wagner arrives at the exact time and enters the burger joint. I wait five minutes before following him. When I sit down, there's an unspoken agreement between us that I'd arrived thirty minutes early to watch him. His shiny tie and silk shirt proclaim his status as an important cog somewhere in the corporate world.

"You know," he says by way of greeting. "I find it highly coincidental that you walk through my doors the same time your high school running mate emerges as the next Malcom X."

"Crazy, right?" I reply. "Maybe I should have picked up a lottery ticket instead."

"I don't care for your humor."

"Get in line."

We engage in a few seconds of silent dick measuring before he changes tack. "I'd be overly suspicious of your motives it I hadn't seen some of your interviews. You are dumb even for an athlete, and that's saying something."

"Are you hitting on me?"

He sighs under his breath. For some reason this guy is indulging me and I have to wonder why.

"Tell me what we're doing here," he says.

"Actually, the better question is 'Why are you here?' You clearly don't like me."

"I've been asked to accommodate you. You have ascending celebrity status that might come in useful."

The implications in his words hover over me, ominous. Someone's watching from afar while I try to find them. It would be funny if it wasn't frightening.

"Who asked?"

"That's not your business to know. Let's get back on track. What do you want?"

A waitress approaches. I order soda, Wagner orders an iced tea. I snicker and tell him today's special is chocolate chip crumpets. He doesn't respond.

"So I've been told your group follows the principles of Odinism," I say when our drinks arrive. "That interests me, but I didn't see any evidence of it at your little circle jerk the other night."

Wagner's eyebrow rises. "You're an Odinist? I'd figure you for a hedonist before anything else."

Oh, *now* he wants to be funny.

"It's in my family, all the way through my Nordic genes. It's what I grew up on."

He grunts, studying me. Wagner probably thought his beady eyes gave him some type of edge in face to face dealings, but I've had a little experience in personal confrontation too. I don't back down easily.

"Let me describe the structure and nature of our organization."

"Are you going to whip out an org chart or something? I might just swoon."

"We are divided into chapters, loosely based on regional breakdown. Each chapter is run by a Grand Dragon, who reports directly to the Grand Lord Vizier. I am under the Grand Dragon for the Midwest chapter. A dozen direct reports in my command handle the recruiting and operational demands of our chapter."

"And you're just laying this all out on the table? If you dislike me so much, why risk it?"

"I risk nothing. What I have told you is available in our charter. The Covenant Church of the New Millennium is a movement no different than any other start-up religion."

"Only you have chosen Odinism to wave your flag over."

He smiles and it's a reptilian look. "We are protected by the Constitutional right to free assembly. So if you thought you could run right to your friend, give him grist for the mill of his next speech, you are sorely disappointed, Killing. We are a public entity and proud of it. There is nothing to hide."

"Then why are you being hunted?"

That catches him by surprise. It's a flick of emotion but I have quick vision. I was the first one to pass my own test. He doesn't know why or who is doing the hunting. Interesting.

"Change is not accepted by everyone," he says after a second. "Some people would prefer to stay in place and lick their wounds rather than progress into the new millennium."

"Resistance to change is a long way from premeditated murder. Someone doesn't like what you represent enough to make a statement. Sutton and the two others were not random acts. You've got opposition and they are willing to take extreme measures. Are you? What about Jerome Carter? Was that your answer?"

"That did not come from us. We do not promote violence, we're not like some of those gangster clubs who use any means to unleash their rage. Our methods are clear and philosophical."

Either he's a convincing liar or he truly believes his words. I can't tell and I'm usually pretty good at reading people. Galen admitted that the riot action was planned; is there a splinter group within the Covenant taking things into their own hands? Or did some of the kids take action on their own?

"You know, not everyone in your church is rowing the same direction. I think you've got some members who are less clear and more action."

At this he shrugs and makes no comment. I can see I'm not going to get much more out of him. He may have been ordered to accommodate me, but it seems there's a limit to what he'll offer up. I change tactics.

"So what do I need in order to join?"

"Your entry fee, monthly tithe and a realization that if you proceed, your career as a professional athlete will be over before it began. No team will touch a player who belongs to an organization dedicated to racial separation."

That's a sobering thought.

He slides a newsprint magazine across the table. It's titled *The Covenant Call*. The Odinism brand occupies the upper left corner of each page and most of the articles preach a version of hate speech, sedition and propaganda. One long diatribe called out the supposed agenda of the US government in collecting our taxes in order to wage war on innocent citizens. It had plenty of spelling errors and bad grammar.

It was not, however, confined to a racial rant. These guys are all over the place.

"Maybe you should take some of that pledge money and hire yourself an editor. Hell, someone who managed to pass English 101 could probably do the job."

"Read it on your own time, not mine." Wagner stands up to leave, throwing a couple bills down on the table. "The list of upcoming meetings is in the back. Don't leave this lying around. If the Jews get their grubby hands on this, we'll get even more zoning inspections and tax audits."

He turns and walks away without another word. Prick.

I leave shortly after, but not before writing on the bills he left.

Jonathan Wagner records *Soul Train*.

Jonathan Wagner slept with Aunt Jemima.

Jonathan Wagner is Shaft.

True to his claims, the mission of the Covenant is outlined on their web site. Not much else though. It was pretty basic and earned a dismissive snort from Maya. It did not have the technical chops to pass her muster.

The magazine proves more useful. The number of meeting notices in the back is staggering. How can all these be going on without someone noticing? Or am I just that far out of the loop for this kind of notice?

On a hunch I grab one of the local free papers that shows up in our mailbox every Wednesday. It's mostly a classified ad collection, but it also has sections devoted to community events. Things like self-defense classes for women, or pick-up litter days at local parks.

I'd looked through this publication in the past, out of sheer boredom, and wondered who read or cared about this stuff.

As I matched up dates of meetings from the Covenant magazine with postings for the community, it became readily apparent that the Covenant chooses many of those events to disrupt and spout their rhetoric. The goal could be either recruitment or plain old subversion and dickheadedness.

Some of the meeting notices were classified as "discovery assemblies." Those coincided with advertised events that clearly targeted certain segments of society. Is Sutton's killer embedded within one of those segments?

Suddenly I became one of those people who cared what was in the paper.

If they're simply handing out leaflets or trying to disrupt the agenda of a gathering, that's one thing. But somewhere in there is someone with a killer instinct, from both sides of the color fence. And I needed to find out whom.

Probably the same person who ordered Wagner to meet with me.

After a couple hours of squinting, cross-referencing and writing down dates, I've had enough. It's nearly 10pm. No sign of Maya. No call, no other contact. The fact that I had no idea where she was says something about the state of our marriage. The additional fact that I didn't bother to call her cell phone says even more.

I flip on the TV for background noise and wash up in the kitchen sink. My hands feel filthy from handling the Covenant mag. I grab a bottle of water just as the evening news opens with a breaking report.

Galen had been found murdered within the last hour.

The water goes down the wrong tube as I process this information and devolve into a fit of coughing.

His face had been painted black with white lips, like that of old time actor Al Jolson. Police had received an anonymous tip and found the body hanging from a tree several miles outside of town. Cause of death was attributed to asphyxiation but numerous bruises, abrasions and dried blood indicated that someone had brutally beaten him before hanging.

While the loss of life was tragic, I don't get too worked up over Galen. He crawled into bed with a group that's been targeted already, he assumed the risk. I don't feel sad over him, but I am concerned.

Someone could be saying the same thing about me if they didn't know the true facts.

Undoubtedly Galen's links to white supremacy would emerge. Whether or not the Covenant name emerged is irrelevant; he would be chalked up as a notch in the same class as Sutton. Galen would quickly become a statistic in a war John Q. Public may not realize is being waged. But I had a feeling that the core answer still would not be found.

Who is hunting the white people?

Jonathan Wagner's body turns up two nights later. He'd been burned nearly beyond recognition and after the flames had been put out, someone draped him in a white robe and hood. The red cross adorning his hood would prove to be drawn from his own blood.

The originality of the murders is waning. My paranoid feeling is increasing.

This is not mere coincidence. Someone is watching me and cleaning up my trail, but why? It's scary as hell, but also reaffirming. Am I making that someone nervous? Did I cause enough concern within the upper ranks that they needed to sever the links binding us? And why would they do that? To prevent me from finding out who killed Carter, maybe?

After a few weeks of calm, North Haven once again became a destination for national shows like

20/20 and *Nightline*. Reporters re-surfaced, asking their inane questions, stopping people on the street for those all-important human perspective quotes.

Dee also received a lot more attention. This I knew not because we spoke, but because his face started appearing left and right, only on a larger stage. No longer was he the property of North Haven, he'd gone big time.

Overnight, it seemed everything changed. The streets grew eerily silent after dark. I'd drive home from work after a late shift and the number of people visible was much less than normal. No one walked alone.

Oddly, both black and white acted as if they were next on the target list.

Protest groups formed every day, little spurts of ten, twelve, fifteen people coming together to demand action of the police, chanting, marching. Most ended in a spat of violence, a fight that left more than one bleeding, maybe some fractures.

It seems the Covenant has a full plate disrupting these groups.

Most surprisingly – or perhaps not in hindsight – I receive a visit one early Saturday morning. Detective George Warren swings by the store to talk; witness interviews had placed me in contact with both recent victims.

"How do you know it was me?" I ask as I motion him to sit in the other chair in my office.

He looks down at the bolts and handcuff rings before replying. "Look at you. You're not exactly background scenery. How many other blond muscle-head football players live around here?"

"Would you say I'm dumb even for an athlete?"

"What?"

"Never mind."

He glances back down at his notebook, recovering his train of thought. "Back to Galen Schroeder and Jonathan Wagner. Did you know them both?"

"A little."

"What's 'a little' mean?"

"It means I met them, but didn't know them long."

He flips a page and jots something down. "I've got you drinking with Schroeder at Vandy's the night of the riot. You bought. Galen left drunk. Then several nights later you are seen at the 22nd Street Grill with Wagner, the same night Galen was killed. For some reason you felt compelled to deface paper currency with his name. Two nights later Wagner comes up dead too. You have to admit this all sounds a bit too coincidental."

"I am the bastard child of long odds."

"Stop being a smartass, Killing."

"You know what I find funny? A couple of months ago I called you with information that could have been helpful to all this and you blew me off. Now here you are asking for my help."

Warren snaps his notebook shut with obvious irritation. "I'm not asking for your help. I'm trying to eliminate you as a person of interest."

CHAPTER TWENTY-ONE

Vandals

I take a minute, hiding my emotion. Person of interest?

"Do you really think I had anything to do with all this?"

"Good detective work means following all leads and either confirming or eliminating them. You were with both men just days before their murder and by your own admission you didn't know them long. Those two facts alone warrant taking a second look at you. Do I think you had a hand in murdering them? No. You're a pain in the ass, but that's about it. Tell me what the thread is linking you three together?"

Either Warren hasn't put together the Covenant connection, or he has and is giving me enough rope to hang myself.

It's my opportunity to let him know everything I do, to show him that I'm not just a hobby cop running around trying to be useful. It's a chance at minor redemption.

"Sorry, Warren. Can't help you. But imagine how I feel? Two guys that I just met have been killed in an awful way. Maybe I'm next. Maybe you should put some hounds at my door for protection. That could be your way to find a lead."

He snorts. "Tell me why the trail leads to your door and I'll think about it." He stands to leave, but I halt him.

"Hey, on another subject, did you ever find anything out with those prints Allan passed up to you from me?"

"Print work gets assigned to the lab guys. It doesn't have to route through me. Why? What are the prints for?" He stares at me, trying to connect the dots.

"Some guy that's been ripping us blind here. I want to see who he is, see if he's known to any of the other stores and for what."

"Oh," he says dismissively. "Tell Borden to re-run through the lab, send me the results and I'll get it to you." There's an unspoken trade there: Give up Wagner and Schroeder and I'll get you your print info.

He leaves without another word.

Less than five minutes after that, Kevin knocks. "There's someone else here to see you. Want me to bring her back?"

Her. I nod.

He returns with my mother. Her eyes are red and swollen from crying. My pulse hammers.

"What happened." It's not a question. "Dad?"

Mom shakes her head and slowly sits in the bolted chair. It certainly was seeing use this morning.

"He's still at the house. I had to get away."

"Did you guys have a fight?"

"No. I almost wish we did. That I know how to handle." She sniffs and retrieves a tissue from her purse, wiping at her nose. "It happened while we slept. They came in the middle of the night. Spray painted the house, awful things all over the walls, the windows, doors. They ripped up lawn ornaments and flowers. I can't believe we didn't hear them."

My blood starts heating up. "You're hours away from here in the middle of nowhere. Who would do this?"

"I don't know. But they left terrible things. Racial slurs. Even the 'C' word. I couldn't look at it anymore. Why would someone do this to us?"

I know exactly why.

But I don't know exactly who.

Mom declines my offer to stay with us. I'm actually thankful. Things are getting weird, who knows what can of worms I've exposed. I give her the business card of the alarm monitoring service my stores uses. They can have one installed in 48 hours and she'll even get a discount with my referral. I promise to stop out and help clean up but she waves away my offer. Dad has it under control.

As soon as she leaves I dart out the side exit without notifying anyone I'm going.

The connection between the vandalism is obvious. Someone in the Covenant doesn't buy my cover. Wagner flat out said it, but also said he'd been ordered to accept me, from someone high enough on the food chain that he listened. Would he burn both ends of the candle like that? Did he take action on his own before getting toasted to a crisp?

That didn't seem likely. He didn't know who hunted members of the Covenant. He didn't know he was on their list. So that had probably come as quite a shock to him.

Was it Galen? He didn't seem capable of that kind of aggressiveness, but what if the wounds to his body were not from a beating, but rather torture?

What did he say about Kimber and me? What did he remember?

Crap, crap, crap.

I skid to a halt in front of her house, hands shaking with anger and impotence. Urgency superseded etiquette; I yank open her door without knocking and barge inside.

Kimber is kneeling on the floor of the tiny living room. All about her are strewn decorations and other detritus of a life made cozy. It looks like an earthquake caused everything to crumble inwards. Her couch spilled stuffing from the sliced cushions. Her TV lay on the floor, tube smashed into glittering confetti. The only nice piece of furniture she owns is a corner hutch with glass doors, glass shelves and a little light mounted inside. She'd used it to display her collection of crystal figurines and blown-glass ornaments. I couldn't even recall how many of those things I'd given her over the years as gifts. Now, not a single one remains whole.

I knelt down to her. "You didn't answer your phone. Are you alright?"

She's got a couple of crystal fragments in her hands, like she was trying to fit them back together. Her eyes are haunted. "I...one of the girls called in last night. I covered her shift and stayed there overnight. Came home to this..."

It wrenches my soul to see her like this, a lost girl hurt on the inside and failing to understand why. This was because of me.

"Kimber, I'm so sorry. If you had been here last night...Where's Sebastian?"

She shares the same look as my mother. They don't understand a world where this kind of hate can exist. They don't belong in such a world. "He's at Jeff's." She drops the fragments and looks around again. "Why would someone do this?"

I take a deep breath and let it slowly out, dreading. "Because of me. From last weekend, from that guy that came out."

Footsteps sound from the basement stairs, stomping up through the kitchen. Jeff emerges into the living room, face red with emotion.

"Did you say you had something to do with this?"

Jeff's not a big guy. Kimber might actually be taller. On top of that he looks like a twit, a stats nerd with floppy brown hair. I think she overcompensated for me by choosing the exact opposite type of boyfriend. I had nothing against him personally, outside of the fact that he was her boyfriend.

"All this is my fault."

He yells in anger and charges, responding to ageless instinct of territorial knights. Kimber is his girl, she's under his protection and as such, it was his duty to avenger her honor. Since he can't take it out on the actual criminals, he chooses the next closest object. His intentions are honorable, but he needs to work on selecting his targets better.

I stop him dead in his tracks with a two-handed shove to the chest, sending him flying backwards. Somehow he gets twisted in the air and slams into a window, spraying shattered glass all over the lawn. His eyes widen in pain and shock as dozens of shards carve up his back. A high-pitched yelp escapes his mouth.

Kimber doesn't even react. She's still staring at the floor.

Striding over, I offer my hand to him. "Better get that looked at." There's no heat to my words. Like I said, I have nothing against the guy. He just needs to be somewhere else. Rhode Island is fine.

He slaps my hand away and slowly gets up, swearing under his breath. The fight's been taken right out of him. That has to be humiliating. Not only did he fail in his attack, he failed in a spectacular manner, right in front of the girl he wanted to protect. I almost felt sorry for the guy.

"Honey, can you drive me to the hospital? I might need stitches."

"You go, I'll be fine. Rick is here." That's probably the last thing he wants to hear.

"Well, then I should stay too."

"No. Go."

"But —"

"You're bleeding on my rug."

"Oh, sorry. Shoot. Okay, I'm going." He leans down with a wince and pecks her on the cheek. "Don't forget the police will be here soon. Be truthful. Tell them why you think this happened and who's responsible."

He glares at me as he passes and minces down the front stairs. His Ford Explorer roars away.

I give a tiny wave, wiggling my fingers. "What a wimp."

"Shut up, Rick," Kimber says, exhaustion in her voice as she levers herself up. "Tell me again how this is your fault."

I point to the far wall of the kitchen, visible at the end of the hallway. Profanities have been sprayed in blood-red paint. "Somebody in that supremacist gang is sending me a message. They hit my parents' place last night, too."

A quick intake of breath. "Are they okay?"

"Fine. A little shook up, like you." I stalk through the house, looking at the destruction. Every single room had been savaged, from broken dishes and appliances in the kitchen, to holes in the bedroom wall and a torn up mattress. Even the toilet bowl had been smashed, water spreading across the tile floor. Who does that?

The back door appears to be the entry point. It's smashed off the hinges and there are large gouges in the jamb.

Just the violence inherent in this damage is frightening. What would have happened if she'd been home? I shudder at the thought and let the back of my hand brush against hers, taking comfort in the warmth of her reality.

The police arrive and she spends a half hour giving them a report. Afterwards I stay, helping her clean up the mess.

Eventually she asks me to leave, needing time alone. She won't listen to my argument, so I make her promise to call me later. We stand in a silent hug on her front step, returning to a different time. In that moment, with the late spring air settling on us, it feels as if she too wants to peel away the layers that have accumulated since our paths separated.

The solemn nature of the scene is torn apart when I fire up the Cobra.

This is too dangerous now, I tell myself as I turn the wheel back home. People are getting hurt, people close to me. Last night was the houses. What's next? The people themselves?

I think it's time to turn this over the professionals. Maybe a call to Allan and Warren is in order. I can give them everything I know about the Covenant, Wagner and Galen, the schedule of public disruptions.

My cell phone rings, startling me from my thoughts. Considering the type of day I've had so far, I almost throw it out the window. What else can go wrong?

It's Dee. "Dawg, help me. I think I'm in trouble."

CHAPTER TWENTY-TWO

List

I grind on my brakes and yank the Cobra over to the curb. "What do you mean?"

A horn blares and the driver behind me flips the bird as he swerves around. I wave back using all five fingers and cut the ignition.

"It's Moller. He's planning a huge press conference. These last two white guys that got killed has everyone in a panic. Two in one week."

"No shit. As a white guy, I'm a little disturbed. How is that your problem?" I let a little edge seep into my tone. Shut me out for weeks and call when you need help? What a crock.

"Killer, listen. Moller has pulled together a list of names he wants read out. These are all people who don't have a neutral stance on equality, people who could potentially be adding fuel to the fire. Some of them are public figures. I'm 'sposed to denounce them at the conference."

"Denounce? You mean the opposite of pronounce? Wouldn't that be something like mumbling their names?"

"Knock it off, man. I ain't kidding 'round."

"Well, what are you? Some puppet with no mind of your own?" I'm not going to let him up off the mat quickly. It's a hallmark of our relationship: nothing easy, everything earned.

"You know I ain't nobody's puppet. But it's hard to say no, especially when he shows me what kind of difference I can make."

Meaning: Dee can't stand up to the guy. He doesn't have the chops. Having been around Moller, I can understand, if not forgive.

"Yeah, that was some difference at your rally last week. How many got injured again?"

"That ain't my fault, man. You know it. And anyway, how you going to turn your back on a friend when he's down? I know you saw me, and you walk away with that little white guy? Explain that."

"That little white guy was hit this week, the first one."

"Seriously?" Dee doesn't sound surprised, which tells me he already knew something. There's a game being played but I don't know the rules.

"Why not just do what Moller wants?" I ask, switching us back on topic. "Maybe it will do some good."

"You don't single out someone like that. There are names on that list that no one would suspect. Politicians, local businessmen, a city council member —"

"So? Maybe they have it coming. How good is the info? Is it grounded?"

Dee stays silent for a second. "Killer, you on that list. You."

"*What?*"

"I saw it. Says you been hanging out with both guys got killed. You just confirmed one of them."

Who is watching me so closely that even Dee knows? My stomach sinks.

"Killer?" He repeats. "That true? You not saying something says something."

"Yes, both of them. Met them both recently."

"Then you know what they were involved in, you know about that Covenant group. The little white guy joined just a couple months ago."

"I know that."

He sighs. "Then you gotta know it don't look good. You running in those circles put your name on my list. What the hell, man."

"I'm working a different angle than you. We each try to make things better in our own way."

"Not everyone will see it that way."

I scrub at my forehead, rubbing hard. "Listen up, Dee. Something more is going on here. We're both being handled. The pieces are all out there, but I can't connect them. Someone is using everything you stand for to kill others, but I don't know what the end goal is. And if we don't figure it all out soon, it's going to end badly."

"Badly meaning what?"

"I don't know, but I think the schedule is increasing fast. Those murders aren't the last, just the latest." I start telling him about my parents and Kimber, but he cuts me off.

"Really? You think this is some kind of master plan? Dawg, stop crying conspiracy. This ain't no puzzle to be solved. It's people killing each other because of color, like Alabama in the sixties. History repeats when we don't learn the lesson."

"No, you're wrong. Different age, different place. It's not Klan, no matter how much the signs point that way. Have you seen a single white-robe wandering around? No, because it isn't them. Someone just wants us to think so, and I think the Covenant is the true target, for whatever reason. That's what I need to find out."

"Klan, Covenant, Aryan Nation, White Knights...it don't matter none. If I don't speak out and help my people, it's going to keep happening. That's what I know."

He's not seeing the big picture, just his little portion, and it frustrates me. "Do you really think marching around town with candles and signing goofy peace contracts are helping? Look at how your last attempt turned out. There's a program going on in the background and it involves killing people who stand in the way. You want to help? Find out who the blacks are knocking off the Covenant."

"What blacks?"

"The ones who started all this."

"Whoa, whoa, Killer. You are jumping logic. How do you know it's not other groups? More minorities than the black man live around here." An edge creeps into his voice. I'd touched on a subject near and dear to his activist heart.

I ignore the warning signs. "Did you miss the message in those murders? Choosing to ignore it isn't much different than condoning it."

That pisses him off. He goes formal on me. "Killer. Rick. How long we been friends? You not speaking…you *are* not speaking right. If this can come between us, it tells me that the bridge for others is longer than anyone thinks. Be part of the solution, not the problem."

"Knock it off. Did you read that from an index card? You sound like Moller now. Don't forget who your true friends are."

"My friends understand the struggle I have."

I snort loudly, on purpose. "What struggle? You make millions playing a game. You have any idea how many people would love that kind of struggle?"

"You, for one. Oh, but that's right. You can't. It's easier to quit." He's nettling me, goading me on.

It works. I feel myself getting pissy and try to hold my temper. "This isn't about me. Stop digging."

"It's always about the Killer. Always has been. You make sure of that." He stiffens up his tone even more, raising the wall higher. "Now that I think about it, maybe there need to be people exposed around here. Local cats who've picked a side. They want to stay hidden but we want them known. I think you've cleared things up for me."

"Godammit, Dee..." But the line goes dead. I punch back his number but he doesn't answer.

Swearing out loud, I fire the car back up and tear away from the curb. That earns me several more honks and yells, but I flip them all off before they beat me to the punch.

It's six pm. I should have just enough time.

Leaving the Cobra idling in the driveway, I push through the front door of my house and spy my papers still lying on the coffee table where I left them. I vaguely remembered a meeting scheduled for later tonight and now more than ever, I need to attend it. Not only do I expect they'll talk about the murders, I might be able to clue into which ones were the vandals.

I can smack them in the mouth right then and there.

Plus, if word has leaked out about Dee's plans for his next press conference – and I have to believe they have – then I want to hear what the response will be. My finger traces down my page of notes, seeking the correct time and location.

"Rick."

I jump, startled. Maya is standing in the doorway to her office. I'm so intent on my own mission I didn't even notice she was home. Was her Jeep in the garage? Matter of fact, was the garage even open? I don't remember. So much for my vaunted powers of observation.

"What's up?" I reply, turning back to my notes. The meeting starts in thirty-five minutes. If I leave now, I can just make it.

"Can we talk for a minute?" Her voice is neutral. I fail to notice that particular warning sign, so wrapped up am I in my own thoughts.

"How about later? I'm in the middle of something."

"No, Rick. *Now.*" Her pitch sharpens, spearing my attention. I look up, confused. What have I done wrong now?

Maya sits next to me on the couch, an expression of intensity on her flawless face. I resist the urge to glance at the clock.

"I have something to tell you," she starts, holding my gaze. "It's about a company that specializes in disaster recovery for other technical companies. When the clock hits midnight at the end of the year, there are going to be a lot of businesses scrambling to keep things going. This company – it's a start up – is in the perfect position to explode from the opportunities. They have a new product that will really sell to the small business owner desperate to keep his systems running."

Really? This is the talk we need to have right this moment? "So are you talking like investing in it? How much?"

"No, something more. I've been offered the Director of Information Security job."

That catches my attention. "When have you been looking?"

"Well, Tom and I..."

"Tom Simmons?"

Now she's the one who looks startled. "Yes, how did you know?"

"Never mind. When are you supposed to start?"

"Any time now. All I have to do is say yes. That's why I had to talk to you first. Tom was hired as CEO and wants to bring me on."

Grabbing my file, I stand up. "Well, whatever. You know your career better than me. If you think it's a step up, you don't need my permission."

"This one I do. It's in San Francisco, Rick."

I stop in the foyer. "California?"

"Yes, in California."

"Wait, you want me to just pack up and leave?"

"That's where all the good tech companies are. It works out well since you'd have to move to play football anyway."

"But..."

"But nothing. You're my husband. Where we go, we go together." She applies the full court press. "I've done some homework on this. Training camp for you goes end of July through end of August. You can just rent a hotel room. The early schedule has the Vikings on the road for a month. Most players maintain separate homes. While you're on the road, I could research some places in Minneapolis and we could lease one during your off week when you come back. It makes perfect sense. There's nothing here for you any more so why stay?"

"Well, my parents are still around, for one."

"Your dad upsets you every time we visit. Why would you want to continue that? Since they've moved, you barely see them anyway."

"Yeah, but..."

"But what? Is there another reason?" Her eyes pin me, daring me to say it. Even I am not that much of a fool.

"I can't talk about this right now. I have to go. We'll talk later."

"Be sure we will," she calls after me as I exit the house. "This is a dream come true, Rick. We'll be millionaires this time next year."

But would we be rich in the ways that matter? I wonder.

CHAPTER TWENTY-THREE

Rock and Roll

I pull up to an old VFW building with only minutes to spare. Cars spilled from the blacktop onto the grass yard. Crowded meeting.

With Wagner and Galen's demise the beehive has taken on an increased energy level and that does not bode well for anything Dee has planned.

The basement smells like mold. The ancient wood paneling is offensive even to my limited interior design sensibility. This is the type of place where old men in suspenders sit on folding chairs and bitch about kids nowadays.

Tonight the demographic *is* those kids.

I see a few familiar faces, including Seal the social wart. He waves frantically at me from across the room, but I pretend like I don't see him and keep turning. There are a lot of brands on display tonight, far more than my first meeting.

I wonder if somewhere in this collection of Abercrombie & Fitch facades there is a hunter killer squad planning their next action.

People take their seats and I end up sitting next to a girl I'd never seen before. The slam of a closing door rolled down the stairwell, letting everyone know we're locked in.

"Isn't that against fire code?" I ask her.

She just gives a look and seems nervous.

We open with the pledge once again: "To be born white is a privilege and an honor. To protect the purity of our blood is a duty and an oath. We pledge allegiance to the Covenant Church of the New Millennium..."

Blah, blah, blah.

Two younger men take turns moderating the meeting. They look to be in their later twenties, early thirties. Maybe the Covenant is running out of elder statesmen, seeing as how they keep turning up dead and all.

There are the usual speeches about tithing correctly, a recap of recent events, which took quite a while considering everything that's happened in the last couple of weeks, and an introduction of new members. I note how many more there are than in my first meeting. Perhaps the killings of white folk had driven more applicants to the Covenant's books.

After forty minutes of that blather, the agenda rotates to the upcoming press conference and rally. A number of calls go up for violence, for showing "them uppity blacks" that we protect our own.

Uppity? Who says that?

The moderators shoot down every proposed action that had an element of revenge. Counter-protests, handing out flyers, placing people in the crowd to shout down any speakers; these things they endorsed.

I find that troubling.

Where are the planners behind the attack on those four black kids? Where are the instigators of the riot? Two carloads left Colonial Estates. Are those occupants absent from the crowd tonight? Or have the moderators already shut them down?

Behind the makeshift stage hangs a scarlet curtain, emblazoned with the Odinism brand, made from a thin material. A light flicks on somewhere in the back, turning the fabric translucent.

I can see the faint outline of a head and shoulders, someone standing behind the curtain. It's not the minute taker, he sat behind the moderators.

The figure turns and appears to speak to someone out of sight. The light snaps off, making the fabric opaque again.

What was that? Why is someone staying hidden?

They didn't want to be seen by people in the audience. That's why.

What if that's me? I'm already marked and watched, the vandalism has proven that. Is the person behind those actions the person behind the stage? Could I really be that close to the shot caller?

I'm tempted to rush the stage, rip away the curtain and expose whoever that is. But one look around the room stifles the impulse. I'm surrounded by a hundred members, and each one of them is a potential enemy if I show my hand. Even Seal. The Carter murderers may even be hidden in this crowd.

I know a bad move when I see one.

So I fidget my way through the rest of the meeting, thirty more minutes of torture. When it ends I immediately start working my way forward. People are knotted in groups of discontent, forcing me to wind a circuitous route. Along the way I hear snatches of dissatisfaction, embryonic plans of retribution and more than one indicator that Dee's rally is in big trouble.

North Haven is already sizzling with division and things will only keep getting worse.

A single door is set in the back wall behind the curtain. It was this door that probably opened and allowed light through. I open it slowly, clenching my gut against the possibility that there were people on the other side.

No outcry follows so I duck inside and close the door.

It's your typical storage room, stacked full of tables, old banners and broken bar stools. This is where all the folding chairs from the meeting will be brought.

I cross to the opposite wall and open a door set in the brickwork. I'm a little bolder now. Whoever I'm chasing is moving along this path and I can't afford to lose him. On the other side is a long hallway, dank and dark except for a single bulb at the far end. Steps lead upward, presumably to the back parking lot area.

Feet scuff the top of the stairs and faint shadows play as bodies exit the building.

I'm seconds away from my target.

Moving down the hallway quickly and quietly, I pause at the bottom. Low voices drift back down, too low for me to understand. I sneak up one step at a time, pausing just below the top. It seems like they're still close enough that I will have a good view.

Taking a deep breath, I start to rise up. Let's get a good look at you Mister.

My cell phone rings, startling me nearly into losing my bladder. I stumble back and slide down a couple of steps, twisting my ankle. A squelch of pain slips from me and I struggle back up, but now there's no one in sight. The sound of an engine comes from around the side of the building.

Limping, I move towards my car, snatching the cell phone from its clip. "What?" I bark.

"Rick, James here."

"And I said 'What'?"

"Is this a bad time? I know it's late."

Yeah, it's a bad time, pal. I almost identified the target I've been chasing for weeks. I think.

Instead I sigh. "No, you're fine. What you got?"

He launches into something about my legal issues. A dark SUV negotiates the far end of the parking lot. Only the roofline is visible over the cars between us. I match the engine sounds. My man is in there, getting away. Snatching up a chunk of rock, I let it fly. I may not have a pro-level arm, but it's enough.

Stone bangs off the rear window, undoubtedly cracking it. Brake lights flash in response, then the truck speeds away.

James is prattling on about lawyers and hearings and something about my not paying attention. I don't really catch everything as I hobble to my car, focused on the fading truck.

"Fine, whatever," I interrupt him. "Just remind me closer to the dates." I hang up even though it sounds like he wants to say more.

I burn a half hour driving around the area in a fruitless search to pick up the truck. By the time I arrive home, it's fully dark and the neighborhood has gone to bed for the night.

Standing outside my garage, I look down the street to Moller's house. We need to have words, Geoff and I. This list is his creation and I want to know how he got it. What does he truly hope to gain by having Dee read aloud the names? Is placing public pressure on people really the best way to force change?

Maybe I could break Nathan's other wrist in the process, just for kicks and giggles.

I turn, entering my house. Tomorrow then, gentlemen, we will have ourselves a little talk.

CHAPTER TWENTY-FOUR

Speech, Speech

I wake groggy, as if I hadn't slept at all, to find Maya banging away on her computer. She immediately starts in on the San Francisco gig, but I cut her off. I'm not in the mood. Her response is to hand me some printouts on California real estate.

I take them into the bathroom in case we're out of toilet paper.

I'm out of the house forty minutes later, showered and fed, but feeling no better for the effort.

Someone has dragged this dog behind the car for several miles.

The sun hangs low, bright in a clear sky, temps already warm. It's going to be a great day but I realize that such promise is not mine alone. Others are banking on a great day as well and their success is my failure.

My ankle throbs as I limp down the street. James mentioned that my arrest will likely be bargained down to a misdemeanor, which means I still have a felony to give. If Nathan is home, maybe I'll use it up, this time on purpose.

Curtains flicker in the house across the street. Probably a neighbor peeking out at the crazy jock who seems to be making news in all sorts of the wrong ways.

Moller's house looks quiet. The mailbox is empty, so someone has been home recently. Striding up the driveway, I detour around back. The garage is open, only the Jag visible. I start towards it.

"And what are you about?" Geoffrey asks from behind me.

He's sitting in the courtyard patio with a cup of coffee, paper folded neatly across his knee. Christ, is this guy posing for a Folger's commercial?

"Looking for you. Where are the boys this morning?"

"Lance left an hour ago to run some errands for me. Nathan I haven't seen in a day or so, though I have heard him moving about the house."

He sips his coffee. "Surely you haven't come here looking for either of them. What can I do for you?"

"You know why I'm here: the names on your list. My name. What's your game?"

"I understand your concern, but Damonti and I are only doing what we think will most help this community. Even you have to recognize the increasing signs of conflict. This century is winding down and people are nervous about what the next will bring. In many ways."

"Dee I get. But why is it important to you? This isn't your town; you've only been here a few months. Why do you care?"

Moller shrugs and smiles. "It's in my nature, perhaps. I want only to see everyone receive what they deserve."

Maybe it's my mood, maybe I'm wound so tight by the shadows jumping all around me, but I listen to his words and hear something different. I take a step forward onto his patio.

A growl stops my progress as Tyr raises his head. The monster lounged behind Moller, so quiet that I didn't even notice him. There's no doubt what will happen if I keep moving towards his master.

Why couldn't Moller be a cat person?

He smiles, a faint thing that touches only the corners of his eyes. "Rick, you act as if I am the architect of some nefarious scheme. Trust me when I say that is a theory bordering on mad."

"I don't even know what nefarious means. Does that make you a good guy or bad?"

If he thinks I'm kidding, he doesn't show it. I'm not, by the way.

"You've known Damonti your whole life, you know as well as anyone his activist nature. We all have the potential to leave a larger footprint in our passing and this is Damonti's manner. I'm only trying to guide and help him fulfill that desire."

"How did you get my name on that list?"

"That I cannot reveal without breaking trusts of several close associates. It does beg a closer inspection, though. What were you doing with two men actively campaigning for racial separation? You, who has a proven past just the opposite."

"We were selling Tupperware."

"I hope your flippant nature takes you far. It surely doesn't engender any confidence in others. Rick, I'd like to give you a piece of advice."

"Give means free. You get what you pay for."

"People have many paths open to them. It is fine for these paths to diverge, no matter how deep the history between two people is. Damonti has chosen his, so should you do the same. Go play football. I have heard you can be quite good, perhaps that should be your focus and your path. It does not mean you will lose Damonti's friendship, which appears to be a frightening aspect for you." He leans forward, intense look in his eyes. "Be a man, Killing. Be the man you can be."

That doesn't even make sense to me. "Are you going downtown with Dee today?"

Moller shakes his head and leans back, refolding his paper. "This is not about me. These are his people, his efforts, his moment of light."

"Sounds like you're just hiding in the shadows."

Moller spreads his hands in a theatrical wave. "Tomato, tomahto."

And that was that. I had nothing left, no counter arguments. Clearly this guy gives out only what he wants and I'm overmatched in that way. He'd be a hell of an interrogator. I turn to leave.

Of course, there's also the matter of getting the last word.

I spin back and feint a charge at him, yelling loudly. Tyr, lulled into a sense of complacency by our conversation, startles awake and scrambles up with a growl. His reaction knocks Moller over, spilling coffee everywhere.

I take off running, hell bent for leather towards home, ankle screaming.

Take that.

The press conference is slated for noon. High noon.

This time there is no winding path, no march for peace, not considering the outcome of the last one. The police probably wanted more control and keeping things stationary helps that.

My intricate plan involves showing up and waiting for something to happen.

If the Covenant wants to disrupt the event in the same manner, I hope Seal was involved in the planning. His incompetence would lead to them firebombing a hot dog stand in Provo, Utah. On the other hand, if there really is a sub-group within the Covenant responsible for the riot, then we've got a bigger problem.

I pick the SuperHawk for this trip, for more maneuverability. And, unlike its stable mate, it also has all working parts.

An hour before the festivities begin, I pull into a slot too small for a car, across the street from the city square. Police have already cordoned off the perimeter of the park, creating a protected area several blocks around. I spot variations on the theme of riot gear, meaning other jurisdictions had sent reinforcements. Nobody is taking chances today.

A platform had been erected at the outer edge of the park for cameras, raising them up. Technicians scramble over the scaffolding, draping it in fabric to hide the structure, doing sound checks with audio. The center of the square held a fountain. A lower platform stood there, with a podium for the speakers. The angle of the cameras would place the wide steps of City Hall in the background.

Very dramatic, Dee. Or should I say, Geoffrey.

I wander the area, watching people gather. They looked suspiciously at the cops, who looked just as suspiciously back. The core crowd is mostly black, sprinkled with other races in support of the cause. Many carried signs of peace and their body language said they intended to honor it.

The outer edges consist of the white folk. Interesting that they maintained a distance. Maybe they figure this is a black thing and not part of their problem, or they didn't want to get too close in case another riot blew up.

Either way, I'd never seen such a clear demarcation between two colors.

Beyond all the collected groups stood news vans and the sheer number staggers me. Cables run from them to the camera platform. Others have cameramen staged on top of the van for a distance shot. Reporters work the crowd, easy to spot with their fancy clothes and retinue of equipment handlers following in their wake. I take care to avoid them all.

Dee arrives twenty minutes later, escorted by police and men in dark suits. I assume these are guys hired for the occasion, professional security with special expertise in protection.

By now the park is at capacity, citizens of North Haven and surrounding towns standing shoulder to shoulder in the most significant cultural moment most of us have ever seen. A hush falls over the crowd as Dee joins the Mayor and several council members, shaking hands like a politician.

Several voices in the crowd yell out, supporting his cause. An answering call comes back, decidedly negative. I recognize the face from my first Covenant meeting, but the kid doesn't do anything more than respond. He does look angry though.

As the Mayor opens the conference with a scripted summary of recent events, I stare at my friend. It seems like he's staring back, but I can't see his eyes behind the sunglasses.

What is he thinking?

After ten minutes of narrative, the Mayor cedes the mic to North Haven's newest activist. Dee steps up to the podium and pauses for a long two-count, almost like a soap opera moment.

Good lord.

"Mayor Schneck, members of the council, thank you." He begins, giving a half nod in their direction. Everyone nods back as I'm sure they practiced. "People of North Haven, I come to you today not as a ball player, but as a fellow citizen of humanity. As recent tragic events have shown, we teeter on the brink as a town, a culture, a living entity. The old century gives way to the new, and so should old hates be paved over by new promise. We cannot enter the new millennium divided by race, by color, by prejudice. Yet certain factions within our society resist the change that will see us into a better age. Certain factions cling to old wounds, repeating the ugliness that existed in our past."

Another whoop of support goes up but he does not acknowledge it.

"Brothers and sisters of all colors, do not let us succumb to the savage. Do not look across the barrier with distrust, but rather with acceptance. Together we can break the cycle of chains and hate. As one humanity we can forge new bonds and finally put to an end the things that should be left behind. Today I come to you with a plea for tolerance."

This speech is as bad as the one he wrote in ninth grade about growing cauliflower.

Turning my back on my friend's performance, I make my way to the edges. The full gamut of emotion is displayed before me, black, white and all those in between. I see hope, fear, hostility. On too many of the faces, something simmers just below the surface, waiting to be triggered. Part of me understands.

White people are dying left and right, yet here's a black man speaking to his people. Where is the champion for my people? If the minority is represented by Dee, does he also carry the banner for the majority? Is our hope wrapped up in a guy who still struggles with sinker pitches low and inside?

I stop and lean against the side of a building, letting my eyes roam. The day is growing hot, but I'm not getting the location of real heat. If the Covenant wants to disrupt this event, when will they strike? The police presence is strong. Is that preventing them from doing anything?

As my thoughts wander, a flash of light catches the corner of my eye. It comes from between two news vans, across the way. I can just make out the rear of a black Chevy Tahoe.

A web of cracks is spread across the back window.

Gotcha.

Chapter Twenty-Five

Gun Runner

I start making my way around the edges of the crowd, circling towards the truck. Is my guy in there now?

Maybe I'll get another chance after blowing it last night.

The density of the crowd makes it hard to move quickly and the line of vans blocks my sight. No one pays attention to me, other than a few people irritated by my passing. They are all focused front and center on the performance being enacted there.

Several police watch me, their riot helmets slowly tracking my progress and it makes me feel a little better. If something does go down, I've got professionals at my back.

I finally get behind the line of vans. Now the Tahoe is firmly in my crosshairs, at the end of the block. It's in three-quarter profile to me, with those barn-style rear doors that open out wide. I can see that the driver's side door is cracked open just a bit. Alarms start a low jangle in my head. My feet begin to move faster.

One cop barks an order for me to stop but I ignore him. There aren't any more cops between me and the truck.

As I pick up my pace, there's movement at the rear of the Tahoe, just shadowy motion that I can't see clearly because of the window tint.

Something slim and long pokes out the crack of the doors. I squint. What is that?

I realize it's the barrel of a rifle.

"Gun!" I roar, launching into a sprint. "GUN!"

The barrel wavers a second then swings my direction. At least, I think it does. I can't really tell.

I panic and throw myself off to the side, behind a building. There's a small parking lot and I slam up against a car, rocking it. A man is on the other side, in the process of closing and locking his door. He stands there, key in hand, quizzical expression on his face.

It must have looked really random, this guy flying out of nowhere, for no understandable reason, plastering himself against his car. I don't have time to explain.

I run to the corner of the building, peeking around it.

The truck's reverse lights flash as the driver slides it into gear and starts pulling away. They were going to assassinate Dee, in front of every camera here.

THAT was the Covenant's grand plan. Holy shit.

Several nearby cops are on their radios, moving quickly in my direction. I hope they saw what I did.

The Tahoe drives down the block, signals and turns. It doesn't drive like a getaway vehicle. My nerves are a mess and I'm suddenly too chicken to run after it. If they were willing to sniper my friend on stage, there's no way they'd hesitate to blow a hole in me if I ran after them.

Plus, what would I do if I caught it? Jump on the roof? Rip open a door and drag out the shooter? Neither of those ideas seem particularly realistic options.

I feel way over my head.

Then it occurs to me. If they really were willing to pull the trigger on this, did they have a backup plan? What if there's another vehicle with a gunman inside? This is their big moment, their best opportunity. Who knows when Dee will be teed up in a public park again?

I scan the area but it's just cops running towards me. Vans and the backs of people watching the stage form a backdrop. There's too much stuff blocking my way.

Fine, if I can't find the suspect, I'll remove the target.

I dart away from a cop reaching for me. He's yelling something but I can't hear him. The thoughts in my head are too loud.

It will be like that Kevin Costner bodyguard movie, at the end where he saves Whitney Houston. I'll save Dee from another assassination attempt, the police will catch the shooter and everyone will realize that I'm not off my rocker.

I use some football moves to juke out two cops blocking my path. I'm off to the side of the stage now. There's all sorts of commotion in the crowd. Maybe they finally understand that something is going on. Peripherally, I see a bunch of fingers pointing in my direction.

That's right, Rick Killing knows what's going down.

I lower my shoulder into another guy, completely blowing him off his feet. Now there's just one older pudgy cop between me and the stage. I see Dee turn his head towards me. He doesn't even know what kind of danger he's in.

The cop is backing up, reaching behind him. He's probably never been charged by two hundred and twenty five pounds of pure adrenaline bent on saving a life.

He whips out a Taser and pulls the trigger.

Two little barbs stick into my chest. I stop and look down at them, tracing the filament wires back up until our eyes meet.

He triggers the charge.

I wet my pants.

Someone is slapping my face. It stings. Three more. Now I'm annoyed. I punch back blindly, eyes unwilling to open, insides feeling like distant vibrations.

My hand connects with something.

"Hey, watch it Killer!" Dee's voice is tiny, a long way from my ears.

I peel open my eyes to find his ebony face hovering over me, zooming in and out of focus. Hands are pressing my shoulders down, strange hands. They belong to EMTs. I shove them aside and sit up.

Cops stand outside the ambulance, watching me, probably waiting to see what crazy thing I'd do next.

Dee moves to the bench across from me. "Dawg, what the hell you doing?"

Good question. This is going to sound stupid. "There was a gun. In a Tahoe with a cracked window. I cracked it. It was pointed at you. Black Tahoe." I sound like an idiot even to myself, but my brain couldn't seem to hold a coherent thought.

One of the officers gives a short shake of his head to Dee.

"Killer, no one saw such a truck. You sure?"

"Yes, I'm sure. Why else would I say it? There was a guy and girl, I hit their car. Find them and ask. They had to have seen it too."

The expressions surrounding me said: Yeah, we'll get right on that, pal.

Dee nods slowly. "Okay, if you say so. I already called Maya and she's waiting on you. Someone will get you home."

I stumble getting out of the ambulance and he catches me. I grip his arm. "Dee, you have to drop out of sight. I'm serious, there was someone taking aim at you. It's the Covenant Church of the New Millennium. I think they're marking you as retaliation for the two latest murders."

"You sound pretty convinced. How do you know?"

"I've been investigating them, trying to find out who's behind it all. I think the guy was in that Tahoe."

Pain pricks my eyes as the sun drills into them. To my disgust, I really did piss my pants. How humiliating.

Dee doesn't answer as he walks me towards a waiting squad car, so I press him. "Did you at least finish your speech?"

"To the point where you got all frantic in the crowd." He smiles to blunt the edge. "But I think the message got across. We have to stop the killing, dawg. I don't need an hour to say that."

"And did you read out your list?" I stop and square up, confronting him. "Did you sell me down the river?"

He stares at me through his stupid gold-rimmed sunglasses. "No, it's not worth it. I can't be pissing off the people who care. It turns out I got friends watching my back; can't ignore that. They deserve better."

Damn right, man. But you could at least say sorry.

A young sheriff's deputy in a too big uniform opens the passenger door for me.

"Dee, he looks like Opie. Is he even old enough to drive?"

"Go easy on him. He's a cadet. Go change your nasty pants. I'll call you later."

"Remember what I said. Hunker down and watch your back. Hire more protection."

We pull away, parting the crowd of onlookers. At least I'm not in back. This little episode will make the news, I have no doubt. There's nothing else for all those news cameras to film right now. I dread the call from James that will come at some point. He has to be thinking I'm insane.

Opie maneuvers the car free of the crowd and we accelerate down the street. He turns to me, all freckles and buzz-cut hair. "You know, my brother played on your high school team. He wasn't a starter so you probably don't remember him. But I remember homecoming in your junior year. You threw four touchdowns against Brookside. I was only thirteen then, but it was awesome."

I lean my head against the window and close my eyes. Somebody shoot me.

By the time we reach home, the window is nearly cracked from me beating my head against it. Stupid Opie talked the entire time.

I exit the car without another word and ignore his offer of more help. I feel a little more normal, as much as one can with urine-soaked pants.

After washing up, I find Maya downstairs working out. The TV in the corner is set to a local news channel and of course, my face appears. There I am, running like a maniac through the crowd, knocking cops aside like bowling pins. At least my form is still good.

And there I am taking 50,000 volts to the nipples, curling up in a ball and twitching. Attractive.

Maya gives me a scathing look but for once doesn't say a word. That's how I know she wants something. I should join her in a workout since it's been a couple of days and I've eaten nothing but crap. What I really need though is a drink.

One Captain later, I'm up in my loft checking messages. The machine is filled to capacity. People I know and people I don't, all looking for a story. One message came from Kimber, as requested, telling me she was going to bed and that everything was fine. I can't detect any undertones in her voice, she sounded like a girl whose house had just been vandalized. She doesn't answer when I call her back.

James, however, is another matter. He picks up before the first ring is done and I spend the next half hour trying to keep him from screeching.

The final message is the most surprising. It's Detective Warren, asking me to call back. He left both direct office and home line numbers. Seeing as it was Sunday afternoon, I took a chance.

He answers on the third ring. "Warren."

"Wow, that's exactly how you answer at work. Is it rehearsed?"

"Is this Killing? Jesus, you are a smart ass. Good thing you're big or someone might pummel you for your lip."

"Maybe God made me big so I could freely explore my smart ass nature."

He is quiet a second, perhaps awed by my philosophical statement. "Then how do you explain your moronic side?"

Or maybe not.

I switch topics. "Do you have something for me?"

"Yeah, those prints. Where'd you get those again?" With his Chicago accent, it comes out sounding like: 'Dose prents. Where'd youse get dose gen?'

I rummage through my memory, dredging up my cover story. "They came from a guy that we think has been stealing from us. Just looking to put a name to him so we can track our records."

"Okay, how does Geoffrey Moller sound then?"

"Sounds like a first and last name combo. Anything you can tell me about this Moller?" Other than the fact that he lives down the street from me; I already know that part.

"Not much. There's no theft arrests. A few unlawful assembly and disorderly conduct citations, years ago down south. Nothing within the last ten."

"Oh, that's disappointing."

"Yeah, he's your average schmoe. Except for one thing."

Now I perk up. "One thing?"

"There's a watch flag on his record."

"Meaning what?"

Warren sounds hesitant. "I'm not sure. I've never seen this before. I sent off the request for more information. He could be somebody pretty important. Tell me again how you pulled the prints?"

"They came off a shelf he touched," I lie.

"Well, they're pretty smudged so it could be a bad read."

No, you have the right guy.

"Okay," I say. "How long before your request comes back?"

"Probably be a while. These things never process fast unless we have a reason to fast track them."

"And I suppose retail theft is not a reason?"

Warren laughs, condescending. "Yeah, sure, Killing. You're just that important. When I get it, you'll get it." And he hangs up without another word.

By the time I descend from the loft, Maya is freshly showered and standing naked in our bedroom, brushing her hair. Her eyes flick to me in the mirror when I walk into the bedroom.

"Have you thought more about San Francisco?"

The question knocks me out of my mental wandering. "What?"

"San Francisco. City by the Bay. Journey. 49ers. Golden Gate. Have you thought more about moving out there with me?"

"Good lord, Maya. You just told me yesterday. I'm supposed to make a life-changing decision overnight? What's the rush anyway?"

"Honey, we're in the digital age. Everything happens fast. You have to jump on opportunities when they come along or someone else will. We don't want to miss out on this one."

I lean against the dresser on the opposite wall, keeping my eyes fixed on hers. "Why do you *really* want this?"

The answer has never been spoken between us, and may never be. She wants to take me away from my hometown, from everything – and everyone – North Haven offers.

"Why do I want this?" She turns to face me and I make sure to keep my eyes up. No sense in getting distracted. "I want this for us, to build some security in a fragile world. Being a consultant is not secure. Being a technical commodity is not secure. There's no severance package, no pension for my kind. If I strike while the iron is still hot, I can parlay my skills into a position at a higher level that is indispensable. This tech boom won't last forever, maybe another five or six years. By 2005, I want to be well situated."

Her reasoning is sound, not at all like a person who flicks shrimp at Japanese ladies. That doesn't mean I'm sold though. There's a big gap between creating gee-whiz gadgets and making gee-whiz career moves. I'm not sure Maya knows the difference.

My reluctance must have shown in my face. She studies me for a few heartbeats then walks over and lies down on the bed. Mind you, she is still buck naked and her walk is now a slink. Her long legs stretch out, toes pointing to emphasize the line of thigh and calf.

"Why don't you come here, Rick?" Her fingers begin a trace dance around her ribs, stomach, breasts. "Anything you want, right now. *Anything.*"

Not long ago, I would have already been devouring her, falling headlong into her web. She's as sexy a woman as I've ever met, seductive in all the right ways, and she knows how to please a man. My blood stirs just thinking about past times.

But things have changed over the last few months. Even before the murders, before football came around again, I changed. I can sense the manipulation and know the game. Once we were finished with round one and lying there in post-coital comfort, she would start selling me on the move, using hands and lips to drive home her argument.

Eventually I'd give into her advances for round two and that would somehow translate into a victory for her. I'd come home the next day to a moving van parked in the driveway. Ask me how I know.

I'm sick of being manipulated. Everywhere I turn someone is trying to get me to do something. My wife wants me to move away from everything I've known. A white supremacist watches me from afar, laughing at my crude attempts to find him. My agent fed me answers to questions I shouldn't have to answer, gives me tips on how to speak and act. My best friend wants me to join his peace parade.

Where are the things Rick Killing wants?

I push off the dresser and move towards the bed. It's time.

Immediately Maya's hand reaches up to the front of my shorts. Her other hand drifts between her legs.

"Maya, it's not going to work."

"It will if you let me take over. How do you want me?"

I step back before her magic powers start to take effect. "No, not just this. Us. We're not working."

There, it's out. No going back now.

She rolls over and pulls herself up into a submissive kneeling position, arching her back. We've played this game before. "Would you like me to beg?"

"Knock it off. I'm not going." My voice is sharp.

That stops her little play. Her eyes narrow. "Not going where? San Francisco?"

"Yes, I don't want to live there."

Maya stands, coming up to me and holding my eyes with hers. "Think carefully on this, Rick. Very carefully. It's a great move upwards, for me, for us."

"Then you should go, with my blessing."

Her eyes dilate and she sits back down on the bed. Most girls would have tried to cover their nudity, feeling vulnerable. Not Maya. She's too proud. The anger builds in her face.

"What the fuck, Rick. You think I won't go?"

"Oh, I know you will."

"You're damn right I will. I'll leave your sorry ass here and in a year I'll be worth millions. Where will you be? Playing a silly game that you've already failed at? This is a chance to redeem your screw ups."

Okay, that's it.

There's nothing more to be gained here. I've seen it one too many times. Her anger will escalate, allowing it full rein until it controls her, causing her to say things that should never be said between husband and wife. She'd apologize later, but only if she got her way, and that does me no good. I exit the bedroom.

"Don't you walk away, Rick! We need to talk. Rick? Fine, fuck you! You hear me? Fuck and you!" Her voice chased me through the house, but she didn't. She wouldn't. That's not her style. In her experience, men came after her.

I need a long motorcycle ride, to escape, to clear my head, to start thinking through the days and weeks ahead. But one is damaged in the garage and the other is still parked in an alley near the park. I'm having a bad year for two-wheeled transportation.

So I lace on a pair of running shoes and take off. It's the one thing I've always excelled at. No one has to tell me how to do it. No one does it as well.

Fate works in odd ways. It was a significant moment for Maya and me, one that she did not appreciate the way I did. It marked a clear point in our relationship where divergence became clear and declared. From this moment onward, we could look back and see what an effect my pronouncement had.

It also forced me to the couch for the night. And because I slept in the living room, I heard them coming for us.

CHAPTER TWENTY-SIX

Attack

The sound of cracking glass startles me awake. It's sometime after midnight, but I can't see the clock clearly.

At first I think I'm imagining things. Nights are weird that way, playing tricks on your mind. My body is sore and stiff from the Taser, maybe I just heard one of my muscles groan in dismay.

The next sound pegs my adrenaline at eleven. Someone had smacked their knee against the treadmill. It sticks out from a corner wall by the French doors. I've done it enough to recognize the sound.

Intruders are in my basement. Burglars, coming after my stuff.

The glass was probably the French door. They'll be coming up the stairs like nightmare monsters from the depths of Hell.

My breathing goes ragged and I stifle it. I don't know what the hell to do. Maya is asleep behind a locked bedroom door, so that's one small favor. But it also means she won't hear me whisper for her to call 911. The woman sleeps the sleep of the dead.

I tip-toe over to the kitchen, breath held tight. For once I'm happy with tile. It doesn't squeak like wood floors. However, I'm certain everyone within a three block radius can hear my heart hammering.

Retrieving the cordless handset, I stuff it under a couch pillow, dial 9-1-1 by touch and press Dial. I hear the number tones and shove it deeper in between the cushions.

That done, I make my way to the stairs and peek over the wooden rail. Flickers of faint light pan back and forth as the burglars cup hands over flashlights to see where they're going. God, please tell me Maya left dumbbells strewn all over the floor like she usually does. But the lack of any clinking or swearing tells me she cleaned up after herself. Of all times...

The light grows stronger as they near the bottom of the stairs.

My fear morphs into anger. This is my house, my stuff. If they want it, they need to come through me. The police won't be here for another ten minutes, responding lazily to an off-the-hook call. I'm on my own.

Gripping my runaway nerves and harnessing my anger, I cast a look around for weapons. Why couldn't I be one of those guys who collected guns? Like Uzis and big bore hunting rifles. Maybe the odd grenade launcher here and there. Hell, we didn't even have a fireplace set with a poker I could use.

I palm one of my old trophies from a display case next to the couch. It came from the Associated Press for making their All-America team in college. It's a football set atop a fluted column and weighs over ten pounds.

We all have different weapons at our disposal. Now it's time to take the fight to them.

With a three step run-up, I vault over the railing, not knowing what will happen at the bottom.

All two hundred twenty-five pounds of me lands on top of someone, my foot catching another in the head. They yell and we tumble down the stairs together. I lash out wildly with the trophy, not caring who or what I hit. A cry of pain goes up when I feel it connect.

The body beneath me squirms and I smash at it until the movement stops. I have no idea what I was hitting.

Hands grab at me, punching, pulling. The darkness serves to heighten my fear, transforming my attackers from punks intent on stealing my stuff to nighttime slayers and monsters.

Struggling to my feet, I throw off one body and flail around until I feel the trophy connect again. I leap towards the direction of the body and continue punching. I manage to grab a handful of hair and use that to zero in my punches on his face. The form goes limp.

The sound of feet comes from behind.

Before I can turn, I'm tackled from behind, momentum carrying us into the weight bench and knocking it over. Iron thuds off the thick rubber mats covering the floor.

Fingers claw at my face. I can smell stale breath.

Twisting my head away from the blows – and taking a couple shots off my ear in the process – I realize the trophy has slipped from my grasp. Now what?

My hand scrabbles and lands on a plate lying on the floor. A five-pounder. Perfect.

I pummel the body over me, yanking forth a cry as I crack ribs. A couple more blows to the head silences him. I grab another five pound plate as I gain my feet, sliding my fingers through the center holes. Now I've got iron knuckles.

Come and get it.

The sound of squirming bodies fills the space. Three, I think. The moon is only a sliver, not bright enough to send light through the doors. I want to flip a light switch, but don't really want to move.

"Rick? What the hell are you doing down there?" Maya's sleepy voice comes from upstairs, from the hallway to our bedroom. Oh, now she wakes up.

"Get back in our room and lock the door! Go! *Go*!"

Less than a minute has passed since I vaulted the stairs. When no other attack comes, I step back and hit the lights.

Feet sound on the stairs and I spin around, weights up and ready.

Maya lets loose a little scream and stops midway down. Her eyes go wide. I turn my attention back to the basement.

Four young men lay scattered about. Two of them are on the bottom landing, those who I landed on. One looks unconscious, the other cradles an arm with bone sticking out of the wrist area. Tears glint in his eyes as he breathes sharply through clenched teeth.

The third kid lies near the weight bench. This is the one who tackled me. Blood pools around his head and he doesn't move.

The fourth assailant does. Move, that is. He scrambles to his feet, blood running from nose and mouth, trying to squirt past me to the patio doors. I catch him by the hair and punch him square with my ad-hoc knuckles. He cries and drops to his knees, hand pressed against his bleeding nose. I yank his head forward on a hunch.

Son of a bitch.

The Covenant brand. Old and settled under the hairline. A quick check of the other three reveals the same thing. But none of these guys look familiar.

"What the hell are you doing here?"

Neither of the conscious kids responds; they are too deep in their own wounds.

It all clicks.

I'd exposed myself in front of the town yesterday, trying to save Dee. The Covenant couldn't have that, not in their group. An example had to be made. Some vandalism and graffiti might make me think twice about my place in North Haven's current state of affairs.

Maya stands silent behind me, hands tight over her mouth. I point back up the stairs. She goes without comment. That's a first.

"You're the ones who vandalized my parents, Kimber; you came here to do the same. I should fucking beat you both senseless."

Problem is they already are. Neither even seems aware of me.

I inspect the French door. A hole had been cleanly cut into the pane next to the knob. Outside, a circular collection of glass shards indicated where the cut out had been dropped on the patio, probably by accident. That's the sound that woke me. Thank goodness for the clumsy.

On the patio sits a black bag, like one for hockey gear. I walk out and open it, expecting cans of spray paint, hammers, saws; anything that can be used to damage property.

The blood drains from my face.

Inside: white robes, KKK-style hoods, rope, wooden crosses, and jugs of liquid that smell like gas.

Oh God.

It was the Covenant all along.

I was supposed to be the next victim, the next sacrificial lamb intended to send a message. Christ it was so simple; I can't believe I didn't see it earlier. Create a threat to one race and it attracts those who sit on the fence of racial divide. Increase your membership and you increase the ability to attract more members. It becomes a rolling snowball, growing larger with each revolution.

That has to be it.

I sink to one knee, trembling. Then I go inside and kick each kid once. Because they frighten the hell out of me and their willingness to cross the line far exceeds my own. I may have beaten them all down tonight, but I'd lose a war simply because I have limits.

If the assassination attempt had succeeded on Dee, it would drive the minority stake to his side. The Covenant would have started a self-fulfilling prophecy and they could just stand back and watch. It would be Mississippi and Alabama of the sixties all over again.

The doorbell rings and I take the stairs two at a time. I don't see Maya; maybe she's retreated back to the bedroom.

Two officers stand outside. There's no heightened sense of alertness in their expressions. Maybe they think such a nice neighborhood couldn't have any real crime.

Wait until they see the basement.

"We traced a 911 call from this address, sir. Is there an emergency?"

I just motion them inside. Pausing at the couch, I pull the phone out and shut it off. One cop nods as he understands my action and he moves a hand to his gun butt.

"You don't need that. Not anymore."

I walk them downstairs and they immediately go into securing the scene. It feels surreal, watching them work, like it happened to someone else. They cuff the conscious kids, radio for extra units and medical. We go through the sequence of events. I don't mention my role in the Covenant, but I do point out the brands. If either of them recognizes me as the lunatic on the receiving end of a Taser yesterday, they remain professional enough to keep it tight.

After they've logged all my words, I motion outside with one hand. "That's not all. Come see this."

Walking them out to the patio, I use my toe to flip open the bag so they can see the hoods and ropes. Both cops stare, assembling the model in their head and I can see the startling realization flood their faces. One turns to me.

"More than a break in."

I nod. "Way more. Not the first time either. I've been targeted before, indirectly. Just last week vandals hit my..."

Oh shit. Mom, dad.

Kimber.

CHAPTER TWENTY-SEVEN

Taken

Panic seizes my muscles. Forgotten are the residual effects of the Taser. "Call my parents, get someone out to their house!" I bark at the cops as I turn for the stairs. "My wife will get you the contact info."

"Hold on. Where are you going?" One cop puts up his hand to halt my progress.

I push his hand away and run upstairs. They yell after me but I'm not stopping.

Maya is standing in the living room, cloaked in sweats, arms wrapped around her body. She looks at me but says nothing.

"Get them my parents' number," I say as I stride past her. "Take care of yourself."

The police cruiser occupies the middle of the drive, blocking my way. I spin the Cobra around it, running over shrubs and decorative rock in the process. I hadn't planted them, couldn't pronounce them, wouldn't miss them.

Farther down the street, a black Tahoe sat across from Moller's house. I don't need to take a second look to know it sports a cracked rear window. They left it there and walked to my house, keeping the element of surprise. Piece after piece is falling into place. I'd have to let the cops know about it, if for no other reason than to show I wasn't crazy yesterday. Maybe I'd even get to show it to the old fart who Tasered me. Bastard. My left foot still shudders at random.

As I push my car through the 3am streets, the specter of someone looms over my shoulder. Someone knew a lot about me. I never gave my real address. Everything about the house was placed in Maya's name. I'm not an easy guy to track. I've done it on purpose.

Yet, less than ten hours after I thwart a planned attack, I've got racist killers on my doorstep with custom fit robes. That tells me they knew all along where I lived.

And that's creepy.

My hands start to shake as I think about it. If I'd known those kids were killers, would I have been so bold as to bring the fight to them? If I didn't would I be hanging from a tree right now? What would they have done to Maya if they'd come across her first?

What would they do to Kimber?

The Cobra leaps forward in response to my prodding, roaring through the quiet streets. The safety of people I love pressed down on my shoulders, crushing. It feels like I'm the only one who can prevent the worst.

Hang on, babe.

I skid to a halt in front of her house. She never answered her cell when I called and I don't know her home number. The air stinks of burned rubber as I leap onto the porch over a row of hedges and begin yanking on the doorknob. It's locked.

"Kimberly! Open the door. It's Rick!" I keep pounding and rattling the knob, as if it will suddenly unlock.

An eternity of heartbeats later, lights flick on upstairs and I hear movement within. I force the door open as soon as the lock releases.

"What the hell is your problem?" Jeff looks up at me, squinting with sleepy eyes.

"Where's Kimber?"

"It's Kimberly, and she's not here. Are you drunk?"

I shove past him. "Shut up, Jeffy. Where is she?" I call her name up the stairs.

He pushes back, trying to exert some measure of dominance. "Get out of here before I call the cops."

"Do it. She needs them right now." I call her name again.

"God, you're such an idiot!" He yells. "She's not here. Not here! What's going on?"

"Then where is she?" I keep looking up the stairs, as if he hid her there. He keeps trying to push me back out. Geez, he is one weak man. What the hell does she see in him?

Across the street a light fires up in a window. Our shouting is waking people up.

"She's at work," he replies. "Covering another night shift--"

I spin and return to my car, ignoring his questions.

Another twelve minutes tick by as I make a beeline for her job. The facility keeps a skeleton crew overnight every night. The rotation is supposed to be carried equally, yet somehow Kimber ends up with the lion's share. She needed to learn the word No.

Once the building had been an elementary school. Now it's a semi-guarded facility for housing troubled youth. I pound on the main door, noting the wire mesh over windows. A chain link fence surrounded the property and I was forced to scale it.

An extremely large man opens the door and his scowl could send hounds scurrying. He's my height but thirty pounds heavier and looks Italian mean. Beady eyes pierce me. "Whaddya want?"

I know who the muscle in this place is now. The name Anthony is emblazoned across a patch on his left pec.

"I need to see Kimberly Tadisch. It's an emergency."

Anthony just stares. "What kind of emergency?"

"There are categories? Just let me into see her. Please."

Stiffly, he cracks open the door and peers past me. He's looking to make sure I'm alone. "How'd you get in the courtyard?"

"Portable trampoline. What does it matter? C'mon, help me out pal. Ten minutes then I'm out. I just need to make sure she's okay."

He leads me down several hallways, past rooms shut away behind frosted glass doors. Nightlights burn in more than one room and I imagine kids too tough to admit fear of the dark, using the light to keep at bay the monsters that haunted them. If only they knew the real monsters sported brands on the back of their necks.

At the end of the hallway, he opens a door into a large room. It's sectioned off into sleeping areas, separated by ceiling height cube walls, with curtains covering each opening.

Two cubes have their curtains drawn, at the far end.

"Kim? Hey Kim?" He raps his knuckles against the wall as he walks towards the cube. I don't wait for an answer, ripping open the curtain to find an empty bed. It looked like someone had slept in it.

I round on him. "When did you last see her? Could she be making rounds? Where else would she be right now?"

My questions are rapid fire and apparently quick thinking isn't his strong suit. Ripping phone books in half probably is.

"Uh...she turned in...uh, around eleven. My cube is in the men's area. Other end. I don't...I'm not..."

I yank open the curtain to the other cube, stumble back from the sight, swear.

A black woman lies there. At least once she was black. Now she wears whiteface like a negative of Galen. A wad of cloth plugs her mouth and sprouting from her chest is a wooden cross. She doesn't look like she put up a struggle; they must have stabbed her while she slept and stuffed the cloth in her mouth to prevent sounds as she died.

Blood drips to the floor, a spreading pool growing one drop at a time.

Bile rises in my throat. Anthony gasps and his breath shudders. Half-incoherent words burble from his mouth. My eyes burn. This woman has been killed for no other reason than her color and her location. The Covenant came to call for Kimberly. I force down black thoughts and fears.

"Call the cops," I direct Anthony, voice hoarse with emotion. "I'll check the rest of this place."

Please don't let me find her body crumpled in a corner somewhere.

He gapes at his dead coworker for several moments longer before my words sink in. He backs slowly to a phone hanging on the opposite wall, afraid to turn away. Maybe he fears the dead will rise and come for him.

We all have our nightmares.

Mine stalk me as I move down the hallways, pushing open door after door. Several kids woke as I peered into their room, muttering fuzzy questions I didn't answer.

Five minutes later I return to find Anthony standing in the middle of the room, gaze transfixed on the dead woman. He's looking straight in the mouth of his own mortality, I think. That easily could have been him had he slept in this room with them.

"She's not here," I say. "But there are two empty beds in room 14 that look like they've been used."

He shakes himself, returning to our reality. "What? Fourteen?" He walks over to a desk and picks up a clipboard. "That's not right."

We enter room fourteen and flick on the light to find three kids sitting up, sleepy confusion in their looks. I point to the two empty beds in the corner.

One of them follows my gesture. "That's Brad and Jamie. They were here at bed check." He turns to one of the others. "Right, Rob?"

Rob shrugs, immediately defensive. "I didn't have anything to do with it. Whatever it is. I fell asleep before them but I could hear them whispering. They were just talking stuff."

"Like what stuff?" I interject.

"Stuff. Girls. Sports."

"Any girls in particular? Like Kimberly Tadisch?"

His face colors slightly and that's my answer. I flip a look to Anthony. "When did those two arrive?"

He pages through the clipboard. "Ten days ago, it says here."

"Get their history; the cops will need that." I motion him out of the room and we leave, snapping off the lights and ignoring questions from the boys.

I guide him back towards the staff sleeping room. "Did either of them have any distinguishing marks? Tattoos? Brands?"

"I don't remember, but we catalog all that stuff during intake, in case of gang affiliation."

My thoughts are racing far ahead. "Do me a favor, check the files before the cops arrive. I'm looking for a brand on the back of their head or neck. Hurry."

Anthony walks quickly past the open door, keeping his eyes focused forward. He's purposely avoiding the dead woman's body. I wonder how well they knew each other.

Retracing my steps back outside, I walk the perimeter of the grounds, studying the chain link fence. At the back of the building a service gate hung open. The padlock chain has been severed with a bolt cutter. How the hell did they sneak that in here?

Or was it planted out here for them to find?

Beyond the gate there's nothing but a field choked with new growth, giving way to wooded slopes. It wouldn't be hard to slip into that and disappear.

A camera hangs from one corner of the roof, covering the back entrance area. I recognize the model as a competitor to my store setup. We didn't choose them because they lacked an auto-rotate feature. If they weren't facing in the right direction, they were no help.

Walking around the building, I spot several more.

Anthony meets me in the main hallway as I re-enter, two file folders in his meat hooks. He looks to have regained some color and composure. "Who are you anyway?"

"Your friendly neighborhood vigilante." But the joke falls flat, given my current mood and circumstance.

I take the folders from him and flip through both. Pictures of the two missing boys — from all sides — were interspersed with detail images of all significant marks. Sure enough, the one named Brad wore the brand under his close-shaved skull. Jamie had longer hair, hiding it. Both boys fit the Covenant mold: young, clean looks hiding evil behind the eyes.

In the distance, sirens begin to wail. The cops are minutes away. I look Anthony in the eye. "Jamie and Brad made this happen. If they didn't actually kill your friend, then they helped the ones who did. You have a cut lock on the back gate and a fire door pried open. Where's the rear camera aimed?"

"Basketball courts."

"No good. The angle doesn't cover the back gate. You need better surveillance."

"This isn't a prison."

"Whatever. They took Kimber tonight. You saw what they did already; you think they won't do it again?" I struggle to keep my voice from cracking.

"But why?" Then the light bulb goes off for him. "Shit. It's the murders, isn't it? It's all tied together."

"Tighter than you can imagine."

We turn to watch the flashing lights of police cars as they wind up the entrance road.

CHAPTER TWENTY-EIGHT

Sociopath

The early dawn light causes the front of my house to glow as I pull into the driveway. I had told the detectives everything: my suspicions about the Covenant, my actions in trying to uncover them, my findings thus far. A month ago my words would have fallen on deaf ears, chalked up to Killing being Killing.

Now, they listened intently and asked the right questions. Having a dead body in the next room will do wonders for your credibility.

The detectives promised to keep me in the loop. I told them to bring in Warren.

The Tahoe is no longer parked down the block, probably towed and impounded. Decorative rock is scattered across my yard and driveway. I take a broom and sweep the driveway clean, mind far away.

She was taken because of me. But why?

What did I have that the Covenant could possibly want? What did I know?

It has to be Dee.

They still have him in their crosshairs. Eliminate him in a public way and you create a stir in the minority quarter. Use that strife to pull more soldiers into your cause. Build your army.

Why build an army though?

You need armies to fight a war, but if the Covenant is the one creating the war, what's the point? I'm missing some crucial point and it's that point that will resolve this whole puzzle. I'm getting a headache from all the thoughts spinning wildly around me and I still don't have answers, just worries.

They took Kimber.

The police know everything I know. They know about Kimber. They have manpower and experience in tracking missing persons. I'm just an outsider now, looking in, helpless to control events. I'm impotent.

When I enter the house, Maya turns to me. She's sitting on the couch, eyes reddened and hurt, abandoned. But she says nothing, biting back the anger. Something in my face must have warned her off.

I fall into bed, mind still rumbling. Against my will, sleep takes me.

Several hours later I startle awake, immediately angry with myself. I should have been doing something; what, I don't know, but not sleeping.

A shower scrubs the horror of the night from me, but not the memories. Those may never leave.

When I step out of the bedroom, Maya is standing there, sheaf of papers in her hand. I explode.

"Jesus fucking Christ, Maya. I'm not in the mood to talk about San Fran—"

"It's not about that. These came through your fax while you were in the shower. And your phone kept ringing. What's going on, Rick?"

I take the papers and flip through them. It's the file on Moller, sent by Warren. I guess appearing at two consecutive crime scenes made me a more important man than he thought. But I don't feel any satisfaction over it.

My eyes widen as I skim the contents that fill three pages.

Moller lied about his wife and daughter. Allison was not in her last year of high school. Katrina was not living in their other house.

March 1995. On a fateful Tuesday night, mother and daughter left the movie theater after a show in the downtown part of Detroit. They got hassled by a group of black youths. Katrina, apparently quite the spitfire, gave as good as she got and refused to back down. One thing led to another.

The mutilated bodies of both women turned up several days later, raped and tortured. Police rounded up five boys, each of which confessed to a role in the tragedy.

None of them made it to trial.

All five bodies were found weeks later, hanging from trees, identifiable only through dental records. Coroner reports confirmed that each victim had been kept alive and repeatedly tortured over the course of many days. Authorities never made any arrests in connection to this crime. There's no notation of why the record is flagged.

"Rick," Maya repeats. "What is going on? Does this have something to do with Geoff?"

"Geoffrey," I mutter, stunned but continuing to read. "And no, this is just something I stumbled across."

Jesus. His wife and daughter.

How could anyone hold it together after something like that? It's an event that triggers a complete change in a person. Some would go into a shell and never come out. Some would take up a cause and march with the name of victims splashed across their banner.

Some might become white supremacists.

Could he?

The motivation was there, but the more I think about it, the less likely it seems. He runs a company that preaches diversity. He took on the task of transforming Dee into the activist that could speak to the black community of North Haven. He's never shown any sign of animosity towards Dee or anyone else.

No one can be all that and still plan systematic murders of others. No one is that sociopathic.

Nathan, on the other hand...

He had the same motivation but his crucible was forged at a critically different stage, in his late teens. It could have left a much deeper scar.

Plus, the guy is really weird.

But does that make him a killer?

I replay all our interactions through my head and the more I recall, the more things start to click into place. He may not be the top dog, but I can picture him being a high lieutenant in the army. I can envision a name tag with the title of Grand Dragon spelled out.

A feeling of dread steals up my spine.

That's how the Covenant knew my address so quickly. One of the killers lives right down the street. He'd used his father's tutorship of Dee to create an opportunity to escalate a race war. He's been the one feeding information back to his leaders. No wonder it felt like they were watching me closely, all they had to do was ask him to look out the window.

Christ, it fit so perfectly. Why didn't I see it earlier?

He's been playing his father and me like a fiddle, hiding it from his brother. Now that's sociopathic.

Maya interrupts my thoughts. "Then what exactly is going on? I called your parents. Cops are sitting outside their house but nothing has happened. Rick, there is blood all over my basement. Why is it there?"

"Because you never put away the weights when you're done."

"This isn't the time for your lip."

"You're right. Sorry. I've gotten caught up in something and people are sending messages."

"How did you get caught up?"

"Like I do every other time. I just don't know when to quit, I guess. Look, you need to get yourself out of here. Go someplace where no one will look for you. Get a hotel room and keep your head down. They came for me once, they could again and I don't want you left here alone."

"Alone? Why would I be alone? Where are you going?"

I turn away. "'I'm already gone, Maya. I think I have been for a long time. It's a place I have to go solo and I won't be coming back, not to here anyway."

"What? That makes no sense. Are you using metaphors again?"

I don't answer as I slam the front door closed, knowing what I have to do.

I'm going to kill someone.

CHAPTER TWENTY-NINE

Clubhouse

I storm down the driveway, eyes fixed on Moller's house. If Nathan's in there, I'll beat him senseless until he talks. Then I'll keep going until I feel better.

The flag to my mailbox is standing straight up. I hadn't placed anything in there, and Maya would never stoop to snail mail. I'm not even sure she knows we have one.

I yank open the door to find a single index card lying inside.

Back off. Wait for our word. She depends on you.

The letters are blocky, like the font from architecture plans, revealing no personality. I read much into it, though. Hate, an agenda, a finality to their plans. Whatever the Covenant has planned, they need me for some part of it. I don't know what and didn't plan to find out.

I debate on calling Warren. He had to have been informed by now. Maybe this card will help him, fingerprints or something. Then I realize I've already polluted it with my own, and my hands are sweaty.

Plus, I want Nathan first. I want to watch his face as I cave it in. Nobody hurts someone close to me and gets away with it.

I walk up their driveway, casual in case any of the neighbors are paying attention. Bypassing the front door, I stroll to the back of the house. No cars are visible, in or out of the garage.

No Tyr either. Good. That thing scares the shit out of me.

All the doors are locked, but some of the curtains are still open. It's clear no one is home. I guess it makes sense. It's a Monday; most normal folk are at work, like I should be.

So, no Nathan here. Guess I have to do it the hard way.

I'd given the detectives the location of Colonial Estates and the other complex, but there were several others I failed to tell them, mostly because I couldn't remember the names or addresses.

I'll start with those places.

I drive the Cobra downtown and swap it out with my motorcycle. I need to be agile and quick for the recon activities, just like Jack B. Nimble. The bike is still in the alley where I left it yesterday, although it seems like days ago.

The early afternoon sun casts slim shadows as I pull out my cell phone and dial. Dee answers on the fourth ring.

"This better be good, dawg." His voice sounds a little slurry.

"They took Kimber, Dee. Last night."

This sharpened him right up. "What? Who is they? How...?"

So I gave him the condensed version of what I knew. The small part of me that wants to say 'I told you so' remains quiet and easy to ignore. More important things were at stake now and I can feel the enormous weight of a clock counting down to something I could not predict.

Afterwards he still sounds a bit skeptical. "You're serious about all this? White people murdering their own just to start a war? And somehow they're now after you?"

"I know, it sounds out there, but trust me, it is happening. You're in this too, Dee. You're a target, whether you believe it or not. Take you out in front of an audience and the hornet's nest gets stirred up just that much more. Think about it, it makes perfect sense."

"No, it makes crazy sense. I'm just a ball player."

"You *were* a ball player, now you're something more. A beacon, a symbol, an anchor for those people who are confused and angry and wondering what in the world is going on. You are that voice in the storm they need to hear."

"You make it sound bigger than it is. I didn't even write that speech."

"Accept it, pal. Are you home now?"

"Yeah, night game tonight and doubleheader tomorrow."

"Keep your head down. People are gunning for you, don't give them an easy target."

He mumbles a few words I can't make out, but I know he's coming around. He won't say it for a few days – and even then he'll make it sound like his idea – but deep down he understands what I'm saying and what's at stake.

"When did you last see Moller?" I ask, getting to the meat of my call.

"Uh, Friday maybe?"

"Was Nathan with him then?"

"No. Just Geoffrey and Lance. I guess Nathan was off doing something else."

Damn right he was.

"Did Moller get you those bodyguards?"

"Yeah, mostly brothers but a few white guys too. Got two of them with me now."

"Perfect. Keep them close. I got to run."

"Where to?"

"To find Kimber and kill Nathan."

I pressed End before he could ask more and fired up my bike.

Pointing it in the general direction of my first destination, I twist the throttle in desperation and try to ignore the tick-tock in my head.

Hang on, Kimber. Hang on.

The first stop is only twenty minutes away. Like the others I've seen, it's tucked back from the road and has a community clubhouse. I don't have the time to go apartment by apartment, but since the Covenant likes to gather as a group, the clubhouse is a good place to start. I don't know exactly what I'm looking for, but I'll know it when I see it.

At least, that's my plan.

The door is locked, so I punch out a pane of glass right next to the doorknob, gashing my knuckles in the process. I search the room but there's not much here. I'm not sure what I thought I'd find. Maybe Kimberly tied to the Ping-Pong table in the middle of the room with a thug standing guard over her, pool cue for a weapon, just like a bad movie.

Instead I spend fifteen minutes making a general mess of the place. I break chairs, tear up the felt on the pool table, pull light fixtures out of the wall and piss in the fridge.

Let's see them get their deposit back after this.

As I'm exiting, my blood is boiling out of frustration. A young guy is trotting across the courtyard towards me. His expression is sour and pissed off. Well so am I.

"Hey, what the hell is going on in there? I heard something." His tone comes off like he expects me to answer.

I don't. I let him get close.

Then I punch him in the face as hard as I can. Right in the kisser. It hurts like hell, but feels better than I thought.

He drops to the ground, hands over his mouth. Blood leaks between the fingers and I see what looks like a tooth lying next to him.

I check the back of his skull just for good measure and find the brand. I'm seeing this thing everywhere, especially in my nightmares.

My work here is done.

Next.

CHAPTER THIRTY

Unmasked

I hit two more complexes, all based on my notes taken from the advertising rag and the Covenant magazine. The first one doesn't appear to be anything more than a regular housing area with a few Covenant members embedded inside.

I root around it but don't make the same general mess. There's nothing in it for clues and I didn't have to punch anyone.

The second one is different though.

Like Colonial Estates, it's a closed complex made up of Covenant members. I can see the Odinism flag through several windows and the central clubhouse has a large version hanging inside behind the bar.

This one is also nicer. It has a pool and carpet on the floor. Despite the gorgeous heat of mid-afternoon, no one is lounging around the pool deck. Maybe these white dips are afraid to get too tanned.

I spy a couple of girls walking between buildings across the parking lot and stay hidden. They appear at first like any other pair of girls in their twenties, but I've made a living watching people for those subtle signals.

And now my instincts are setting off little alarms.

There's something furtive in the way they move, the way their heads keep darting around. I watch them traverse the length of the parking lot, get into a car and leave. If they were in my store, I'd zero in on them as potential targets. Body language is body language and I think they know something is going down.

That focuses my intensity.

The clubhouse is empty but next to the pool sits a squat gray building. I assume it's a locker room and changing area. The door is open so I don't have to sacrifice any more knuckles.

The place has been made over to another lounge area, with some old futon couches against the wall, coffee tables and magazine rack. The mags are five year old *Sports Illustrated*, *People* and one *Cosmopolitan*.

Clothing is strewn across the floor and the first impression is the aftermath of a rocking party last night, minus the beer cans and random sleeping person no one wanted to take home.

But as I look closer, those alarms grow louder.

Several pieces are ripped. A sock lay forgotten. A white t-shirt peeks out from under one of the futons. The inside of the sleeve has three letters written on the hem: KKT.

As in Kimberly Katherine Tadisch.

She's done that as long I've known her. Short sleeve shirts get initials on the inside seam of the left sleeve, long sleeve shirts get them on the left cuff. She once wanted to do it to my underwear, which set off a rollicking love session.

Kimber was here, they brought her here.

My breath starts coming faster as I roll through scenarios in my head. She'd fought back. Got her shirt ripped and torn off. They either forgot it or didn't think it mattered. No one bothered to clean up afterwards and that speaks to the arrogance of their actions.

This is all the evidence I need; now I just have to do something with it.

I tear through the rest of the room, but there is nothing more. How long were they here? Where did they go after this?

Standing outside the shack, I stare at the apartment windows. They stare back, a showdown. She could be in any one of those right now, but how can I go through each one? That would take forever and give them time to escape. If she's here, the place needs to be locked down.

Cutting around behind the building, I come across a lone parking lot, small and forgotten, like they added it on long after all the structures were in place.

Just as alone and forgotten sat the black Tahoe, broken back window winking at me sarcastically.

My mind stuttered.

It hadn't been impounded after all. They must have retrieved it, dropping off a love note to me in the process. Maybe Nathan had driven it away, right under the noses of the cops at my house.

That's ballsy. And frightening.

Then again, these are kids who kill in drastic ways. I can't measure them by any normal scale.

I spring across the lot and yank open the passenger door. There is no plan in my mind if the vehicle is occupied, just pure reaction and response.

It's empty. I crawl through the interior, looking for further evidence, sweating in the stifling heat of a dark truck left under the sun. There's some dark crusty stuff smeared on one window and I'm afraid it's blood. That makes me stop and clamber out. I sink to the ground, shuddering breaths causing my chest to shake. My fear for Kimberly is paralyzing me. I can't get the terrible images out of my mind, all sorts of worst case scenarios creating the paralysis.

I'm in over my head. Time for the pros. I need help.

With shaking fingers I fumble my cell phone out and flip it open. The 'No Signal' light flashes back, mocking me and my emergency.

Mumbling swear words, I start moving in ever-widening circles, eyes glued to the screen. Finally, as I pass under the shadow of a building, the light flashes green and I punch in the number.

"Warren."

"Warren, it's Rick Killing. I need help." I stand motionless, afraid to move lest my phone drop the signal.

"Killing, what the hell? I've been looking for you all morning. What is going on? You've been involved in two scenes that suddenly have made you very important to me."

"I'm out in the boonies. I found something you guys need to check out. It's the truck. The black one. It's here. Here. The window's broken. Come out."

"Slow down, dammit. You sound like you're hyperventilating. What are you doing right now?"

I take a deep breath and hold it for a long count. "I've been checking out places where I know the Covenant group hides. They are the ones who took Kimber. I'm at a place out in Marengo and found evidence that she was here. I also found the truck that tried to shoot Dee...Damonti Davis yesterday."

"A truck tried to shoot your friend?"

Why does everyone pick the wrong time to play the funny guy?

"Warren, listen to me. Kimberly Tadisch was out here. I found a piece of ripped clothing that belongs to her. You need to get someone out. Dust it for prints, check out some dried fluid, that kind of stuff."

"How about you leave the cop business to me and I won't tell you how to play football. That sound fair?"

"I'm just trying to help. She's in danger."

That's all fine and dandy, but you might be making things worse. This truck, you go into it?"

"Yeah."

"Did you wear gloves?"

"No."

"Leave everything just as you found it?"

"No."

"Retrace your steps out of the truck so we can rule out your set?"

"No."

"You see the point I'm trying to make here? You've just made our jobs a lot harder. Everything we collect now will be contaminated with your evidence."

"Warren, I get it. Can you just send someone out? Based on what's happened in the last twenty four hours, don't you think I've earned some credibility?" I snap a glance at my watch. "She's been gone already at least ten hours. Maybe more."

"No, you *think* she's been gone. So far we have no evidence showing that."

"And I am fucking telling you that I have the evidence in my goddamn hand! How many more bodies do you need?"

"This isn't a novel, Killing, it is real life. My work is all about concrete pieces of the story, not hunches. You say you have clothing that belonged to her. How do you know?"

I rub my thumb over her initials, as if I could actually feel them. "Because I know. Trust me, it's hers."

My tone must betray some emotion because Warren doesn't answer right away. "Killing. Look, it isn't my business what you're doing with your life, but don't you have a wife? After what happened at your place last night, don't you think she could use you right now? Shouldn't she be your priority?"

"Here's the bottom line, Detective. Kimberly is an ex-girlfriend and still very much a friend. I've known her forever, so when I see a torn sleeve from a t-shirt belonging to her, I damn well know it. Now, are you going to send someone out, or do I have to tear this place apart myself?"

"All right, all right. Calm down. Let's backtrack and get some details. Marengo is a small force, only one detective but also a K-9 unit."

I reiterate my findings on the Covenant, this time roping in Nathan's connection. Even though he doesn't say anything, I can sense the concern in his voice. He's not blind. Any fool can look around and see the brewing blood fire. If it isn't stopped, it will consume all of North Haven and surrounding areas.

He agrees to phone it into Marengo but makes no other promises past that. It isn't what I want to hear, but better than nothing. I hang up the phone.

So that leaves me with what, exactly?

Do I stand around and wait? Start going through each building in case I can find something? I stand there at the corner of the building, undecided. There's still one more complex I have on my list. She could be there, but I don't want to leave this one because I know she's been here. Bird in hand versus two in the bush and that sort of thing.

Maybe I can set up outside the entrance to flag down any cops and watch for anyone leaving. That seems like a more responsible plan than blindly bumbling around and making a further mess of the scene. It's probably what I should have done in the first place.

Mind made up, I turn and walk around the corner, headed for my bike.

And run smack dab into Lance Moller.

He smiles, a broad innocent expression. "Hi, Rick."

Then he jabs a stun gun into my gut and pulls the trigger.

CHAPTER THIRTY-ONE

Revelations

Tasers are generally used in one of two ways. The first is to fire a set of barbs into the opponent and trigger 50,000 volts along the wires connected to those barbs. It's enough to knock anyone down. Sometimes it even makes them pee their pants.

The other way is called drive stun. This is where the Taser is placed against the victim's skin and triggered. It's a close quarters tactic, great for if you happened to be locked in a closet together.

Fortunately for me – if that term can be used in this situation – Lance chose the latter method.

I'd been shocked once already, possess the reflexes of a professional athlete, and was completely startled by his appearance. This provides my opportunity.

I leap back, slapping his hand away in the motion. My stomach tingles where the Taser tips had made brief contact.

The stun gun goes flying, landing in the grass ten yards away. "Lance! What the hell!" Connections start firing in my brain. Oh, no...

Backing up further, I open space between us. He comes after me, feral look across his face. Two months ago I would have called the expression wild glee.

"You're a part of this? You and Nathan? Why? How could you...?"

"Lots of questions, one answer."

I remembered the night in his father's basement, drinking up a storm. The glittering look in his eyes wasn't alcohol, it was utter madness. How could I have missed it?

Lance stalks after me, hands curled into fists. "You're so stupid, Killing. Stupid. Do you even know what the hell is going on?"

"Know? Know what? That you're involved in the murders?"

Lance lets loose a short bark of a laugh. I can see the personality of the person I thought he was; it just doesn't come through in the same light any more. He half turns his head to the buildings behind him and yells without taking his eyes off me. "He doesn't even know, you guys!"

Movement registers behind some of the windows, several opening. Faces appear, staring down at me, silent and spooky. "You have no idea how funny this has all been. You ran your ass ragged all morning and are still no closer than you were. The message was sent. 'Back off. She depends on you.' How hard is that to understand? Even for an idiot like you."

"You have Kimber? If you've hurt her at all, I will end you."

"Oooh, listen to the tough guy. You have no idea where she's at, no idea what I'm going to do to her. And it's going to be fun. She's a spitfire, no wonder she's got you by the balls."

"Fuck you."

"But those were my friends last night. You smashed up Alex so bad, he might never be the same. I have to make sure you pay for it."

With that, he leaps at me, fingers in claws.

I stumble back, mentally and physically off balance. Half-formed words dribble from my mouth as my heel catches something and I fall backwards.

In an instant Lance is on top of me, fingers going for my throat. Spittle flies from his mouth as he yells a string of swear words. Stars dance in my head as he connects a glancing blow off my temple and I panic.

Heaving him off me, I scramble to my feet. Other kids were streaming out of the buildings now, running towards us. I can't let them surround me. I know exactly where I'd end up.

As Lance rolls over, I catch him under the jaw with the point of my shoe. He flops over with a groan. I want nothing more than to kick his head until it caves in. He has Kimber. I'll kill him.

A guy with tattoos up and down his left arm is the first to reach me, slowing slightly and launching a poorly balanced swing. I may not be a fighter, but even I'm better than that.

I duck under the clumsy attempt and give him a shove, propelling him in his original direction of travel. He spills ass over teakettle onto Lance. Both grunt and swear.

Then I kick in my own engine. I have to get out of here. It's the only way I can save her.

Veering off at a sharp angle from the approaching crowd of Covenant members, I avoid two guys blocking my way. Suddenly the juke move I'd perfected as a college receiver became the most important move I made all day. If anyone slows me up in the slightest, eight – make that nine – more Covenant members would be on me.

I sprint across the open yard, making my way towards the entrance. Yells follow in my wake, alerting anyone else around the area that something is going down. More faces appear in the windows and doors.

Time is my enemy.

I spot my motorcycle at the far end of the lot, glimpsed between two buildings. The clubhouse and pool structures stand between me and it.

Two guys and a girl round the corners of the clubhouse, moving to intercept. I didn't worry about any of them being able to stop me on their own, but they don't need to. They only need to slow me and allow the rest to catch up. Football defenses work on the same principle. It's a serious danger.

I vault on top of the AC unit outside the clubhouse, using that momentum to catch the lip of the roof. The shortest distance between any two points is a straight line. Mine runs through this building. Or over it, as the case may be.

Pulling myself up, I run up one side of the roof and down the other. Voices raise the alarm, telling others my movement, but they are lost in all the other yelling.

I drop from the roof into a mulch bed, behind a young girl, sore ankle protesting. She jumps and lets out a high scream, startled by my appearance. I knock her over.

Another guy nearby spins and lunges for me. I twist to escape, feeling the pull on my jeans, but he can't hang on. I tear free and the path to my bike is wide open now.

The SuperHawk fires up and I rip out of the parking lot, accelerating through the gears faster than I ever have. The sound of car engines tells me the chase isn't over, it's just moved to machines.

Lance and Nathan Moller. Damn damn damn.

There's no doubt in my mind that Nathan is with her right now. One sent to capture me, the other to babysit her. That's what brothers do, right?

I can outrace any car on my bike, but I'm also more vulnerable. All they need to do is tap my rear end and that could send me spinning off into a ditch somewhere. The lead car is several blocks back but holding firm. I have to make sure no one gets close enough to knock me off. The winding two lane country roads between Marengo and North Haven play to my favor. I can fly down them maintaining speed while the cars have to slow slightly.

Within five minutes there are no longer cars in my mirror. But I keep the throttle pegged, even though tears are streaming from my eyes and making everything blurry. My sunglasses are lying somewhere back at the complex. I lean forward, trying to get behind the windscreen.

Does Geoffrey know?

I'm not sure. How can he not know what his sons are up to? But that thought is offset by his actions and words. He never came off like a man hiding a secret.

I have to assume he knows. Maybe he's even the master mind behind it all.

And that's a thought that staggers me. Every interaction we've had plays through my mind as I race towards North Haven. Have they been plotting this all along? Or am I just a sudden loose end that needs to be severed? My thoughts are an incoherent jumble as I try to grasp the implications of the Mollers and the Covenant.

I reach for my back pocket, only to find it flapping in the wind, cell phone gone. I thought of the kid that grabbed me.

Shit.

At the first gas station, I find a pay phone and throw some coins in the slot; punch in Warren's number.

"Hello, you have reached the desk of Detective George Warren. I am either on my phone or away from my desk..."

Double shit.

I leave a hurried voicemail, which probably sounded nuts, implicating the Mollers. A plan forms in my head as I talk but I don't leave those details.

Then I speed off for cultured lawns of Windermere Fields.

Coming for you, Geoff.

CHAPTER THIRTY-TWO

Sardis

My house is locked up, forcing me to enter through the garage. I never carry house keys. Maya's Jeep is gone. I find a note from her though, on the kitchen counter.

You selfish bastard. I hate you. Clean up the blood yourself.

Well, I guess she left safely then. One less thing for me to worry about.

I rummage through my closet until I find one of my sports bags and pull out a baseball bat. It's a DeMarini Voodoo. The double-wall technology should make a nice sound when I bang it off Nathan's head. Their warranty provides me a replacement for a dented bat, but I don't know if I still have the receipt.

Oh well.

The Jaguar is now parked in Moller's driveway. I stride down the block, bat firmly in hand, murder in my eyes. Next door to his house, a lady is on her front porch and she looks at me strangely. I'm just paranoid enough that I think everyone is in on this plot.

"Call anyone and you're next," I say, pointing with the bat. I don't know her last name, or her first.

I don't bother knocking. I shove open Moller's front door. Thankfully it's unlocked, so I don't have to kick it down. It's a pretty solid looking door.

The sounds of a TV come from downstairs so I head there immediately.

Geoffrey is sitting calmly at the table, phone to ear. His pet rhino Tyr lies on the floor next to him, watching me. As I step off the last stair, Moller looks at me with no expression of surprise and nods towards the chair opposite of him. I don't sit.

"Yes, yes," he says into the mouthpiece. "No, he's here now. I will handle it."

The TV in the corner is set to a local station. A Breaking News logo hangs in the corner as the camera pans across the face of Kimber's group home. Yellow crime scene tape crisscrosses the front door; investigators and other official personnel can be seen milling around and doing their respective jobs.

He hangs up the phone. "Hello, Rick."

I start towards him, bat lifted high. "Tell me where she is."

Tyr scrambles up from his resting spot behind the table, growling. That halts my progress. The table only comes to his shoulder. Christ, this creature is ridiculous.

"There is no need for this. She is fine," Moller says, and motions again for me to take a seat across from him. "We should speak."

This time I do sit. "You know. You know everything, don't you?"

He leans back, thoughtful look on his face, tapping a pen against the table surface. "It's important that a father know his sons; that he understands what they can and cannot do. I am no different than any other parent in that regard. My sons are different, from each other, from all others. I have tried my best to mold, to shape their thoughts and raise them in a way that honors us all. As with many parental intentions, there have been successes and failures along the way. For the most part, they make me proud. So, to answer your inquiry: Yes, I know everything."

"If he's hurt her, I'll kill –"

"Rick, you will cease this display of movie hero antics. It is 1999. We have evolved past those notions. The new millennium will bring about massive change and it all starts here."

I hear a faint noise from the second floor, but my eyes are fixed on him. "You're as nuts as your kids." My knuckles tighten on the DeMarini.

"You pose an interesting dichotomy, Rick. Do you realize that? By apprehending a couple of young people with a brand you'd never seen on their necks, you went down an investigatory path with the most tenuous of connections. There were some extraordinary leaps of logic required there. You are either utterly paranoid or deceivingly intelligent. I must admit, I thought you were little more than a smart aleck, hotshot athlete who never really had to think for himself because others did it for you. In that vein, I was mistaken, so please accept my apologies."

"You're kidding right? I'm about to smash your head into pulp and you want to apologize for reading me wrong? Seriously?"

Moller makes a soft snapping sound and Tyr pads closer to me, rumbling deep in his throat. The thing is only two feet away. Some laws of nature had been violated in the creation of it, I'm positive.

"You will do nothing of the kind. There's still a role for you to play, but it is not that of the hero."

He holds up a hand to forestall any reply and leans back in his chair. "In ancient times there existed a city named Sardis. Do you know of it?"

"Geoff, I am serious. I'll kill—"

"Geoffrey. *Geoffrey!* How many times now?" It's the first outburst of emotion I've ever seen from him. There's hope.

He takes a deep breath and composes himself. "Sardis suffered greatly at the hands of invaders. The Cimmerians in 700 BC; Persians in 600 BC and Athenians less than a hundred years after that. One could say conquest became the city's legacy. As you can imagine, thousands were raped, beaten and slaughtered during each one of these invasions. Many children were orphaned beginning with the first conquest. So many in fact, it presented an enormous problem for the remaining elders. Lineages from the higher houses were lost. Children of royal blood ratted through the streets alongside bastards and slave-born, creating a political nightmare. The lines of ascension were sundered, placing the future of Sardis in jeopardy even before the Cimmerians moved on. The entire city hovered at the brink of chaos, as families jockeyed for position to rule the future. Yet, no one had clear claim."

I shift slightly in my seat, watching to see how Tyr reacted. The hell hound's eyes are pinned to me, probably thinking of his next meal. Another thump comes from upstairs, louder now.

"To avert this crisis, the city leaders decreed that all newborns be branded with the mark of their house. The brand was placed at the base of their neck. It was a most effective campaign and became such a success that brands evolved into a fashionable accessory. Within a decade, many children bore some kind of mark, whether high born or low."

He stands and stretches, beginning to pace. I notice he keeps the table between us though. "Understand this: a brand, while disfiguring, provides a clear message. It is a lifelong commitment. One cannot simply excise a brand when he tires of it, unlike a simple tattoo. A brand is permanent, a brand is identifying. And one of the biggest problems with America is that we are no longer identifiable. We have become a stew of all kinds."

"So that's what you're doing? Trying to re-create something from a long dead city that kept getting attacked over and over? That's a lousy plan."

Geoffrey smiles. "Sardis is a tale of redemption, of surviving crushing odds. From the blood of conquest it arose to become the source of gold currency. From Sardis emerged gold coin purity that had never been seen before. It became a major trade center, all on the backs of branded children."

He places both hands on the table, leaning towards me. "From the devastation of the old millennium, we will forge a new identity. We will eliminate the impurities in our own gold and restore our standing as a world power. This year ends many things, none the least of which is the erosion of our pride and our power."

"You mean like white power, right?"

And with that I fling the bat over Tyr's head. "Fetch!"

The dog is well trained, but it's still a dog. Tyr flinches and spins to follow the bat before his training takes over. But that gives me all the time I need.

Leaping from my chair, I vault up the stairs three at a time and slam the door shut. Tyr collides with it, growling and barking and clawing at the wood.

That was close.

CHAPTER THIRTY-THREE

Lance

I lean against the door for a heartbeat, feeling the wood tremble from Tyr's assaults.

Grabbing one of the counter stools from the kitchen island, I jam it under the doorknob. It always works in movies, so why not here?

The first floor is empty and I can hear faint thumping sounds from above. The second floor is arranged in a square, with an open rail. A central loft is ringed by closed doors all around. The third door is locked. Remembering the cop movies I've seen, I back up, lower my shoulder and charge. It's a six-panel oak door, but I'm a whole lot of pissed off. The door doesn't stand a chance.

Wood splinters spin through the air as the jamb shatters and I fall into the room.

Kimber is on the bed, spread eagle, tied at ankle and wrist to the four corner posts. She's wearing only a set of silk boxers and it confirms that the two boys took her while she slept. She's worn a t-shirt and boxers to bed as long as I've known her. I already know where the shirt ended up.

A white hood covers her head, emblazoned with the Odinist symbol in stark, obscene red.

At my entrance she bucks against her restraints, causing one of the posts to bang the wall. That was the sound I heard.

I run to the bed and rip off the hood.

Kimber's eyes fix on me, red and filled with tears. A wad of cloth is stuffed in her mouth, expanded from saliva. I pry it out and untie her wrists.

"Are you hurt?" I ask, pulling her close.

"No, I'm pissed off. Some prick touched me. What the hell is going on? How did you know where I was?"

"It's a long story and when you hear it all, you're going to be more pissed off."

"Oh, Jesus. This is you? I'm strapped to a bed half naked because of you?"

Many replies come to my head right then, but most aren't the right time, right place.

"Here," I say, yanking off my own t-shirt. "No charge."

"Not even close to square, Killing." She pulls it on and I go to work on the rope binding her ankles. "They sprayed something over my nose and mouth; I can barely remember anything. Everything is fuzzy. What was it? Chloroform? I thought that was just a movie thing."

"Not chloroform. That's a myth. More likely you got a fentanyl derivative," I reply, working at the knots. Who was the Boy Scout that tied these, for Christ's sake?

"You know something like that and yet you have never finished reading a book in your life? That's rich."

Is she really busting my balls right now? Really?

Kimber rubs her head. "It gives a headache, whatever it was. What happened to Lora?"

"Who?"

"Lora. My partner at work. She was in the cube next to mine. I thought I heard some noise as I went down."

I don't answer right away and concentrate on the rope. Finally: "She's dead, Kimber. They killed her."

She sips her breath and I pull her head to mine, whispering 'sorry' in her ear. The clock ticks away in the back of my mind. We have to get out of here.

"Why, Rick? She didn't do anything." Her voice cracks as she struggles to hold back a sob.

"Because she was black. Because she slept in the space next to you. Because they wanted to. These people are insane." I go back to the knot. Her left foot is free, but the right one is stubborn.

And we are in significant danger.

The frustration and desperation are not helping. My fingers keep slipping and there's a lot of wasted motion. I can't focus. It's only been a minute but feels like forever. Kimber is quiet, eyes closed, mourning the loss of her friend.

"Where are we?" She whispers. "This looks like a nice place."

"You wouldn't believe me if I told you."

Finally the knot works free and I yank the rope away from her ankle. "Come on, we need to go now."

I help her stand, but she's unsteady on her feet. Her balance is off from whatever drug they used. She places both hands against my chest. "Just a second. I'm dizzy."

"Kimber, we have—"

"Rick! I said one second." Her eyes flash up mine, full of fire. But then they widen and focus on something past me. "Oh! Watch ou—"

I feel the familiar prick of Taser barbs, followed by a jolt and blackness.

Not again.

Warm hands rub my forehead, over and over, the touch light. I don't need to open my eyes to see who is doing it. These fingers I know.

My head rests in Kimber's lap. Cold concrete is beneath my back, which feels oddly good. Keeping my eyes closed, I tilt my head towards her belly and whisper: "Where are we?"

"Garage, I guess," she whispers back.

"Anyone else here?"

"Yeah, stud. Me," Lance calls from somewhere off to my left. I sigh and open my eyes. It was worth a shot.

Sure enough, we're in a garage; Moller's it seems. How surreal is that? One block away is my own welcoming abode, yet here I am, trying to clear the fuzz from my head.

"I'm getting pretty sick and tired of being Tased," I announce, not caring whether I get a response. Now my back hurts even more. Knife wound, stun gun darts, betrayal by neighbors who really did seem cool at first. All that makes me crabby.

The four-car space is empty of the usual implements. No lawnmower, no rolling toolbox, no rakes, hoes or shovels. The only tool I see is called a Lance.

All the overhead doors are shut, but sunlight streams in through the windows at the top of each door. It looks like late afternoon still, around supper time. We've got maybe two more hours of sun.

We're in the first stall, closest to the door leading inside the house. I wonder where Geoffrey is.

Lance is sitting in a folding chair a few feet away, leaning over and staring at us with his stupid grin. I'm beginning to think he's not insane, just missing a significant number of brain cells. Next to him is a camera mounted on a tripod. That can't be good.

"It sure took you long enough to wake up. I didn't even give you a full shot. What a puss."

"You're right, I bet you wake up sooner than me. Let's test it."

He shakes his head, bright wide eyes never leaving my face. He looks so happy that I'm spooked from looking at him. I can feel the tension in

Kimber's body. She's wisely biting her tongue, smart not to antagonize him.

"You think you're so funny, so smug. I can't wait to slice that smirk right off your face. Then I'm going to take that little piece of ass behind you for a test drive. Your wife has too much taint in her so she's safe, but your mom...that woman still has it going on. She probably could use a real man for once."

I, on the other hand, am not so smart. "You plan on bringing one along?"

Lance and his father are two different kinds of crazy. One, cool and calm, planning murders with the same kind of reserve meant for corporate strategy meetings. The other, happy go lucky and completely unhinged inside. Where on that spectrum does Nathan fall? The stereotype killer full of hate, daddy issues and repressed memories?

I hope we don't have to find out.

Time to see if I can exploit his cracks. "Why don't you try to take me man up, instead of hiding behind a stun gun? I'll bet my entire salary you can't. I'm bigger, stronger, faster and a whole hell of a lot smarter."

He smiles with those creepy eyes. "I've seen your pay checks. Pass."

Ouch. I hate it when assholes are right. I try a different tack.

"Are you the one who trashed her house?" I nod over my shoulder to Kimber.

"No, I took a little trip up to see your mommy. Did you know I could have killed her that night? I stood over her bed, listening to your dad snore, watching her. She sleeps like one of those Disney princesses, both hands tucked under her cheek. So beautiful and elegant. I was tempted just to tear that shit up. It would have been glorious. I could have been her frog."

Kimber's body trembles and I can tell she's close to losing it. This is her first exposure to Lance; it has to be overwhelming. At least I'd drank with him once before, not that it makes it any better for me.

"She'd have broken you in half."

The door leading from the house interrupts our witty repartee as Geoffrey pushes it open and steps into the garage. He's changed into Gabardine slacks and a pressed white shirt, just like any other white supremacist dressing for a long day of plotting murder.

He pauses and stares at us, eyes sparkling with mad clarity, tapping a cell phone against his chin. He gives a quick glance at his watch.

"I suppose I have no one to blame but myself for all this," he starts, giving a vague wave that I took to mean our current predicament. "You've always had a role to play, Rick, I just never thought you'd be able to piece anything together. Your calls to Detective Warren have created a bit of a situation that we must adjust for. I can adapt, but I dislike it."

"What are you talking about? What role?"

Keep him talking, Rick, keep him talking.

"Hero or martyr. I could have used you in either manner. It's apparent, though, that you have chosen the route of martyr."

He looks out the garage windows, gaze faraway. "You had so much potential. It will bother me to kill you."

CHAPTER THIRTY-FOUR

Nathan

Geoffrey steeples his fingers and rubs the point against his forehead, like he's got a headache.

"Understand that a movement of this magnitude takes extreme foresight, incredible amounts of planning and even more patience. A substantial amount of funding is also required. It took me quite a while to find you, or should I say someone who fulfilled the role the way you could. I moved to this ridiculously large house to have casual access. I walked down the street that day on purpose. I purchased that old Corvette – a beastly machine, by the way – in order to draw you closer."

"How did you know?"

He smiles. "You really must reprimand your employees when they don't lock doors. Your adolescent car fixation is on full display in your office. Unfortunately, it cost a small fortune to buy something remotely close to your dream car. This was a point where I wished I knew more about cars. A financial lesson, I suppose."

Damn. I don't even know what to say.

Moller reads my look. "My actions for the past year have been carefully calculated and performed, a one-man show."

"Why?" Kimber interjects. "What does all this get you?"

I know.

"Dee. That's what he gets. Someone he can get close to, place before cameras, and murder in public."

"Partly right, Rick. Partly right."

Kimber must have a confused look, for Moller continues, never taking his eyes off me.

"I want to change things, Miss Tadisch. To right this ship called America by putting everything, and everyone, back in their correct places. Our country has become filled with subversives, all working on their own goals to collectively erode the common interest. To make us robust again, the strong must rise up and take control. I liken it to the founding fathers rising up against England. Many feared rebelling against the Queen, but we turned out all right afterwards, I dare say."

Moller rocks back and forth on his heels, hands clasped behind his back. A professor deep in lecture.

"The world is a much more complicated place in 1999 as compared to 1776. Too many of our rules are created to accommodate minorities, for those screaming equality when what they really mean is increased power. The pie is only so large and if one group grows their slice, then another group loses. None of this is my own unique viewpoint, mind. Nor is it a new perspective; there are plenty of groups who share the same opinion. Some are infamous, others unknown. I could have joined the Klan or Christian Knights, but they are worse than Congress. You've never seen so much squabbling. I might as well have joined a book review club. No, I required more immediate results."

"Like a race war," I say. Slowly, I shift my center of balance, preparing myself for sudden movement.

Behind Geoffrey, Lance fidgets with the Taser, probably trying to extract more voltage from it. I'm going to beat him senseless with it, then Tase him right in the balls.

"Well, nothing galvanizes individuals into action like a threat to their way of life. Think about it. The times of greatest prosperity in this country have revolved around wars. This current boom lacks that. I needed to create an enemy around which we could rally. Only I don't seek to have us united as a population, I want us divided."

"You are stark raving nuts." I stand up, slow and purposeful, hands away from my sides. Lance instantly comes alert. "You killed your own."

"That, I will assign to Lance. He prefers dramatic messages. I had hoped to be more subtle, but the millennium closes fast upon us and I need to begin the new one correctly. I do admit that it made things easier. Sutton and Wagner never shared my vision."

"And Wagner squealed like a little girl," Lance chirps.

"Nathan probably loved it too. You raised weirdos, Geoff."

"Nathan," Moller repeats and looks over to Lance, as if to ask a question. His cell phone rings at that moment and he turns away, speaking lowly into it.

I mouth the words 'I will kill you' to Lance and wink.

Moller turns back and addresses his son. "They'll be here in five minutes. Nathan is with them. Have the truck back into the garage."

I wonder if I can yell loud enough for the next door lady to hear when the door opens. God, I wished I'd taken the time to meet her, learn her name. And not threaten her on my way here; definitely don't threaten your neighbors if they could be the key to saving your life.

"Wait," I say as Moller turns to re-enter the house. Keep him talking, Rick. "Where does Odinism come into all this? That's a nature religion and you're using it to brand a bunch of lost kids."

He pauses and slowly spins back to me. "Do you even know the true nature of those who practiced it? They were men of a Viking age, men of hard times and harder desires. They came and conquered, they lay waste to the lands before them. They were who we are, Rick. And they did not forebear other races well at all. In Odinism we find the link to our past, a way to right this vessel, a rudder for our lost values. Should you take up the brand, you are instantly one with a brotherhood and sisterhood, part of a family that can resist the racial erosion occurring all around us."

I say nothing, at a loss for words.

He brightens. "How did that sound? It's my elevator speech. My recruiting pitch is much more persuasive."

"So, you're a killer and a fraud. You probably wear women's underwear too."

Moller's eyebrow rises. "Really? That is your comeback? Goodness gracious, Rick." And with that he goes into the kitchen. I can see him on his phone through the cracked door.

I turn to Lance. "What's your half-twit brother been doing? Shouldn't he be here for all this wondrous hand jerking?"

Lance just gives me a glance and moves back against the far wall. He's keeping distance between us now that he is alone. Either he's smart, or afraid.

I hope afraid.

Kimber is standing now too. I pull her close and wrap one arm around. It's an old habit position and still feels the same. She doesn't resist.

"What are you going to do?" She whispers.

"Die," says Lance.

Christ, is this guy a bat? How does he hear us?

"I'm going to stomp Lance's face into a potpie and stick that stupid Taser up his ass." I made sure to say it aloud.

Lance just laughs.

In truth, I don't know what I'm going to do. This whole thing is completely surreal. Here we are, gorgeous spring day, standing in the garage of a dream house Victorian, with the architects of North Haven's murder club. I can see the roof my own house through the garage windows. My own house!

How messed up is that?

It doesn't seem like any help is going to arrive. No one knows where we are. Moller is far too smart and methodical to allow random chance to disrupt his machine.

I'm going to have to improvise.

"What are we waiting for? Don't you have places to go, insane things to do?"

Lance is sticking his tongue on the electrodes of the stun gun. Now that the barbs have been used, he's removed the cartridge, meaning he'll have to be in close proximity to use it. Good.

He just shrugs and continues playing. God, that kid is wired backwards.

I survey our surroundings. It's a garage, not a prison fortress. Couldn't I just dive through a window? Problem is, Kimber. I could probably dash for one of the windows and escape before Lance can get close enough to hit me with the gun. But I can't leave her behind. He knows it, too.

As indecision grips me, I hear the sound of an approaching vehicle. It's a truck, pulling up the driveway. I want to believe it's a police SWAT van, but I'm not counting on it.

The last stall door opens. As it does, Lance steps forward, placing himself between us and the opening. The Taser is held up in strike position, warning me off.

A Tahoe with a starred rear window backs into the stall. The garage door closes before the truck shuts off. Two men in dark suits exit the front seats and I feel my stomach sink. They are dressed like bodyguards. I'm not surprised when they open the door and I see Dee's face.

They pull him from his seated position and he tumbles to the concrete floor, heavily and limp-limbed. Blood begins to pool around his head.

"Is he dead?" I say lowly, fearing to make it true by speaking any louder.

No one answers.

Then they yank another body out and toss it on the floor.

It's Nathan.

Now I'm surprised.

CHAPTER THIRTY-FIVE

Tripod

Dee's body moves slightly and he groans softly. I let out pent-up breath.

Nathan remains still, eyes closed, body limp.

What the hell is going on?

Lance stares down at his brother, face devoid of emotion. The two security guys station themselves next to the truck. They're white, of course, burly with concealed muscle and the blank stares of men who never question orders.

Geoffrey exits the house again. "Ah, good."

"What are you going to do with us?" Kimber asks, taking the offensive. Her tone is not weak, it's challenging. She's going down swinging. That's my girl.

"Probably not what you think. Well, let me correct that. You will die, but I promise it will be swift and painless. You will not be harmed, raped or mutilated."

"Well, that makes me happy."

"You say that now. Any good plan has contingencies built in. Your presence here created some kinks. I thought for a moment that we could create a lover's triangle scenario."

"Did you whiteboard it?" I ask, needling him.

"Imagine this," he continues, ignoring me. "Damonti and Kimberly, found dead, shot while in the middle of a secret tryst at some seedy hotel. Shortly thereafter, Rick disappears. It comes out later that he used Kimberly's address for entry to a religious movement, while still married to his wife.

Why would he do that? Wait, the religious movement is tied to white supremacy? And he supposedly found his black friend tangled up naked with his white girlfriend; perhaps his mistress? Oh my, the speculation that would generate. Of course, his body is never found, leading many to suspect he killed them both and fled. You must admit, that is juicy."

"You should have run with it. Why didn't you?"

"Because, Rick, I genuinely like you and do not wish to drag your legacy through the muck like that. You could be a poster boy for everything we promote. Tall, strong, Aryan through and through, quick-witted to a fault. A true alpha male in all ways, Mr. Killing."

"Is that a joke?"

"Plus, you serve a better purpose. I told you earlier: hero or martyr. If you won't stand at the head of my table, then you will lay before me, a sacrifice. When North Haven's prodigal son is the next victim, think how that will incite the masses. I don't have to be the bad guy creating a tableau that demeans your life; you are just another victim in this vicious world. Further, sports channels will provide more coverage over your murder than I could ever purchase. There is nothing more tragic than a comeback tale aborted through unforeseen circumstance."

"If you don't want to be the bad guy, how about letting us go? And buying us ice cream."

I don't think he even hears me anymore. "The resulting furor over your discovery could actually lead other whites to retaliate, could drive more members into our fold. If not, well, then I have North Haven's other son to sacrifice and create a revenge scene. There is simply no downside to any of this."

"The dying part is a bit depressing."

Moller laughs. "Yes, I suppose so."

I nod over to the camera and tripod. "What's that for?"

"These days, you need proof of everything. No one trusts anymore, everyone suspects the worst of each other."

"I can't imagine how that happens."

Nathan stirs just then, giving a grunt and rolling over. No one moves, just watching him slowly come back to the surface. He looks around and judging by his expression, he knows why he is here.

"You really are going through with this?" He asks, piercing stare on his father. The kid looks like he's trying to use his heat vision.

"I warned you many a time, Nathan. Either you are with us, or you are against us."

"I'm with you in pushing for separation. I'm not willing to commit mass murder to do it. Not innocent people with no dog in the fight." He glances over at his brother. "I'm not warped."

Now I'm disturbed. Usually I can judge other people pretty well, I think. With Nathan I completely missed the boat. I dislike being wrong. Maybe I should start feeling bad for breaking his wrist.

Geoffrey shakes his head. "And that is most unfortunate. You have been rather disappointing throughout all this."

"So you sacrifice me, like I'm some stranger? That's your solution?"

He says it with building heat, letting the emotions rise. And here I thought my dad was a prick. I'm seriously going to buy him a Father's Day card this year.

"There's a compelling storyline to it," Geoffrey replies. "I become the distraught father, the tragic victim who has buried three family members over racial matters. Public sentiment will swing heavily towards me, making me a sympathetic figure. The Covenant will follow me to the ends of the earth after that."

"None of this will make up for the tragedy that happened to your wife and daughter," I say.

He looks at me, measuring. "Again, you surprise me, Rick. You have obviously snuck around my past. Impressive, your tenacity is greater than I imagined. But you're wrong. They were not innocent victims in this war. Katrina was my partner in all things; she died standing firm on the ground we tilled. If anything, it made me more focused, more determined to honor her last act."

Great, a family that hates together, stays together. I wonder if I can buy that saying on a wall plaque at the white supremacy theme park.

Nathan stands up, a bit shakily. He shrugs his shoulders to clear the webs. "You don't really expect me to take it lying down, do you?" Lance moves closer, standing behind him, ready. "To let you use me as just another pawn in your game?"

"You have shown a singular lack of spine, son, so yes, actually."

"Fuck you." His face is red. There's a lot of pressure behind it, even though his body is completely still.

"Yes, go with vulgarity, Nathan. The last bastion of the cultured and the first resort for the weak minded."

"He's right, though," I add. "Fuck you."

Geoffrey goes to laugh. Nathan explodes.

He drops to a crouch and sweeps backwards with his leg. Lance goes to leap over it but is a fraction of a second late. He tumbles back, landing heavily on the concrete. The Taser goes skidding across the floor.

Both bodyguards are a moment delayed in reacting. They're not seasoned or practiced, just big. So am I.

And I'm also used to throwing my body around. A life of football has taught many lessons in angles, momentum and pain tolerance. Hitting someone else often hurts, but you accept it as part of the price and make sure the blow counts.

I launch myself across the space. The nearest bodyguard flinches and trips over Dee's inert form, falling awkwardly.

My form isn't great, and my linebacker buddies would razz me about it, but I collide with the other bodyguard, smashing him against the Tahoe door. He grunts and his lungs expel air with a loud whoosh. I've heard that sound many times in games; I've made that sound before when getting hit. It's not a good sign for the tacklee, but great for the tackler.

He drops down, slides to his back. Right now his mind is blank; his body is overcome with the urgent need to replenish its oxygen supply. I scramble on top of him and use my forearm. One, two, three times, I land blows on his forehead, causing the back of his head to impact the concrete. The sound is nasty. His eyes roll back and he goes limp.

I learned that from watching mixed martial arts.

Rolling over, knowing I'm late for the first bodyguard, I scramble to my knees in time to see Kimber place the Taser against the guy's temple and pull the trigger. The t-shirt rides up her spine, revealing the white cotton boxers. Nice.

The scream that erupts from his mouth is horrifying. His hand spasms in the act of pulling a gun from under his jacket. It clatters to the ground with a metallic stutter. Christ, a gun.

Nathan is jabbing at Lance's ribs with stiffened fingers. It looks like a practiced move, some kind of kung-fu thing. Now he's Jackie Chan? I really need to reassess my ability to read people. But the move works. Lance curls up into a fetal ball, not even fighting back.

This entire time, all ten seconds of it, Geoffrey has not moved, watching the scene as if reviewing a movie. I don't know what he's doing. If he thinks things are still under his control, he's dead wrong. A half-smile graces his mouth, as if all this is according to plan.

The guy is completely detached from reality.

Moving straight from his brother to his dad, Nathan leaps up. "You think I'm a sacrifice?!" he yells, consumed by fury. "*A sacrifice? I will fucking end you, father!*"

Before Geoffrey can open his smooth-talking maw, his son snares the tripod, whips it around in a vicious circle and smashes him right in the throat. The attack is suffused with raw hate and violence, accompanied by a scream ripping from the mouth of a betrayed son.

Even I'm stunned. And I've wanted to do it for the last hour.

He goes down in a heap. Nathan pounces on him and starts punching. Geoffrey puts up minimal resistance; I can hear him gagging. His hands flail uncontrollably.

He's a dead man.

CHAPTER THIRTY-SIX

Father

I scramble to my feet at the same time Lance does. His eyes are wide and bugging out. "Father!"

He moves to attack his brother, but loses his balance and stumbles, not quite tipping over.

It's Dee, bear-hugging his ankles. Blood streams down his forehead, across his face, grotesque. I can see the pain in his eyes.

He grasps Lance's legs and doesn't let go. That's my chance.

I take two strides and land my best haymaker right on his jaw. Smile at that, asshole.

The blow knocks Lance over and he lets out a groan as he impacts the floor. I reach down and help Dee to his feet.

"Killer," he says, voice scratchy and low; confused. "What the hell happened?"

I don't answer. He's barely able to stand. Kimber rushes over to help me support him. She's still clutching the Taser, instinctively refusing to let it go.

Nathan is raining blows down on his father still, screaming obscenities with each swing. Geoffrey's form jerks and shudders.

Motion out of the corner of my eye is Lance grasping for the fallen gun.

Shit.

I pull Kimber and Dee and turn for the door, mental clock counting off the heartbeats. Too late, too late.

A gunshot rings out, causing me to flinch, expecting to feel a flare of pain blossom in my back. Instead it's a cry from Nathan.

I shove the other two towards the garage door and fling a quick glance over my shoulder.

Nathan is twisted, half-reaching around for the entry wound in his back. His eyes are squinted in pain. At one time I thought that was his normal look.

Another shot rings out and his forehead explodes as the round exits. Gore sprays across his father's twitching body. Lance strides over and points the gun down at his brother. I don't think it's necessary, Nathan's brain is all over the floor.

We stumble through the garage door to the driveway just as two more shots are fired. I can't get the image of Lance's face from my mind. He just murdered his own brother and those eyes were dead calm. He could have been watching a commercial for all the emotion in them.

I've never met a more frightening person.

"*Go, go!*" I yell, half-carrying, half-pulling Dee. His entire bulk is on me, one arm draped over my shoulder. Kimber is trying to help but she's just not strong enough. Tears stream down her face, from fear, from helplessness. Never do I want to see that again.

There's nowhere we can go. We're completely exposed. Mindlessly, I turn us up the street towards my house, as if that's some kind of haven.

I don't know what else to do.

We're running, stumbling, trying to maintain our balance. Kimber is screaming for help. Where's that lady now? She could call the police. Did no one else hear gunshots in Windermere Fields?

The garage door slams open, a nightmare sound, and I don't want to look back. It's like looking back at the face of your monster, the one you cannot outrun no matter how much you churn your legs. But I can't resist.

Lance is walking after us, gun down by his side, eyes boring holes. The stare alone could kill. He's going to assassinate us in the middle of Hunter Run.

I scream at the other two, something unintelligible, because I'm more scared than I've ever been.

Ahead, Warren is standing at my door, arm raised to knock, confused look on his face. It would be comical, if not for the fact that a murderer stalked us. His expression flares from confusion to alarm and he spins, grasping for the revolver strapped to his waist.

Lance is thirty feet away and closing fast. He's smiling again and I know he wants to place a round in each of our heads while looking us in the eye.

I shove Dee and Kimber forward, causing them to fall in a heap, as I round back on Lance. I told you, anyone intent on coming for my friends needs to pass through me first. And I meant it.

He raises the gun, sighting down the barrel. I tense.

The crack of a gun nearly causes me to piss.

Lance jerks and surprise colors his face. A red entry point appears on his right shoulder. He moves his eyes over my shoulder to Warren. The gun follows his focus.

Another crack.

This one scores, knocking Lance down. He drops to his knees, staring down at the red flower blooming from his stomach, smile frozen on his face. The gun falls from limp fingers as he grasps at the wound.

Then he tilts and tips over, squirming on the smooth asphalt. Pain removes that stupid grin.

Snatching the Taser from Kimber, I rush over, jam it hard into his balls and pull the trigger. A resulting scream soars up into the air and now it's my turn to smile.

I drop the weapon and crawl over to my friends. I pull them close and hug them like I'll never let go.

CHAPTER THIRTY-SEVEN

November

I'm standing in the open garage of my soon-to-be former house at 620 Hunter Run, staring out. The realtor sign has a SOLD banner slapped across it, resulting from an accepted offer last week.

The weather has turned, the air gone thin and brittle. For those who believe the new millennium will bring massive amounts of change, today is that kind of harbinger. Gray skies smother the land;

trees stand stark and bare. Just the other day I read a report suggesting that people store food in watertight containers and drop them into lakes or ponds, in case refrigeration capability is lost. Christ. This year really needs to end.

For the rest of us, today is little more than warning of yet another winter around the corner.

Maya is long gone, off to California with Tom Simmons and her new job. I wish her nothing but good fortune. We didn't part amicably – which surprised no one – and we'll probably never see each other again.

With the SOLD sign, the last anchor to my old life has been pulled.

Turns out, luck did play in our favor when the Mollers had us captive. Warren heard my panicked voicemail and, unable to reach me, drove out personally. I guess he'd come around to realizing that maybe, just maybe, I was on to something. Better late than never.

Geoffrey survived, if that's what you can call it. He's in a coma, breathing through a tube. The news reported that it is unlikely he'll ever leave hospice care. They also discovered that Asatru Convergence Inc. is not a real company. Asatru is, however, a growing supremacy religion in prisons.

Weirdly enough, Lance fared the best of all the Mollers. The one who killed and loved it, survived to full recovery. Of course, he'll probably never get out of prison, but still, karma works in odd ways. Maybe he can find his new religion in there.

The sound of an approaching car rolls over my garage. I play the game. It's a police vehicle.

Allan Borden pulls his cruiser into my driveway and exits. I move over by the service door and lean up against the side.

"I got your message. You have some more information on the Covenant? Why didn't you call Warren?"

"Because he's not guilty." I have no time for small talk, might as well cut right to it.

That stops Allan's advance. He's two arm lengths away. "What did you say?"

"I should have seen it earlier, figured it out long before this. But I've been a little preoccupied."

He nods slowly, still recalibrating. "Uh, yeah, good game last week."

I remain in place. "One thing I never got was how the Mollers knew so much about me. Things that they shouldn't. Kimberly, my habits, the inside scoop on my calls to Warren. How did I come to their attention anyway? Pure coincidence? Or was I offered up?"

"What are you talking about?" Allan's eyes are guarded, his body stilled to the point of frozen, like he's reluctant to move.

"It must have given you some kind of perverse joy to be the one to arrest me. I've known you since we were ten. Granted, we've never been close friends, but that's mostly because I thought you were a stiff. Turns out you're worse. When did that happen?"

His mouth opens and closes several times as he tests out different responses. Finally, he decides to drop the act.

"You want to know when it changed? When I started having to deal with the shit day after day in this job. That's where you see just how bad this country has gotten. Immigrants stream over the border, blacks sink into the welfare cycle, trash from all over the place think they deserve something for nothing. If we don't do something soon to clean up the dregs, we're all going to suffer."

"Well, your exalted leader is the only one suffering right now. He's fed through a tube and will never talk again, even if he wakes up from the coma. You guys are going nowhere."

Now Allan changes. His frozen posture loosens a bit and he draws his weapon, holding it down at his side.

"There will be another. Someone else to fill the void. This thing is started and has life of its own. Geoffrey had big plans, we can still follow them. It may not happen by New Years, but eventually it will. You're an afterthought now, Rick. No one needs to listen to your lip anymore."

I nod to the gun. "So you shoot me? Finish what he started? Really?"

"There will be an investigation, but it will be based on my report. As long as I'm thorough and show appropriate action on my part, I'll be cleared.

Your habit of seeing conspiracy in everything is still well known. You got lucky with the Covenant, but even a blind squirrel finds the occasional nut. If I write that you accused me of aiding the Mollers and attacked me, it will sell pretty easily. I'm a decorated officer with no affiliation to any race movement. My laundry is clean."

"So, more cover up. Like you did with the murders? Did you make sure no patrols would interrupt their activities? Did you give them places you knew would be safe to commit their kills? Some of those scenes were pretty elaborate. They needed time, time that you could guarantee."

"Okay, whatever Killing. I've heard enough." He raises the gun, drawing a bead between my eyes.

I raise my hands and back up a step. "Think about this, Allan. Think about what you're doing."

"Oh, I have. For the last five months I've thought about it. You did your bull-in-the-china shop routine, and completely fucked everything up. Geoffrey wanted so badly for you to come aboard with us; he never saw the truth about you. He either overestimated his powers of persuasion, or underestimated your loyalty. I told him many times, your friendship with Damonti defined your stance. And sure enough; you got in deep, did everything we needed you to, and somehow still came out clean. That's quite a magic trick. I never figured I'd get a chance to balance the scales. Then, you just had to get in one last shot. Your arrogance couldn't just leave it alone. Now it's my turn. So, thanks for that."

"Don't thank anyone yet. Look behind me. On the shelf next to the toolbox."

He re-grips his gun, moving into a Weaver combat stance and darts his glance over my shoulder. "Is that a surveillance camera?"

"Yeah. I'm still popular enough at the Hyper-Mart that I can borrow equipment for the important things. Go figure. Don't shoot that, though. I promised them I'd bring it back whole."

"Son of a bitch."

"Oh, and I did call Warren. He's inside watching the live feed, with audio. I needed help hooking that part up."

Now comes the tense part. Allan has to make a decision, but I don't know which way he'll go. Fight or flight?

I hear the front door open and Allan glances over. His shoulders sag.

Slowly, I let my breath out, low enough so he doesn't hear. I won't give him the satisfaction of knowing.

He looks back at me with questions written across his face and I didn't need to hear them to know what he asked. "It was one little thing that finally pulled it all together for me. You had a copy of *A Bleeding Nation* in the back of your squad car the day you arrested me. It was half-covered by file folders. I saw it but didn't pay much attention. That was a rather busy day for me."

Allan gives me a look of disbelief as Warren comes into view, his own gun drawn.

I point to my right eye. "Quick vision."

Kimber is lying on the couch when I return to her – our – house, reading. I'm not familiar with the object but it appears to be this thing called a book.

The TV plays in the background, showing some local afternoon talk program. Dee's mug fills the screen as he speaks with the host. He returned to the Cubs after nearly a month away for injury. His bat and defense was missed as the team fluttered down to last place. Some days I still think there are lingering issues with his head. He doesn't speak much about what happened to him. But he forged on, continuing to speak out on social issues, only now he's more selective and in control of who stands beside him. I have, on the few occasions when we allowed the media to tell our tale. But we're both wary of giving too much information, knowing how true stories become wild tales when left to idiots with an agenda.

"Where were you?"

"Oh, I just had to clean up a few things at the house. You know, for the inspection. I'd left one of my tool boxes in the garage."

"Oh," her eyes hold me steady, but I don't crack. No sense dredging up worry.

It's been a ride over the last few months. After that day at Moller's, Kimber and I came back into a shared orbit quickly. As in next day quickly. You don't go through an experience like that and expect to remain distant.

I moved in with her four weeks later.

Who knows what the future will bring, but I'm not so concerned any more. When I'm with her, the tumblers of my life click into place, cleanly and correctly. I'm where I need to be, everything else will shake out just fine.

She sets down the book and sits up. "So, Mr. Rookie of the Month for October, you have a bye week. What do you plan to do with yourself?"

"I don't know. The last game went to overtime and I'm pretty sore. For a crappy team, the Bears hit hard. Maybe a nice long massage will help me." I lay down on the couch, placing my head in her lap.

"Oh, really. And I'm supposed to drop everything I'm doing to service you?" She leans over and brushes her lips across my forehead. Her fingers tickle along my rib cage.

This is so right.

On that fateful day back in April, when I looked around and tried to see down my path, it was Kimber's face I saw, distant yet distinct, whether I realized it or not. It's always been there, just waiting on the right circumstance. Everything I did, everything that happened since, has been about her.

In the end, she's what it was all about.

~ FIN ~

Post- script

The July sun beats hot on my shoulders as I stand on the back patio, staring across my yard. I'm not thinking anything in particular, other than I need to stay out here while Maya slams things into boxes and yells at me through the screen door.

June ended with a bang. July should get better. Training camp starts soon, bringing a change of scenery for a few weeks. I'm excited, yet wary. The gridiron feels so far away.

My cell rings and I flip it open. It's Warren.

"You're getting visitors." He says in greeting.

"More Covenant? Because I've about had it with those shits."

He laughs. "No, couple of detectives from Chicago. They need some info on Moller."

I do the math. "They're not coming for general case questions. Something has happened, right? Something that involves all of us." My stomach tumbles and sinks.

"You ever heard of Noah Bell?"

"The black guy from Chicago trying to make the world a better place? Sure, who hasn't? Dee wants to be him when he grows up."

"Well, there's a vacancy for the position. Bell was found dead this morning, beaten to death."

I get the sense that my run with the Covenant Church of the New Millennium is not quite over.

To be continued in The Killing Face, *2015...*